Resort

Resort

ANDREW DALEY

TIGHTROPE BOOKS

Tightrope Books
#207-2 College Street,
Toronto Ontario, Canada M5G 1K3
tightropebooks.com
bookinfo@tightropebooks.com

EDITOR: Deanna Janovski
COVER PHOTO TOP: David Jang
COVER PHOTO BOTTOM: Jordan Liles
COVER & LAYOUT DESIGN: David Jang

 Canada Council   Conseil des arts
for the Arts   du Canada

 ONTARIO ARTS COUNCIL
CONSEIL DES ARTS DE L'ONTARIO
an Ontario government agency
un organisme du gouvernement de l'Ontario

Produced with the assistance of the Canada Council for the Arts and the Ontario Arts Council.

Library and Archives Canada Cataloguing in Publication

Daley, Andrew, author
      Resort / Andrew Daley.

ISBN 978-1-988040-36-3 (softcover)

      I. Title.

PS8607.A44R47 2017   C813'.6   C2017-904309-9

"Ever get the feeling you've been cheated?"
—Johnny Rotten

Prologue

THE FIRST TIME WE WERE ROBBED, IN
Mexico City, I thought we deserved it.

We were on a sort of honeymoon, meandering through the
leafy streets of luxury cars and bougainvillea in the posh suburb
of Coyoacán. I was new to Mexico, recently reunited with Jill, and
enthralled by her and the curious way of living she'd presented to me.

It was a sticky summer day, the heat like a cranky child, and I
wanted to return to our hotel for a siesta. Jill had other plans. She'd
heard that somewhere in the maze of drowsy streets was the house
where Leon Trotsky had received an ice pick to the head. I was asking
why she was interested in a long-dead Russian revolutionary when
footsteps rapidly approached us from behind, and a rush of motion
spun me around.

Two young men stood before us. One waved a large clasp knife
unsteadily in my direction, and the other was slowly opening a
second knife. For an instant, I thought it was a joke, that this couldn't
be happening, even as my hands went up, instinctively, and I took a
step back, muttering, "Okay, okay," and reaching for my wallet.

Jill refused to surrender her handbag and was instead digging for
cash in the pocket of her jeans. Luckily, she was facing the less-than-
malevolent sidekick, a handsome kid with strong native features, who
had yet to open his blade and stood waiting for her.

The jittery thief facing me was unsatisfied with the 200 pesos in my wallet. Nor did he want my credit cards, since he probably knew better than to get involved with them. He pressed the knife to my stomach, forcing a slick terror through me, while he rifled through the pockets of my shorts. With those empty save for a tourist map, he nodded toward my new sneakers.

I was crouching to remove them when Jill saved our skins, and my feet, by pulling from her pocket the 1000 pesos she'd withdrawn from an ATM that morning. That was enough for the patient thief facing her, who grabbed the cash and ran. His companion, now alone, lunged once for Jill's bag before changing his mind and likewise running off.

The ordeal barely lasted a minute, yet had seemed far longer. I might have keeled over had Jill not lifted me from the sidewalk and into her arms. We held each other as best we could with the shock shuddering through us. Jill sobbed quietly, and I felt sick, the more so when I saw, at the top of the street, police officers maintaining a roadblock. They had likely watched, or even sanctioned, our robbery.

Welcome to Mexico. Beware of thieves.

Still clinging to each other, we slipped past the police to find another ATM. In a taxi heading back downtown, I finally knew how our victims felt: the stomach-dropping panic, the greasy sweats, the burn of shame at being violated. The way Jill curled into me suggested she was struggling with the same ugliness.

We hid in our hotel room the rest of the day, and the following morning caught a flight to the Dominican Republic.

The second time we were robbed was at a taco restaurant on a highway lined with resort hotels in Puerto Vallarta. We were working an American couple—squeezing our limes, we call it. When in Mexico, you're always squeezing limes, into your beer or over your taco. Except our limes were American or English or Canadian or sometimes German or Dutch.

The restaurant was open to the traffic rushing along the dusty road, headlights coming on in the tangerine January twilight. Jill and I were tired from a sun-baked day of pretending to be on vacation with some new friends from San Francisco. She was a marketing consultant who could speak only of the software she sold, and he was a lawyer with a foreclosure firm. We four were the only customers in the place, probably because the tacos weren't very good.

This time there were three thieves, two to brace us at our table, a third to watch the road. A curly haired youth showed us a handgun stuffed into the waistband of his jeans and demanded, in English, our money. The waiter, I noticed, had conveniently disappeared.

The lawyer objected, rising from his seat. The gun came out, and God knows what would have happened if Jill hadn't hauled his stupid ass back down. She opened her purse and urged the marketing lady to do the same. We knew the routine. I doubt they would have shot us. Still, we all had roles to play in this particular drama.

The thieves collected a few thousand pesos and the Americans' phones before flitting back into the night. The worst for us wasn't the loss of money, but the indignant reaction of the Americans, who insisted on reporting the theft. The waiter returned and did a poor job acting outraged. Despite Jill explaining that the authorities wouldn't care, that we should return to the gated security of our resort, the lawyer ran to the highway to flag down a police cruiser. Unfortunately, one happened to be passing at that moment, which prevented Jill and me from just walking away.

Not much later, Jill and I sat glumly on a bench in an outpost of the Jalisco state police, playing the heartbroken holidayers. It didn't matter that we'd never complete this squeeze, nor was I concerned at that moment that we deserved this second robbery no less than the first. Our priority was keeping our identities secret.

The police didn't care who we were. But after yawning through an account of the robbery, they reluctantly allowed the lawyer to use their phone. An official at the American consulate, after the lawyer tracked one down, invited us to visit their office in the morning. The official asked us to give our names and passport numbers to the police. Jill and I had to happily comply.

When the call was over, the police cheerfully drove us back to our resort. The Americans suggested a nightcap, but we were too rattled from the robbery. We made plans to meet for breakfast instead and returned to our room.

Of course we had no intention of meeting with the consular official. We'd last used those names at Christmas when we fleeced an Australian couple, and it was possible that some database might connect our passports with the earlier robbery.

We were packed by midnight and spent the night in a different hotel along the strip. I lay awake for hours, feeling clever about our escape and our future in general. Having been mugged twice in Mexico, I couldn't imagine any sort of further trouble on the horizon.

By noon the following day, we'd taken a bus south to the city of Mazatlán, where we checked into a large resort with different passports and got ready to try our luck again.

Day 1

Acapulco

THE DAY OUR LIVES IN THE RESORTS began unravelling, I woke early to swim in the ocean.

It was our first morning of a week at Costa de Paraiso, a hotel near the southern end of the Acapulco strip. Though we'd hit a dead end—no money left, no progress with our scams—Jill and I were still optimistic of an upswing in fortune in the next six days. We'd been successful in Acapulco before and were betting the last of our savings we would be again.

I arrived at the beach even before the Germans and Brits, who routinely claimed their daily beach chairs with their towels before breakfast. Fishermen were still unloading their catch for the day or eating tortillas and fish cooked by women in the shadowed lanes between hotel towers.

My goal that morning was a sandbar I'd glimpsed the previous afternoon, a pale sliver of aqua in the navy surf. When I'd reached it and stood, panting and pleased with my effort, chest-deep in the water two hundred yards out, I turned to contemplate the shoreline.

Guests at Costa de Paraiso stayed in low-rise apartment blocks orbiting a main building with a timbered cathedral ceiling. Landscaped paths zigzagged between these room-blocks, linking tennis courts, bars, and swimming pools, all honeycombed into the gentle slope to the sea. A pedestrian avenue lined with royal palms carved directly through these grounds to the beach.

And yet our resort, somehow, had vanished. With the sun cresting the coastal mountains, all the waterslides, beach umbrellas, and hotel towers blurred together before my eyes. I'd swum so far out, I'd lost Paraiso among the miles of attractions curving along the bay.

But with the tide rushing in, and the undertow sucking beneath me, there wasn't time for contemplation. I treaded water, the sand shifting beneath me until at last I surrendered, letting the waves take me, unwillingly, into shore.

Our room was on a ground floor and featured brochure-perfect ocean views. Jill had retrieved breakfast from the dining room and spread it over our patio table. Yogurt and granola, hard-boiled eggs, cubed papaya. She insisted on us eating together whenever possible, breakfast especially. Every morning, we resolved to do the same thing with our day: get close to vacationers, preferably a couple under forty, and make friends with them.

Lately, the stress of our situation had cut into my appetite. I ate an egg and most of a banana. Jill's disapproving glance suggested that wasn't enough.

"Danny, seriously. Try a little more. You're getting too thin." She nodded toward an overweight couple walking up the slope to the main building. "Look at those two there. They'll never believe you're one of them."

I laughed because she was probably serious. "I promise I'll eat a big lunch, okay?"

"We should meet for it. I've got flamenco dancing at ten thirty, then I want to hit the shops and bars in the lobby."

"I'll be back by then."

"Good. It's a date." There, on that sunny patio, she shone just a little more brightly. "I've got a good feeling about this place. It's time, you know?"

My activity for that morning was a walk through a mountain nature preserve, arranged by the hotel, that I would use to troll for lonely hearts or bickering couples. In my three years down south with Jill, I'd trekked over a dozen tropical islands and long stretches of Mexico's coastline. The highlights never changed: rocky archipelagos, palm trees, pounding surf, and the majestic sheen of the Pacific, the Atlantic, or the Caribbean.

That particular hike I should have abandoned before it got underway. Trailing the guide was an impenetrably lovey-dovey pair of Chileans, three giggly, hungover Mexican girls, and two sunburned middle-aged English couples with incomprehensible accents.

Without possibilities, I brought up the rear. Jill and I had last scored in mid-January and, in the three fruitless months since, had gone broke chasing our lost luck. It was the end of March, the high tourist season winding down.With no other prospects, if we failed at Paraiso, we'd be homeless and so easy prey for real criminals and the police.

It was noon when the hiking group emerged from the forest, wilted and mute in the dense heat. A passenger van conveyed us down the mountainside, then a short distance along Costera Miguel Alemán, Acapulco's perpetually snarled, exhaust-smeared main thoroughfare.

The streetside of Paraiso was a chaotic forecourt of airport shuttles, tourist coaches, and taxis. In a row of scooters for rent, I spotted a purse dangling from a seat. I veered toward it, ashamed by my instinctual reaction, when, to my relief, a woman returned for it.

I pretended our situation wasn't that desperate yet and reset my happy tourist face.

A revolving door spun me into a lobby jammed with holidayers wearing the most ghastly beachwear available for purchase in the shopping malls of Pittsburgh, Glasgow, or Calgary. I knew it well. It was the uniform I wore to work every day.

Cooled by whirring ceiling fans, I was passing the wood-panelled lobby bar when I spotted Jill in the gift shop. She was speaking to two women with long, highlighted hair. Midwesterners, by my guess. I could hear their brash voices over the canned mariachi music.

Jill's freshly blond tresses let me know how she'd passed the morning. But I couldn't complain, as she had two fish on her line and I had none. I sat at a table where she might see me.

Because she sometimes worked alone, I left it to her to decide when, or if, she would invite me into her game. So far, I'd been blessed. She'd been including me in the fun since our days in the drama program at Ryerson University, when she brought this loner kid into her circle of friends. It's her generosity I love most of all, which is no less genuine for how she utilizes it.

While waiting, I was struck by how little she resembled the two other women. Her now-blond hair fell messily over her shoulders, and in her raspberry one-piece swimsuit and yellow sarong, she displayed a confidence alien to the other women.

If I saw this difference, why couldn't they? Because people are

13

generally trusting and want to believe in the goodness of others. We earned our living off this.

Jill did most of our work. With women, she told them what they already knew about their children or their mothers-in-law. If they were quitting smoking, she either urged them to stay strong or snuck out with them for a puff. Her friendliness was central to our schemes. A broken sandal strap always elicited comment. Compliments never hurt. And most women have a moment to hear, in overpriced hotel gift shops, where they can find an item cheaper.

She ushered the two women to the checkout, where one of them charged flip flops and potato chips to a Citibank Visa. From my table, I watched Jill's eyes scan the card.

A waiter brought me a lunch menu. I examined this until I heard: "Steve, there you are. You were supposed to meet me here an hour ago."

If I was Steve, then she was Gina. Her slipshod English accent meant I would be an American for the rest of our stay at this resort.

"The tour guide got lost," I said. "I thought we were going to die out there."

"I'm glad you didn't. Honey, this is Lori, and this is Shauna. They're from Omaha."

The women were our age, early thirties. Jill and I walked with them as they exited the lobby for the pool. "I hear Omaha's a great town," I said.

"Really?" Shauna gushed. "Thanks. It's a good place to be from."

"Steve books shows for theatres," Jill said, which meant, in our arrangement, that she was an actress I'd met ten years before. It was her favourite role, and the one nearest the truth.

"Wow, that's cool," Lori, said.

"It's not that exciting," I said. "I do kids' theatre. Puppet shows and stuff."

"Are you ready for lunch?" Jill said to me.

"Can I take a shower first? I feel like I just ran a marathon." Time out for a little family meeting. For this to work as quickly as we needed it to, I had to be clear on her plan of approach.

"If you hurry. I don't know why I'm so hungry. All I've done since we got here is eat."

"Tell me about it," Shauna said. "Did you see that dessert table last night?"

14

"I bloody well did," Jill said, sounding more Scottish than English. "Three different kinds of chocolate cake."

"A week here and I'll be the size of a house," said Lori.

"That's not true," Jill said. "And it doesn't count when you're on holiday."

"Come get me in a few minutes," I said to Jill before turning to the two other women. "See you on the beach, I guess."

"Or at the bar," Lori said, and both she and Shauna laughed.

I set off across the lush grounds, my optimism in check. We'd worked plenty of limes these past three frustrating months, yet for some baffling reason hadn't made them pay.

Our room appeared far more lived-in than it had that morning. We'd stayed just one night at Paraiso, and already I had to kick a path through the clothing overflowing from Jill's many suitcases onto the floor. It was the same back when we lived together during university. I'd always known what I was getting into.

The room was further cramped by two double beds. According to Jill, my insomnia, which had lately been pretty bad, had been keeping her up. Not surprisingly, since we often woke up in separate beds, our sex life had suffered.

Far more alarming was that we had just over 3500 pesos left in the world, or roughly $350. We'd also maxed out Jill's last credit card paying for the week at Paraiso, an irony neither of us had mentioned. We had a bed and food at Paraiso for six more days. After that, we'd ... burglarize hotel rooms for valuables to pawn? Mug people?

The place to avoid was a Mexican prison, which by anyone's description is a unique hell. Filthy and unsanitary. Overcrowded. Ruled by drug gangs. Survival in one was impossible without money to purchase drinkable water, adequate food, health care, and clothing. And to bribe a corrupt public defender with access to the right judges.

Nor was there anyone to bail us out. Neither of us had family of any use, and I'm sure the consulate would have had questions about our years down here without visas. Not that they'd be able to get us out of prison. Our isolation was an additional strain on our relationship.

Even more dispiriting was how far off we remained from our dream of opening a small English-language theatre in a sunny tourist town. Our hurricane escape route, Jill called it. We planned to do

15

popular shows and musicals in rep and occasionally something slightly more daring. Plus we'd have a stage for comics and a bar worth drinking at.

The theatre was Jill's dream, but one I eagerly supported, and not just because it brought us back together after a short separation last fall. We each had a ton of talent going to waste, and our schemes were no means to a real end. They weren't even fun anymore.

All we needed was a lot of money, say $50,000.

That wouldn't have been impossible in the glory days of our scams, when we accessed over ten cards a week and some months netted up to $15,000. But as I've said, we hadn't scored in months and had almost no cash left.

To pull us out of our nosedive, I'd lately been suggesting we regroup by getting service jobs in a country less volatile than Mexico. Jill refused, insisting our luck would change, like it always did, and that entertaining other ideas undermined our confidence.

As much as I disagreed, she was right: we'd never raise the funds we needed for our dream by making margaritas for tourists. And we were too broke to even reach a place where foreigners could get jobs. So we were trapped, and robbing people—or as we told ourselves, robbing the greedy banks through people—remained our only plan. But without money to pay for the resorts, we'd soon be unable even to do that.

The worst of it was that neither of us had mentioned our little theatre in months.

Among the usual bathroom clutter were the tubes of a L'Oréal product promising *el mejor rubio* for 200 pesos. Jill had been especially energetic with her dye job, leopard-printing the white countertop with stains. That too was sloppy, since the housekeeping staff would notice them.

The "best blond" bounded into the room as I was towelling off, a jagged excitement in her eyes for the first time in months. I was glad to see it. Her response to our situation was to paint a performer's smile over her broody introversion and to sleep a lot. Like many couples, our issues were financial in origin and hampered by poor communication.

"Those girls are cousins," she said. "And best friends."

"Meaning their husbands might not be," I said. "But they could be."

"Exactly. Maybe they're buds, too. We should find out."

"Let me go make their acquaintance."

In our favoured divide-and-conquer tactic, my role was to distract the men with anything competitive—dune buggies, tennis, boozing—while Jill worked her magic with the women.

"They're on the beach." She was pawing through a bag, no doubt for something appropriately shapeless to wear for the American women. Her willingness to immerse herself in a role was inspiring. "I already have one card number."

"I saw you get it. While I'm gone, you should work on that accent. It's all over the place. And what's with the dye job? I thought we were bankrupt."

"Do you like it?"

"I do," I said, reaching for the drawstring of her sarong. She spun away from me and tripped backwards onto a bed tangled with the clothing of her many disguises: tube tops, straw hats, sundresses, underwear and G-strings, capri pants, halters, plus uncountable shoes and sandals. I dove after her.

Not now, I was told. There was work to do.

Typically, the voice telling me this was so impeccably English you'd swear she was born and raised there. Not that I needed reminding, as I ventured back into the furious glare of the afternoon, that she could be perfect anytime she chose.

The husbands were easy to spot in the beachside tiki bar. The big one talking animatedly, the shorter, balding one only half listening. The big one was with Lori, I decided, the shorter one with Shauna. Their pale softness suggested office jobs or businesses of their own.

I sat at the far end of the bar, my sunglasses reflecting the sandy sea of sunbathers, just another husband bored by all the relaxation underway. I heard more Spanish being spoken than English—a bad sign. Whether it was the global recession keeping Anglos away or the gun battles between drug gangs on Acapulco's streets, it limited our opportunities.

This troubled city probably wasn't the best place for us. Our run down the Pacific coast of Mexico had started badly when we were robbed at that taco place in Puerto Vallarta just after the New Year. Jill liked our chances in Acapulco better than anywhere else, and I trusted her instincts more than my own. We also couldn't afford the flight to another country.

I ordered coffee and water from the barman, taking care to not engage him too closely. Nor did I intend on speaking to the husbands. The idea was to let them see me, so that when we later met I'd appear, somehow, reassuringly familiar.

The shorter guy was a bit anxious, and the big guy affably drunk as he glared at women in swimsuits. They seemed to get along all right, although self-satisfied people like the big guy can be tough to befriend or to convince you have something they need, like where to find the best seafood. Conversely, people distracted by hating their holiday, like the shorter guy, or fretting over its cost, can be easy to squeeze. Jill and I liked to widen the cracks already evident in relationships.

When there was anything to squeeze. Twice that spring, when we got card numbers, Jill's contact reported them overdrawn and so useless to us. It was too bad we couldn't run credit checks on people.

Also, by the time we'd reached Acapulco, I'd decided that our movements were being tracked by some law enforcement agency or other. My suspicions began after Puerto Vallarta, where we'd had to give the police our passport numbers after being robbed. Within a week, I read about the break-up of a huge credit-card ring in Miami. Was that Jill's fence, I wondered. Was our gig up? That sharp rap at our hotel room door or the hand grasping my arm at a bar could be just around the corner.

Apparently not, because a day later, Jill sent our last useful card numbers to her contact.

The husbands drained their drinks and exited the bar. I lingered, rattling a few precious coins. Despite our cash-flow crisis, I left ten pesos for a tip to avoid standing out.

On the beach, I paused to let a crowd of yammering Chinese tourists pass before me. When they'd cleared, I saw that Jill was waiting for me in the shade of a palm-thatched umbrella. She was stealthy that way, always a few steps ahead of everyone else (and sometimes herself). She had that loopy grin on her face, the one only I could put there. I loved that seeing me still made her happy.

"The big guy will be a handful," I said. "I'd say wait and see what else turns up. But we can't."

"No, we can't. Trust me on this, all right?" To illustrate her point, she let herself tumble backwards, like a falling tree. If I hadn't caught her, she'd have cracked her head on a beach chair. We'd played the game before. I always caught her.

She pulled me into her embrace, and for a long moment, I succumbed to the comfort she offered. How many beaches had we stood on together? In front of how many hotels?

We actually first met on a beach in Mexico. Well, more or less. It was on the beach in Cancun, during a university reading-week trip, that I fell hard for a girl I'd previously admired from afar. We were misfits who shared a love of acting, and who discovered that we really only belonged with each other. When she took off shortly after graduating—and when I foolishly failed to go after her—I was shattered. The few years of semi-fame I enjoyed from some television roles, followed by a sharp decline, were haunted by her absence.

Then three years ago, she reached out to me, and I joined her down south. On those many beaches and in countless indistinguishable hotel rooms, we made a home.

I held her like I wanted to that long ago first night in Cancun. With a card number in hand, two couples to work, and Jill in my arms, my morning funk was lifting. "Let's get lunch at that diner we like. I want pancakes."

"With what money, Danny? Lunch is on the buffet in the dining room. But you have to get it for us because I don't want to run into those women again until dinner."

There was that discipline, when I'd have spent the afternoon snoozing in front of the television. Every day she reminded me how much work went into being a successful actor.

And so Steve Sawyer, theatrical booker, and Regina Bóccia, English actress turned American homemaker, with two kids and a mortgage back in Buffalo—or anywhere far away from where our limes lived—ate take-out in their room. Then we ran memorization drills from our university days and rehearsed potential scenarios. When at last Jill was satisfied that we'd scraped the rust from our roles, I snuck off for a late-afternoon swim.

For dinner at the better resorts, guests dress slightly less garishly than they do during the day. Slacks and collars for the men, skirts or dresses for the women. The clamorous dining room contained more Mexicans than Anglos, and also many Asians, who were equally useless to us. They all crowded a massive roast pig, their plates held out expectantly.

Jill contrived to seat us near the two American couples, whom we studiously ignored. Camouflaged in a tan skirt and a flowery blouse, her hair in a schoolgirl ponytail, Jill could have been mistaken for another cousin of the girls.

Jill ate sea bass and lasagna while I pushed salad greens around my plate. When this earned me an eye roll, I joined the American men at the dessert table, letting them sniff me out again. Back at our table, Jill helped me through a big hunk of blueberry cheesecake.

We lingered over coffee. To get what you're after there's sometimes no easier way than to leave things to chance. Like when we heard, moments later: "Cal, this is the English lady I told you about. The actress."

One of the Nebraskan women approached, her three companions looking on. "What are you guys doing?" she said. "'Cause we're going to the pool bar for the show."

I swallowed a huge grin. Beside me, Jill shivered in anticipation.

The big guy was Cal Umberger. He and his wife, Lori, could put back a lot of booze. The shorter one was Evan Biddle, husband of Shauna, who in our time at the pool bar nursed a single piña colada. The cheesy dance routines underway poolside provided Jill and I with sufficient pauses in the conversation to process all we were learning about our new friends, and to tweak Steve and Gina's identities accordingly. Jill's accent, of course, was flawless.

When the cabaret was over, Cal invited us back to their room for more drinks.

"We're turning in," Evan said, yawning.

"Speak for yourself," Shauna said. "I'm having a good time."

I always hated visiting other people's hotel rooms. They were jammed with information useful to a squeeze, but far too humanizing. Seeing their pajamas flung over a chair or learning their choice of toothpaste raised more issues with our livelihood than I could ignore at once.

Cal unloaded bottles of Budweiser from the mini-fridge and made margaritas for the girls. Except for Shauna, who had a Sprite. If I noticed that, why didn't they notice that Jill returned from the washroom with her fresh drink half empty?

Cal owned a Ford dealership and expounded at length about his sales techniques. We also heard how much he hoped the Republicans would choose Mitt Romney to defeat Obama later in the year. I picked at the label of my beer, then stopped for fear of revealing my boredom.

"And your buy-back option, Cal?" Evan asked, his smirk too sly for Cal to notice.

Cal answered, again at length, and I noted Evan wasn't the dud he'd first appeared to be.

Shauna had an iPhone and asked if we were on Facebook. My pat answer was not yet, although I'd heard it could be great for work. Jill agreed. Social media was another reason to quit our game. There was nowhere to hide on it, though to ignore it was deeply suspicious.

Inevitably, Lori handed some photos of her kids to Jill. She and Cal had three boys under ten. Shauna and Evan were still trying. When Lori asked if we had any kids, Jill coolly produced two wallet-sized photos of kids she claimed were ours—Brayden and Janey, apparently—then praised women who give their children the benefit of a full-time mom.

She turned to me. "I forgot to tell you your mom said Janey lost another tooth."

"We can put pesos under her pillow when we get back," I said. "She'll love that."

Jill handed the photos around. "Brayden's my little hero," she said. "He told me, 'Mommy, you can go on vacation because I'm big enough to look after Janey all by myself.'"

In the next few minutes, she provided such captivating details on these two little strangers that I was genuinely moved by how deeply she loved and missed her children. All this from a woman who'd never expressed interest in having children, and yet, whom I'd catch, as far back as our university days, peering into baby carriages and beaming at happy toddlers.

The Biddles left soon after, which was a shame. Evan was funny and Shauna had spunk. They were the kind of couple friends I wanted us to have when we got out of this life.

In their absence, Lori bummed a cigarette off Jill and then dished on Shauna's marriage. Evan was having difficulty settling down. He didn't enjoy accounting work and wanted to move to a larger city and become a photographer. We all agreed that children of his own would provide Evan the routine and responsibility he needed.

By midnight, when there was no chance of seeing their cards, I'd had enough blather.

Footlights marked the gravel path to the beach. Smog moon big and orange over the bay. Jill clutched at me, drunker than I'd thought, a fact that, ever the performer, she'd kept to herself. "Let's go to Puerto Escondido this summer," she said. "We've never been there, have we?"

She was referring to my favourite part of our game: each summer, in the low season, we'd drop out and rent a house on some secluded beach, unpack our bags, sleep a lot, cook our own food, and pretend we didn't live off robbing the working poor.

But weren't we supposed to be free of this life by then? "This summer?" I said. "There's no 'this summer.' We're getting out of this. That was the deal. That's why I came back."

"Yes, yes. Everything will work out. You'll see." She hiccupped and veered us toward a bench with a view of the moonlit bay. "Sit. Please."

Once settled on the bench, she reclined against me. "I meant we should go there. To put on our shows," she said. "There's lotsa Americans go there. Brits and Aussies, too. Surfers. Yes, I know you want to get out of Mexico, but that might be the right town for us."

Hearing her say that got me excited. We'd gone so long without discussing our theatre that I feared she'd decided it carried too much real risk and responsibility. Her silence on the subject was odd because she was its largest proponent. "We can check it out. First we need a lot more couples like the ones you met today."

She was a dead weight against me, and more drunk than I'd ever seen her on the job.

"We definitely do. And those guys aren't the big one we need," she said, waving in the direction of the Umbergers' room. "But it's coming. The big one."

Whatever that meant. She slumped ever further into me, drifting off.

I let her because thanks to her work that day we had a chance— the first in weeks—of fulfilling our dream. Nor could I forget she'd rescued me from the ashes of a once-successful acting career and a lifelong death through waiting tables and telemarketing.

So I'd trust her again, like I always did. Yet, not for the first time, I questioned whether she'd be able to leave the thrills our thieving provided for a more settled life.

Or if I could, for that matter.

Day 2

Acapulco

EXTENDED FAMILIES OF VENDORS,
from grandparents to babies, were arranging portable display racks
of beach toys when I arrived at the shore the following morning.
Uniformed hotel employees raised umbrellas and raked the sand free
of debris. As they had yesterday. As they would tomorrow.

Only the sea ever changed. That morning it was a choppy teal,
unwelcoming and conceivably portentous. I swam against the surf
inshore, this time never losing sight of Paraiso.

Back in our room, I let Jill sleep while I got us breakfast from the
buffet. When I'd roused her and we sat to eat, her usual volume and
enthusiasm were muted by her hangover. It didn't matter because
that day, our second at Paraiso, our focus was on execution rather
than strategy.

After we ate, she laid out chinos and the last clean shirt for me to
wear, then handed me a can of sunblock. "For after your shower," she
said. "And every two hours you're in the sun."

At the door, I got a goodbye kiss from my bed-headed wife in
her bathrobe, like an ordinary man leaving for an ordinary job. I
also received the floppy hat I hate wearing. "I know you didn't wear
it on the hike yesterday," she said. "But you need it. There's no
shade out there."

Jill and the American women were going shopping.
Unfortunately, this happy hubby wasn't able to offer cash from his

wallet for her to buy herself something nice. "I should be back by early afternoon," I said.

"I might be later than that. Whoever gets back first should do some laundry."

Soon Cal, Evan, and I were in a Volkswagen Beetle taxi jostling down Costera. The driver already had a sweat towel around his neck, letting us know how hot the day would get.

The Campo de Golf, midway along the bay, was the local country club for the better-heeled. The greens fees cost me 300 pesos, and the rental of a new-ish set of Callaways another 400. It was a significant outlay, leaving us with just over 2500 pesos. This had to work.

Golf was a skill I brought to the job. Growing up, my musician father had no interest in sports on which he couldn't place an easy wager. It was only after I landed my first starring role in a television series—as the handsome maverick Crown prosecutor Tom Walker in *Legal Ease*—and had scads of money and free time to spend it, that I took up the game. In ten years of playing, three on the finest courses in the Caribbean, I'd become a formidable opponent.

The boys had brought their own clubs, and for once I was evenly matched. Having played the course often, I was ahead by the third hole, when Cal began complaining—justifiably— about the scrubby, sun-baked grass and the sand on the greens. Evan kept pace until halfway, then lost interest. I let Cal get within a stroke on the seventh, then birdied to put it away.

Nine holes was sufficient, we agreed, beneath the brutal sun. I wheeled our cart up to the clubhouse. "How about some breakfast?" Evan said. "I'm sick of the food on the buffet."

I agreed, hoping the boys, who so far had paid cash, would use their cards.

The clubhouse restaurant had a patio overlooking the tennis courts and the parking lot. Beyond these, central Acapulco was lost in a sulphurous yellow haze. As we ate, SUVs rolled up and disgorged Mexican men in suits. *Narcotraficantes*? Lately they'd developed a lucrative alternate trade in kidnapping. That too was keeping me up nights.

The *huevos rancheros* were decent, but the coffee, typically, was instant. Cal pushed his mug aside. "You'd think a country that grows it would brew a decent cup."

"They export all the good stuff," Evan said. "To you. You drink it at home."

Cal took out his overstuffed wallet, flipped through a stack of credit cards, then set an American Express card beside his plate. My heart fluttered. "Excuse me," he said, standing. "If the waiter comes back, put it on that."

Some facts: Cal had never been ripped off before. Otherwise, he wouldn't have left his card so readily. And yes, sometimes it was that easy.

I hauled out my own wallet. "Cal, I can't let you do that."

"Sure you can," Evan said. "He'll just sell a few more cars."

I was glad it was Cal's card on the table, not Evan's. I liked Evan, who seemed genuine. He reminded me of a friend and fellow actor from university named Warren who used to have a hard time speaking up for himself.

The Amex card sparkled silver-blue in the sunshine, and my conscience prickled me. I pictured Cal and Lori stopping for groceries on their way home from the airport. I saw their shopping cart piled with Tater Tots and soft drinks, and the cashier explaining their card was maxed-out they'd have to call Amex. The shock and disbelief on their faces.

When the waiter brought the bill, Evan pulled a coupon from his shirt pocket and presented it to him. "Shauna gave me this. Makes sense to use it, I guess."

I'd seen coupons like it before. Teenagers handed them out at information kiosks along the strip. They offered discounts at restaurants and attractions across Acapulco and came in books of perforated pages. I'd just never seen anyone use them.

"*Gracias, gracias,*" Evan said to the waiter. And then to me: "How do you say that's not ten percent off your tip?"

The waiter smiled, nodding.

"You just did," I said.

Minutes later, I made a show of watching the waiter approach with the revised bill. In the few seconds it took for Evan to follow my gaze to him, I glanced down and memorized the numbers, aligned sideways to me, on Cal's card. I had Jill to thank for that trick.

From there, more patience was required. I still needed his four-digit pin number. Once we had that, Jill waited until the lime left the hotel before sending the numbers to her contact. On rare occasions, she'd "borrowed" a card long enough to clone it in a portable burner. Yet with newer cards proving impossible to clone, I insisted she stop stealing them. Until a few months ago, we'd been doing well enough to avoid the risk of getting caught red-handed.

We told ourselves that ours was a victimless crime, that the losses were handled by the banks and card companies and their immeasurable billions of dollars in reserve. In truth, I'm sure many people got hassled because of what we do. The waiter cleared our plates in silence, taking the card. Sorry for the trouble, *amigo*.

Cal proposed we walk back to Paraiso, forgetting it was a couple miles distant—a tough hump on shade-less Costera. I thanked Jill for my floppy hat. We'd strolled less than two hundred yards before he stopped at a restaurant patio. "Who wants a cold one?" he said, confirming my suspicion about why he wanted to walk.

It was early afternoon. Evan reluctantly assented, and ordered a Diet Coke. I joined Cal in a first Corona. He alone drank a second.

In letting Cal pay, I prayed to see his Amex pin number, but instead got the numbers of a Citibank Visa, again without the pin number. Disappointing, surely, but overall I was pleased with the developments since yesterday's dispiriting hike. Happier days shone on our horizon.

Back on the street, the boys uneasily marked the passing of two military trucks loaded with fully armed, black-masked soldiers. "They ought to keep you in line," Evan said to Cal.

They were Marines from the naval base at the end of the bay. When the drug war opened up a front in Acapulco, the city became, not surprisingly, less hospitable and occasionally hostile. Precisely the place for a desperate pair of gringo con artists to make a last stand.

We passed a dingy cantina advertising tacos, its lemony walls mudded by exhaust fumes. "Fish tacos?" Cal said. "Who wants to try a fish taco?"

I did, though it was scarcely an hour since we'd eaten. I badly wanted to finish this.

Evan chuckled to himself. "I'm out," he said, raising his hand for a taxi. "Cal, why don't you give me your clubs. I'll take them back for you."

A battered Beetle swung to the curb. It took the boys five sweat-inducing minutes to cram both sets of clubs into the tiny car. I marked their mutual concern and easy camaraderie.

As Steve Sawyer, I couldn't tell Cal he'd selected a Mexican, not a tourist, cantina, a grimy, dangerous place where Mexican men drink and fight. There were some men lounging within its murky depths and staring back at us. Also, the tacos would be awful. If Jill and I weren't so hard up, I'd have caught a ride with Evan.

Cal chose a seat on the patio, the better to ogle the promenading *chicas*, and ordered two Budweisers from an old man. "What we need is a boys' night out," he said. "Downtown, where the action is. You know what I mean?"

I did and had half-expected his suggestion. "I'm not sure that I do."

"Let's you and me and Ev go see the naked ladies. All these tourist towns have them."

A familiar weariness settled over me. I knew the location of every miserable strip joint in Acapulco. Evenings in them were expensive odysseys involving taxis and rambunctious drunkenness. But they were also superb opportunities to get card numbers. If you had the cash that sort of night required.

The beers arrived. Cal clinked my bottleneck. "You know who we ask?" he said. "The little guy on the front desk of our hotel. He'll know the score."

My memory of the rest of that afternoon is hazy. There was a Rolling Stones-themed bar and a humorous encounter with the *Policia Turistica*, chipper teenagers in crisp white uniforms offering directions and those books of coupons. Save for a round I got at a wine bar, Cal paid for everything, easily a dozen beers, plus platefuls of tacos to cram down his gullet. Tequila, too, that vilest of liquors. My excuse was that Jill had confiscated my credit cards. Now the onus was on me to return the courtesy of a bender.

Alas, in each place we visited, Cal paid cash, so I didn't get his pin numbers. My hope, each time he pulled pesos from his wallet, was that Jill had fared better with the girls, that between us we had complete sets of numbers.

The sun was setting when we returned to Paraiso. I saw Cal to his room, outside of which Lori was playing poker with Evan and Shauna at a patio table. From her attitude, I gathered it wasn't the first time Cal had come home tight. Cal and I made fuzzy plans to rent scooters the next day. The girls hadn't seen Jill since they returned from shopping late in the afternoon.

I said goodnight and reeled away toward our room. Twilight made long shadows of the umbrellas at the pool bar, hurricane lamps glowing rosily. Most people were heading for the bright cacophony of the dining room atop the hill. I nodded to them, feeling buoyant about our progress that day. I squinted for Jill in vain, anxious to share my excitement with her.

Then I saw them: Jill and a man descending the steps from the dining room. He was mid-fifties, darkly handsome, and wearing a perfectly rumpled linen suit. Meet Nick Vandal, actor, film producer, and former rock star.

Jill and Nick paused on a pathway, a rigid Jill intent on something he was saying. I watched her hand alight on his arm for a moment, and a slick dread cut through my beery glee. Nick reminded me of a raffish older man I'd seen Jill with a year ago, just before Jill and I were forced to temporarily separate

Then the wife entered the scene, inserting herself between Jill and Nick. Brenda Vandal was a tall, sharply angled, and deeply tanned woman with kinky blond hair. Jill would have said her pink mini-skirt and flowing white Mayan blouse were too youthful for a woman of her age.

I skirted the edge of the pool and darted behind some flowering bushes as the trio ambled toward the beach. The Vandals looked English, or maybe European, and more sophisticated than the tourists we usually robbed. Had Jill started a second squeeze? Our need certainly warranted it, although it could be impractical and dangerous.

They halted where two paths met so Nick could make an important point, allowing me to observe the stiff artificiality with which Jill held herself. I couldn't tell if it was Nick Vandal distressing her, or the woman who'd joined them. From the calculating glare Brenda kept levelled at Jill, I saw that she was another dreadful matter entirely.

I let them march on. If Jill was working the couple, I was too drunk to be of any use. Nor did she appear to be in any danger. I decided she was just being friendly, and staggered off in the direction of our room to wait there to share my good news.

Day 3

Acapulco

THAT THIRD MORNING AT PARAISO, despite a vigorous swim, I was feeling the worse for two nights of drinking. Still dripping seawater, I sat reading emails in the internet café off the main lobby.

My friend Warren had sent new photos of his son from Toronto, a jolly little guy about nine months old. I hung out with baby Ben last summer during my brief separation from Jill and got quite attached to him. Ben was modelling a sky-blue snowsuit in Riverdale Park, fresh snow heaped around him. Already drooping in the heat, in a swimsuit and t-shirt, I endured a pang for home and frigid winter days.

Warren wrote that the theatre company he'd joined last year was taking their homegrown black comedy, *Bumpercars*, to Boston and Providence. Great news. It was Jill who introduced me to Warren, way back in our first year at Ryerson. Like her, he'd been lucky enough to not have succeeded at acting when he was younger.

There were birthday wishes—I turned thirty-two last month—from my father, Earl Drake. I also stayed with Earl last summer, in the house I'd bought for him back when I was on television. He wrote that he was having heart trouble again. That was no surprise: his heart's been broken since my mother and her girlfriend died in a house fire when I was an infant. According to Granny Drake—Earl's mother, who was babysitting me elsewhere at the time—the fire was Earl's fault for letting the women fall asleep with candles still burning after a party.

In this latest instance, my dad had fallen ill at a card game. An ambulance was summoned—he probably loved that, the grand departure, his cronies concerned—and an emergency room doctor got him to a cardiologist straightaway. I was reading that Earl was awaiting test results, when I heard a loud thud followed by orders barked in angry Spanish spoken with an English accent.

In the lobby, the man I'd seen last night with Jill was shouting at a bellhop who was frantically righting an overturned luggage cart. Let him be leaving, I thought. Yet the cart, upright again, rolled deeper into the lobby. The bellhop chased after it, tossing bags aboard.

"Here, fucking watch yourself," Nick shouted at him. "You'll knock it over again."

A young manager-type in a suit stepped between Nick and the bellhop. As the only other non-Mexican male at hand, Nick sought me out for commiseration. "They lose your bags, then they knock them around for you. How's that for a welcome?"

I held up my open hands and turned back to my terminal to log off. I wanted to hear what Jill had to say about this pair. I'd passed out last night before I could show her the numbers I'd got from Cal, and she'd still been asleep when I left for my swim.

But first, needing something to read, I detoured to the games room for the communal shelf of books and magazines tucked away in the corner of every resort hotel. Among the chick lit and terrorist thrillers, behind a ping-pong table, was a crumbling copy of *King Lear*, *Macbeth*, and *Hamlet* in one volume. Of the three plays, this drama school near-graduate and former star of shows like *Street Heat* had only read *Hamlet*. And there wasn't room for Shakespeare in our present repertoire, since reading itself was often suspect with the people we got to know. I grabbed an Elmore Leonard novel for myself and some glossy magazines for Jill.

Borne upon clouds of steam, the aroma of Jill's many soaps and lotions ushered me into our room. Add her Camel cigarettes, plus the bourbon she enjoyed when she didn't have to drink what others were having, and you have the comforting scent of my ever-transitory home.

Jill was completing her make-up and preparing for a day at the beach. I tried to recall if I'd known we were going to the beach that day, as my forgetfulness was also an issue in our relationship. Jill complained that I never listened to her, and so never remembered what she told me. While that wasn't untrue, she often forgot to tell me things.

She emerged from the bathroom wrapped in a towel as I tossed the magazines onto one of her suitcases. "Are those for me?" she said. "Thank you."

"And this." I held up the sheet of hotel stationery on which I'd scrawled Cal's numbers.

Without her contact lenses in, she squinted at the page. "I got the same Visa number. But I didn't get the pin number. Did you?"

"I'll get it today. Both pin numbers. The big guy's a sloppy drunk. We're going to rent some scooters. What's up with the girls?"

"Nothing. I don't know if it was something I said. I mean, it was fine, but we didn't talk about hanging out again, and I didn't want to get pushy."

"It's okay. That happens. Is there a way back in?"

"I don't know. Do you think I'm losing my touch?"

That was a question I heard a few times each week in those last days. "No. I think we're both just really tired of doing this."

Which was what she needed to hear. "Guess they're getting lucky not knowing us."

"Don't worry. I've still got the guys."

She handed me some sunblock. "Never mind them now. I told this English couple I met last night we'd maybe do something today. He used to be a famous singer. You'll like them."

I dutifully smeared 45 over her back, my frustration evident. "Look, we should stick with the Americans. One more day and they'll be done. It's stupid to walk away now."

"Maybe we'll come back to them. Right now, this English couple will be faster." She tied on her bikini top, picked up her beach basket, and put on her sunglasses before sashaying to the door. "You coming?"

I'd no intention of abandoning the work I'd done on Cal and Evan. In fact, the beach was the best place to look for them. I swung my towel around my neck. "Right behind you."

Noon was a stupid time to arrive at the beach. There weren't any chairs available in our hotel's fenced-off *privada* section. We wound up in a cramped section of the *pública* beach, squeezed between a clump of rocks and a squabbling Mexican family.

Regardless, Jill thrived on the beach and in the heat, though wisely avoided the sun. "We won't see anyone here," she said, resplendent in her chair. "But we can move later."

"There'll be more chairs when people go up for lunch. So where's this English couple?"

"You'll see them." She stared at a Spanish edition of *Vogue*. "They definitely stand out."

That they did. "I'm getting a coffee," I said. "Do you want anything?"

"I'm fine. Hey, that was good work yesterday. I forgot to say thank you."

"Good work from you, too." Then I added, with some extra certainty more for myself than for her, "We'll be all right."

I returned to the tiki bar where two days ago I'd first espied Cal and Evan. A warm breeze rattled strings of coloured lights overhead. Sipping espresso, I glanced around in time to see Lori leave the bar with three plastic cups held aloft. I looked in the direction she was headed and spotted Shauna stretched out beneath an umbrella of palm fronds in the *privada* section.

By marching double-time over the sand in a wide arc, I managed to reach Shauna just as Lori did. "You girls got a good spot," I said.

"Hey, there you are." Shauna hauled herself upright. "Where's that pretty wife of yours?"

"We're at the other end. We got up late today."

Lori handed Shauna a drink. "You guys should move over here," she said.

"We're working on it," I said.

Cal and Evan sloshed in from the surf. "Stevie," Cal said. "How you feeling today?"

"About how you'd expect. I haven't been that drunk in a while."

Cal held an emerald starfish in his left hand. It pulsed slightly, suffocating. I wasn't surprised to see it in his hand so much as I was surprised to see it at all. In so far as possible, resort beaches are sanitized of any unnecessary, holiday-ruining wildlife. There were occasional warnings regarding jellyfish, but never anything menacing or fun.

Cal, however, I'd pegged for a predatory brute the instant I laid eyes on him. Had he never seen a starfish before? "What time do you want to get those scooters?" I said.

"That's not happening today, *hombre*. Last night put me in the doghouse."

Lori ignored his comment. "Cal, what the hell you got there?" she said.

Cal unzipped the pocket of a fanny pack hanging from a beach chair. I knew it was a knife he was after, and what he intended to do with it. "Please don't," I said, weakly.

Evan came up to watch. "Where's its mouth?" Cal said, slipping the short blade of a pen knife into one of the poor creature's arms. "How do you think it eats?"

"Turn it over," Evan said. "You see, there. It eats through all those feeler things."

I could have yanked the starfish from Cal's hands. But that would have meant the sacrifice of two starfish that day, not just one. I was wasting my time. I needed Cal alone, preferably late in the afternoon when he needed some hair of the dog. I told them I'd check in again later and excused myself.

Ahead of me, a silvery heat shimmered over the thousands of souls jammed along the twenty-mile curve of Acapulco Bay. Meandering between them, I felt a little woozy. When at last I found Jill again, I reported that the American couples wanted us to join them by the tiki bar.

Jill flapped magazine pages and smoked. "But there's nowhere to sit, is there?"

"No, not yet." I sank into my chair and opened a much-thumbed copy of *People* over my face. The roaring surf and the laughter and shrieks along the shore combined to lull me into a dangerous complacency about our situation, and so to sleep.

I woke to an English voice booming over me. Before I could react, the magazine was whipped from my face, and I lay exposed, blinking in the white fire of mid-afternoon, to the man I'd seen a few hours ago in the hotel lobby.

"Gina, I frightened him," Nick said. With his dark features, he sounded more English than he looked.

Jill handed me my sunglasses. "Steve, this is the couple I met. Nick's a film producer." Her English accent was gone, I noted, not twenty yards from the Americans.

"I thought you said he was a singer." I sort of recognized him as a musical somebody from way before my time. His wife stood speaking into a phone not far off.

"That too." Nick loomed over me. "I want mussels for my dinner, mate. Gina says you know a good spot. Mussels and beer."

"Remember we went to that place the other day?" Jill said.

The restaurant she likely meant was on the far side of Acapulco, and we'd eaten there with a Canadian couple a year ago. "What part of town is it in?" Nick said.

"Downtown, I think." I wondered how Jill proposed to pay for this meal. "It's a long way. I'm sure there's places closer just as good."

"We'll take a taxi then," Nick said before lurching across the sand to where his wife stood. "Tell him I'm not paying that much to have the option extended," he shouted at her.

Brenda tossed the phone at him. "Why don't you? He put me on hold." Her frantic eyes searched me, looking for I don't know what. I shuddered. Fair warning.

Nick walked back toward us. "So what are we doing before dinner? It's just gone two."

"Have you seen the cliff divers?" Jill said.

I sensed a chance to get out of the killer sun. "There's the old fort downtown," I said.

"How about something a little less touristy?" Brenda said.

"What the fuck," Nick said. "We've got to do something."

We decided to get changed and meet outside of the lobby. Jill repacked her basket, and we trooped across the sand. I steered us from the section where I'd last seen the Americans to avoid any cross-pollination of our scams.

Beside me, Nick snarled into the phone then returned it to his wife. "You, Steve," he said. "Where've I seen you before?"

I faced a delicate decision. Nick might have seen me on *Legal Ease*, which was syndicated in twenty countries. Or in my last role, before my career collapsed, as a turncoat informer in a BBC miniseries shot cheaply in Toronto, with a week of atmospheric exteriors in London of places like Big Ben and Piccadilly. If Nick was a producer, maybe he'd been involved in that?

Yet as much as I'd always wanted to be recognized as a former television star, it had never happened. "You saw me this morning. You were yelling at a valet about your luggage."

"Yeah, that monkey. Used our bags for football practice. You can tell a lot about a place by the way they treat you when you're checking in."

"You just got in today?"

"Yeah, this morning."

Before I could contemplate that falsehood, I spotted Lori and Shauna near the bar. I veered right into a grove of palm trees, but it was too late. Lori and Shauna waved, their voices screeching for Gina above the din of the beach.

"Gina, there's somebody calling you," Nick said.

Jill offered the girls a friendly wave. I did too, for good measure.

So did Nick Vandal, like the star he purported to be. My gut said he'd be more trouble than he was worth, and I regretted again the chance we might miss with the Americans. The morning had me feeling deflated and a little dizzy. I should have listened to Jill and worn my hat. I reminded myself the Americans still had a few days left at Paraiso, and led Jill and the Vandals through the palms toward the main building.

One of my favourite things in Acapulco is the tricked-out, chromed public buses plying the streets. Christened *Fantomas* or *Dios Es Amor* and painted with Catholic saints or superheroes like the Fantastic Four, at ten pesos, their jarring, diesel-choked rides are a bargain.

If you aren't in a hurry. Like much of Mexico, they're more enchanting than efficient, the drivers pausing to chat with girls en route or eat a taco from a vendor's cart. Dozens rattled past, blasting hip hop, while the Vandals kept us waiting on the streetside of Paraiso. Jill was bubbling happiness, the Vandals having allowed her to jettison the Walmart crap she'd worn for the Americans. And, I think, because I'd agreed to her abrupt change of plan.

When the Vandals arrived, I suggested a bus to cover the five miles to the fort. We needed to keep this excursion as inexpensive as possible.

"What, and get stabbed?" Nick snorted. "Not if you paid me."

Steve cranked up his tourist enthusiasm. "C'mon. Don't they look, like, neat?"

"The taxi will be air-conditioned," Jill said, meaning for me to leave off. So I did, bringing up the rear as our foursome joined the perpetual parade along Costera.

Jill and I were by no means the first crooks to set up shop in Mexico. Centuries ago, the Spanish murdered the native population with broadswords, Christianity, and disease. *Conquistadors*, they called themselves. Conquerors. Pirates soon followed, raiding the coastal

35

towns. Later, the French took over and installed an emperor. The Americans invaded, ditto the British. The Mexicans have had quite enough trouble with foreigners.

The Vandals were here before us, too. Or so I suspected, during our prolonged transit of Costera in our *un*-air-conditioned taxi, from their references to other cities they'd visited in Mexico. And from how comfortable Nick was in giving orders to the driver in Spanish.

I sat sweating in the backseat, sinking from pessimism into despair. If they lived in Mexico, and had credit cards issued by Mexican banks, they were of no use to us.

The *Fuerte de San Diego*, perched atop a rock shelf in the old centre of town, dated from the days of the pirates. Or so I recalled from visiting it with a couple from Maine. In addition to a history lesson, Jill got their MasterCard number in the gift shop, and that night I scored their pin number when the husband and I made a midnight run for quesadillas. A textbook squeeze from the good old days. Gone now. All of it. Oh, the money and the luck we took for granted.

The taxi dropped us behind a motorcoach offloading a gaggle of Scandinavians. The Vandals—Nick in his wrinkled linen suit, and gangly Brenda in a skin-tight, tie-dyed dress—drew stares and murmurs. Seeing Nick inhale the attention like air left me hopeful he'd be so blinded by his own importance that he'd be careless with his credit cards.

A switchback path led up the cliff face, then over a moat and drawbridge. Nick paid Jill's admission from a healthy roll of pesos, leaving me to do the same for Brenda. Apparently, this allowed him to take Jill by the waist and steer her down an arched tunnel into a dusty courtyard. She flinched at his touch, almost violently so. Flirting and touching were part of the job, so I was surprised to see her react that way.

Ever the professional, she quickly recovered. When Nick's fat hand brushed her bottom, she easily removed it. I watched as she laughed at something Nick said, her hand searching for a strand of hair taken by a hot rush of wind. Her wry grin, when I reached her, assured me she'd handled lecherous old fools before.

My task was to distract Brenda, who straggled behind either yammering into her phone or texting. She made no secret of her lack of interest in the fort or in me.

"Cellphones make it tough to really get away, don't they?" I said.

"I'm arranging a solo retrospective at a gallery in Mexico next month."

"Wow. Great," Steve Sawyer was obliged to say. "By Mexico you mean the city, right?"

Brenda sort of grimaced in response as she made another call. She spoke Spanish with an American accent, which puzzled me. Not that Steve Sawyer understood what she was saying. I moved off, confused and irritated. Body language conveys our true feelings for other people, and I needed a moment to reorganize mine.

Bleached-white stone battlements. Cannons pointing out to sea, pyramids of balls at the ready. Inspired by Brenda's condescension, I broadly played the hapless tourist with my camera.

The best part of the fort was the view of the real Acapulco straggling up the velvety green mountainsides. The impenetrable barrios visible through the trees were where our Mexican hosts called home. At the moment, Jill and I couldn't even afford to live there.

Nick interrupted my contemplation. "Acapulco's a stupid place. Filthy. Dangerous, too, now that the drug cartels are fighting over it. Have you ever been to Veracruz?"

Steve Sawyer certainly hadn't. Neither had I. "No. Where's that?"

"Opposite coast. It's where we live. Be easy to arrange a visit, if you'd like." Before I could respond, he exited down a cobblestone ramp to the museum housed in the barracks under the walls. I clung to the view, baffled by why he'd make such an offer to a stranger.

Downstairs, among the rusty swords and sea chests, was the diorama of colonial Acapulco from which I had learned about the pirates. Model corsairs fired their guns into the city, where the miniature invading swashbucklers met stiff resistance from the locals. The museum was a bust otherwise, the tiny rooms stifling.

It was cooler back on Costera in the greasy breeze created by the traffic rushing past. Nick wanted to visit a big park containing some tropical gardens. According to Steve's tourist map, the park was halfway back to our hotel.

"Another day," Brenda said. "I've had enough sun. Let's get a drink in the zócalo."

"I didn't say we'd walk," Nick said. "What are taxis for?"

Brenda answered with her feet, turning toward the centre of town. I flapped the map open again to show Nick that the main square was nearby, but he pushed passed it. "Don't fucking show your back to me," he shouted after his wife. "Where're you off to?"

Jill and I trailed at a safe distance. "I'm not taking Mexican cards," I said. "No way."

Jill's mouth formed a single, solemn line. "Let's hope we don't have to."

We caught up to them where the knotted streets of central Acapulco reached around the mass of rock supporting the fort. A densely packed area of cheap hotels and eateries opened up. On our left, the shiny yachts of a better class bumped at anchor against the sea wall.

Acapulco's thickly treed zócalo rose from Costera to the steps of the cathedral. We settled on the terrace of an Italian restaurant in the shade of a banyan tree. Although the Vandals had made up, or postponed their tiff, Nick's scowl frightened away any vendors who approached our table. Without consulting anyone, he ordered a margherita pizza and a litre of white wine. I ordered an orange soda, Jill a beer. I trusted we were going Dutch.

Once she got some wine into her, Brenda warmed to Steve, listening with apparent interest to his account of his communications job at an insurance firm. She and Nick hadn't glanced at one another since we sat down. So much for having to find that wedge.

Nick, meanwhile, regaled Jill with stories of movie stars he'd recently met, his busy hands dropping from his glass to alight on her crossed legs. She appeared to be following amiably, but I sensed an odd detachment from her. She always excelled at creating a rapport, becoming the easiest companion to the dullest or least likable people. Not so with Nick, whose relentless narcissism made him a difficult case.

Brenda poured the last of the wine into her glass and ordered another litre. I suspected she might be a Jekyll and Hyde drunk— always unpredictable and rarely profitable. Fresh out of stories of our life in Buffalo, I held my nose and asked about her art. Big mistake: "… weaving images from Aztec mythology into urban landscapes. I'm re-interpreting the sun god …"

As Brenda droned on about herself, I detected odd tonal shifts in her accent, which at times sounded as inconstant as Jill's had two days ago. Midway through her mini-manifesto, a foot brushed against my bare leg beneath the table. Since Jill sometimes offered reassuring pats while on the job, I enthusiastically returned it. Only then did I consider that my distance from Jill made it impossible for her to reach me.

Brenda beamed at me. I was saved by her ringing phone, which she instantly answered.

Nick continued nattering at Jill, who was doing a great job of looking interested. "Why keep chasing it?" he was saying of his musical career. "Did I want to be the next David Bowie? Definitely. But it wasn't in the cards, so fuck it. You've got to try new things."

I wanted to ask if he ever got recognized, or if he still cared to be. But that would have been Daniel Drake asking, not Steve Sawyer. I didn't regret the years I wasted trying to revive my acting career because if I hadn't failed so spectacularly, I'd have never been reunited with Jill.

Brenda tossed her phone onto the table. "The gallery couldn't open the files. I have to go back and resend them."

Nick resented the interruption. "What, now?"

"Yes now or the catalogue won't be ready in time."

Nick took Jill's hands in his own. "Gina, love. We'll have to postpone this until dinner."

Distracted by Nick's forwardness, I missed the waiter delivering the cheque. Brenda gave him a credit card so quickly I saw only that it was a Visa. And Jill, focused on the syrup Nick was feeding her, couldn't have seen it from her side of the table.

That Brenda managed the cards was potentially telling. These sorts of expatriates were older, educated, and in semi-retirement. Many owed the IRS or Her Majesty's Revenue and Customs back taxes. Working them was often tedious because they rarely used credit cards.

The waiter returned with a debit machine. Brenda paid and pocketed her card so rapidly, all I got was a foreboding sense that she was on to us.

"Thanks for the drinks," I said. "We'll get you back another time."

"Looking forward to it."

In the interval between acts, we returned to our room until dinner. While Jill showered, I caught an episode of the steamy telenovela we'd been following the last three months. *Lo que les falta a los ricos*, it was called. *What the Rich Lack*. Subtlety, foremost. And while the poor did as well, I was pleased I understood most of the dialogue. The way things were headed, I'd need Spanish in prison.

I woke to Jill leaning over me in a towel. Seeing an opportunity, my hands reached up, but she pulled herself away. "I said get into the shower. Let's not keep them waiting."

The Vandals, she meant. Why bring them into this? I made room for her to join me in bed, tugging at her arm. When she didn't, I said, "What happened to you this afternoon? When that asshole was going on about himself. You zone out a bit?"

"I'm tired, I guess. All this worrying about money."

"Yeah, me too. So tell me how we're going to pay for this dinner. How much is left?"

"About 2000 pesos."

"That's not enough. Were you hoping to find some money on the way to the restaurant?"

"I don't know. But I need you to get ready because I can't do this without you."

A comforting thought, except I couldn't overlook that the Vandals had her a bit rattled. That became further evident in the complicated updo she made of her hair while I showered. And in the slinky dress I'd not seen before and the fresh polish on her nails. She looked magnificent, but the special effort rankled me, and I couldn't say why.

She tossed me the crumpled chinos I'd worn golfing with Cal and Evan. "You should give those an iron."

"You do it. If these English idiots are so important to you." I stormed out the patio doors into the milky twilight and slumped in a deck chair. By now, Cal would likely be two beers into his recovery. If Jill and I wanted to open that little theatre, I needed to be with guys like him.

"C'mon, Danny," she called after me. "We don't have time for one of your tantrums."

Tarty pop songs, the tinkling of glassware, and the throaty laughter of drinkers drifted over from the pool bar. To be fair, Jill's preparations weren't any more elaborate than they were for other dinners. Something about the Vandals felt wrong and had us both off our game.

My unease reminded me that I still didn't know much about her life during the five years we were apart after university. She modelled for a time, she'd said, then taught English in Mexico City. When the school abruptly closed, she drifted back into the scams that had sustained her when she was younger.

Not that I wanted to know everything about her, like the details of her criminal contacts. And there were things about myself in those five years that I wouldn't have been comfortable sharing with her. What mattered was that we had each other and a shared respect and trust. Considering the many unhappy couples we encountered, that was rare.

With that in mind, I stuck my head back into our room. "Sorry. That was uncalled for."

The freshly ironed chinos and a lavender shirt hung from a standing lamp. "Apology accepted. Now can you please get dressed? Please. We have to work."

The Argentine steakhouse Nick chose for dinner had a nautical theme and was finished in gilt and French blue. The Vandals were munching salad, something only done by residents of Mexico or poorly informed tourists, and had drained a bottle of wine. Nick smacked his lips as he chewed, making horrible noises. I steered a disgusted Jill into the seat beside him.

The prices on the menu were blinding. The appetizers alone could have finished us.

More wine arrived, then bloody steaks. As we ate, the Vandals tried to outdo each other with stories of celebrities they knew. Jill was more of a presence than earlier but less than her usual sparkling self. She played the quiet, introspective type in a way I'd rarely seen from her. I tried to meet her eyes to offer some support. You can get lonely in a squeeze.

Brenda was also a performer and had enjoyed a role on a long-running British hospital drama. Of the pair, she was the worse for drink, at one point tilting sideways into me, arms flailing to catch herself, her many silver bracelets clattering against the table. As the meal progressed, she conceded the table to Nick, enduring his stories in a surly silence.

Nick chewed some steak then looked at me as if for the first time. "What is it you do?"

I repeated that I did internal communications for an insurance firm.

"Really? That's boring. Doesn't sound like you at all."

"Steve's an actor too," Jill said. "He won an award last year."

News to me. I couldn't understand why she'd offered that or where she might be going with it. Considering I actually had been a professional actor, it was potentially a problematic thing to say. "Just for community theatre," I said. "But it felt great to get it."

"Tough work, isn't it?" Nick said. "Acting. I had a rough go the first few movies I did."

"I knew there was a reason I liked you," Brenda said to me.

I lifted her hand from my thigh. "If you think of it as work," I said to Nick. "So what are you producing?"

He peered at me over his goblet of merlot. "Action picture. Commandoes. We're talking to Jason Statham. I'm meeting some investors tomorrow. You want a part?"

"Are you serious?" Steve and I were equally thrilled. "Absolutely."

"There's one that might interest you. School mate of the hero. Not a big role, but meaty."

Brenda snorted into her wine. I felt unreasonably excited, especially since I knew nothing ever came of these seemingly divine encounters.

Anxiety clouded Jill's face. "I guess we'll have to stay in touch, hey Steve?"

I heard her concern. She'd just been trying to include me in the conversation. Now thanks to my over-inflated ego, our situation with the Vandals was more complicated.

"Of course you should," Brenda said, her hand returning to my thigh.

A light went on within me: they were swingers. The icky couple pairings, Nick's weird invitation to their home, and their overall smarminess. Jill and I had a rule against swappers and had twice refused invitations from some lusty German couples.

Another rule was that Jill never called her contact with card numbers while we were still at the same hotel as the cardholders. We also avoided drugs of any sort. We never worked more than one scam at a time or switched scams mid-stream to new subjects at the same hotel. And we no longer stole cards, since being caught with them would involve the local police.

The meal dragged on, the Vandals sniping at each other and drinking themselves into a stupor. Eventually, Nick rose unsteadily and paid for our feast from his endless stack of pesos. It was a great relief, and a huge setback.

Nick leaned on Jill, and I attended to Brenda. While we steered the Vandals between tables of gawking diners, I couldn't help but notice Nick mutter conspiratorially into Jill's ear. Here again, a lime's flirty familiarity with Jill usually wouldn't have bothered me. But in this instance, for reasons I couldn't yet fathom, I hated it.

Outside, a salty mist softened the edges of the city. Jill plonked Nick onto a curb and escaped his eager hands to smoke a cigarette. Brenda wandered off toward the Elcano hotel. Was I supposed to chase after her? I didn't.

It was after midnight, and the taxis swirling out of the fog were all occupied. Two American couples emerged from the restaurant, talking and laughing loudly. Jill and I both turned their way, expectantly, and caught each other doing so. Of course it wasn't our friends from the night before. The glance we shared conveyed all our frustration and disappointment.

I looked away first, hoping to conceal my blame. We'd probably squandered yesterday's gains when we might have finished the American couples by now and been on our way to a new hotel. Instead, with only four days remaining at Paraiso, we'd reached another dead end.

Part 1

King's Reach

WELCOME TO KING'S REACH
Correctional Institution, a minimum-security prison housing over two
hundred inmates on a jagged corner of Vancouver Island.

Welcome also to the place I've called home since those last days
in Mexico with Jill. And to the most difficult and dangerous role of
my career: a prison inmate. I've been at King's Reach for one year
and nine days and need to serve three more years, or a full third
of my twelve-year sentence for drug trafficking, before I'm eligible
for parole. At least, that's my hope. Lately there's been evidence to
believe I'll soon be facing new charges.

Before arriving here, I spent seven months in a detention centre
in Vancouver awaiting trial. That puts the events in Mexico eighteen
months distant, although it often feels like less.

King's Reach houses white-collar criminals and other offenders
nearing the end of their sentences. Save for the fence marking the
perimeter, it more resembles a place for a corporate retreat than a
jail. That prisoners don't walk away is due to the facility's isolation.
It's a half hour drive through heavily forested country to the fishing
town of Gracechurch. King's Reach is an island on an island. There's
also a fully equipped gym, pool tables, and a fifty-seat screening
room left over from the days before inmates had laptops and tablets.
Why would anyone leave?

After a rough adjustment to life in prison, I now do two things here. I'm writing a day-by-day account of my last days in Mexico to help me understand what happened down there, and I'm directing a production of The Tempest starring myself as Prospero.

The day my future at King's Reach became a lot brighter began as usual with thirty laps of the swimming pool. After breakfast in the dining room, I re-read the little I'd written in the notebook provided for my account by the prison psychiatrist. For a while now, I've been stuck on those first few days in Acapulco. That morning, it was easier to gaze out the window at the rare winter sunshine than try to make sense of that mess down south.

I was also puzzling over the length of The Tempest. It takes Prospero and the gang a long time to get off that island. I shared my concerns with a convicted arms smuggler named Hassan, who's playing Stephano in our production. He agreed that parts of the text could be trimmed.

At mid-morning, I headed out to the tennis courts in search of a match. Here I discovered the position of a ball was in dispute. Two men circled each other, probing for weaknesses. One was a burly member of the Warlords biker club, our local baddies. The other was a handsome young hothead named Tyler who's playing Ferdinand, the love interest in The Tempest.

"Tyler, don't," I shouted, my voice lost among other inmates urging them to fight.

Here in prison, I've learned the hard way that fighting bikers is like playing Whac-A-Mole. If you beat one, another turns up, then another or a gang of them. Tyler fighting was bad for the show. I needed my Ferdinand intact.

I took his arm to restrain him, but he shook himself from my grasp. The racquets clattered to the court, the taunts turned to blows, and a sick roar rose from the spectators. I grabbed my towel and returned to the main prison complex to ask the warden to not punish Tyler. With The Tempest opening in the screening room in two weeks, there wasn't time to rehearse someone new for the role.

During my first months in prison, I got into many fights thanks in part to all the media attention my arrest and conviction received. ("Hard Time for TV's Hunky Tom Walker" was my favourite headline.) A year ago, at my sentencing in a Vancouver courtroom, I was ordered to the Kent Institution, a maximum-security prison with a mean reputation, to await a permanent placement in the penal system. I was told I might languish at the Kent for a year before being transferred to a medium-security facility.

The inmates at the Kent prepared a brutal welcome for me. They attacked me in the gym, in the shower, even in my cell. They beat me in shifts, relieving each other like wrestling tag teams. Yet if I hadn't endured it, I wouldn't now be in King's Reach procrastinating on an assignment from a shrink while I mount productions of Shakespeare. In a roundabout way, I can thank my fame for that.

Doubtless there are people who'd insist I deserved every blow I received, that I got off easy with the drug conviction—I think I did—and still need to answer for my real crimes. If so, they'll be glad to hear I'm expecting the new charges. They'd also be disappointed by how desperately I fought back. A childhood in which I started at new schools sometimes twice a year meant facing more than my share of schoolyard bullies. The thugs at the Kent weren't the first to be shocked by how well I defended myself.

In those dark days last year, all that I'd recently lost in Mexico left me unhinged in a way I still don't understand. I'd leap at my attackers like I wanted a beating. Or fight through convulsions of sobs that forced them to back off in confusion and fear. Which, I guess, was a method of self-preservation? Once, when I could no longer stand up, I was bundled into a corner and beaten with a table leg. I woke up in the infirmary. I'd had three teeth knocked out, both eyes had been battered shut, and my nose and three ribs were broken. Pretty boy no more.

With the clarity a few boots to the head brings, I saw how my need for attention would only make prison more difficult to endure. The authorities agreed: I was a flashpoint and was immediately transferred to a less dangerous prison.

Within days of arriving at King's Reach, I was summoned to the office of the warden, Sherman Carr, upstairs in the administrative wing. The hour he kept me waiting, I passed gazing from a window that offered the prison's only view of the rocky shoreline of the Strait of Georgia. On stormy nights, when my roommate wasn't snoring, I'd heard the distant sound of the surf.

Warden Carr is a precise man in his fifties who wears his thinning hair cut short. He told me that my rescue from the Kent, and what he called my celebrity, would not translate into continued special treatment. He also shared his goal of rehabilitating every convict in his prison via addiction therapies and pioneering anger-management and alternatives-to-violence clinics. My continued presence at King's Reach depended on my participation in the services available to me, and on my demonstrated commitment to self-improvement.

I left our chat determined to serve my time as quietly as possible and avoid this fussily ambitious man. Unfortunately, the fighting had reawakened an older, harder version of myself. I raged against my confinement, filling my days with garbage television, paperback thrillers, and the internet. None of the warden's programs appealed to me: I'd mostly completed university, I wasn't addicted to anything worse than fame, and I didn't care to learn a trade. I stumbled about obsessed by the fatal decisions I made in those last days in Mexico. What a fool I'd been.

Meanwhile, my fellow inmates thumbed game controllers for days on end or slept their lives away in thirteen-hour nights. I couldn't see they offered friendship and the secrets to surviving in prison. My isolation was perfect. I read online that Shakespeare was thirty-seven when *Hamlet* was first performed. I was thirty-four and could look forward to reaching thirty-seven without a change of scenery.

Word of my attitude eventually reached the upstairs offices. At our second meeting, two months into my stay at King's Reach, Warden Carr asked why I'd been snubbing his programs and avoiding the communal tasks like kitchen duty and groundskeeping. I wasn't keeping my half of the bargain. Did I want to participate or return to the Kent?

Since he put it that way, I told him to sign me up for whatever he wanted.

Fortunately for me, it wasn't that simple. To convince me to want to participate, the warden insisted I consult with a shrink named Dr. K who was occasionally available to inmates.

In my salad days on *Legal Ease*, I was briefly involved with a vain co-star named Hannah Dyer. The same Hannah whose character survived that show's sudden demise to live on as a private investigator in a spin-off. During our difficult month together, Hannah would update me on what she'd learned about herself "in session" with her psychiatrist. She also played a homemaker in a series of television commercials and once claimed to have used the insights psychoanalysis provided in pitching a fabric softener. Her analyst helped her dig deeper, she said, to fully flesh out her character.

Nonsense, I told her. What a load of psychobabble. Yet she must be doing something right, as her show is in its sixth season, a huge hit in Europe, and I'm in prison.

Dr. K isn't a real psychiatrist, he's a psychotherapist named Kyle Moran who reminds me of a fortysomething version of that jock-ish, chummy guy everyone knew in high school. In my thieving days down south, guys like him, with no natural predators, were easy to befriend.

We first met—and still meet—in a beige room in the administrative wing. The wooden table separating us is scarred with inmates' names and suggestions for sexual positions. At our first meeting, he smiled like a friend and thanked me for coming, as if I'd had a choice. He said that both the warden and a doctor at the detention centre in Vancouver had noted that I displayed a lack of interest in my own affairs.

"Does that sound familiar?" Dr. K asked. "Do you feel hopeless at times?"

"Depends on what you mean by hopeless," I said.

The man nodded, essentially saying: so it'll be like that, will it?

Dr. K lives in the Vancouver suburbs and commutes across British Columbia for chats with inmates in different prisons. Although he loves his work, he misses his wife and two young sons so much that he wants a job closer to home. He usually looks tired and harried. The road will wear you out.

He told me about himself, I suspect, so I'd share the truth about myself. But there is no truth. Everyone's in character, making this up as we go along. Or so I believed at the time.

"How do we do this?" I said. "Since I have to. I mean, when do we start?"

"Now's good," he said. "Start at the beginning. Where you grew up, your parents, that sort of thing, and we'll see where that takes us."

I told him I had no solid memories of my mother, who died before I was two.

"My father raised me while moving us between towns in search of work. He had—he has—a gambling problem, so there were often bookies dogging our trail. When I got fed up with that life, I moved in with Granny Drake, his mother, to attend high school in the town where I was born. Granny was a kleptomaniac. The police were always bringing her home from stores. I thought it was because she was old, but my dad said she'd had itchy fingers even when he was a kid."

Dr. K nodded again. He was tough to read, though that was likely part of his shtick.

"I started acting in grade school," I continued, "and kept at it in high school. Then I went to Ryerson University for drama. But before I graduated, I got a role in a television series, so I dropped out. When that show ended, I moved to Mexico to teach English. And when the school went out of business, I got involved with drugs, and that's how I ended up in prison."

Hearing this, Dr. K jerked forward in his seat, unable to contain his smirk. "Teaching English, huh?" he said. "That's not what I heard you were doing down there."

I shrugged. The old me, the thief from the resorts, suspected I had a mook.

"All right," he said. "What can you tell me about your girlfriend?"

"She wasn't into drugs," I said, "so she doesn't factor in this."

About Jill, he was relentless. "You were students together at Ryerson, right?" he said.

"Yes. Then after graduation, she went to Mexico. I stayed because of the shows. Then when I couldn't get any more acting jobs in Toronto, I went to Mexico, and we hooked up again."

The doctor weighed this for a moment. "That's it?" he said. "Nothing else to add?"

I had to be careful here. "I miss her," I said. "A lot. And I'm still pissed that I haven't heard from her, but I'm sure she has her reasons."

To avoid discussing Jill, I talked about my father, blaming him for turning me into a bad egg, when of course the fault was entirely my own. This blah blah flowed beautifully until midway through our fifth or sixth session, when Dr. K abruptly cut me off. "I've heard all this before," he said. "You're just flapping your lips. Are you sure you want to continue with this?"

"The warden says I have to be here."

"That's not my problem," he said. "There's lots you're not telling me. Come back when you really feel like talking."

A week later, I got into an argument in the kitchen over a dirty pot that I claimed a fellow inmate hadn't cleaned properly. A taller, bulkier fellow inmate. I was definitely the aggressor. Inexplicably so, for my heart wasn't in the fight, and I ended up the worse for it. The warden warned me that if I got into another one, I'd be shipped back to the Kent. With cartoon stars still circling my head,

I didn't understand what I'd become and hated it. I was also feeling increasingly awful about everything Jill and I had done down south.

I next saw Dr. K in the lounge area, speaking with a man whose son had just been killed in a boating accident. In his baggy jeans and Canucks jersey, Dr. K looked like another inmate. Where before I couldn't understand what he gained from hearing so many sob stories, I now considered that he genuinely liked helping people. That made him unique.

I waited until he was free, my latest black eye shining, and asked if I could see him again. He very graciously said that I could and, at our next meeting, asked again about my girlfriend and what had driven me out of Mexico.

"Why?" I said. "I told you. It's over. She's gone."

"Look how upset you get when I mention her," he said. "Can't you see we have to start there?"

To assist me in accessing how I felt about my situation, he told me to write an account of my last weeks down south. It was important to consider the emotional circumstances of that time as much as the events themselves. "Make it a diary," he said, offering a hardbound notebook. "Break it down day by day. And don't leave out your girlfriend. We need to know everything about her. This is the only way forward for us."

Until my assignment was ready, we'd find ways for me to fit in at King's Reach and avoid further conflict. Then he asked if I knew what I wanted to do after my release.

"Bit early for that, isn't it?" I said. "The old-timers say take one day after the other."

"They're old-timers because they never figured it out. Daniel, let me ask you: what do you want to do when you get out of here?"

Act. I want to act. Then. Now. Always. It's what I do. Even down in the resorts with Jill, I treated my "roles" with the utmost respect, inhabiting my characters to the best of my ability. But I know how rare it is for washed-up television actors to successfully relaunch their careers after a stint in prison. A career, I must add, that had tanked years before my incarceration.

"Act," I said. There was an odd constriction in my throat. "Act. I want to act again."

"Now we're getting somewhere," Dr. K said. "Would you consider putting on a show?"

"In prison? I'd just get beat up again. You're joking, right?"

I had to respond carefully. Like Jill, Dr. K has the gift of putting an idea in your head and making it seem like your own. "How would I do that?" I said. "If I was interested."

"I'd talk to the warden if I were you. Did you know he used to be an actor? He tried to start a drama program here a few years ago, but no one was interested."

Apparently Warden Carr had been, decades ago, a drama student at college before transferring to correctional studies when his wife became pregnant. It jived with his egoism and need to control. Once a performer, always a performer.

With our time at an end, Dr. K opened the door for me. "Think about it," he said. "Or let me know if you get a better idea. You need to be busier."

Downstairs a dour line of convicts had formed at the locked doors to the dining room, waiting for the evening meal. They weren't anticipating a lack of food or a shortage in seating. They simply didn't have anything else to do. I joined the queue instead of walking back to my room only to have to leave again.

There was no point in staging a show where no one acted and fewer still would care to watch. Generally, acting for theatre is tougher work than acting for television, and there's no money in it. The most you can hope for is the respect of your peers.

And yet, I couldn't deny my growing excitement over the prospect of performing again. I'd really missed it.

The doors to the dining room opened, and the line slouched forward. I slipped out of it.

He had me. By appealing to my vanity, Dr. K had shown me a path out of my funk.

I jogged back upstairs to book a meeting with the warden, who wasn't free until next week. Ample time, I recall thinking, to polish my pitch, having decided that, without question, King's Reach needed a production of *You're a Good Man, Charlie Brown*.

Warden Carr was initially cool to *Charlie Brown* and waited a week before summoning me back to his office to re-pitch the show to me on his terms: he would be the artistic director and have the last word on casting. There was that ambition again.

"Great," I said. "So long as we understand that the role of Snoopy is already filled."

Interest in the show grew slowly. No one wanted to audition, and I had to lean on two inmates with acting experience to play Charlie Brown and Linus. That got everyone's attention, and on the day of the open call, thirty men waited in line outside the screening room. The old Steinway was rolled in from the lounge, and an inmate found to hammer out the score. I scrounged a dog food bowl and scrap lumber from the woodworking shop to build a doghouse. That's how, a few months after my conviction, the newly formed King's Reach Players mounted a successful production of *Charlie Brown*—so successful that we're now greatly expanding our range with *The Tempest*.

The path through the pine trees back to the prison complex was still silvered with overnight frost. Two guards lumbered past me, heading to the tennis courts. They never hurried to a fight, and often let men batter themselves into exhaustion before pulling them from harm.

I share a room in the main corridor with a hulking Serb immigrant named Dragan Saranovic, who told me I'd just missed the old man who delivers the mail. Dragan showed me a crayon Christmas scene he'd received from one of his young daughters. There were colourful paintings and drawings plastered on the wall over his bed. Dragan is a few months shy of being paroled, and one of the happier men in King's Reach.

"I like that her Christmas tree is orange," I said. The wall over my bed was achingly bare in comparison. "And that there's tons of presents."

Dragan once owned a roofing business in Vancouver, where he also coached kids' soccer and arranged international tournaments. A few years ago, he accepted payment for a trip to Japan from dozens of parents then absconded with the money. When the police tracked him to Serbia, he took off again. Six months later, he surrendered in Prague, destitute and asking to be taken into custody.

When I heard his story from another inmate, I wondered how a father of three swindled other kids. I never asked, because Dragan's friendly with the Warlord bikers, who control the contraband here, and has a stash of phones and tablets under his bed. He passes his days playing chess in a disused room with other brainy eastern Europeans. As my game's not horrible, I sometimes join him there when the Players' production schedule allows it.

I reached into my locker for the notebook Dr. K provided me, figuring I'd work on my journal while waiting to speak to the warden about Tyler. I was surprised to find it on some socks when I thought I'd left it beneath them. Lately, it never seemed to be where I'd placed it last.

Dragan said, "You're like my oldest girl, always writing in your diary."

"If it's a diary, why would I keep it somewhere you can read it?"

"Don't worry about that. With three girls and a wife, why would I read your diary?"

Back in the main corridor, I made way for the tennis court combatants, battered and cuffed, being led by guards to the holding cells in the basement. Tyler was less bloody than the biker, if that counted for anything.

They were also escorted by Bobcat, the gnome-ish biker boss whom the warden had originally insisted upon for the role of Caliban, Prospero's subhuman servant in *The Tempest*. Bobcat would be a bad choice for any activity that didn't involve rage and brutality. Because the warden is determined to encourage the bikers into the mainstream of the prison community, I'd been forced to bargain Bobcat into a lesser role. Now Bobcat's drug-addled presence in the company was a distraction I needed to remove.

"Fuckin' jumped my boy on the tennis court," he said to me. "Good thing the guards got to him first."

Evidently, Bobcat had forgotten he'd seen me on the tennis court during the fight. Or that Tyler was a fellow Player. He wasn't bright to begin with, and the drugs had taken a toll.

Outside the chess room, I caught up to old Steyne, the mailman. His release date was even sooner than Dragan's, next week I'd been told. He was so nervous about it he couldn't stand to have it mentioned.

"What have you got for me today?" I said. "Any good news? Who still loves me?"

The old man picked through his satchel and handed me a drab business envelope that I instantly decided to ignore. "I don't like the look of that one, Danny."

In the hoopla of my arrest and conviction, I was thrilled to receive a flurry of mail, some of it even friendly. Nowadays all I receive are bills for credit cards I long ago maxed out and for a storage locker I'm apparently still renting in Toronto. And a lot of brown envelopes containing bad news from lawyers in faraway places like Tennessee and New Hampshire. One was all I ever needed to open to convince me to hide them all under my bed.

Today's letter was from my lawyer, McKeon, who badly botched my defense. Although he swore to appeal a sentence he considered harsh for a first offender, I rarely hear from him.

"Danny, wait." Steyne also had a box containing, I hoped, a book on Elizabethan magic from a university. Necromancy. Occultism. It's a factor in my portrayal of Prospero. Not that I've given my role much thought, as I'm so busy directing and sweating over Dr. K's assignment.

Half an hour later, I was pacing by the window upstairs that overlooked the shoreline. The many hours I've had to wait for the warden have allowed me to make a friend of Edith Orson, the administrative officer at King's Reach. She's been at the prison since it opened in the early 1980s. Of the five different wardens she's served under, she assures me that Sherman Carr is the most insufferable.

Edith and I often speculate on what Carr does in his office. He has no lack of assistants and excels at delegation, leaving him ample time to monkey in the affairs of others. He also golfs a lot, which anyone not incarcerated can do nearly year-round out here on the West Coast.

"What kind of mood is His Highness in today?" I asked her.

"Exceptional. He's been asked to speak at a conference in Australia. Plus he's got news that's not really news to you and me. If you know what I mean." Edith offered an elaborate wink.

Given its many luxuries, King's Reach is a sore point for the residents of Gracechurch, who form the bulk of the staff. They were recently outraged by the warden's plan to build a permanent ice rink, since the nearest rink available to them is an hour's drive away in Nanaimo. If I were struggling with a mortgage in this economy, I'd be pissed off too.

After half an hour, I was ushered into the inner sanctum. The warden's a hand-shaker, his moist grasp weighing you for weaknesses. Pretending to like him exhausts me.

"Danny, there you are," he said, like he hadn't known I was waiting. "I was going to send for you. There's good news. I just got off the phone with the mayor of Gracechurch. Do you know him? No, you wouldn't. How could you?"

I'd met the mayor last summer, having invited him and other local notables to a performance of *Charlie Brown*. The one at which, with the media in attendance, the warden fully realized the opportunities his drama program might provide to polish his own star, thereby practically guaranteeing me a second production.

Also at that performance, I was introduced to a local journalist named Stephen Kasey, who wrote a great piece on the transformative power of theatre. The piece was picked up by the media giant that owns the Gracechurch paper and appeared online and in papers across the country, providing me far more exposure than I was comfortable receiving.

Since then, Stephen Kasey and I have had an arrangement. In exchange for information on the warden's plans for King's Reach—funnelled to me from Edith Orson—he would approach a town councillor with the idea of staging *The Tempest* at a venue outside the prison, so residents could see for themselves that our rehabilitation is possible.

Now a beaming warden announced that the town had offered the use of a renovated one-room schoolhouse for three performances of *The Tempest*. He said it like he'd secretly nurtured the idea through many cleverly worded emails over five months. Like he believed the men under his direction had worked so hard they deserved a wider audience.

I'd found out in an email last night. With Carr informed, now I could present the news to the Players as a gift from their benevolent warden. Letting him take the credit for the additional shows would hopefully keep me out of the spotlight. Considering the bullet I dodged at my trial, I want the public to forget I even existed.

Speaking with Carr, my surprise had to be genuine and, worse, grateful. "Three shows?" I said. "We're going to need real lights. What's left in the budget?"

"Nothing. Before you get too excited, there's a problem. We have to get approval for everyone who leaves the grounds. I'm telling you now, not everyone's going to qualify."

I hadn't anticipated this sort of snag. "Who won't be able to leave?"

"I don't know yet. The parole board has to consider each inmate individually."

"They'll be away from here for three hours at a time and under guard. These guys are focused like you wouldn't believe. What kind of trouble can they get into?"

"Some might consider you a flight risk," Carr warned. "Maybe I should keep you here."

"That's ridiculous. Why would I start something like this and then abandon it?"

"We've all heard the stories, Danny."

Carr had me scrambling, and I hadn't even asked for what I needed. "Tyler Mullins," I said. "From this morning. Don't send him back to the Kent. Not if I have to cut other Players."

It took a moment for the warden to connect the fight on the tennis court to *The Tempest*. "I can't show favouritism. It's out of the question."

"We need him. If I have to recast too many roles, we won't be ready in two weeks."

"You're pushing your luck today, pal." Carr couldn't agree to my request because he hadn't yet determined what he'd ask of me for it. It was my signal to leave, the need to tell him that I'd arranged all of this burning in my chest.

I brought my frustration to the resource centre, where I'd been refining my script and managing the Players among day-old newspapers and dozing old men. Christmas decorations were going up. Garland and tinsel over the book racks. A plastic tree in the common area. I sat at the table that had been allocated to me. Dragan had reminded me that his patient wife, Margot, would visit this week. She had kindly offered to scour thrift shops and Salvation Army tables for our costumes, and I needed to print off a request for the cash to pay her for them.

I have Margot to thank for the clothes I'm presently wearing, having arrived at King's Reach in the bloodstained prison greens issued at the Kent and a borrowed tuxedo jacket. One day, Dragan discovered me shivering in the pervasive West Coast damp and asked Margot to shop for me. The first time I met her on a family day, she surprised me with jeans, shirts, and wool socks. How she paid for it, I didn't ask. I have much to be grateful for at King's Reach. It's the closest thing I've had to a home in years.

The cash request in hand, I slumped in my seat. With *The Tempest* on a potential hold, there was no excuse for me to not work on Dr. K's assignment. For months I'd been stuck at the steakhouse with the Vandals, when things still made their usual lack of sense. Thereafter, events and individuals' motivations were murky, and my various approaches to the story had failed.

Because I wanted to keep Dr. K happy and keep myself at comfy

King's Reach, my first, highly fictionalized account presented me as a bad guy seeking rehabilitation. I figured an actor and con artist should be able to write that in a few hours. It was a confessionary tale about how selling drugs while teaching English in Mexico nearly got my unwitting girlfriend arrested.

Unfortunately, Dr. K wouldn't be fooled by such a hollow story, and I was getting tired of lying.

Then I remembered that while awaiting trial in Vancouver, an American agent had offered to represent me after my acquittal. My second approach to the assignment was to develop my story into a treatment for a film or television series, which I could later sell to restart my acting career. In this version, I portrayed myself as a vain former actor who tricks a lovely young woman teaching English in Acapulco into becoming a drug mule. When she's kidnapped by *narcotraficantes* over an unpaid debt, I reluctantly attempt to rescue her. This change of heart ultimately leads me to repent my evil ways, which naturally is rewarded with the true love of the teacher.

My rehash of Hollywood plots took a week to write. If I didn't feel bad about stealing from credit card companies, I definitely had no qualms with ripping off hackneyed scripts. But it too went nowhere because acting in television is much easier than writing it. Three months of work had produced nothing of value, and Dr. K was asking about my progress. His concern deserved the truth, as did my welling guilt and remorse.

What kind of a convict is fool enough to write a confession of his true crimes while he's serving time for another conviction? This one, that's who.

The truth? By this point, those last days in paradise had blurred together into a smear of sunlight, alcohol, and deceit. Making notes took a month, strains of mariachi music ringing in my head. Eventually, I got the first three days of Paraiso down on paper. As I wrote, I was revisited by all the anxiety and insomnia I'd known then. The further I dug, the more I appreciated how the doc's method allowed me to confront what I'd done, if not quite accept it. It was a worthy task.

Yet something about my portrayal of the Vandals, and my story in general, seemed off. A specific truth, one that tied everything together, lay just out of reach. Was that because the writing forced me down uncountable memory lanes with Jill? That happened every day, only now the challenge was to weigh our many half-remembered conversations or her gestures for indications of what was to come.

I also had to reconcile those inconsistencies with sweeter reminiscences. Like when, a month before we reached Paraiso, we learned a couple we'd been squeezing had a disabled son at home and were taking their first vacation since their honeymoon. Despite my protests, Jill abruptly ended our squeeze and treated the couple to lunch with our limited funds. That didn't fit into the timeframe I was writing about, but it certainly weighed on the tone of my assignment. These emotional detours to happier days have left me stuck for two months, unsure of the truth.

My notes offered no solutions. I was flipping through them when I spotted Dr. K heading my way. Despite his paunch, he moved with a loose, youthful confidence. He wasn't much older than me and had far more of a life built. But if I believed in what he preached, then all things were still possible for me.

"Look at you, Daniel. Hard at it. How's that book coming?"

"Great," I said, closing it.

A moment passed in which we recognized we had no capacity for conversation outside of our sessions. Which is not to say we didn't like and respect each other.

"If you're stuck, try starting at the beginning," he said, laughing as he moved off. "See you on Thursday, I think it is."

His jokes always served to amuse himself and to clarify a point I'd missed. His speech was slyly economical that way. And he was right to suggest the beginning was easy. It was everything that followed that didn't make sense.

Among the post-lunch crowd drifting into the resource centre was Patrice, a tiny, wiry Quebecois. Last month, he nailed the role of Ariel, the prickly spirit Prospero uses to do his magical bidding, in his first audition. That would have been an achievement for a seasoned actor. For an insurance fraud and arsonist-for-hire who hadn't seen theatre since school, it was destiny.

"Patrice," I said. "Rehearsal starts at three today. We're nearly ready for a full run-through. I want to start with the shipwreck, so I don't need you off the top but soon after."

"Okay, boss. When do we get the stage in?"

"Next week, I hope. Gabe and Tyler are almost finished."

"Let me know if I can help, yeah?"

Everyone wanted to help. The Players are better carpenters and painters than they are actors. But they're becoming actors, and that should be applauded.

Start at the beginning, the doc had said.

The do-it-yourself spirit of the Players, first on *Charlie Brown* and now on *The Tempest*, reminds me of my student days and that, of course, reminds me of Jill.

Actually, almost everything reminds me of Jill.

The first time we spoke, in our first year at Ryerson, there was construction underway for our production of *All My Sons*. On the stage of the Theatre School, Jill and a few other students were raising a wall of the Keller house and needed extra hands. I happened to be crossing through the backstage just then and heard her call my name.

The wall secured, she introduced herself. That wasn't necessary. Everyone knew Jill Charles as an enthusiastic if private girl with more talent than a few of us combined. She wore men's dress shirts and long skirts. There was a rumour she'd been disowned by her wealthy family for choosing to act, and another that her boyfriend had directed her in an indie film (which no one had seen or could name). I realize now she did nothing to dispel them.

No such intrigue dogged me. An understudy for a bit part in *All My Sons*, I'd enjoyed limited fame acting in school plays in the small towns where I was raised. That counted for nothing in the big city, where I was a bewildered outsider. Jill's voice, calling my name, offered the possibility of a more sophisticated world.

That first winter at university, I observed that the guys who approached her were always politely rebuffed. She caught me looking at her once and didn't care. It was only on the beach in Cancun, during a spring-break trip with our class, that I found the courage to speak to her. I don't know why I went to Mexico. Probably I wanted to fit in. I do recall I'd never have afforded the trip if my father hadn't done well at a racetrack out west and FedExed me ten crisp American hundred-dollar bills.

Mexico was the first foreign country I'd travelled to, and I was enthralled by its vibrant colours and crazy heat, visiting a jungle wildlife reserve and some Mayan ruins. To avoid my drunken classmates, I slept in the afternoons. That's how, one midnight, I ran into Jill on the beach, tears streaming down her cheeks. The only other time I'd seen her in Cancun, she'd been with two older men. A gossiping classmate claimed they were producers from Los Angeles.

That night on the beach, she nearly slipped past me into the darkness. But I snagged her wrist—and my fate—and suggested she rest in an empty beach chair.

I cheered her up with stories from my itinerant childhood. Earl plying a landlord with wine so we could abscond with our belongings, our rent unpaid, when the man passed out. Or Earl taking my deliberately disheveled seven-year-old self door-to-door, pretending to represent a children's charity. My father's always been a crowd pleaser, and soon Jill was laughing. I never learned why she was crying. Back then, I took it for granted that sensitive girls cried every day for some reason or another.

She told me her parents were English stage actors, living in California, who rescued her from an orphanage near San Diego. Her discovery so near to Mexico, she said, combined with her brown hair and eyes, had convinced her she was part-Mexican by birth.

"Your hair isn't brown," I said. "It's sort of a dark blond."

"A joke," she explained. "Wouldn't it be cool to not know where you're from?"

Even then she wouldn't let the truth get in the way of a good story.

She said she was from Montreal and had attended a private girls' school in Toronto. She was two years older than me and had been doing a psychology degree at McGill University when she saw Jennifer Jason Leigh in *Last Exit to Brooklyn*. I'd seen that film too, and later realized she'd always been engaged with the demons and insecurities that fuelled her creativity.

As soon as she graduated, she was heading to Broadway. Her father was American, so she could apply for dual citizenship. First she'd do musicals, since she loved to sing, then focus on dramatic roles. Not that she wasn't interested in Hollywood. But being a great performer had nothing to do with being a movie star.

"It's good to have a plan" was all I could think to say. I'd been acting since grade school and had a vague notion I could make money from it. At the time, my main concern was finding a place for the summer so I wouldn't have to live with my grandmother in that small town again.

After an hour or so of talking, she asked if I was hungry. "I know this all-night place," she said. "But I have to get some money first."

What cash I had left was earmarked for a trip to more Mayan ruins down the coast at Tulum. But they could wait. "I can pay," I said.

She laughed. "No you can't. You don't have any money."

We entered a massive bar where hundreds of students were cheering a wet t-shirt contest. Girls paraded their dripping breasts, the lustful assembled howling. Jill ignored it, leading us into a murky corner where drunk kids slumped in banquettes and couples made out in the darkness.

A few women's purses sat unattended on a table. Jill opened one seemingly at random and extracted a wallet. "It's my friend Heather's," she said. "She owes me money from lunch."

"Sure," I said.

There was a Heather with us on the trip, a rich kid I'd never seen Jill with. More curious than shocked, I watched her pocket some cash and return the wallet to the purse. It wasn't anything I'd do, yet I couldn't see how it was my business to question her.

That night in Cancun, I learned there was a lot of my father in me after all.

The restaurant she had in mind catered to Mexicans working in the hotels nearby. It wasn't a place I'd have entered by myself. More impressive was that Jill ordered in Spanish. She'd been to Mexico before on vacations, she explained when I asked.

As we ate, we divided our classmates into two groups: those who cared about acting and those seeking a shortcut to money and fame. Jill was playing Ann Deever in All My Sons. I said I liked her portrayal, and that I especially admired a classmate named Warren Gillies, who was playing Chris Keller, the surviving son of the war-profiteer father.

Jill agreed. "He's the best in our year," she said. "Only he doesn't know it. There's, like, no ego to the guy."

The meal over, she had to meet a friend. What kind of friend do you meet at three in the morning? I wondered yet didn't ask as we strolled a stretch of sidewalk in the zona hotelera. Her arrival at the Coco Loco Bar brought a smile to the doorman's face. Her admission was free. Mine would cost 200 pesos. I hesitated in withdrawing my wallet.

"Sure you want to come in?" she said.

A poor excuse for music boomed behind a metal door. "Do you want me to?" I said.

She shook her head. "This isn't our kind of place," she said.

61

"Thanks. I had a great time."

I received a delicate kiss on the cheek, after which I floated above the beach and the strip until dawn. "Our kind of place," she'd said. For there to be an "our," there had to be an "us."

In my shared hotel room, two guys I didn't recognize were passed out in one bed, and the other bed had mysteriously disappeared. It didn't matter. I lay awake on the floor until noon, replaying the night in my head and imagining many happy endings for Jill and me.

I didn't see her again in the remaining two days in Cancun. Nor was she on the hungover return flight.

Back in Toronto, she wasn't in class or the Theatre School hallways. A week passed, then another. Someone said she'd stayed in Cancun to model. The understudy for Ann Deever was given Jill's role and wasn't as interesting in it. My days were full with class work, a job bussing tables at the Hard Rock Cafe, and *All My Sons*. Run-throughs, technical rehearsals, dress rehearsals. Another rumour placed her in Hollywood with her producer boyfriend. No one could say for certain, and to ask anyone risked revealing my crush.

When next I saw her, she was sloshing through a spring snowstorm of fat wet flakes on Yonge Street. Cloaked in a man's overcoat, toque pulled down to her eyes, she weaved between hunched pedestrians. I caught up to her by the ticket booth in Dundas subway station.

"Wouldn't you rather be in Mexico today?" I said.

"Excuse me? Oh, Danny. It's you."

"Where have you been? People were getting worried."

"I was in Montreal helping my mom move."

"So you didn't go away to do a movie?"

The look she gave me told me to get used to hearing things like that. A train rumbled into the station. She dug a token from her coat pocket then pushed herself through the turnstiles. "I wish," she said. "Gotta go. See you soon, okay?"

I lost her in the heaving after-work crush, no longer smitten, but entranced.

The next year, she attended class more regularly and invited me into her crowd, where I made friends with Warren Gillies. Warren and I marvelled at her eerie ability to vanish into a role and her skill at memorization. She was our resident genius and everyone's secret favourite, a position she continually shored up through her encouragement of others.

Too bad that passion, and her insularity, convinced jealous classmates that she had a drug habit or was sleeping with a teacher. Few looked beyond her suburban soccer moms and gender-jamming drag queens to see the sweat and determination creating them. Or that the swagger she displayed on stage masked a brittle self-consciousness.

I enjoyed no such talent or confidence and was discovering there was no lack of Daniel Drakes at Ryerson. I struggled for a reason to talk to her. She knew it, too, and one day asked if she could offer a suggestion to sharpen my characterizations. We chatted for two hours over lunch at the Senator restaurant. Her treat. Spend a day empathizing with everyone you meet, she said. Get inside their heads. Feel who they love. Who they fear. And why. Start thinking like them. That'll help you understand why people do the things they do.

Easy enough with half a psych degree, I thought. Yet it worked. Her approach helped me win the role of Young Man in *Mother Courage and Her Children*, with its eight lines of dialogue. Sadly, none were with Jill because she played Kattrin, Mother Courage's mute daughter. Once again, she showed us how it was done, obsessively researching the Thirty Years' War and the lives of women in seventeenth-century Germany. The result was a Kattrin infused with so much vulnerability that she stole every scene from the fourth-year girl playing Mother Courage.

Extra performances were added after a glowing notice appeared in the *Toronto Star* that made special mention of Jill. That review, and an interview in the student paper, unnerved her as much as it excited her. (There was no mention anywhere of Daniel Drake as Young Man.)

In our improv class, she was lightning fast and wickedly funny. In English lit, she led the class through the Brontës. She seemed happier to me. We had lunch a few more times, talking actors and directors. She wanted to direct films, too, and had an idea for a screenplay. Many considered us an item. Just friends, I'd have to say.

One day, she surprised me with tickets to see Christopher Plummer in a show at the Royal Alex. For my birthday, she said. I was stunned. The only other person who even knew it was my birthday was my Granny Drake, who'd mailed a card.

Soon she was waiting for me after class, anxious to gossip or complain about her problems with a fastidious roommate. She'd talk non-stop about the day-to-day, though was guarded about her earlier life. People jump to conclusions about who you are, she explained.

I could appreciate why it was difficult to share. Her American father had vanished back into the States when she was seven, and she had a younger brother in New York with whom she rarely spoke. Her mother, in Montreal, was a lonely poet who worked retail jobs. Jill fled home at fourteen, living with foster families and then on her own. She was eventually corralled and sent to school in Toronto on a trust fund created by her father's parents. It would last until she ran through it or turned twenty-five, whichever came first.

What a perfect pair of half-orphans we made, I thought. To my amazement, she let herself be swept along beside me. She even admitted to having purposefully strayed near me on the beach that night in Cancun. Still, it took an elaborate play on her part one night, after we fled a professor's dull cocktail party, for me to realize she was courting me. That fantastic truth smacked me in the head much like her elbow did as we hurriedly undressed in her bedroom while her uptight roommate paced and muttered in the kitchen.

I'd had a few girlfriends, though none lately and none who consumed me nearly as much as she did. None who ever invited me for dinner, half-destroying an oven in the process. And none who bought me a new pair of jeans when I tore my last, ragged pair painting a set.

In the summer after *Mother Courage*, she visited her mother in Montreal for a week. I ached for her so much that I understood I'd never truly missed anyone before. So much so, I was glad she'd refused to get a cellphone. What a love-sick fool I'd have made of myself with it.

When two weeks passed and she hadn't returned, I feared I'd never see her again. Before she'd left, she'd moved into a tiny bachelor apartment of her own in a ratty building on George Street. I'd spent a few happy days and nights there with her.

My father once showed me how to jimmy locked doors with a bank card. That day my student card worked just as well. Presumably, I was looking for Jill, though not in the physical sense. I didn't see anything new to me, just the futon, the Ikea table, and the clothing of an aspiring young actress. The real discovery was that breaking in wasn't just easy, it brought a rush unlike any I'd experienced. I fled like a thief, but locking the door behind me.

Two days later, a postcard arrived from Jamaica. An impromptu holiday with her mother. She apologized for not calling, missed me, and would see me soon. The gushing relief I felt was unlike anything I'd known before.

Upon her return, our romance proceeded slowly, given her zeal for rehearsal and my part-time job. By Halloween, she asked me to commit to dating her exclusively. Fine by me, since that was already occurring. I couldn't believe my luck when by Christmas she clung to me as much as I did her. We'd become each other's unexpected anchors in a delirious time.

In January, she started skipping classes again. When I asked why, her reasons were vague: a sick aunt (whom she'd never previously mentioned) or a subway delay (when she lived almost beside campus). This concerned me, as did her occasional requests for some time alone when earlier she couldn't get enough of me. Yet as long as she kept returning to me—and she did, continually—I didn't dig any deeper.

Meanwhile, I'd noticed that fragments of other people in her life were showing up in the characters she created. Her building superintendent's habit of sighing after he spoke. The dismissive goodbye wave of the Korean woman who sold her cigarettes. A week with Jill demonstrated more about an actor's creative methods than a year with any instructor.

That year our springtime production, *The Rocky Horror Show*, promised tons of fun for both techies and performers. Jill assumed she'd be playing Janet, even though she was still missing classes. Our professor warned her that raw talent was ephemeral. If she didn't return to the daily grind of classwork, there'd be no Janet for her, no matter how brilliant her audition.

"He's right," I said to her. "You've got to work for it. What's going on with you?"

"I don't know. Sometimes I don't like people looking at me or feel like talking to anyone."

"You know you'll get the part if you just do what he says. Is it like stage fright?"

"Not really. It's hard to explain. I'll be okay. It's not your problem."

Yet it was, since she was struggling with it and I wanted her to be happy. "What about pretending no one's looking at you?" I said. "That you're alone on stage?"

"I want people to see me. To see what I'm doing. That's what I don't get."

That night, she called to say she was staying with her aunt to rest for a bit. This was deep mid-winter. Almost everyone had the blues. "We should go back to Mexico," I said.

"Don't even joke about that. I'll see you in a few days, okay?"

When she returned, she was calmer. We visited the greenhouses in Allan Gardens, passing from a frigid city to the tropics in a single step. Among the palms, orchids, and ferns, she chatted happily about us getting two houses, both near the water. One in the Beaches, the other on an island like St. Lucia. Or somewhere in the States, if we were working in Los Angeles. Or up north in Muskoka. Did I want those too?

I did, so long as we could always luxuriate in the sense of belonging we created.

That was the right answer. I just needed to get warm again, she said, folding herself into me. We fit together very well.

That spring she was a wonderful Janet and turned many heads her way again. None were members of her family, I noted. But none of mine came, either. No matter: we had each other.

We got an apartment that June, a one-bedroom in a house in Cabbagetown. To pay for it, I worked loading produce trucks at a suburban food terminal. I'd rise before dawn to find Jill had packed me a lunch while I slept. Some days she'd include notes detailing the special treatment I could expect when I came home to her. If this was love, I was all for it.

One day, we went to see a talent agent in Yorkville. Some of our classmates were working as extras in movies. The pay was great, and the hours you put in counted toward your union card. Jill covered both our sets of headshots, telling me I could pay her back when I got my first role.

As our final year at school began, she brought more order to my life than I'd ever known. Multivitamins appeared, along with instructions to take them. Moisturizers. Vegetables. Regular bed times. The attention was occasionally overwhelming and alarming. What if I got used to it? What if it suddenly vanished?

Another joy was witnessing her making more friends, particularly with other women. The men's shirts disappeared as her clothing became brighter and more flattering to her figure. She'd model new outfits for me in impromptu fashion shows. She even asked my opinion on her hair, a lovely honey-brown mess streaked with red and blond, which she dismissed as mousy and wore in a ponytail or piled atop her head. Instinctively, I told her to ask her girlfriends.

"I will," she said. "What do you think? Since you see it most. Should I cut it?"

I loved its varying moods and its boundless potential. "Don't touch it," I said.

"Thank you. That's what I wanted you to say."

We'd take off for autumn afternoons on the island. There'd be a picnic and make-up sex without the fight on the cold sands of Hanlan's Point. Or I'd return from work to find our kitchen half-painted hot pink and Jill drunk on bourbon and anxious to welcome me home.

I also began to notice inexplicable absences and evenings when she wasn't home when I got in. One month, she asked if I could pay the rent. There was an error at the bank managing her fund, she said. Then she covered all of the rent for the next two months. She'd linger before me, waiting for me to ask. I never did, I think because I didn't know how to phrase it.

How long had this been occurring, I wondered. How long had I been ignoring it?

In November, I heard I wouldn't be receiving a student loan until my father paid his taxes. Since he'd never filed taxes in his life, I was in a jam. I couldn't work more hours at the Hard Rock Cafe and still attend school. Nor could I finish the drama program as a part-time student.

On a cold night, I lay in bed beside Jill, stressing over the situation. Even then I slept poorly and sometimes moved to the couch in the living room so I wouldn't disturb her.

She curled into me, burrowing for warmth. "Why don't you let me help you?" she said.

"Help me how?" I said, although I knew what she meant.

"Isn't it time you let me?" she said. "Why haven't you ever asked me?"

By now I'd guessed there was no trust fund. She never received any mail or phone calls concerning it. And I couldn't forget her with that purse in Cancun. Money was fluid to her, not a thing to be feared and hoarded, like it was for me. I was concerned that asking where hers came from risked snapping the spell of our bond. Yet she was right: it was time.

"We can't really be together if you don't know about this part of me," she said.

"Do I have to know it all?" I said. "Just give me an outline. The basics."

She laughed. "Don't worry. It's not dangerous, and no one gets hurt."

"How's that possible? Of course someone gets hurt. Or loses. That's stealing."

"I'm not stealing from people. I'm stealing from the banks through them."

My first thought was that my father would be impressed. "Is that why you were stressed out last winter?" I said. "Is that why you go away sometimes?"

"Yes."

"Okay, so now I know. I'm not getting involved in it with you."

"I'm not asking you to. Look, I know it isn't right, and it's not forever. But it's how I've had to get through things, and it's all I've got right now."

"You've got me," I said.

That got me kisses, and more, after which I slept better than I had in months.

The next day, she handed me a roll of twenties worth $3000.

As our lives went on as before, I rarely wondered what she might actually be doing. I never asked anything more of her, nor did I worry for her safety. I'd overlooked much the same with my father for years, and he never cared for me nearly as much as Jill did. I couldn't see how what she did mattered if we loved each other and did well in school.

That winter, Warren and I were both called to read for a day-part as a drug dealer in a television series called The Badge. Under Jill's direction, I watched episodes of the show, chatted with drug peddlers on Yonge Street, and bought a red Adidas tracksuit at the Salvation Army. En route to the audition, a few people on the subway gave me anxious second glances. Thanks to them, I felt the character inhabit me and again appreciated the genius of Jill's methods.

Our agent called the same afternoon. My first paying role, from my first audition. Who said this was tough? For three days of work, I earned close to $5000. I paid a beaming Jill back for the headshots and my tuition. Warren, ever the gentleman, took the news well.

In that episode of The Badge, my hoodrat character runs out of luck slumped against a bullet-riddled SUV, blood bubbling at his lips. My own luck, inexplicably, sailed on when I was offered the role of a hot-headed young cop in another forgettable show, *Street Heat*. Even Jill, the theatrical purist, agreed I should drop out of school for it. Those chances don't come often.

Her year hadn't been as positive. She'd been passed over for Gertrude in *Hamlet* and was finding Ophelia dull. There wasn't any mistaking that my sudden success rankled her. Given her talent and ambition, I would have been surprised if it hadn't.

I dove into the series. Who wouldn't? What I failed to appreciate was that it meant much less time for Jill and me. Complicating our situation was my role as *Street Heat's* ladies' man, a stretch for a kid who'd shied away from women much of his life. Jill began reading my call sheet to see which actresses I'd be working with that day.

"I see you've got another closed set scene with Jeanette," she said one morning. "Soon you'll be getting so much at work you won't want anything to do with me."

Her pettiness was new. "Do you know how hard it is pretending to be into someone when you're not?" I said. "Because the person I'm into is you."

"I don't know. You seem pretty happy these days."

"I've seen you kiss men on stage, so what's this about, really? Are there problems in your other world? Why don't you leave it behind and let me pay for things while I've got the money?"

"I'm not living off you or anyone else," she said. "I need an audition, that's all."

"You're still in school. And you keep forgetting I got really lucky."

A day later, she apologized. I sensed there was more than jealously troubling her, and rooms in her heart no one was permitted to enter. How many, I doubt even she knew.

That spring, she completed her degree in theatre arts. Like many students, she graduated to nothing. For weeks, she flitted around the city missing the buzz and adulation of performing and not finding any chances to get it. She landed an audition at The Second City and was told to try again in a few years. She agreed to collaborate with Warren on a piece for the Fringe Festival and then found reasons to avoid meeting him until he finally took his ideas somewhere else.

The only thing she enjoyed was a brief position with a drama program for kids in a city park. She'd bring stories home about how much the kids loved playing make believe. The kids adored her. Everyone did. But when the funding dried up, she was adrift again.

We spoke of a holiday when *Street Heat* finished shooting and never chose a destination. We'd get Sundays together, during which I'd reassure her there isn't a finite amount of success in the world. Just because I was enjoying some didn't mean she'd be denied it.

The unexplained absences began reoccurring. She told our agent not to put her up for any roles. "Maybe it's not for me," she said. "All those people judging you. See how upset I get?"

I was worried about her, and now really wish I'd been more available.

More than once I cancelled our Sunday when I had to shoot on a second unit or rehearse script changes. I'd suggest dinner and then get home too late. A tense evening would be cut short because I had to get up very early again the following morning for work.

I particularly recall her disgust at my sulk over not getting a role in a big Hollywood film when I was already starring in a television series. What kind of monster was I becoming? Living with my inflated sense of worth and entitlement, when she doubted her own talent and fortune, must have been exhausting.

I began suggesting that we move to a two-bedroom condo in a better neighbourhood, for which I'd happily pay. Jill repeated that she could look after herself and took a gig performing on a cruise ship plying the Caribbean. Four weeks on board, two off. Variety shows, clown outfits, and frothy musicals. I wasn't aware she'd even auditioned.

She cut her hair for the job so that it curled gently against her shoulders. She also dyed it blond, foreshadowing the Jill I would fall for again in Mexico. She looked great, although the blondness had a limiting singularity to it. Not that I told her.

The morning of her flight to Tampa, I had to be at the studio across town by 5:30 a.m. We shared a strained goodbye at our apartment door. Jill's eyes were hot and welling with tears, but the actor who could bawl on command retained her composure. I didn't cry until I reached my tiny trailer at the studio and was late getting into hair and make-up.

We'd boarded the proverbial train by this point and were hurtling toward an end neither of us wanted. I retreated into self-pity. What was I supposed to do? Quit a job everyone wanted just so she'd feel better? Would she have done that for me? I told myself we'd be all right after a short break from whatever had been making her crazy.

She was back in two weeks, having quit the cruise ship over the crappy living quarters and a creepy male colleague. I foolishly asked if there was more to the situation with this colleague. This led to a massive, door-slamming argument the likes of which we'd never had before. Like something from a play, actually.

I slept on the couch that night, and in the morning, softened my approach. "I told you I didn't want to know," I said. "But what's going on? Are you in trouble? Like, with the cops?"

"I'm fine. I don't know. Danny, I don't think I can do this anymore."

"What can't you do anymore? Us? Are you breaking up with me?"

"I don't know. Everything. God, you're so linear. I love you, but I can't take this."

I gave her what she wanted that evening, what she couldn't bring herself to do, intending to relieve the strain. I viewed the break-up as us resting between rounds until we sorted things out. I never once believed it was forever.

For the next few nights, we alternated on the couch. Slowly the tension dissipated and laughter returned. I apologized for being so self-absorbed and insensitive. She apologized for being so difficult to read. As I flew off on a press junket for the premiere of Street Heat, I felt that our recovery was well underway.

I left two messages for her in the four days I was away. We didn't speak because she still refused to get a cellphone and only rarely checked her email.

When I returned, the creaking floorboards let me know that no one had walked over them in days. All her keepsakes and treasures were gone, as was her clothing. (Actually, this being Jill, some bits of clothing remained scattered about.) I was struck by how few possessions she'd had, and by how little space a woman who could be so large on stage occupied in the real world.

By that evening, I had everyone I knew making enquiries. None of her friends had spoken to her since she returned from Florida. Jill had seemingly disappeared. I called in sick to work and flew to Montreal. But I couldn't locate her mother and didn't know the woman's maiden name. Back in Toronto, I charmed the registrar at Ryerson into pulling Jill's records. The address on them was for the girls' school she'd attended, which refused to allow me access to their records.

The fact I was ignoring was that she'd planned to leave, and that if she'd wanted me to come with her, or to know where she was, she would have told me.

The following week, a postcard arrived from Acapulco. She was sorry to have vanished, but she needed to get some perspective from far away. She was fine and missed me.

I booked a flight to Acapulco and told the producer of Street Heat that I'd be gone a few days, maybe a week. He said that if I didn't come to work when I was expected, he wouldn't just sue me for breach of contract, he'd make certain other producers knew I was unreliable. "Get a new girlfriend," he said. "Or a new career."

I reconsidered Jill's postcard. It was written so quickly in a jittery hand that she forgot to sign it or even say goodbye. I shredded it and tossed the pieces around our love nest. These lay undisturbed while I rented the swanky condo I wanted in the St. Lawrence Market area and plunged ahead as if I wasn't the least bit affected by her absence.

A few weeks later, I was visited in my trailer by a Toronto cop and an RCMP detective. A part of myself I'd been suppressing instantly admired Jill for her nimble escape. That's when I knew how badly she had me.

Did I know where Jill was? When did I last see her? Was there anything odd about her actions or travels in those last few days?

As a boy, I'd lied to the police about my father's whereabouts, so why wouldn't I lie for Jill? It never occurred to me to help them find her so she could straighten out her life. I wanted her to have whatever life she wanted, even if I didn't fit into her plans.

The cops wouldn't tell me why they wanted to talk to her. Evidently, it was about more than a few wallets. They assured me they had no reason to suspect she was in danger, and then showed me photographs of two middle-aged men. I could honestly say I'd never seen them before. Later, I realized I must have appeared suspicious to them as well. I didn't care.

I read in a newspaper around that time about a vixen in her early thirties who seduced lonely money managers and bankers to milk them of their savings. It wasn't that, I told myself. Whatever her crimes, she'd never cheated on me.

Each day, I missed her ever more deeply. It was a fundamental longing. A grief. Her absence nurtured the delicious conflict that I loved about our relationship. Everyone said I must be furious.

Sure, I'd say. Instead, I preferred to talk about a new television series I'd be appearing in.

Street Heat had tanked. And that was fine by me because soon I was appearing every Tuesday night as Tom Walker, the crusading Crown attorney in Legal Ease. The $20,000 I received each episode, in a thirteen-episode season, was more money than I ever imagined possible. A car and driver to work, the best parties. It's an old story. Except in my version, I was an imposter and knew the good times wouldn't last.

There were other women in this time, attracted by my success (and my producer friends). Yet they didn't read the label of every product we purchased in the grocery store, infuriating me in a way I never thought I'd miss. Nor did they make me feel I was the only man they'd ever loved. Quite the opposite: with these other women I sensed I was playing a role any actor could have filled. And there was no point searching for a better match with the torch I still carried for Jill held defiantly high.

After a year, I realized I'd taken our happiness for granted. And that I'd watched her lose herself when I could have done more to help. A second postcard arrived saying she'd be gone indefinitely, like I didn't know. I stuck it to the bathroom mirror to rebuke me every morning.

I remembered that night in Cancun and wondered if she'd dismiss me as an actor solely interested in money and fame. If I could've, I'd have told her that I felt like I was trespassing. That I was bored with television, of a life, however lucrative, playing the same character over and over. I missed the stage and the creative process. I missed the excitement Jill generated, and the energy her turmoil provided. The rush I got from her was greater than anything a role on a television show could provide.

In its second season, Legal Ease was picked up by an American network. Everyone from the producers to the interns—myself, definitely—prepared for megabucks and superstardom. In the meantime, money sifted through my fingers like beach sand. Trips abroad, $4000 couches, cocaine. My father resurfaced, penniless, so I bought him a house in his hometown, mostly to keep him out of my life. I don't like the person I became during that time.

Rumours reached me about Jill. She was in Berlin, studying art. She was in Japan, teaching drama. Each one landed like a gut punch, leaving me breathless and desolate.

The American network broadcast three episodes before dropping us because their viewers couldn't understand our accents or why the lawyers wore black capes like vampires.

Panic in the production office. Ratings plummeted. Advertisers fled. To reach a younger, more female audience, the remaining scripts were rewritten to focus on the romances underway at the fictional law firm. Tom Walker was stupidly assigned to start a relationship with the character played by Hannah Dyer, with whom I'd just ended a stupid affair.

Bitter over our split, Hannah wouldn't play nice. Our scenes together were dreadful and the tension palpable. The crew grumbled about cranky cast members and the toxic environment on set. The show took a second hiatus while the remaining episodes were re-rewritten.

A week later, I learned *Legal Ease* was wrapping up and moving to Vancouver, where Hannah's character would carry on as a private investigator in a series of her own. The other female lead would also survive in this spin-off. Her and Hannah's characters would now be lovers. A show with two lesbian characters in starring roles. It was a daring move, I was told, for network television.

The problem with heydays is you never know when yours is at an end.

I had a few day-parts playing cops, crooks, and lawyers. When those roles dried up, I played the schmucky dad-who's-left-with-the-kids-while-Mom-takes-the-night-off in a frozen pizza commercial. For two years, my savings evaporated while I harassed my agent. Or my second agent, as I fired the first one when work failed to materialize.

My first non-acting job was with a catering company. At one party, an older woman, having accepted an *hors d'oeuvre* from my tray, asked where she'd seen me before. Hope lit me up. Unfortunately, she and another woman couldn't place me and claimed to have never heard of *Legal Ease*. They helped themselves to another mini-samosa and returned to their conversation.

I sought anonymity in telemarketing, selling window cleaning services and newspaper subscriptions. My income barely covered the rent, so things like my gym membership and union dues went on my credit card. My fall was legendary among colleagues who were writing plays, buying houses, having children, and making films.

Warren took pity on me. He'd moved in with his girlfriend and was getting some small roles while selling tickets for imported Broadway musicals. He arranged a similar job for me. For reasons I can't recall, it too was short lived.

Around this time, my agent—the fourth, I think—dropped me for failing to generate any revenue. Creditors were circling. I wasn't yet thirty. I'd downsized to two rooms near Allan Gardens. Tilted floors, gurgling radiators, mouse shit. I spent my days tripping over the pricey furniture I'd accumulated. I didn't have many friends, nor did I deserve them.

Late one March afternoon, things became bleaker when I was laid off by another catering company. I could have gotten a real job, or I could have returned to school for some practical skills. Instead, I found myself imagining the kind of scams Jill had run. Credit cards? Fake financial documents? My father had passed bad cheques for a while. Even as a kid, I saw how clumsy he was at it. He had the right pieces of paper and the signatures, but he never believed in what he was selling. Without that confidence, you can't expect to succeed.

Whatever Jill's game was, she'd been good enough to fool a lot of people for a long time.

On my last catering job, at the home of a Rosedale billionaire, I'd considered fingering a few items, the way my father would to sweeten his bottom line for the week. I could pretend that being a thief was a temporary role I had to play. From that angle, it wasn't a bad idea.

My phone rang again, startling me. It didn't ring often, and the last time it did, a few days ago, a rude man informed me I had a week to pay my phone bill or he'd cancel my service.

"Danny?" Jill said. "Hey, it's been a while, huh?"

Four years, nine months, and seven days, actually. A great burden was lifted. This call was always coming.

The warmth in her voice was tempered with a hardness. "What are you doing these days?" she said. "I heard about your show. Good for you."

"I'm between gigs right now," I said. It was what I'd been saying for three years.

Reeling, needing air, I opened the balcony door to the winter dusk. Where before the grey monotony of Jarvis Street at rush hour was a horror to avoid, I now looked out over a city transformed by the energy and warmth of an orangey twilight.

"If you're not busy," she said, "do you want to come work with me? I've been teaching English in Mexico, plus I've got some other sidelines. I could use your help with them."

Jill had never asked for my help before, least of all with her sidelines. A second act to this love story was in the offing, with a scene and a costume change.

A blast of frigid wind rattled the balcony. A new beginning with Jill in Mexico or more garnished minimum wages and self-pity? I sensed her shifting on the line and pictured the hopeful if vaguely impatient look on her face. Her timing had always been superb.

"All right," I said. "But I don't have any money."

"I know. I'll get you a flight. Is Tuesday good? How long do you need to get ready?"

Nighttime was best for the preparations that lay ahead. One night to sneak some personal items to a storage unit, a second to assure the building manager, by my presence, that my rent would be paid. Then as soon as his back was turned, I'd vanish. My father had taught me well.

"Make it Wednesday," I said.

"Sure. And Danny, get rid of your credit cards, okay? Cut them up and throw them away. Get rid of your cellphone, too. You're not going to need it here."

Day 4

Acapulco

LATE ON THE FOURTH DAY AT PARAISO,
I was strolling the gravelled paths between guest rooms when I heard
someone calling my name. A woman holding a glass of champagne
leaned from a second-floor balcony. There was movement behind her
and raucous voices radiating like light.

This time she shouted: "Steve Sawyer."

What does it say about Jill and me that I didn't instantly recognize
her? I stopped beneath the balcony. "I need your help," she said.
"Where the hell have you been?"

Looking for the two American couples to finish that squeeze.
Swimming. Reading Shakespeare in the games room. Anything to
avoid encountering the Vandals, as Jill had set out to do at mid-
afternoon. "I guess they're up there with you?" I said.

Nick appeared behind her and wrapped a furry arm around her
waist. This time, Jill didn't flinch. "There's some people you should
meet," he said. "Remember last night? The producers?"

"Let me get dressed." All I had on was my swimming trunks and
a towel.

"They're not people you keep waiting, Stevie. The stairs are around
on the left."

Normally I wouldn't stand to be ordered around, but during my
afternoon off duty I'd resolved to ignore my reservations about the
Vandals and let Jill run things as she saw fit. Her instincts were better

than mine. Perhaps she'd seen something I'd missed.

Upstairs in a suite of rooms, twenty or so people mingled by a makeshift bar. Brenda pounced on me in the doorway. "These are the investors we told you about. Don't be afraid to embellish a bit. About your roles."

"I won't." I gently extracted her claws from my arm. "Thank you. I'm going to check in with Gina first."

Jill was as relieved by my arrival as she was miffed by my absence. She led me deeper into the room, where Nick was regaling a handful of people from an armchair.

"This was the eighties," he was saying, "when ethnics started showing up on the telly. I said to myself: there's money in them. So I started knocking on the doors of all the shops in Finsbury Park, telling the shopgirls I could put them on TV."

The party-goers possessed the calm assurance of wealth, the first we'd encountered in weeks. Jill's money-meter wasn't to be doubted. Unfortunately, most were Mexican. Worse, I noticed again her struggle to create that easy familiarity with them, or to even be a presence in the room. I helped myself to a glass of champagne to put a shine on our situation.

"This one guy from Pakistan didn't like me talking to his wife. They don't like their women talking to other men. Screams at me that I was dishonouring his house. Rubbish like that. Comes at me with a cricket bat, chasing me into the park. Me, I'm lugging this Betacam, two steps ahead ..."

Nick's audience laughed and swilled more bubbly. He motioned me toward himself and a barrel-chested Mexican man in his sixties with a young woman at his side. "Here's the fellow I told you about," Nick said. "He'd be perfect for the school friend, don't you think?"

"He's too old." The man had a thick accent. "What about the other guy?"

"Too old?" I said. At this point, in my actual life, I'd have told them both to get stuffed. I struggled to recall that Steve Sawyer, amateur actor, did not have the same stock of experiences.

Jill averted disaster by marching us off stage. More champagne got me chatting with a deeply tanned couple from Florida. He was in trucking, and she did interior design. Steve introduced Gina, and we all agreed it was wonderful to drink champagne in Mexico on a sunny afternoon. If nothing else, I reckoned, we could start over with them.

Someone announced a move to the beach. People grabbed bottles of wine and plastic cups. Jill followed Nick, and I was following Jill until Brenda cornered me, her sour wine breath hot against my face. "Where're you going in such a hurry?" she said.

I guess she was trying to be funny. "Not right now, Brenda."

"Wait with me a bit. I've got something to tell you."

Not a chance. It was more important to show Jill I was back on the job than listen to her.

On the beach, two young Mexican men in dark suits kept some beach chairs reserved for our party in the hotel's *privada* section. That they did, with just a flimsy rope fence separating them from the crowds in the *pública* section, further indicated the unsuitability of Nick and his friends. And all the more reason, with just three days remaining to us at Paraiso, to abandon them for some average tourists.

The old Mexican man held court beneath a palm umbrella. Having been soundly rejected, my motivation was no longer clear. The booze had given a headache, and I'd misplaced the couple from Florida. I wanted to ask Jill how we were supposed to get card numbers on the beach.

Nick walked up. "Don't be put off. You want to play the role a bit."

"What role am I supposed to be playing?" Despite evidence to the contrary, the film felt like a ruse. For what, I couldn't imagine. "Can I at least see a script?"

"Easy, mate. The script's in flux at the moment. Rewrites."

Jill came between us. "Why not just talk to Nick's friends. Let them get to know you."

"How do I even know there is a movie?"

Nick laughed. "There isn't one yet, fool. It's what we're talking about."

He abruptly left us. I turned to Jill. "What about us, huh? How's this helping us?"

"Now's not the time for this."

"There's something weird about those two. They're trouble."

A commotion interrupted us. A security guard was arguing with two teenagers hawking cans of soda and beer. Presumably, no one told them Paraiso was all-inclusive, that anything we wanted was ours for the asking. More likely, the concept was inconceivable to them.

The guard shoved one of the teenagers. I'd had enough of beaches that didn't belong to us. And of all the double-speak necessary for a game I no longer had the stomach to play.

Jill knew what was coming next. "Don't you walk away again," she warned.

I set off across the burning sands without answering. Another swim was in order, to rinse me clean of this mess. I waded through the surf until it swallowed me.

An hour later, I was sulking in the internet café

My father wrote that his cardiologist had declared his heart a ticking time bomb. He'd be travelling to Toronto for surgery as soon as a hospital bed was free. He was worried about what he'd do for income while he recovered and wished there was someone to drive him to and from the city.

Annoyingly, he'd neglected to state the kind of operation he was having. Was it a simple valve shunt or a chest-cracking, elbow-in-guts bypass? I couldn't gauge how worried I should be. As for his lost income, how to advise a man who, not yet sixty, had been "retired'" for a decade, existing, as he had all his life, through petty scams, gambling, welfare fraud, and the charity of others? Some days, I half-regretted hooking him up with a computer. But he's the only family I've got. When I have a son, I'd like him to look me up occasionally.

I got down to work. The accounts I found of Nick's career didn't differ much from what I'd gleaned myself. Born Nicholas Colleoni in London in 1956. Lead singer for Romany Stomp, a late punk band manufactured by a record label, a kind of sneering boy band. They hit it big in 1981 and toured the world. Soon after this, the Stomp morphed into a new wave outfit and prettified their image by jettisoning the snide Colleoni.

Colleoni became Vandal and launched a solo career that peaked early with the hit "Streets of Her Love." I half-remembered it as a synth-pop ballad tarted up with the electronic noises then in vogue, the kind of song now heard in grocery stores and soft drink ads. A fan page dedicated to preserving the spirit of '85 offered a sound bite of the song, which I declined to hear again. I clicked through websites, marvelling at the ridiculous haircuts of that era.

As I suspected, Brenda Swain, born Harlinson, was American, from Peoria, Illinois. At seventeen, she lit out to New York. After modelling and roles in the choruses of various Broadway shows, she wound up in London's West End around the time Nick Vandal's second solo record sputtered on the British charts. Married in 1985, they separated within a year.

Brenda was best known for her role as flinty Inspector Dalrymple on the BBC police series, *Suspect*. Nick likewise turned to acting, appearing in some forgettable British films. There was also a short stint as the lead in a *Phantom*-like rock musical in the 1990s. And three more solo records, each on different labels, though none in years.

The unearned plummet from stardom. The drift into obscurity. What I read reminded me I was wise to have accepted Jill's offer of a new life rather than chasing a fleeting dream. Down there in the sunshine, we acted every day, each hotel a new stage, with no hope of acclaim.

There was no mention of the Vandals moving to Mexico, but lots of has-beens turned up there, where it's always warm and their dollar goes further. Even though it all checked out, there remained something inexplicably repulsive about them. I sat considering how to move Jill away from them, when the opportunity I'd sought rumbled into the room.

"Told you we'd find him here," Evan said.

"No, you said he'd be reading," Cal said.

"Just checking my email." I closed the page of the *Miami Herald* before they saw it. I often checked for updates on the break-up of the credit-card ring there. In another bust I'd read about, the leaders received multiple fifteen-year sentences for fraud.

The boys, on their second last night at Paraiso, had been granted a night of carousing by their wives. "We're going to hit those bars I told you about," Cal said.

The strip joints. But it was barely six o'clock. "Bit early, isn't it?"

"We're going to eat first," Evan said. "Food's free here."

"Meet you in the dining room," I said. It was rare that a lime asked to be squeezed.

I set off running, feeling stupid for having stormed away from Jill like I did. I wasn't pulling my weight, and she deserved better. And with just 700 pesos in my wallet—roughly seventy dollars—I needed as much capital as she could spare for this fresh enterprise.

On the beach, yet another golden sunset made long shadows of the remaining sunbathers. The *privada* section was empty, as was the guest room from which Jill had called down to me. The party must have gone to dinner, whether at Paraiso or elsewhere.

I cleaned up in our room then dressed so much like Cal and Evan, in jeans and a Hawaiian shirt, that we'd be mistaken for brothers. Before leaving, I scrawled a note for Jill on some hotel stationery and left it on top of the television convertor.

A sickly sweet aroma billowed from the dining room. Seafood night. A pink pyramid of lobster tails on ice. Tureens of bubbling butter. Cal and Evan were already shovelling it down. I wasn't hungry, but worked steadily at a plate of crab legs. There was little table talk, just cracking shells and grunts of satisfaction.

Because strip joints don't open until later in the evening, I suggested we stroll across Costera to digest a bit. Near the Hard Rock Cafe, we passed a legless beggar with his back against the broken wall of an abandoned mini-golf. I'd been seeing him along the strip for years, and his eyes, when they met mine, said he'd been seeing me, too. I dropped some coins into his frayed Starbucks cup, seeking good karma and his continued silence.

Our destination, Samantha's, was in an area of nightclubs that was deserted so early in the evening. We passed an hour in the Buccaneer Bar, which offered views of a bungee jump tower reaching over the beach. Something on a television monitor about the Republican primary caught Cal's eye, and he ranted at length again about Obama. I sat listening while a listless Evan watched the sun melt into the Pacific. Just one man jumped from the bungee tower in our time there. When he did, Evan inexplicably stood and applauded this feat.

The doorman at Samantha's wanted a hundred pesos to get past him. That early, we could have haggled for a better price. But Steve Sawyer couldn't have known that, and Cal, grinning like an idiot, wouldn't have cared. The happier he was, the sooner I'd have his pin number.

Strip clubs the world over are alike. A black stage outlined with rope lights. Lonely, drunken, and often menacing men. The difference in the developing world, where the girls aren't organized to demand fair wages or health care, is that the desperation is overwhelming.

Cal chose a table discreetly back from the stage, where a skinny girl spun around a pole. Beer was pricey: seventy pesos for Budweiser, which was advertised as "imported." Hoping to piggy-back on the boys' cards, I made a big show of paying for the first round.

The bar was half full, the clientele exclusively Mexican. Cal clinked our bottle necks and hooted loudly, which drew prickly looks from adjacent tables. Cal waved back. If he did it again, I'd have to step out of character and warn him that he wouldn't make any new pals here.

The hip hop was so loud it reverberated within me. Conversation was difficult, an unfortunate handicap because limes are less likely to notice you watching their hands when they're talking. Cal showed the Visa I'd already seen to our waitress, which kept the tequila and beer flowing. A matronly woman circulated between tables, speaking closely to patrons. Cal was excited by what she had to say. "Ready for a table dance, fellahs?" he shouted.

Evan said no. As I'd have said, if I were speaking for myself rather than Steve Sawyer. I felt crappy for deserting the only woman I wanted to see naked, and hoped she'd read my note by now. Jill could handle the Vandals, but as soon as I finished with the boys I'd hurry back to help her. It was too bad we never used cellphones.

There is much to be said for strip clubs as a means of revealing a man's character. Cal stared at the short, brown-skinned girls, his obsession apparent. Evan preferred the masked combatants in a *lucha libre* match on a television above the bar and drank heavily. Our table was largely silent, overcome by a quiet despair. When Evan shouted in Cal's ear, only their body language was audible: he wanted to leave. Cal did not.

At a corner table, two men were cutting lines. Narcotics have always had a home in Acapulco, though I'd never seen them used so brazenly. This town had gone to hell, and the rest of the country was tumbling after it. Jill and I needed out.

Returning from the washroom, Cal had a new plan. The matron had offered him a private massage with a girl of his choice. Evan visibly squirmed. "I told you I wasn't doing that."

I didn't want one either, and not just because it wouldn't secure the numbers I required.

A table beside us invited a girl to dance for them. She slipped while mounting the little stool she carried between customers, her sleek, bare behind brushing against Evan's shoulder. He abruptly stood up and headed for the door.

I looked to Cal, who was laughing too hard to notice me. Seeing his pin number in the dim light would be tough. Evan had the right idea. "I'll see what's up with him," I said.

Outside, Evan had cadged a cigarette and was pacing the sidewalk. The night was no cooler than the day. "Some place, huh?" I said. "I don't think Gina would like me being here."

"Don't tell her, okay? Shauna wouldn't like it either, and I got enough to worry about."

I let him slump a little lower, then said, "What's up, buddy?"

"Oh, I got some news today. Shauna's pregnant. She did one of those home tests."

"Congratulations."

"Yeah, thanks. It's not like I've got a choice, do I?"

The bouncer approached us. "Uds. *no pueden estar aquí. Regresen adentro, o váyanse de aquí.*" His tone did not require translation.

"I'll get Cal," I said, sensing an opportunity to really celebrate.

"You can't tell him. You can't tell anyone. But I'm sure he already knows because Shauna can't keep her mouth shut about anything."

A home, a steady job, a wife, a kid on the way—what a problem to have.

Cal stepped onto the street. "Are you guys coming back in or what?"

"I'm not," Evan said. "That place is all wrong."

A moment passed in which Cal judged their friendship to be worth more than naked women. I envied them their bond. "Okay," Cal said. "But I'm not going back to the hotel."

And then opportunity knocked again: Cal needed an ATM and veered into a Banamex. Evan and I took up defensive positions flanking him, and seconds later I had the pin number from the Amex he'd used at the golf course.

Our first complete set of numbers in two months. I longed to race back to Jill, but my job then was to avoid arousing suspicion by finishing the night. Plus, I wanted more numbers.

Containing my exuberance wasn't easy. Costera was swinging, the bars pumping. But our trio trudged along in glum silence, our big night going nowhere fast. Evan was lost in his head, and I felt Cal drifting away before he stopped and announced: "Fellahs, I'm going back."

Evan looked like he might cry. "Are you kidding?"

"It's my one chance for some fun. Our secret, okay Ev? See you guys later."

Evan watched his friend depart then shuffled off, dragging his sorrow. I trailed like the loyal dog he'd left back in Omaha.

A Hooters appeared around a bend in the road, its rosy interior offering a comforting familiarity. Evan chose a table beneath some monitors showing pop videos and sports highlights. We might have been in Delaware or Nevada, were it not for all the Mexicans within.

Our waitress wore the requisite orange short shorts and tight t-shirt. She spoke English, though was less flirty after noting how drunk Evan was.

I ordered two light beers and water. Evan unwisely insisted on more tequila, which all but blinded him. He boo-hoo'd about never becoming a rock photographer, a dream now dashed by his impending fatherhood. He was a childish bore. I changed my mind about us being friends.

The waitress brought us the bill, unasked, a manager looking on. Evan clumsily dug a Citibank Visa from his wallet. He tried to focus on it then handed it to me. "Help. Me pay."

Twice in one night. Fortune was smiling again.

In taking his card, I purposefully forgot I'd liked Evan until an hour ago. I ran a finger over the embossed letters—Evan Gregory Biddle Jr.—and examined the three-digit security number on the back.

The waitress left to retrieve a credit card machine. In her absence, Evan struggled to extract something from the pocket of his jeans. I leaned over to help. "What do you need?" I asked.

He brandished the dog-eared coupon book. "Check to see. A coupon. For here."

Unbelievable. "No. It's too late. She's already done the bill."

"Please. Shauna said. Use it."

The Hooters coupon offered a free drink and ten percent off an entrée. I tore it out and handed it to the waitress. It was quite a rigmarole to save a few pesos.

In a few minutes, the waitress was back with the new bill. With Evan unable to even hold the credit card machine, I swiped his card then took his hand and pressed his index finger against the four numbers he mumbled aloud. Then I placed a pen in his hand and scribbled on the receipt. The waitress laughed at us. We were a comedy duo.

I excused myself for the washroom to write down Evan's numbers and Cal's pin number on a matchbook. It wasn't something I would normally have done so close to the source, but I was fairly drunk.

When I returned, Evan was face down on the table, the receipt and his wallet and credit card scattered in front of him. I slipped the Visa into my pocket with the matchbook, hauled Evan to his feet, and stuffed the receipt and his wallet into the front pocket of his jeans.

The manager helped me steer him to the door. Too many witnesses, I thought. Desperation, and Evan's card, had left me careless. And the CCTV cameras watching us. I hadn't considered those. I told myself we hadn't fleeced him yet. Which did nothing to quell my alarm over having just stolen his credit card and become the sort of petty thief I despised.

Success had brought my appetite roaring back. To sober up before I brought the good news home to Jill, I steered us along Costera into a twenty-four-hour Sanborns, a popular family-dining chain. Jill would appreciate my hard work, I reckoned. However angry she was about being abandoned, there was no question I'd just redeemed myself.

The Sanborns staff was less than welcoming. I poured Evan into a banquette and ordered some French fries. His card burned a hole in my pocket as I ate. Let it, I thought, staring down the welling remorse. I justified the theft by telling myself that it practically guaranteed two flights out of Mexico. I'd insist on somewhere safe, like the Bahamas, where we'd work harder than ever to fill our coffers. Our little theatre emerged from the fog that had obscured it.

By the time I'd finished eating, the booze had caught up to me as well. Evan was a dead weight. I should have hauled him back to Paraiso while he could still zombie-march one foot in front of the other. The taxi driver asked for a hundred peso premium in advance against any bodily seepages. I was in no shape to argue.

I remember the lights of the Costera strip blurring past the taxi window and how happy I was to be returning to Jill victorious. I remember Evan slumped in the backseat. I don't know how I got him to his room, or that I even knew his room number, so maybe I left him in the lobby? That would have been sloppy of me.

My next definite memory is my happiness at discovering Jill asleep in bed. I tickled her under the chin with Evan's Visa. When she saw the card, she threw her arms around me. I got kisses, too, many more than I'd had in months. Too bad it soon became apparent that I'd drunk myself incapable of capitalizing on the praise being heaped upon me.

We kissed for a while again, then I said, "Sorry about leaving you on the beach earlier. That was mean of me. I wanted to apologize, but the guys were ready to leave."

"It was dangerous, too. Why didn't you wait around? You've got to be more patient."

I didn't have an answer. It mattered only that we had some cards and that I was forgiven.

"Forget it now," she said. "I've got good news, too. Nick and Brenda have invited us to stay with them in Veracruz."

I recalled Nick making the same offer at the fort, which I'd been trying to forget. The joy of my accomplishment was replaced by a dull foreboding. "Why? We don't need to go now."

"The American guys won't be enough, honey, considering how much we need to save up. I was worried about how we'd get to Veracruz." She wagged the Visa like a cat does a mouse. "Now I'm not."

Day 5

Acapulco

I WOKE WITH A SANDPAPER TONGUE
and a fiery ache in my head. I reached for Jill and found only her
comforting aromas. Letting them embrace me, I dozed in and out.

When eventually I crawled into the bathroom, the face in the
mirror was bloated and bleary, the yellowy eyes bloodshot. A smirk
slowly cracked it as I recalled my achievements of the night before.
Who's the star today?

Jill returned as I re-entered the room. "You're up early," I said.
"Where've you been?"

She tossed her handbag onto a chair. "I couldn't get anything out
of Evan's card. Doesn't anyone pay their bills anymore?"

"You did that now? But we're still at the same hotel."

"I had to. Before he cancelled it. Anyway, I called my guy with the
other number."

I couldn't believe what I was hearing. "Are you fucking crazy?
They'll think it was me."

"No, they won't. Even if they do, we'll be in Veracruz by then. Nick
says they're leaving today, so we should start packing."

Only then did I notice Jill's many suitcases stacked on the other
bed. "Did you use the right pin number? Because the card I gave you
worked last night."

"Yes I did. I'll call my guy and see how the other card did. Do you
want to fly tonight or in the morning?"

In answer, I hauled on my swimming trunks and slammed out of the room.

The beach was emptying, the sunbathers scattered to lunch by a strong offshore breeze. I paddled out to my sand bar, where I decided the big risks Jill had taken were necessary. So we should probably continue with the Vandals as well. Depending on what Cal's card paid, that is. Maybe we wouldn't have to go anywhere with them. And once they were finished, we were leaving Mexico. Forever.

Jill wasn't in our room when I returned to it, although our bed was made and my two bags sat on top of it. My worldly possessions were easily contained within a suitcase and a knapsack. I was halfway through packing them when she rushed in, a pale spectre of the woman I knew, her eyes red and puffy. Jill almost never cried, so something must have been very wrong.

"My guy's gone, his number's cut off." Breathless, she tripped on her words. "So I called his cell. He said to hang up and never call again."

I was confused. "So how do we get in touch with him?"

"We don't. The bank closed his accounts. Someone's cards were no good."

"What about the other card I got? The Amex?"

"I checked my account. There's nothing in it. I have to find Nick. I need his address."

"Fuck Nick. And Veracruz. We can't even buy lunch. What are we going to do now?"

It was Jill's turn to rush off, which was also unlike her. I took my pounding head in my hands. How could both cards have failed so spectacularly?

Then I remembered the cash I'd set aside for a crisis. I upended my suitcase and reached inside it for the seam into which I'd slipped five American twenty-dollar bills. I tried another seam, then a third, tearing at the lining. In vain. The bills were gone.

Somewhere a maid was laughing at me. I figured I deserved that and more for what we'd done. I threw the suitcase across the room, sending clothing after it. The money wouldn't have gotten us far and then what? I wanted to cry too.

Of the two evils, I more feared homelessness in Acapulco than the Vandals in Veracruz. So now we needed to go, if we could get there. Then I understood: it was over. Without a contact for the cards, we were free of that life. My dread changed to a quiet elation. Possibly we'd look back on this day as the turning point.

I was lying on the bed, watching our new, crime-free life unfold on the ceiling, when Jill charged back into the room. "I can't find Nick anywhere. And they're leaving soon."

"Did you try their room?"

"I never went there. I don't know where it is."

Her voice had an edge of hysteria in it that I'd never heard before. I took her in my arms, hoping to soothe the turmoil boiling within her. A big hug settled me down, too.

We hurried down the palm-lined avenue to the beach, zigzagging between apartment blocks. The sun was at its zenith, hammering down. Anyone with any sense was indoors.

"I can't believe I'm looking for that asswipe," I said. "What if they're gone already?"

"We'll cover more ground if we split up." She would search for the Vandals along the shore and in the beach bars while I checked the main building. "Meet me here in fifteen minutes, with or without them."

I started in the games room, which was empty at that hour. I remembered the three-in-one volume of Shakespeare and found it beneath some cowboy novels. It was heavier fare than I was used to reading, so it would certainly keep me occupied wherever I was headed.

From that point on, it's impossible to say when or if I was making critical mistakes. One decision simply followed another and to speculate on what may have occurred had I made different choices, or when the most fatal decision was made, is useless.

For example, wanting a beer to cut the fog of my hangover, I entered the lobby. Was that a mistake? Or was choosing Paraiso in the first place? Or Acapulco?

Near the bar, Cal and Evan waved to me from reception. Should I have reconnoitered the foyer before entering it? Definitely. Or was my mistake to not run away then?

Steve Sawyer decided to accept their invitation. He didn't have anything to hide.

The boys were rumpled, their skin a sickly grey beneath their tans. With them was the manager who'd endured Nick's verbal barrage two days earlier.

"Ev's Visa card is missing," Cal said. "Someone tried to use it this morning."

I felt all the colour drain from my face. I'm sure I looked as poorly as they did.

"Mr. Cabreza here has been helping us," Evan said, indicating the manager. "The service has been great so far."

"You don't have to thank them for doing their jobs," Cal said.

"I remember you using it at Hooters," I said to Evan. "Did you lose it there?"

Evan wouldn't meet my eye. "Yeah, we checked with them. They don't have it."

Cal smelled of stale booze. "Ev says he remembers you making the payment with it. That you were the last person to use it."

"But then he put it away," I said. "And I paid cash for the taxi back here."

"I'm sure I lost it," Evan said. "And someone tried to use it. I was pretty drunk."

"Yeah, but that someone wouldn't have known your pin number," Cal said. "Steve, the police want to ask you a few questions. We think you've got some explaining to do."

Real fear, distinct from the irritation I'd felt all morning, icily spiked through me.

The manager smiled as if showing us one of the resort's amenities and led us into a tiny, tunnel-like office crammed beneath the main staircase. Within was a heavy-set man in his fifties fiddling with a phone. On the desk were two American passports and a small black detective's notebook like my character on *Street Heat* had used.

"Ud. es el tercer *hombre*?" the cop said to the manager. "*Yo necesito ver su identificación también.*"

It was unbearably hot in the airless office, and the sweat poured from me. They wanted my identification, naturally. Not wanting to let on that I understood him, I said, without much enthusiasm: "I didn't take Evan's card."

"It's not just that," Cal said. "My office called this morning. Apparently Amex called to say someone tried to use my card at a Target in Miami this morning. It's a pretty goddamn big coincidence, don't you think?"

"Not really. I'm sure it's the Mexican banking system. It's not as sophisticated as ours."

The cop flinched at this, revealing his knowledge of English. Unfortunately he caught me noticing him, and that piqued his

91

interest in me. What kind of actor can't keep a poker face?

"Sir," the manager said to me. "The officer would like to see your identification."

In my wallet was a New York state driver's licence for Steven Lawrence Sawyer. To hand it over, I had to duck my head beneath the slanted ceiling. Hotel employees shouldered past, glaring at the intruders. The cop had chosen a location to his advantage, a trick Tom Walker knew from *Legal Ease*. I envied him the sweat towel he'd draped behind his neck.

The cop jotted Steve's details into his black book. He wasn't introduced to me. I hoped he never would be. "*Ud. tiene otras quejas en contra de él?*" he said to the manager.

"*No, ninguna,*" the manager said. "*Pero, él es muy parlanchín con los otros huéspedes.*"

Chatty with the other guests? Panic prickled my body like a heat rash. I figured Jill and I had an hour before the cop determined the licence was bogus. Maybe less. Once we were in custody, he could take his time tracking our movements and linking us to other swindled tourists. That was the first time I'd witnessed the awful morning-after of one of our squeezes. It was a humbling experience. I'd recommend it to any equivocating thief.

Evan stared blankly at the floor, his innate courteousness disturbed by having to consider me a suspect. Cal kept a hard stare on me. I was glad when he realized there was no point in them remaining in the office and led Evan from it.

The officer returned the licence. "*Pregúntale si tiene problemas con su tarjeta de crédito,*" he said.

"Have you heard from your credit card company?" the manager said to me.

"No, but I only use cash. It's my wife who looks after the cards. I should check with her."

"*¿En qué habitación está él?*" the officer said.

"What room is yours, sir?"

Despite the computer terminal inches from the manager's fingers, I lied about our room number. Anything to give Jill and me a head start. If I got out of there, that is.

"Where is your wife?" the cop said to me in English.

"Right now?" He'd startled me. "I think she went shopping. That's why I need to let her know what's going on."

The cop nodded quickly to the manager and exited the office. "Please wait just a moment, sir," the manager said before following him.

Was I under arrest? The opposite end of the tiny office tapered to a hallway leading to the rear of the shops and services in the lobby. I placed Steve Sawyer's driver's licence back in my pocket. The decision I then made started the clock ticking against us in earnest.

The second door in the hallway opened into the back of the gift shop where I first spotted Jill chatting up Lori and Shauna. Oh, how I wished she'd never done that. Without looking back, I crossed through the shop and into the crowd of holidayers in the main lobby.

Jill was waiting at the designated spot on the path, hands on her hips. From ten yards off, I felt her fear as never before. I slowed to a walk, regretfully realizing that I wouldn't be in this mess if I hadn't returned to "rescue" her after our separation last fall, sold on her dream of opening our theatre. What a moment to be entertaining second thoughts.

As I hesitated, two sixty-something women, beach-bound in sunglasses and sarongs, looked me over as they passed.

Jill at last spotted me, her relief as vivid as her distress, and hurried to me. "I've been waiting twenty minutes. Where have you been?"

"Showing my ID to a cop the Americans called. So we're leaving. I don't care where we go, but we've got to go now."

"What kind of cop?" She found my news sufficiently mortifying to ignore the two women staring at us. "The Acapulco police? Or the state police?"

"How the hell do I know?" I took her by the elbow to lead her on.

"Excuse me," one of the old women said. "Are you Danny Drake, from *Legal Ease*?"

Naturally, the question I'd waited years to hear would come the day after I slept in a tequila bottle and became a fugitive from Mexican justice. The smart answer was no.

"Sure am. But I use Daniel now, not Danny. Big fans, are you? Did you see me in *Street Heat*, too?"

Jill marvelled at this burst of absurdity. "Danny," she said.

"That show was too violent," the woman said. "*Legal Ease* was okay, but I like the show they replaced it with better. The one in Vancouver, with the girl detective. She's so clever. Are you still friends with her?"

Hannah Dyer, she meant, my former co-star. The women were fans of the spin-off created for Hannah that abruptly ended my career in television. For an instant, I succumbed to all the envy and frustration I'd known then. "No. That show's a pile of ..." I trailed off, thinking better of it. "Nice vacation so far, ladies?"

Along the path, Jill was in pursuit of a silver-haired man who might have been Nick tottering toward a block of rooms. She stopped to beckon me forward before continuing after him.

"How come we haven't seen you in anything lately?" the second woman said.

"I've been doing big Hollywood movies. They take a while to come out. You'll see."

I caught up to Jill as she exited the door of a ground-floor guest room. She held a small package wrapped in a plastic bag. I stopped short on the lawn. With my days of grifting over, I was not stepping into the Vandals' room and subjecting myself to the horrors of Nick and Brenda's underwear and luggage.

Nick guarded the doorway, equally disinclined to have me enter. "You look like hell," he said to me. "What happened to you?"

"He was partying at a strip club last night," Jill said.

"Serves him right. Disgusting places. You'll want to get some rest. For your audition."

"What audition? Where?" Beside me, Jill beamed happiness.

"For the film," Nick said. "In Veracruz."

I couldn't understand why he'd want to help a nobody from Buffalo make it in the movies. I wouldn't help a washed-up pop star. I just didn't get it. "News to me."

"That's entertainment, eh? Never dull. Call me when you land, Ginny." He kissy-kissed Jill's cheeks, showbiz style. I could have puked. "We'll pick you up at the airport."

"We might take the bus," Jill said. "To see the countryside."

"Then you'll find there's not much to look at. See you in a few days."

I marched us to our room, keeping an eye out for the police. The audition seemed like a dream, so I'd treat it as such until we were clear of Acapulco. In the meantime, we had a sort-of plan, and I could see as far into my future as a long bus ride. "What's in the bag?" I said.

"Some books Nick said he'd loan me." Jill laughed. "They're leaving for the airport now. Just think. We might have missed them if we'd stayed to chat with your fans."

"They weren't really my fans," I said.

My primary role on travel days was to pace and fume while waiting for Jill, a chronic dawdler and a last-minute packer. We occasionally missed flights and arrived at hotels in the dead of night. She was also, for a drifter, something of a hoarder.

Yet that day she was a blur of motion, cramming her many bags willy-nilly. I kept a lookout through the patio doors, in case the hotel manager had started searching for us. Of greater concern was the fact that we were broke. "How are we going to pay for this?"

"I've got some ideas. Things are working out, don't you see?"

"No, I don't. So what's the plan now, since we can't do the card trick anymore?"

"We can't do *that* card trick anymore," Jill said. "There's others I know, from when I was down here before you. I can look them up when we get to Veracruz."

That was kind of disappointing. And while normally any mention of her criminal contacts forced me to tune out, on that day I pressed on. "That's not much to go on."

"So maybe we'll get jobs like you said. We need to disappear for a bit. If the police are on to us, we shouldn't be checking into any Mexican hotels for a while. Having a place to stay in Veracruz might be exactly what we need."

She had a point. My counterpoint, which wouldn't have been productive at that moment, was that needing a place to lay low hadn't been necessary until she ran the Americans' cards too early.

The room looked like a hurricane had blown through it. I pitied the maid who'd have to reset it, though she'd be compensated by some items of clothing Jill had jettisoned.

Infinitely more frustrating than packing was transporting Jill's many bags. There were eleven in total, not counting the handbags and shopping bags filled with God-knows-what.

To avoid reception, I led us toward the service area behind the main building. Jill trailed, dragging two wheeled suitcases that toppled over every few yards. In righting them, other bags slipped off her shoulders, spilling their contents. I grabbed two of her smaller carry-alls and a plastic bag full of magazines and tossed them aside. That left nine bags, with which we made slow progress.

We reached a greasy laneway of dumpsters and loading docks shared by a number of hotels. Here workers washed taxis, smoked cigarettes, or ate tacos cooked on the back of a pick-up truck. Almost all of them stopped what they were doing to watch this formerly attractive young couple transformed into frazzled hustlers on the lam.

Costera, when we reached it, hummed its usual indifference. The city wouldn't miss us. A Beetle taxi swung to the curb before I raised my arm.

Ten minutes later, when it was clear Jill's luggage couldn't possibly fit into the car, the driver demanded a hundred pesos for his trouble. Stupidly, I refused. The resulting argument drew curious bystanders. And other taxis, none of which had the trunk space we required.

The heat rose in waves from the broiling concrete. To escape the scene, I paid fifty pesos we couldn't afford for a ride we never got. We trundled the bags to a bus stop, where ten buses passed before one rolled up that served the bus terminal. *Acapulquito* was painted a regal purple and trimmed with hot pink, its chrome grille gleaming in the sun.

The working poor of Mexico are generally patient, so no one was offended by the delay we caused in loading our bags, or that Jill and I occupied, all told, three double seats in the centre of the bus. We were grateful to them and to be out of the sun. The driver cued some muddy Spanish rock, and the bus lurched into traffic. At last, I thought. On our way to nowhere.

Soon we were speeding past the elegant palms and the long brick wall of the Campo de Golf. We'd scored a lucky bus, one with a driver in a hurry. People waved from the open windows of the other buses we passed. Jill relaxed against me to enjoy the ride. She was all about the thrills, and heaven help me, but I loved that about her.

A truckload of armed soldiers went by, followed by other military vehicles. The bus pulled to a stop near the entrance to a tennis club, but no one got on.

"Just when the coast was clear," I said, sounding more nervous than I intended.

Raised voices came from in front of the bus. The driver exited and a black-masked soldier, led by his automatic rifle, bounded up the steps. More followed, one leading a German shepherd on a chain. The music cut out, the emptiness filled with leaden footsteps and the hoarse panting of the dog. Having gotten our complete attention, the soldiers started down the aisle. They weren't wearing any insignia, so I couldn't tell if they were military or police.

The soldiers peered into people's bags without much interest. I put an arm around Jill. The dog started barking as it neared us and, after lunging at Jill, was jerked back by its master. I half rose in my seat to protect her, but the soldier gently shoved me back down.

"*El perro piensa que Uds. deberían pagar más por su equipaje suplementario*," he said, and his comrades laughed. He thinks you should have to pay an extra fare for all your luggage.

Two hours later, we reached the bus station on Avenue Cuauhtémoc in an overpriced minivan taxi. Jill paid the driver then hurried inside to check on departures for Mexico City.

As I unloaded the luggage, I recalled that we'd met a couple like ourselves back in December. Our doppelgangers. A bizarro Danny and Jill. We'd been in the Bahamas, at Atlantis, the massive Disney-esque waterworld resort where we'd enjoyed some of our last successful squeezes.

The couple first got friendly at a bar in the network of lagoons and waterslides between hotel towers. He had hollow eyes that never met yours, and she hid her extra years with heavy make-up. They'd ask personal questions, their feelers extending like the tendrils of a creeper, and then be cagey with information about themselves. She was a flight attendant, and he was in real estate, both common professions easy to bullshit about. They were Chicagoans living in San Diego, they said, which perhaps accounted for their tans and oddly unplaceable accents.

At the time, I'd recently returned to Jill after spending a few months alone up north. We were still readjusting to one another and working some couples from Montreal. Yet soon they'd forced so many chance encounters with us it was clear we were trapped in the same sort of web we spun. The reflection of ourselves was unsettling. Were we as obvious? Or as smarmy? We flew to Puerto Vallarta to escape them and commenced our luckless plunge down Mexico's Pacific coast that brought us to a dead end in Acapulco.

Jill returned to where I was waiting on the sidewalk, and together we lugged our worldly possessions up the steps into the terminal. Whoever that couple was, I wondered how they were doing.

The terminal on Avenue Cuauhtémoc wasn't the one we usually used to flit between resort towns in the region. The present station, a hangar-like space open to the busy commercial street, was well off the beaten track in a vast, unchartable area I called "the Real Mexico." Jill and I had become travellers, not tourists, a downgrade in status that required a significant lowering of expectations. No more complimentary saunas or bottomless piña coladas. My chest tightened accordingly.

Buses are the primary mode of transportation for a huge majority of Mexicans. The stations are always thronged, moreso today because it was the Monday of Semana Santa, the Easter holy week. Babies howled, televisions brayed from the ceiling, and departures were announced over a PA system.

To save the cost of a hotel, Jill proposed a midnight bus to Mexico City that arrived at dawn. Sure, but how would we pay for that? Two tickets on the Costa Line all-nighter were 800 pesos. She had about 300 pesos remaining, and I had 67 pesos left to my name.

Jill removed a slim, silver Nikon and an old Samsung flip phone we used as tourist props from her handbag. "We can sell our camera and the phone," she said.

"That phone's not worth anything anymore," I said.

"Yeah?" She took some crumpled bills from a pocket of her capri pants. "Well, I may have reached into the till at one of the beach bars."

"Are you kidding me? Someone will have to account for that."

"Yes, I know. What the fuck, Danny? Do you think I wanted to do that?"

No, I didn't. What she'd done was unfortunate, but necessary.

"Can you stop being so self-righteous?" she said. "Please? And can you watch the bags while I pawn the camera? I'll get a better price if I'm alone."

While she was gone, I stuffed all our luggage, save for an overnight bag she refused to surrender, into three lockers. Then I sat on a bench and watched officers from various police services— city, state, and federal—patrolling the station. There are many different kinds of cops in Mexico, their jurisdictions and loyalties all equally uncertain.

She was back within an hour. I accepted the 200 pesos she handed me and pointed out there were cheaper tickets available for a bus that travelled secondary roads rather than the interstate highway. Jill demurred. Whatever our fate, we were in a hurry to meet it.

The queue for tickets was long enough for me to question our motivation again. "What's in Veracruz? For us, I mean. Tell me again."

"A chance to make some money while we figure out our next

move," Jill said. "What we were doing wasn't going to get us our theatre. Now we have this opportunity."

Optimistic of her, I thought, since this was our only move. At the ticket counter, she counted out cash from a thin roll. "Try your Visa," I said. "It booked us into Paraiso."

"Good idea. There might still be some juice on it."

The card was refused. The woman at the counter nonchalantly exchanged it for cash.

With the tickets secured, our next task was to part with Steve Sawyer and Regina Boccia, or rather their passports. I wanted to destroy any link to our near-miss with the Americans.

"But we need them for Nick and Brenda," Jill said.

"No, we don't. The Vandals are never going to look at our IDs."

Opposite the station was a huge green space, *Parque Papagayo*. There the Real Mexico began in earnest, across a line more psychological than physical. I avoided the Real Mexico because I didn't rob Mexicans and because, frankly, it frightened me.

Once we were inside it, the park was too big to see out of, a source of additional anxiety for me. Among the banana trees and bamboo groves was an overgrown go-cart track, a replica pirate galleon in a scummy duck pond, and tortoises sunning themselves. We might have enjoyed it were we not wasted by the heat and the stress of our sudden banishment from Paraiso.

Also present: so many strolling vacationers we couldn't get a moment alone. Every day is Saturday in Acapulco. Eventually we did, in a petting zoo with an ostrich, a strutting peacock, and a lion that stank so much no one lingered at his cage, which allowed me to bury Steve and Gina forever in a rancid garbage can. The act heralded a new low in our career.

We then sat glumly on a bench with our backs to a wall separating the park from Costera. A massive Mexican flag rising from the *pública* beaches flapped mightily overhead. I'd forgotten this was a city where people came to relax and have fun. "Those other passports should go," I said. "If your contact was arrested, he could tell them our aliases."

"No, we're keeping them. They might still come in handy."

Did she mean for those other contacts who trade in stolen data? I was too hungover and cranky to ask. I should have grabbed some items to pawn like she had. I wasn't contributing or carrying my weight and needed to work harder if we were to get through this all right.

The park closed, the gates clanging shut, at nightfall. We bought water then drifted north along the beach in a depleted silence. The lights of hotel towers, softened by the shroud of smog, reached across the bay. Reduced to black silhouettes, we gladly lost ourselves in the darkness.

In the tranquil zócalo, families sat to dinner at patio tables. Jill chose a small restaurant on a side street, where a year ago I'd eaten with the Englishwoman I'd been working just before Jill and I separated. I didn't mention that. We both ordered the *comida corrida*: soup, rice, and a meatball dish.

When we'd nearly finished, Jill leaned across the table. "It's pretty good, huh?"

I nodded. The meals are always dependable in the smaller family-run restaurants. Real ingredients. Big portions. And for once, I had been hungry.

"I'm glad you like it because we might have enough money left to buy coffee in the morning. After that, we're broke."

She had a mischievous glint in her eye. Immediately, I saw us doing a dine 'n dash, one of my father's favourite tricks when I was on the road with him. I couldn't count how many times he'd lifted me from a restaurant table, my hamburger half-finished, and hustled me through a kitchen into a back alley.

Was she thinking of the same thing? Had it come to that? Her fingernails were bitten, I noticed, for the first time that I'd seen since our university days. I watched as she took in the diners and the harried waitress. She caught me admiring her, half smiled to herself, and continued eating. A sort of calm settled between us.

When the bill came, she offered our Visa again and, by some miracle, it worked. Inspired, we hurried to a Scotiabank ATM guarded by a well-armed young cop. Jill inserted her card and asked for 10,000 pesos. The machine whirred, then flashed: *Tarjeta cancelada. Contacte con su banco.* The card was not returned.

"Now they'll know we were here," I said.

"So what? That's the last they'll hear from us."

Our bus was barely half-full, allowing us to create, after a hot, crowded day, a tiny island of privacy. Among the amenities offered by the Costa Line—a complimentary bottle of water, a bag of almonds—the air-conditioning was the most welcome. In ten minutes, we were so sufficiently chilled that Jill rummaged through her bags for a cardigan.

As the bus left the station, I tensed in dread of the Hollywood films that blasted from overhead monitors on Mexican buses. Wonderfully, they never came on.

We travelled up streets nearly as busy as they'd been at noon, shops and taco stands still open. I was glad to be escaping Acapulco, even if this was the first city Jill brought me to work in, and I was leaving as I'd arrived: penniless, my prospects and destination uncertain.

Soon we were rising, our ears popping, into the mountains. We entered a long tunnel that plunged us into the velvety blackness of the countryside. We huddled together and shared a bottle of water. Then Jill escaped into sleep, curling up against me to share the weight of her need, her hair fanning out.

The rhythmic breathing of other passengers soon filled the quiet. The things Jill and I *weren't* discussing—her sloppy performance with the Americans or her odd attraction to the Vandals—took the seat ahead of us and kept turning to stare at me.

The bus stopped in a town where a solitary soldier boarded. He shared a joke with the driver before exiting just as quickly. If I wanted to leave, as I'd half contemplated that afternoon at Paraiso, this would have been the time. But I probably would have just met a different bad end all by myself. It would be more fun for us to get our just desserts together.

Rolling again, I peered through my ghostly reflection in the window to the blue, moonlit scrublands beyond it. The uncertainty of our situation reminded me that last year, as now, Jill and I weren't communicating very well. I misinterpreted some key signals from her, which led to my foolish pursuit of the Englishwoman.

Unlike now, last year was lucrative, so my first blunder was grasping for more than we required. The debacle began at the pool bar of the El Presidente hotel when I spotted a solidly built woman reading a paperback. Late thirties, I decided at a glance, probably English, and achingly single. I turned to Jill to suggest one last squeeze for the season only to find her seat was empty and her margarita abandoned.

That was the first sign I misread. My greater mistake was

misunderstanding my own motivation. A year ago, I'd already had enough of robbing people and had concluded, without any real proof, that Jill was impatient with my lacklustre effort. A quick solo squeeze, I figured, offered the best way to demonstrate my dedication.

Up in our room, Jill was against the idea. The low season was approaching. "Forget it," she said. "Let's get a beach house and just chill a while. We had a good year."

"We've still got four days here," I said. "Since when do we turn down a job? It'll be fast."

"If you say so," she said.

I chose to be Adam Fowler, a single lawyer from Minnesota whose identity I hadn't used in a while. Returning to the bar, I found a seat near Cheryl. Some easy banter got her name and a smile from her. Then later at dinner, I made sure she saw that we were both dining alone.

Back upstairs, Jill was watching *The Bachelor*. "I'll be keeping an eye on you," she said. "You should be careful. I'm sure she's a nympho."

It's too bad I ignored her insecurity. I'd have saved us a lot of trouble.

The next morning, I waited until Cheryl was eating breakfast before heaping a bowl with granola and conjuring a lost-puppy look. That got me an invitation to join her, and I learned she lived near Nottingham and worked as an accountant at a dairy. Her trip was planned as a fortieth birthday celebration for herself and some girlfriends. When they couldn't escape their jobs, kids, and husbands, she took off by herself. "Bravo," Adam said. I genuinely liked her and resolved to finish this quickly.

Soon after this encounter, en route to the souvenir markets downtown, Cheryl needed an ATM. I steered us into the Playa Suites hotel, where I managed to see her pin number and a few digits of her Barclays Bank Visa before she returned the card to her Hello Kitty wallet.

Vendors pestered us through lunch in the zócalo, none more persistent than a doe-eyed little girl selling coral necklaces. Cheryl twice refused her before succumbing. "I've got a niece her age," she said. Afterwards, we strolled the sea wall then returned to our hotel.

Jill entered our room a few minutes after I did. "Looks like your English bird has you going in circles," she said. "Maybe you should quit while you're ahead."

Foolishly, I interpreted that as a challenge. "I'll be done by tomorrow," I said. "You'll see."

The next evening, Cheryl and I hit a nightclub with a variety show. A Mexican comic with halting English was followed by an ABBA cover band. Cheryl kept the waiter busy delivering bottles of Corona. After a few of these, she abruptly leaned over and kissed me. "Let's go," she said. "I hear crap bands at my local every weekend."

Outside, in the hot-red neon along Costera, she kissed me again.

"Well, that was fun, wasn't it?" I said. "Let me take you somewhere for a nightcap."

She took my hand. "How about the bar at our hotel?" she said.

When we reached the El Presidente, she headed straight to the elevators and called one to go up. The closing doors trapped me with my dilemma. Sex wasn't an option, yet I couldn't deny it was what Adam Fowler should be wanting most at the moment.

Then I caught a break. I sensed something shift in Cheryl, and outside her room, received just a single peck on the cheek. "Sorry," she said. "I mean, thanks for a lovely evening. I'll see you tomorrow, yeah?"

My job now, despite my relief, was to act disappointed in the most gentlemanly way possible. "Why don't we go to the beach tomorrow?" I said. "I'll swing by around eleven."

"Cheers. I'd like that. Thanks, Adam. Goodnight."

I got back into the elevator, wiping strawberry lip gloss from my mouth, frustrated by my frustration. Although Jill was already asleep, I heard her telling me this was all unnecessary.

The day at the beach became a lunch date at our hotel and then daiquiris at the pool bar. Cheryl tipped the waiter with the last of her cash, cause for a small amount of excitement. I'd barely sipped my drink when she quickly rose and led me from the pool.

Midway across the hotel lobby, I spotted Jill in conversation near the front desk with a grizzled, bearded Mexican man I'd never seen before. Naturally I was curious, but if I wanted to complete the squeeze of Cheryl, I couldn't step out of character.

In the elevator, Cheryl's eyes shone with the same heat as last night. Unlike last night, I was distracted by what I'd just seen in the lobby. I told myself Jill was often approached by unknown men, especially macho Mexicans, so there was nothing to worry about.

I entered Cheryl's room without an escape plan. She'd be insulted by an about-face and might not want to see me again. What then would I have to show Jill for my effort? Cheryl tossed her purse onto the bed, out of which tumbled cigarettes, a hairbrush, and the Hello Kitty wallet. Her hands ranged over me. Jill was right: she was a tiger.

Cheryl broke off the kiss. "Stay right there," she said. "I'm going to take a quick shower. There's beer in the little fridge, so help yourself."

"Okay," I said, scarcely believing my luck. I decided to get the card number, pretend I'd fallen ill, then run back to Jill. I heard water splashing in the bathroom. On the bed by Cheryl's purse were the souvenirs she'd purchased: sombreros, t-shirts, and a piñata for her niece. I imagined them brightening her flat in rain-dreary Nottingham. I saw her at the pub regaling her friends with tales of her daring. Ruthlessness is difficult when you feel sorry for people.

Steeling myself, I sifted through the cards in her Hello Kitty wallet—National Health, Tesco Points Club—until I spotted the distinctive royal blue of her Barclays Visa. At that same moment, Cheryl exited the bathroom. "Can you open me a beer?" she said.

Too late, I realized I'd neglected to listen for the sound of the showering water to change when she got beneath it. She was in her bra and underwear, steam billowing behind her. For an instant, I saw reflected in her face the monster who seduced women and robbed them.

Her confusion became astonishment, then anger, then—as she fully understood who or what she'd invited into her room—panic. That was the worst of it, the fear I inspired. I endured the card scams because I told myself it didn't cost the people we robbed. But who wants to frighten them? My determination to move Jill and myself out of that life began that day.

I snapped her wallet closed and tossed it onto the bed. Cheryl stared blankly from the washroom. As I slunk past her to exit, she began to scream. And scream and scream. As if I had her at knifepoint. As if the earth had opened and swallowed her.

I looked back from the door to convey my shame and regret over what she'd witnessed. And to ask if all the hubbub was necessary for a crime that hadn't actually occurred.

Evidently so. Cheryl rushed past me into the hall, shouting and banging for help on the doors of other rooms. I sprinted in the opposite direction, to the stairs, down which I sped to our room on the ninth floor. I blundered into it, panting, raving.

Jill came in from the balcony with a drink in her hand. "We're blown," I said. "We gotta go."

"What do you mean?" Jill said.

"She caught me. My hands. In her purse. We have to go. Now."

"Does she know our room number?"

"I don't think so. No."

I pictured Cheryl at the front desk in her skivvies, bravely brushing tears from her eyes as she reported me. The scene with her wallet I might explain as a mistake. But if they checked my alias or tracked our movements in the past two years.

Jill was stuffing a small dufflebag with a few pieces of my clothing. "Relax," she said. "This happens. You go now, and I'll catch up to you later."

I was thinking about how much I loved her and how I'd failed her. "Who was that guy you were talking to in the lobby?" I said.

My question surprised her. She crumpled a large roll of bills into my hand. "I'll explain later," she said. "Go stay somewhere else tonight. Then tomorrow, go to the Sanborns by the big waterslide. I'll meet you there around lunchtime, after I check out of here."

I took the bag she offered and placed the money inside it. I kissed her even as I stepped backwards to the door. "Tomorrow," she repeated. "The Sanborns by the waterslide."

The door slammed shut, and I was alone in the hallway. And then I was flying back down the stairs, trusting they led to a side street or laneway and not the hotel lobby.

I spent a dull night in another hotel watching television, furious with myself for the mess I'd made. The next day, I ate lunch in the Sanborns around noon, loitering nearby until evening. There was no reason to suspect Jill wouldn't turn up. When she didn't, I cautiously scouted the lobby of the El Presidente and its stretch of beach. Wary of any fallout from Cheryl, I steered clear of the front desk. I wasn't brave enough to visit our room.

On the second day, I staked out a bench across the street from the Sanborns. Various scenarios ran through my head, none of them good. In the knapsack Jill packed for me was underwear, socks, a t-shirt, and close to 10,000 pesos. Enough to live well for a while or for a flight out of the country. Cellphones might have solved everything, if we'd used them. Nor did Jill use email. If only we'd chosen a hotel for our rendezvous rather than a restaurant.

She didn't show up the second day. By the third day, I knew she wasn't coming.

I moved to a cheap motel off the strip. No air-conditioning, no television. Nothing to do but fester with worry. Or haunt all the hotel lobbies and bars along Costera. Or stagger along the beach. Or storm through the Sanborns as diners glared at the ragged gringo interrupting their meals. As if they could tell me where Jill had gone or who that unknown man was.

After five days, I decided she'd been abducted or arrested—things I couldn't do anything about. It was easier than acknowledging I'd been abandoned. There wasn't anyone to contact about her, and I couldn't go to the police. Had she been working a squeeze she hadn't told me about? The man in the lobby? Unlikely, since we didn't steal from Mexicans. Or was there something else going on?

Up on the ninth floor of the El Presidente, my key card no longer opened the door to the room we'd shared. I sat all that evening in the lobby, where no trace of Jill or Cheryl or the mystery man, remained. Good hotels are brand new places every day.

When all I had left was the price of a flight home, I caught a ten-peso bus to the airport.

Toronto's at its best in May. Trees in luscious bloom. Downy twilit evenings. There were worse places to wait for Jill. I converted a few crumpled pesos into less than $200. The price of a hotel room and a meal. And exactly how was Jill supposed to find me?

I took transit into town, drawn to the St. Lawrence Market area where I'd rented a condo during my success. The bleak memory of the days that followed—losing my show, slowly going broke—skulked in the shadow of my old building. Here I was again: just as poor and none the wiser. Yet I was wondrously free of the fear and tension Jill and I had endured almost constantly down south. For the first time in two years, there was no need to look over my shoulder.

I tracked down my friend Warren Gillies at the ticketing agency where he managed the call centre. "Come by our place," he said. "There's something I want you to see."

A chilly night was falling. I'd bought a jacket at an army surplus store, but had larger concerns. "Could I park myself on your couch for the night?" I said.

"Don't see why not. And it will be the couch. Our place is pretty small."

Warren and his wife, Tammy, shared a cramped one-bedroom

basement in Riverdale. They could afford better, Warren explained, but were saving for a down payment on a house.

Tammy arrived shortly after I did. She worked in marketing for a large media provider and was by far the main breadwinner. "Look who," she said. "Our favourite former superstar."

I let that slide because her hugely swelling belly had spoiled Warren's announcement.

"Nice work," I said. "Boy or a girl?"

"Don't want to know," Warren said. "I'm great either way. Alice or Benjamin."

Tammy's blustery unpacking of some groceries belied her semi-welcome. We never agreed, Tammy and I, since our school days, on how much Warren should focus on acting. He was right: the flat was too small for three. I offered to buy him a beer to celebrate.

In a pub on Queen Street, Warren told me he'd been invited to join the Straightaway Theatre Company and was working fewer hours at the ticketing agency to attend other auditions. He deserved it. After Jill, Warren was the best actor I knew, but he was famously unlucky in securing roles. It must have been so discouraging to be continually passed over for mediocrities (like me) with a better smile.

We spoke of other colleagues, many of whom, tired of waiting for that breakout role, were settling into alternate careers. People were surprised, he said, by my sudden departure. I longed to tell him the truth about my life, but my story was that the English language school where I'd worked had closed. Without a job, my work visa automatically expired.

"That sucks," Warren said. "Hey, do you ever hear from Jill? Where's she at?"

"No idea," I said, which was probably the first honest thing I'd said to him.

Late the following morning, I drifted downtown, unsure of every step, looking for Jill along each street. Toronto spun around me, smugly confident in its self-appointed purpose. I passed the storage facility I'd rented the night after Jill called with her offer of rescue. According to my father, bills from it, and other creditors, still reached him. A compelling reason, now that I was back, to not use my real name.

I paused at a bar on King Street, its patio packed in the endless amber afternoon and boisterous enough that I recovered some of my optimism. Halfway through my drink, I saw a television producer and an actress I'd known in my previous incarnation. I slipped out a side door and got a beer in a pub closer to Chinatown. And another. Then another.

The next morning, I woke to a heated conversation underway behind the closed door of Tammy and Warren's bedroom. "He doesn't even have any other clothes" was the phrase that convinced me to begin collecting those few items Tammy had mentioned. My friends were on a separate, more progressive voyage now, one with no room for my shenanigans.

I spared Warren the trouble of turfing me by coughing loudly until the voices subsided. "Thought I'd move on," I said when he exited the bedroom. "I'm going to see my father."

"How is old Earl?" Warren said.

"I'll let you know when I see him," I said.

On the bus out of the city, a calming fatalism muted my remorse. Since our lifestyle had practically guaranteed a cruel goodbye, I should have been grateful for my time with Jill and that I wasn't in jail. Not that I wouldn't have gone back to her in a moment or wasn't sick with worry.

The town of Millward remained a tiny, petty place. When I fled after high school, I was aware that some part of it would stick to me like gum on my shoe for the rest of my life. Big box stores now ringed a doomed downtown that had continued dying in the years I was away. Transport trucks rumbled through it, trailing dust and plastic bags.

I detoured into an older section of town to briefly contemplate the house where I'd lived with Granny Drake while attending high school. Since her death, it had been restored to its gabled Victorian glory.

The bungalow I'd bought for my father faced the county fairgrounds. Earl was in the front yard, trying to start a lawnmower. "Hey, look who," he said. "Are you staying long?"

"I need to make some money," I said. "Then maybe I'll go away to teach again."

That brainstorm had arrived on the bus: a month of ESL training, then off to Asia to teach. Thousands of others did it. Why not me? Jill could follow me for a change.

"That's not a bad idea," Earl said. "Nothing going on here."

"I figured you'd say something like that."

In the evening, we watched a Blue Jays game. Earl lived in a bachelor squalor worse than anything I'd encountered in my student years. I remembered why, at the age of thirteen, I moved in with my grandmother. He didn't, for example, own an extra set of bedsheets. I spent my first night in the house I'd bought under a musty sleeping bag from my brief stint as a Wolf Cub.

Earl grumbled about my presence but enjoyed having an audience for his stories. Like the time out west when he jammed with Randy Bachman. Or the time he stole a Porsche from a man who'd fired him from a bartending job, then sold it. I'd heard them all before.

I drank with him a few evenings, grudgingly. Since returning, I'd unfortunately been hearing the call of a younger, more dissolute version of myself. I never liked that guy.

One night, as I sat wondering why I'd gone after money Jill and I didn't actually need, my father was particularly cranky. The Jays had lost both games of a double-header with the Yankees, and Earl had been sipping beer since mid-afternoon.

"What are you doing here?" he said. "In my house. In my living room. And what happened to that girl down south? The English teacher. Is she what's eating you?"

I threw up my hands. Surely that must be obvious.

"It is her," he said. "You got a bad-girl problem, you know that? Like those girls with loser guys who beat on them and run around. You're like that, only the opposite."

He wasn't entirely wrong. And while the girl in question was certainly bad, there had only ever been one of them. However, an alcoholic widower/bachelor with a gambling addiction who ate tinned stew twice a week was in no position to lecture me on women.

He then got maudlin over a friend with prostate trouble, prompting him into more sodden musings about the good old days. I'd had enough and was heading to bed when he said, "A thing I never told you. Because why did you need to know? Your mother and me weren't living together when she died. We were separated. Temporarily."

I dropped back onto the couch. "What do you mean, separated?"

"She was living with her girlfriend. The one that died with her. You were living there too, but my mom took you that night 'cause the girls were having that party."

"Why are you telling me this now? And what did you do? Why did she leave you?"

"Nothing special. Well, a burglary charge, which I beat. It was just a thing. The separation."

The guilt he'd carried for thirty years slammed into me. "I don't need to know this," I said.

Earl simply glared back at me, ever more resentful of his loss.

I lay awake that night pained not by Earl's awful burden, but by how alike we were. And by my thoughts of Jill. Hopefully my negligence, or stupidity, didn't lead to another tragedy.

Later that week at a card game, Earl heard of a landscaper requiring some help. "You said you wanted to get out of the house more. Not that I'd advise working," he said. "What about acting on TV again? You said it wasn't work at all."

That message I heard. I cut lawns, laid sod, and trimmed hedges. Was there a greater comedown for a former television star than cleaning gutters in his hometown? Even so, I didn't mind. I inspired a few double takes, but people got used to seeing me.

It was a relief to have money and to have legitimately earned it. I cashed my cheques at a payday advance shop in a strip mall, where I chatted in Spanish to Mexican migrant workers hired to do farm work on the cheap. I bought a pay-as-you-go phone for work and would catch myself staring at it dumbly, awaiting a call that would never come.

Though the days exhausted me, I lay sleepless between the sheets I'd bought, Jill leaking from my pores like a sweet poison. I missed her. Overwhelmingly. Jill making dinner. Jill arranging our days. Jill asleep on the beach. Jill in bed. Without her, I was incomplete and adrift, my longing stretching further than the endless swaths of lawn I mowed.

Long hours alone allowed me to continually re-examine those last days at the El Presidente. Where was she when I was with Cheryl? Had that man been present earlier? If it was no one, she would have said as much. Soon I over-obsessed, jumbling the sequence of events so badly that I couldn't trust the accuracy of my memory.

The joy of my return to the working class quickly faded beneath the brutal sun. I missed acting, too. I even missed the thrill of its substitute that Jill had cultivated in the resorts, and finally understood why thieving appealed to her so much. And to me, though less so. Our cons provided her a control over people and circumstances she'd never had in her life and a chance to use a talent that would otherwise have gone to waste.

One night on television, an actor who'd had a bit part on *Legal Ease* turned up on a big Hollywood sitcom. Good for him, I thought. Did I ever truly believe that would be my life, too?

The weeks passed. The actor turned thief turned landscaper got buff wielding a rake and shovel. I bought travel guides to Vietnam and Thailand to help me choose a destination. When I'd saved enough money, I bought a used laptop and arranged for wireless in Earl's bungalow.

The kitchen phone I sat beneath with that laptop never rang.

Inevitably, I ran into a friend from high school. At a barbecue, I met his wife and other people I'd known years ago. As someone who wound up back where he started, I was a novelty and a cautionary tale. Those old shoes, the pair with gum stuck to the sole, still fit just fine.

The more I socialized, the less I thought of Jill—down to every twenty seconds from every fifteen. My old friends owned homes and had kids or were in pursuit of them. Not all of them were happy although they'd all settled into their lives in a way I envied. That kept me at a distance from them. I still couldn't say what I was doing there.

Also inevitably, I re-met Kate Norwood, with whom I'd been involved, via the drama club, in high school. Now she had a five-year-old son, Judah, from a brief marriage. She worked for an auto-parts distributor and lived in fear of being laid off. In fact, no one I spoke to sounded secure in their jobs. Maybe crooks like Earl and Jill—and me—had the right idea.

One evening after work, Earl told me a woman had called for me and would call again. I nearly collapsed. It had been two months since I left Mexico. How could she let me go so long without hearing from her? And was it smart for me to return to our thieving? The odds of getting caught would only increase the longer we kept at it.

The phone rang around eight o'clock. Earl and I exchanged a glance. I answered.

It wasn't Jill—it was Kate asking me to attend a baseball game on Saturday. A date, she meant. Flattered and flustered, I couldn't change mental gears quickly enough. I wanted to say yes, but my yes was to Jill's question about returning to our life together.

Did Kate think I actually lived here? Well, why wouldn't she?

I told her the truth: that I was already attending the game and would see her there. The truth was so novel I spoke it every chance I got.

At the game, Kate asked me to speak to the amateur drama club she'd joined in a larger town closer to the city. Smart of her, I thought, to appeal to my vanity.

The company was producing *The Cherry Orchard*, and I was totally unprepared for how much I envied their opportunity to perform on stage. The depth of the material, the emotional negotiations with colleagues, the camaraderie. Forget LA and shitty sitcoms. Wherever I was headed, I needed the stage back in my life again.

After the rehearsal, I told the company that most television limits your range as an actor, surprising myself with a bitterness I struggled to conceal. I recovered by championing the role of community theatre in the era of streaming and PVRs, and by conducting a spirited Q&A.

There was a junior troupe attached to the company as a teaching component, kids the same age Kate and I had been when we were first bitten by the acting bug. Answering their questions made me feel like one of the older people who'd helped me in my earlier career.

On the drive back to town, Kate talked me into visiting some art galleries the following weekend. It wasn't difficult. I'd forgotten my tendency to flirt, and my need to be adored.

We became a minor item, Kate and I. A platonic item. With Jill still pumping in my veins, I kept my hands to myself. Kate didn't mind. She was playing me longer than that.

In Toronto, Tammy gave birth to baby Benjamin. Warren was ecstatic. I borrowed my boss's pick-up truck a few times to visit the city with baby clothes and diapers. More than once, Warren asked me to stay for a show at Passe Muraille or some other theatre. That each time I had to refuse, saying I had an early start the next day, reminded me how much I missed acting.

In the evenings I continued, with an enthusiasm that felt increasingly forced, to research teaching jobs in Vietnam. Where Jill would never find me. And where there was no English-language theatre so far as I could tell. So why was I going there?

Kate introduced me to Judah, her son, whom I won over with some magic I'd once learned for a movie role. I almost felt like I belonged, and I needed to decide whether to stay in Millward or move on. To where didn't matter because everywhere I went I'd be without Jill.

A few days later, Kate needed help hanging curtains in her apartment. In the parking lot of Home Depot, we unexpectedly met her mother. Was this a setup? I asked myself as I fibbed about remembering Mrs. Norwood from high school. If so, it was cute and well intentioned.

As the two women chatted, I felt removed from the scene, a stranger in a parking lot in a strange town. It wasn't anything out-of-body or mystical, just simply the strongest indication so far that these weren't my people and the town wasn't my place. Later that evening at dinner, Kate set a credit card on the restaurant table while we waited for the bill. I instantly memorized the number, which bounced around my skull for days.

Around this time, I talked a residential customer into some landscaping work at the horseback riding camp he operated. My boss was impressed and offered to hire me as a full-time assistant. I balked, since that would involve putting the real Daniel Drake on the books. He told me to ponder it over the weekend, and that he'd call on Sunday evening. Summer was winding down and lay-offs imminent. I knew that if I didn't say yes, I'd be out of a job, too.

A real job would require a bank account and that would set the collection agents and credit card companies after me. Stupidly, I sought Earl's advice. "Are you nuts?" he said. "Save some cash, then see more of the world. Why would you want to get stuck here?"

You might if you were as tired of rambling as I was. Even Earl had left the road.

On Saturday, Kate, Judah, and I took a picnic lunch to a conservation area. Kate was excited about my job offer, which she presumed would quickly lead to a sales and management role. Eventually, I could start my own landscaping and maintenance business in the area, she said. There was always work in the successive waves of suburbs radiating out of the city.

She had quite a few plans for us, actually, more than she should have starring a man she hadn't yet kissed. I ran with Judah to look for crayfish in a stream, grateful that his presence kept things from getting physical with Kate. The two of them presented a far more daunting decision than that offered by my boss. There could be no halfway with them.

Later at her apartment, I found a lame excuse for leaving after she'd put Judah to bed (my first lie in months). Kate was attending church with her mother the next morning, then spending the day at the family farm. She dangled the idea of me visiting them, and I found another excuse. We had our first kiss at her door. I was sorely tempted to go back inside.

The phone rang Sunday as I was doing the supper dishes. I'd decided to accept my boss's offer, if only to maintain an income for a while—even if it meant becoming myself again and facing my many creditors and the terrible way I'd lived. I'd also decided I wanted a more settled life like Warren and my school pals. And I wanted to be a father. The problem was that I wanted that life with Jill, not with Kate. So maybe I'd run away to Asia after all.

"Hello?" Jill said. "Danny? Is that you?"

I dropped into a kitchen chair, the long receiver cord clattering against the linoleum floor.

"Sorry I didn't call sooner," she said. "I miss you, honey."

Her voice sounded like coconut rum, sunshine, and happiness. "Are you all right?" I said.

"I'm better now. It's been crazy. Do you miss me? Say you miss me."

"Oh yes," I said. Her voice also had a neediness I'd never heard before.

"Are you coming back to me?"

She sounded less like the woman I'd known of late and more like the troubled girl from our last days together in Toronto. The girl I hadn't bothered to go after.

"I don't want to do that anymore," I said. "Why don't you come here? We'll sort this out."

"I can't. Not right now. There's things to finish here. Things I gotta do. Plus I've got this crazy idea you're going to love."

"What kind of idea?"

"You know how you always hated that we weren't working toward anything? Okay, so what if we started putting on shows. For tourists. In English. In a big town like Cancun."

What we needed. And what I should have been thinking. With every hedge I trimmed.

"I need you," she said. "Come work the Christmas season with me. One last run. To make some money. Then we'll find a town with lots of tourists and start putting on shows."

I could help her do that—help us to do that—if it moved us into something real and lasting. I couldn't let her slip away again. But first, I had to get some things straight. "Who was that man you were talking to?" I said. "In the hotel lobby."

"Someone I knew from before you came down south to me."

She must have anticipated the suckerpunch of jealousy that brought. "Not like that," she laughed. "I'll explain later. And I'm sorry I couldn't find you. That English lady sent the cops up to our room. I had to run away from there too."

My other question was why did it take her months to call me when she knew how anxious I'd be? And then, of course, I understood even before I asked: Cheryl.

"Now I gotta ask you," she said. "Why did you go after her? The English lady?"

"I don't know," I said. "To show you I cared."

"But I know you care. That was so stupid."

Earl chose that moment to enter the kitchen in his cut-off shorts and Raptors jersey for a beer from the fridge. "That collection agency called again," he said. "You gotta tell them to fuck off because I'm sick of bullshitting for you."

I watched him exit, a man who'd never gotten a second chance with the woman he loved.

"Danny?" Jill said. "Are you still there? Please say you're coming back. Say you wanna put on some shows with me."

Her timing was impeccable, as usual. "All right," I said. "I'm in. But we have to work hard to make that happen."

"Of course we will. You know me."

In taking charge, she sounded more like herself again. "Write this down," she said. "Delta flight 1497 to Miami tomorrow at one thirty. I'll be there to meet you. See you tomorrow, okay?"

"For sure," I said, hanging up.

Half sobbing with relief, I packed the little I owned into a knapsack. Act III, I was thinking. In which the lost lovers are reunited and a happy ending achieved.

Earl heard my news with a slow nod. Although we'd grown no closer, I'd finally seen him as the conniving and lazy—though not bad—man he was. His criminal days seemed over: no one named Forehead turned up in a panel van half-full of coffee makers anymore.

He lived hand-to-mouth, yet he'd settled, as I'd intended, in the house I bought for him.

He was glad the laptop was remaining and rambled on about it rather than how he felt about me leaving again. I thanked him for putting me up for the summer but not for inadvertently showing me what can happen when you don't make an effort for the people you love.

Later, I withdrew my savings from the sock drawer where I'd hidden them. My Asia fund, I'd called it. Of the $3700 to my name, I pocketed $1000. I stuffed the rest into an old envelope and slipped out into a crisp September night that promised chillier nights to come. Too bad I was leaving: my hometown is gorgeous in autumn.

I put the enveloped bills into Kate's mailbox. That her ex-husband rarely paid his child support didn't make it any less of a kiss-off. What she'd say to Judah I didn't care to consider. I tossed my phone in too, since she needed a new one.

As soon as I was through customs in Miami, Jill was clearing the air between us so we could discuss our plans. She stopped caring about Cheryl once I'd laid out my muddled reasons for insisting on that squeeze. Regarding Kate—about whom, while not ashamed, I wasn't proud—she believed me when I said it never got physical and agreed she should have contacted me sooner. I joked that she was by far my favourite controlling woman. That made her laugh.

The man she'd spoken to in the hotel lobby was someone who'd arranged modelling jobs for her when she first came to Mexico alone. It was a chance encounter, she explained. A brief, friendly exchange. Also, the hotel she checked into after leaving the El Presidente was only a few blocks from where I'd passed that awful week looking for her.

After she'd given up on finding me, she rented a beach house in Mazatlán. Obviously we'd both spent the summer reconsidering our lives and had both, happily, concluded we were better off together. All those rolls of sod, all the sunburns, and all the backache—every moment was worth it now that we'd reconnected to leave our crooked ways behind.

While in Mazatlán she'd seen a production of Grease put on by an English-language summer camp. Midway through, it occurred to her that in all her years down south, she'd never gone to see a live theatrical production. This was because, aside from variety shows in the resorts and comedy nights in larger towns, there weren't any offered in English.

Jill envisioned putting on shows in a tourist town like Puerto Vallarta that regularly received cruise ships. I wanted a port city as well, in a country less volatile than Mexico.

We headed for Costa Rica, which didn't have a town large enough for our theatre but was a great place to pass a month dreaming out loud. With scripts from the internet, we spent happy afternoons on the porch of a beach house blocking them out. Our plan was to do lighter classics like Neil Simon and musicals before moving on to more daring productions. We budgeted how much we'd spend on rent and advertising, the costs involved in setting up a bar, paying locals to work and perform, and of course bribing the right officials and thugs. We also did some necessary work on ourselves, spending entire days just lounging in each other's company.

When our savings ran low, we headed back to the Caribbean, assuming we'd make the capital we required in the hectic Christmas season. Unfortunately, the holidays weren't good to us. We struck out in Cancun, then in Jamaica. We blamed the cooler weather and the economy, but the truth was we'd both lost interest in our cons.

In the new year, we finally got lucky at Atlantis in the Bahamas until that weird couple we suspected of running scams like our own forced us to Puerto Vallarta. It was there that we were robbed over dinner in a taco restaurant one January evening. That marked the return of a persistent dry spell that followed us down the coast to Acapulco and forced us to flee Costa de Paraiso on an all-night bus over the mountains.

King's Reach

Part 2

HANG TIME AT KING'S REACH. WAITING for anything in prison, even a meal or a haircut, is doubly onerous because your whole life is already an exercise in patience.

Typically, Warden Carr took his time letting me know which of the Players wouldn't be cleared to leave the prison for the schoolhouse shows. His obstinacy was baffling since he had much to gain from this opportunity. Meanwhile, my momentum withered into a crippling inertia as days once bursting with tasks and activities stood empty. Worse, all the spare time gave me a chance to work on Dr. K's frustrating assignment.

I did extra kitchen shifts, played tennis, and read. Mostly, I loitered in the resource centre, half asleep at my desk like one of the old timers snoozing out their time. I'd open my notebook and flip through a few pages. My writing had reached the last day at Paraiso, when Jill ran Cal's and Evan's card numbers too soon. The rigmarole of escaping the resort came next and the confusion of the bus stations. Or I thought they did. Determining the why of certain events, which Dr. K wanted me to address, was clouding my memory of them.

Dragan wasn't making things easier for me. One evening, he returned to our room as I sat on my bed with the notebook. "You and your goddamn diary," he said. "Just make it up. It doesn't fucking matter. It won't get you out of here any sooner."

"I tried that," I said. "I guess I'm one of those honest crooks."

Dragan shrugged. "It worked for me."

"Did he give the same assignment to you?" That I believed the doc's assignment was unique to me could be what he meant about my self-delusion.

"Never mind that bullshit. Let's talk business." A few days earlier, he'd asked if I could meet with a friend of his at the schoolhouse, for what he hadn't explained. Nothing legal, that was certain. "Did you think about helping me out?"

I hadn't. The guards would be vigilant for those sorts of rendezvous, and I didn't want to jeopardize the shows or myself. I closed the notebook, thinking I'd take a stroll before lights out to give Dragan a little privacy. Solitude is so hard to come by here.

"Danny, my friend," Dragan called after me. "It will be worth your time."

The point he hadn't made yet was that he'd been very helpful to me. My father would have stepped up and returned the favour. Earl's kind of trouble had been offering itself as a solution my whole life. It was no use denying there was comfort and security in it, and a tension that appealed to me.

In times of indecision, I missed Jill's cool-headedness. She'd know what to do, and if she didn't, we'd find a solution. Except for that last run in Mexico, we'd been a great team. Which of course returned me, as I strolled the empty hallways, to my dilemma with the assignment. And to Jill, whose hold on me remained strong.

The next day, in a concerted effort of avoidance, I wrote a great thumbnail synopsis of The Tempest for the playbill. That got me excited again. It's a deceptively simple play. As it begins, Prospero, the rightful Duke of Milan, and his lovely daughter, Miranda, are living on a deserted island, having been marooned there years earlier by Prospero's usurping brother.

A bookish sorcerer, Prospero conjures a ferocious storm—the tempest—to bring a ship containing his brother and his brother's cronies to the island. Humorous and romantic hijinks ensue. In a solid day's work, aided by the island's spirits, Prospero regains his dukedom and arranges a lovematch for Miranda with a handsome prince named Ferdinand.

In our retelling, the Italian city-states are multinational corporations, and Prospero is the CEO of a pharmaceutical giant forced into exile for refusing to market a cancer drug before it was fully tested. (I stole this premise from a television version I'd seen years ago.) Intrigue and betrayal among sleazeball executives struck a chord with the Players. In this era of economic crises and deepening poverty, even convicted killers agree that multinationals are evil.

Warden Carr found me in the dining room that evening. Finally, a week after we'd received approval for the schoolhouse shows, I learned that of the seventeen Players in the show, only two couldn't leave King's Reach. The two men played members of the evil brother's shipwrecked entourage. Two lords. Adrian and Francisco, to be precise.

"We're a week and a half from the first shows." I said. "How will I fill those roles?"

"That's your problem, isn't it? To help you, I'm keeping Tyler here, on an evening curfew, until the shows are done. You should appreciate that. This could be a lot worse."

Carr was right. I'd feared losing half the company, although it was too bad Bobcat the biker survived the cut. Pondering his unpredictability and the threat he posed to the show, my tongue worried its way into the gaps where I'd had teeth bashed out at the Kent.

In typical weasel behaviour, the warden fled after delivering his message, leaving me to pass the bad news on myself. I went looking for the two convicts.

My least favourite part of the shows was the casting process because it reminded me of how I used to select and manipulate strangers down in the resorts. Yet the casting could also be rewarding and uplifting. Many convicts consider themselves life-long losers, so telling them their reading of Schroeder in *Charlie Brown* or Trinculo in *The Tempest* was outstanding invariably induced a rush of self-esteem.

Now imagine the opposite of those feelings, when you're told you can no longer do the new thing you love. I might as well bring a wheelbarrow to cart their pride away.

I found one inmate in the lounge shooting pool and walked him outside for some privacy. The other was in his room. Both were upset by the news, though not surprised. One was a repeat sex offender on his first stint in minimum security, the other a burglar with a history of escaping custody. We all knew why Carr had to keep them locked up.

Back in the resource centre, I considered how to best plug the two holes in the cast. Our two understudies could step in, but that would mean trusting no one got sick or overdosed. Or I could bring in two entirely new actors. The question was which involved the least amount of work? If I wanted to wow the audience at the schoolhouse shows, I had to choose today.

I turned to the script. Francisco didn't have many lines. Adrian had more, but they were a lot of blather. With so many lords in the play, who'd notice—or care—if I chucked an Antonio, an Adrian, or an Alonzo? For that matter, there were also too many sprites and faeries flouncing about—Juno, Ceres, Iris. Not to mention the Nymphs and Reapers, whatever they are.

The resource centre closes at eight o'clock, and lights out is at ten. Most inmates, lacking anything to do, are asleep soon after. I borrowed a desk lamp from the manager of the centre and talked him into leaving the door unlocked for me.

Eliminating the two roles, by cutting lines or giving them to other characters, took until midnight. I so preferred the improved flow of those scenes I next tackled Gonzalo, another lord who talks a lot of nothing (and who was played by Bobcat, who never got those lines right). Next I cut the faeries, transferring their magical deeds and dialogue to Ariel, Prospero's spirit sidekick. I translated old-timey words, too, or removed them if I didn't understand their meaning. The cutting was liberating. Exhilarating. Sure, it's wrong for a hack television actor to revise a classic. The Tempest is a helluva a play, but after four centuries, it's a bit creaky.

The confusing banquet scene, for which we had no props. Gone. The songs we'd barely rehearsed. Ditto. Eventually, I trimmed anything interfering with the central story of Prospero, Miranda, and the restoration of the natural order of things. So far as I recalled from school, the point of Shakespeare's comedies is to get everything back to normal.

I also tacked on a cheerier ending. Prospero is less than thrilled by winning his freedom and arranging an astute marriage for Miranda. Actually, he's pretty uptight at the end and makes a gloomy farewell speech. People want to leave the theatre whistling a happy tune. Punch it up, my producers used to say.

By dawn, I'd carved the play down by a third. Beside me on the desk was the notebook Dr. K had provided. Naturally, I wondered how I could rewrite Shakespeare yet couldn't write about myself. Nonetheless, giddy with triumph and exhaustion, I staggered back to my room to clean myself up before the manager arrived with the key to the photocopier.

Soon after, I was in the dining room, handing out revised scripts to a few of the Players so we could rehearse that afternoon. Two of my bad guys—Alonso and Antonio—I located in the gym, pumping their sentences away. Both were articulate Montreal mobsters who understood the slippery, neo-feudal world I hoped to create on stage. Both were convicted murderers.

Bobcat arrived as I was leaving, flabby jowls drooping from his dented head. The gym was his realm, the steroid juiceheads, with their shrunken dicks and instant rage, his subjects. None of which concerned me. But he'd lied to the warden about kicking his methamphetamine habit and kept turning up blitzed to rehearsal.

He also so resembled one of the goons who beat on me at the Kent that my hand shook in offering him a script. He dropped it beside a bench press as I explained the changes I'd made.

"Who cares?" he said. "If you're not here to lift, get the fuck out."

After I rejected Bobcat for Caliban, Prospero's subhuman servant, the onus was on me to cast an excellent alternative. Gabriel is a Portuguese immigrant in his sixties, too old for the role. Yet as I said to the warden, years of bricklaying and a drunk-driving accident that killed his wife and two others gave him access to a wisdom and sorrow that greatly enriched his Caliban.

Gabriel also hung out in the resource centre, where he was finishing his high school diploma. His voyage is all the more remarkable since he could barely read when he entered prison two years ago. I suspected he might be the sleeper star of the show.

One reason I chose *The Tempest* is that it has only one female role. Of course, the woman I most wanted for Miranda wasn't available to me. Jill would be old for the role—Shakespeare had in mind a maiden of fifteen—but if it were possible, I'd cast the young woman I remembered from Ryerson. No one I knew could portray better the innocence, optimism, and empathy that make Miranda so compelling.

An imaginary Jill caught up to me as I entered a hallway of inmate rooms. She often drops in at various points in my day to provide some company. Jill from the beach or Jill done up for a night on the town. I tell her about the people I encounter, as if she might soon meet them. It's probably not healthy behaviour.

Today it was the older Jill from Mexico sliding up to say that Shakespeare was too complex for the residents of Gracechurch, I should have chosen something more accessible. It's a good point, although it was coming too late. And she may just be jealous because wherever she is, it's a safe bet she isn't playing Miranda in anyone's production of *The Tempest*.

At King's Reach, there is no one better for the role than Cynthia Sweet, or so she calls herself, a tall, burly drag queen of Asian descent. Even before casting began, I cautiously approached her— she bludgeoned her lover to death with a frying pan—presenting Miranda as a chance for her to showcase her grace and beauty.

To my surprise, she demurred. Cynthia affected a familiarity with actors, claiming to have worked at a Vancouver nightclub popular with visiting Hollywood stars. She told stories of partying with the cast of a schlocky teen horror film. More likely, she sold drugs to them.

Undaunted, I had my mole in administration, Edith Orson, smuggle in a cheesecake, then roses, and finally champagne. When none of that worked, I complained loudly that I'd have to ask another inmate to play the role. Within an hour, Cynthia invited me to sit with her on a sofa in the lounge. "Now Danny, you must know," she said, her fluttering false eyelashes making light of the threat she presented. "If I do this, I'll make my own costumes and do my own make-up."

"Of course," I said. Given the measly budget, I was counting on that.

"I want my own dressing room. And the final word on who plays Ferdinand."

"That I can't do," I said. "That's my job."

"Then you'll have to find another girl. There's not many men around here I'll kiss."

So it went until, in an inspired moment of directorial manipulation, I decided that troubled young Tyler would make an excellent Ferdinand. Cynthia was sold.

Cynthia is one of the few inmates with a room to herself, and so is almost always *en suite*.

"A new script," I said, presenting it with the flourish of an

Elizabethan courtier.

She was watching *The View* on her laptop and muted the volume. "Danny, I'm glad you're here, 'cause we need to talk about giving Miranda a bigger part. She's the reason for the entire show."

"You're right. She is. That's why we're having a special rehearsal this afternoon."

Swaggering, twenty-year-old Tyler is a compulsive gambler who ran through his family's savings before moving on to robbing gas stations and banks. He possessed the height necessary to match Cynthia, plus he was courageous or crazy enough to share a kiss in a place where it can be dangerously misconstrued. Cynthia didn't care what others thought of her, and my guess is that Tyler wanted to see who the kiss might provoke.

I found him in the woodworking shop looking no worse for the punch-up on the tennis court a few days ago. He'd done some construction work in the past, so Gabriel had taken him on as an assistant to build our larger set pieces. He had the chiseled hunkiness to be a successful actor, which I can attest, is usually all it takes. In the meantime, if he also learned a trade through the Players, there'd be no harm in that.

In the only production I've seen of *The Tempest*, the role of Ariel was given to a woman to mitigate the rampaging masculinity on stage, and so she could flirt with her master, Prospero. For my corporate milieu, I wanted as much testosterone as I could lay hands to. Patrice, the Quebecois arsonist, had that and the athleticism required to flit about the stage.

Patrice was often smoking outdoors. I found him sheltering from the drizzle under the gazebo in the flower garden with Hassan, the Lebanese drug trafficker playing Stephano.

At a glance, Hassan agreed with the trimming I'd done. "There was too much. Like in the second act, when they're on the beach after the shipwreck."

Patrice was glad to become the only spirit on stage but wasn't sure about cutting the songs. "The big one in Act III. You keep that?"

"No," I said. "But we can put it back in if we need to. Remember, it's our play."

The Players' rehearsal space is a filthy, unheated store room by the auto shop. Among the engine blocks and bumpers are a few car seats to sit on and just enough room to pace out scenes.

Charlie Brown was an ensemble piece, bursting with goodwill and charm. All it required was six actors, a prop doghouse, and a piano. We patched it together without much difficulty, creating a colourful, if clumsy, evening's entertainment.

The Tempest is far more involved and needs a firm hand. I knew what I wanted before we began to rehearse, if not how to coax it from sixteen other men. From the start, the Players made it easy for me. Some came to the first read-through with their lines memorized. After years among jaded, overpaid television actors (like myself), their energy was refreshing. Still, they were an imposing lot. Home invaders, muggers, thieves—they gaped at me with blank-faced wonder, their trust in me daunting.

Days later, our first blocking was like square-dancing blindfolded, all elbows and hip-checks. I'm more a football coach than a director. My secret is to pretend I know what I'm doing and to trust my actors. The results have been mixed. Many Players shout rather than project, their gestures hugely exaggerated. And no matter how often I remind them, they never learn that a little is enough.

To better observe the first rehearsal of the new text, I asked an understudy named Brooks to play Prospero for me. Proper perspective has been hard to come by because I'm so often on stage. The warden refused my request for a camcorder to record our rehearsals, and Dragan hasn't yet smuggled one in for me.

Brooks is a worn-out junkie and carjacker in his fifties. So far, he's been an excellent Prospero, and is more physically suited for the role than I am. I want him to do some of the later shows here at King's Reach so I can rest for the schoolhouse. (My thirtysomething Prospero—younger than Miranda—is a stretch. The whole show is, actually.)

The Players got underway, displaying as usual more enthusiasm than skill. In the fifth act, just as Prospero instructs Ariel to release the nobles from captivity, the door to the room clicked open, and I heard the ragged smoker's breath of the warden over my shoulder. In so small a space, the Players noticed his appearance. A ripple of self-consciousness interrupted their performance.

"Heard you made some changes," Carr said. "Want to tell me about them?"

Another thing about prison: there are no secrets here. It's more gossipy than the small towns I used to live in.

"Not now," I said without turning around. "Can't you see we're busy?"

The breathing departed, and the door clicked open and shut again.

Fifteen minutes later, I was pleased with my changes and the ease with which the boys adopted them. I'd trimmed the running time down to two hours, including a twenty-minute break.

I stood on a car seat to tell them how well they'd done. "Tomorrow, we're going to do the finale again. There's still guys getting bunched up stage left, watching what's going on. Try to remember you're still performing even if you're not speaking any lines. The audience watches the show. Your job is to act in it."

Another run-through, some work on specific scenes, then we'd try a dress rehearsal in the screening room. I told them to return at noon tomorrow and called an end to the day.

The warden was back immediately, flapping a copy of the revised text at me. "How come I didn't get a copy of this?"

"Didn't think you needed one."

"Danny, you don't get it. Think about all the things I've done for you. Then think of all the stupid things you've done and ask yourself: do I want to fuck up how good I have it here?"

"You told me to cut two characters, so I did."

"Here's how to fix this. I want to be in the show. Nothing fancy, just a walk-on, maybe a few lines. You got that for me?"

"No. There's no walk-ons. Have you read the play?" Trimming characters from Shakespeare is scandalous. Creating new ones is a hanging crime. "I'm not making a part for you. I've already got enough to deal with, like your buddy Bobcat. He never remembers his lines, and he's not taking the show seriously."

Bobcat was also, in my opinion, Carr's spy in the company.

"That's none of your business," Carr said. "You don't decide who's in the show. I do."

"Don't say I didn't warn you." The warden is alone in needing *The Tempest* to succeed. The rest of us are having a great time making art.

"Think about what I said, Danny. 'Cause I can shut you down." The warden turned from the door. "By the way, that Prospero was flat. He should be more mysterious. And inspiring."

"I'd tell him that, but I'm Prospero, remember? You were watching the understudy."

The following day, I was en route to a session with Dr. K when Edith

Orson snagged my arm as I passed the stairs to the administrative office. "Danny, there you are. There's someone waiting for you in the visitors' lounge."

Like the two other times I had a visitor, my heart leapt into my throat in anticipation of the reunion I'd been dreaming of since Mexico. As if summoned, Jill rematerialized beside me as the girl-genius of the Theatre School. I flew through the prison, despite the fact that it was likely Dragan's wife, Margot, waiting for me with the costumes. She'd been my "visitor" the two other times as well. Not that I'm complaining. Some inmates never receive guests.

Dragan gets so many visitors, he's got the gall to complain about them. One saintly wife, a girlfriend, his elderly mother, three beautiful daughters, various friends, lawyers, and an assortment of relatives. Once a week, he's booked into the cottage set aside for spousal visits. The conjugal cabin, it's called. He's there so often I asked the warden to move him there permanently so I could set up the Players' office in our room.

Needless to say, there's been no conjugal visits for me.

The visitors' lounge is a shabby area of brown corduroy couches and chipped end tables that have likely been there for decades. I have it from Edith that the warden is proposing an expensive renovation of this interface with the outside world, and I've shared this information with my journalist friend, Stephen Kasey.

Dragan and Margot stood by the front door, Dragan gesticulating wildly the way he does when he's worked up. Margot kept shaking her head, crying out once as if in pain. I hung by the security desk, watching cars roam the parking lot like this was an office building. Maybe they were discussing the trouble Dragan landed in this week when the warden learned the woman he booked into the conjugal cabin wasn't Margot. How stupid of him: a lie that large might result in charges or time added to his sentence.

A scraping noise drew me back into the room. Margot was dragging a large cardboard box over the floor toward me. Behind her, Dragan stormed back into the prison.

Margot pretended to be unruffled by what had gone down. She's a curly haired brunette with a wide smile, originally from a small town in Ontario like the ones I grew up in. That's all I know about her, except that she has stuck with Dragan as he bankrupted them and landed in jail. He should be grateful to still have her.

The box contained men's suits, white shirts, and a knot of ties. Business attire for our corporate setting.

"Fourteen," she said. "Like you asked for. Plus an extra, just in case."

"Thank you." They'd need a pressing. Someone, Cynthia certainly, must have an iron. I lifted a pinstriped suit from the box, puzzled by its weight. I shook it and turned it over.

"Careful." Margot said quietly. "There's phones in the pockets."

Of course there were. And what else, I didn't care to contemplate. I'd have to let Dragan go through them first. A tiny sigh escaped me. There was that open door again, inviting me to re-enter the criminal world. It was hard to refuse, since the reward might be the camcorder we needed to record a rehearsal. And because I was born to it.

Margot gently laid a hand on my arm. "Don't worry. Everything's looked after with the guard on the desk. Now, check out what I have for you."

From a shopping bag, she shook out a full-length black cloak decorated with patches of Chinese dragons and gold stars. Orange and red flames ran along the hem, and the interior was lined with a reflective silver fabric. Prospero's sorcerer's cape. If someone had asked what I wanted for the role, this is what I'd have described. "Unbelievable. Where did you find it?"

"A movie costume house. An old boyfriend works there."

The cloak fit like it had been made for me. What I lacked in depth for Prospero, I would make up in style. I tied it beneath my neck and stalked through the visitors' lounge, trailing a fine sparkling halo.

"My girls insisted on the glitter powder," Margot said. "There's more in the bag. They said it would make you happy."

"They're right. It does. Thank you again."

Margot was pleased, but distant. Whatever she and Dragan had argued over was punching through her façade of normalcy. "I almost forgot," I said. "How much do I owe you?"

"Eighty bucks for the suits. I bought them by the pound. The cape is free."

"Thank you, but it's the prison's money, not mine. Let me pay you. For your gas too and something for your time."

When I had paid, we stood not knowing what to say. "The weather's been cold so far, huh?" I ventured. "It's not even winter yet."

"It's the damp I hate. I told Dragan we're moving back east when

128

he gets out. I was just home for a few weeks, with the girls, visiting my parents. I forgot how beautiful the trees are in the fall. And the dry air seems so much cleaner."

Barely holding back her tears, she burbled about meeting her ferry to the mainland, Vancouver traffic, and the babysitter. I could only walk her as far as the door. "I'll be back next week," she said. "Email me if there's anything else."

In her wake, I detected an aroma of autumn leaves and frosty nights in little Ontario towns. Not wanting to re-enter the prison, I stood admiring my new cloak. Home, she'd said. Three more Novembers must pass before I can return to those towns, where— despite my best efforts to escape them—I probably belong after all.

As a child, by late November Earl and I were usually established in whichever town we'd migrated to over the summer. We moved thirteen times in ten years, not counting short stays of a few weeks when Earl's plans didn't work out, and there were many times when they did not.

I realized quite young that the towns were selected for their proximity to a racetrack or a casino. Earl's gambling also dictated the length of our stay. Strange men knocked on our doors at all hours. Earl would disappear with them, announcing upon his return that he'd heard of a better job in another town. "Pack your things," he'd say, "we're leaving in the morning."

He worked as a janitor, a carpet salesman, and a cabbie. He was far better at talking himself into work than he was at keeping it. The reasons he gave for losing the jobs were as varied and indeterminate as his skills. In each case, it was wanderlust that did him in. Working's for chumps, he'd tell me. He's not wrong.

He played guitar in those days, fancying himself one lucky break from country music fame. The towns all had taverns or roadhouses with an open stage. Many nights I fell asleep on the coats at the back of the bar and woke up in my own bed. Occasionally, there'd be a woman in our apartment in the morning. They'd almost always leave by noon, but a few stayed long enough for me to witness how badly Earl wanted them there permanently. After they'd left, he'd wonder aloud what their problem was, when it was evident even to my nine-year-old self that he wasn't much of a catch.

Uprooting ourselves was simple. Our few belongings fit easily into the trunk of his Duster. By moving us in summer, Earl never had to explain to school authorities where he was taking me or why. We'd dawdle on the road, looking up a pal who'd promised to record some of his songs or another who owed him money. Someone always owed Earl money.

Travelling in summer allowed us to save on motels by passing warm nights in the car. We parked wherever we pleased. Or we'd drive all night and sleep through the day at truck stops or highway rest stops. Other travellers steered clear of us.

To sweeten our transition, Earl would engage in a little petty thievery prior to our departure. While packing, I'd unearth jewellery, cameras, or stereo components I'd never seen before. He would explain the items belonged to a friend then pawn them along the road. I came to our family vocation as naturally as I did regretfully. Actually, I like to think I've elevated it.

When I was old enough to feed myself, he'd disappear for days at a time. Sometimes I feared he wouldn't return. Yet he always did, with a new bike or a backyard swing set. He'd pull me out of school for a few days while we played with it. A kid couldn't argue with that.

Too often, when we reached our destination, the job he'd heard of was gone or had been hot wind blown by a drinking buddy. Of Earl's many faults, none failed him more reliably than his trustfulness. We'd sleep in the Duster while he scrounged for work at a gas station or in a warehouse. Eventually, we'd take a crappy furnished apartment that was invariably close enough to the railway station that I could hear the diesel engines rumbling through the night. The towns blurred together after a while. They'd have a few churches, a high school, a liquor store, and a co-op feed mill. For much of the year, life revolved around the arena. Even a loner kid who didn't play hockey passed through it a couple of times a week.

It was usually mid-September before Earl enrolled me in school again. I was the perpetual new kid, sticking out in class and ripe for bullies. They'd dog me home for a few days, making their presence felt. Their reasons for picking a fight were as unvarying as the towns: an imagined slight against a sister, the theft of a bicycle.

By my tenth birthday, I'd been in so many scraps I could handle boys two years older than me. Unfortunately, winning meant more fighting: clobbering a first opponent brought more, generally larger, challengers. I discovered that the secret to survival was in performance. I'd land a few decent punches before allowing my opponent to briefly gain the upper hand. Then I'd drop to the ground and begin to wail: fight over. Thereafter, I was left alone.

My last significant childhood punch-up was in the seventh grade in Brantford. The usual pack of bruisers emerged, calling me on until I turned to face them. I must have been tired of losing because this time I didn't turtle. Within minutes, I'd bashed my opponent's nose so badly that blood poured onto his white fisherman's sweater. He started crying that his mother would be furious with him.

I felt awful for what I'd done and decided that the surest way to avoid fighting was to become what people wanted of me. Being a bewildered kid who wished his dad would grow up did me no good. Better to be sports-minded or nerdy and bookish—whatever it took to pretend my life was like other kids'. I developed a knack for not being remembered, a talent for being forgotten.

Orangeville was the next town down the track. The balcony of the grotty apartment Earl had rented in a low-rise building offered a view of the harness racing track. Race days were Tuesdays, Thursdays, and Saturdays. Earl never missed one.

The spirited young woman teaching my eighth grade class—old to me then, though likely fresh from teachers' college—was Sylvia Rupke. A former drama major, Ms. Rupke was producing *You're a Good Man, Charlie Brown*. Principal to first graders, everyone in the school was crazy for it. Auditions were open to every student and mandatory for Ms. Rupke's pupils. She ran a VHS copy of a stage production in class and invited us to choose a number to perform. Competition was fierce, especially among the girls. On the day before the auditions started, I counted five Lucys and four Pattys practicing in the hall.

I couldn't care less about the show. In six months, I'd be living in a different town, my school records scattered like leaves behind the Duster. Would I even attend high school? You'd have to ask Earl if we'd be living in a town with one.

So far in that town, no one had offered to punch me out. My goal was to avoid attracting any attention, so I chose Snoopy's show-stopping musical soliloquy "Suppertime" somewhat ironically. A boy used to scrounging for his own meals would enjoy someone bringing him supper every night. I also believed I'd mangle it so badly I'd be shuffled into the chorus Ms. Rupke was adding to the show for the students who failed to land parts.

My idea backfired. Seconds into my audition something shifted in me. Through some magic, I was overwhelmed by an unaccountable desire to sing and dance to the best of my ability.

In planning to fail, I hadn't rehearsed. Yet by this spell, I remembered all the lyrics of the song, my feet shuffling through the chalk dust beneath the blackboard with a rhythm I hadn't known I possessed. I grabbed an empty plant pot to serve as a supper bowl, holding it hungrily forward as I begged and danced before my classmates, or wearing it as a hat.

When I was done, my classmates roared their approval, clapping and rising from their desks. I stood numbly before them, stupefied by what had occurred. At the back of the room, Ms. Rupke hid her delight behind a geography textbook.

Three other Snoopys followed from boys more popular and gregarious than me. None of them drew even a third of the response I had. As each one walked off to polite applause, I slumped further in my seat, unnerved by this previously un-guessed at passion for performing. The magic was more of a devilment: I couldn't see it doing me any good.

Ms. Rupke asked me to stay back after class. In leaving, some kids congratulated me, and two of my rival Snoopys delivered hard stares.

Ms. Rupke squeezed into the tiny desk beside mine. It was obvious I hadn't practiced, she said, but I was the best Snoopy she'd ever seen. Still, she wondered whether I wanted the role because I didn't seem excited by the great work I'd done.

I recall leaning out of my desk away from her, fearful of exposure, and her flowery perfume. Through her gentle coaxing over the next half hour, my future was determined. I took the role on her guarantee that no harm would come to me from the other wannabe Snoopys.

A month later, Ms. Rupke's *Charlie Brown* gave three performances in the school gymnasium. The local paper called it a resounding success, led by a dynamic performance by thirteen-year-old Danny Drake as Snoopy. That marked the first time I had my name in the paper. Earl made it to the last performance after Ms. Rupke called him at the diner where he worked mornings—the better to hit the track in the afternoon—as a short-order cook. I was happy he came and even happier he enjoyed what he saw. The burden of my new-found talent and affinity became lighter.

As we walked back to our apartment, a springtime scent of lilac in the night air pulled us along quiet, darkened streets. "You looked pretty good up there," Earl said. "You got a bit of the showman in you, like your old man."

Those towns all smelled like lilac in the spring. Late May, early June. And when the lilac peaked, the days warming toward summer, Earl would get restless again.

That weekend at the grocery store, I was recognized as the Kid-Who-Played-Snoopy. A few days later, it happened again as I walked home from school. Even better, the kids I feared would beat me up now wanted to be my friend.

The first vagabond portion of my life ended soon after my triumphant stage debut. One day, Earl returned home with a black eye, a split lip, and two broken fingers in a splint. The owner of the diner called that evening to say he didn't want a punched-out bum scaring customers. Would I please tell my father that he was fired?

It took a week for Earl's face to heal and another until he could use his fingers again. Instead of looking for another job, he announced we'd be moving soon. There were lots of jobs in Niagara Falls, apparently. Even I'd heard of the new casino opening there.

After a decade of upheaval, fistfights, and surprise visits from angry bookies, I'd had enough. Making new friends every year in grade school was a chore I didn't want to repeat in high school. Ms. Rupke's grade-eight class had just graduated in a short ceremony on the same gymnasium stage where we'd performed *Charlie Brown*. Earl chose not to attend because of his face. Since he hadn't yet paid our rent for June, his plan was to avoid the landlord while he collected various monies owed to him. After that, we'd do a midnight dodge in the Duster, a month's rent the richer.

Whether he succeeded in this, I never found out. Two days after graduating, I took fifty dollars from his stash and caught a bus to the town of Millward, where both Earl and I were born and where my mother died when I was two. Millward was also the home of my father's mother, Granny Drake, with whom Earl would sometimes leave me for a week or so when he was especially tired of parenting. My plan was to look so needy and hungry that Granny couldn't turn me away. She didn't believe my explanation that Earl had dropped me off, but since he didn't have a phone, she couldn't demand that he retrieve me.

Granny rented a crumbling house and lived off a number of old age security and welfare cheques (a skill she imparted to my father like a birthright). She was also a furious chimney of cigarette smoke. I'd find a cigarette burning in the living room, where she'd been watching her soaps, and Granny in the kitchen, lighting a new cigarette off the butt of another while peeling potatoes for our supper.

For the luxury of a permanent address, I shovelled snow and handled the yard work. I got a job bagging groceries on weekends and so never asked her for a dime. In return, I got my bed made, my laundry folded, a bagged lunch for school every day. When Granny started rebuking me for staying out too late, I knew I'd won the role of grandson.

Once Earl heard I was safe with her, he carried on down the road, no doubt relieved I was gone. He loved me as best he could, but I reminded him of my mother. Over the next few years, Granny and I would go months at a time without hearing from him.

At Millward Secondary School, I joined the drama club, volunteering as a stagehand in the ninth grade. In my second year, I beat out a dozen other students, including some in their senior year, for the lead in the western crowd-pleaser, Deadwood Dick. Other roles followed, always leads. My high school career culminated with my co-direction of the Victorian melodrama, Lady Audley's Secret. I chose to direct for the experience, and so I wouldn't have the lead stolen from me by some up-and-comer in the tenth grade.

At the end of that year, the principal helped arrange a scholarship for me to Ryerson University. Even better, Granny offered me some of the money she'd squirreled away from her many sources. It wasn't an overwhelming goodbye, since the city was only a couple hours' drive away. Nonetheless, I promised her I'd visit more often than my old man.

Dr. K was packing up as I skidded into our meeting room. He claims I'm late for our sessions because I'm reluctant to confront the reasons why I ended up in prison. He's probably right. But through our chats, I've come to depend on his counsel in the battles to mount first Charlie Brown and now The Tempest. He's the closest a convict could get to having a friend in prison.

"Sorry," I said. "Margot brought the costumes from Vancouver."

"I see that," he said, taking his usual seat at the table. "You've got twenty minutes left. Make it worth the time you wasted."

Removing Margot's cape from my shoulders released a small flurry of sparkles into the dismal room. They were stuck to my hands and likely my face. And yet, they worked in my favour, as Dr. K struggled to conceal his amusement.

Topping my concerns that day was the biker, Bobcat. I needed him cut from the company in a way that didn't reveal I was behind it. How many other theatre directors fear getting shivved by one of their actors?

"Maybe you could mention him to Warden Carr," I said. "Tell him how wrecked the guy is all the time. Get him sent to rehab."

Dr. K laughed. "You want me to do your dirty work?"

"Would you mind? He's shit on stage. What's he even doing in the show?"

"You don't get it. There might be a few keeners in the show, but most of them are there to fuck around. Same's anywhere. Everyone's just doing as little as possible and hoping they don't get caught. Anyhow, I'm not here to talk about some biker jackass. I'm here to talk about you."

Fair enough. Another concern I raised was that I suspected someone of reading my assignment. It was rarely where I left it, whether in my locker or beneath my mattress. If the details of my real crimes made the rounds of the prison, my life could become a lot more unpleasant.

"I'm glad you mentioned that," the doc said, "because we need that notebook in here. We've hit another dead end. How much have you written? Honestly."

"I'm getting there." I didn't like lying to him, especially after he'd given me a second chance at therapy. "I think I've got writer's block."

"Daniel block, more like. Tell you what. We'll keep talking about whatever you bring in here. That's part of the process. But I need your story two sessions from now. We need the real Daniel in here. Or we're done again. For real this time. You got that? Two sessions."

"There's no way I can get it done in time. Especially now with the schoolhouse shows."

"Yeah, I don't care. No more excuses. I've held up my end."

Tough love, as practiced by Dr. K, always got its message across.

Once he'd allowed me to absorb this, the doc suggested I'd been so busy of late I was forgetting where I placed the notebook. He was concerned I was obsessing over the show at the expense of other aspects of my recovery. Which was puzzling, since he suggested I mount the shows in the first place.

"What else should I be doing?" I asked. "Dating? Hanging with my friends?"

"That's not a bad idea. Have you contacted your father yet? Or your friend from school, the other actor? And what about your lawyer? What's up with your appeal?"

We both knew I was too proud to get in touch with my father or Warren. The lawyer, McKeon, I was managing just fine without, thank you. I was playing the ostrich as truckloads of trouble rumbled toward me, although in my case, the sand in which my head was buried was the fine white powder of Turks & Caicos.

Lately Dr. K's been keen on me becoming fluent in Spanish and working in translation. My dubious achievements down south notwithstanding, I had picked up most of another language. There are courses online and native speakers here in King's Reach to practice with. He also thinks the longer I consider myself a criminal, the longer I'll continue to live like one.

I told him that I was having difficulty figuring Prospero out, that I needed to spend more time getting inside his head.

"So you know what you need to do. It's like I told you. You need to listen to your gut instincts, especially about other people. I've never said this to anyone before, but you've got to stop seeing the best in people."

Unfortunately, Dr. K's positivity failed to quell my fears over my assignment. With the long hours I spend out of my room, anyone could access it. There are no locks on the doors, and inmates wander at all hours. I'd have to find a new hiding place or keep it with me all day.

Our time was up. I carefully draped the cape over my arm, trailing yet more glitter.

"Daniel, there's one more thing. If you're going to be more than ten minutes late, don't bother coming. We'll skip the appointment because I've got better things to do."

"Yeah, I know. It's just that today ..."

"Missed appointments will count against the two you've got remaining. You got that?"

A cloud followed me back downstairs. Darkness falling at late afternoon. Winter coming on, my second in here. Chest deep in the day-to-day, it's easy to forget to be grateful for how far I've come in a year. I'd like to arrange a meeting between the wretch I'd been at the Kent and the purposeful and hopefully better man I was becoming. Those beatings did me a world of good.

The lunch hour had largely emptied the resource centre of inmates. I flipped open my notebook to see what I'd last written, in a marathon of fidgeting and fretting, about the day we fled Acapulco in tatters. And now, my small satisfaction at having completed that much had been wiped out by Dr. K's impossible new deadline

If the doc was right—and he hasn't been wrong yet—I was stuck because I was closing in on truths I wouldn't like. So what were those truths, and where were they hidden?

For example, why had I chosen to write about a boys' night out that was indistinguishable from so many others? To play up my role at the expense of Jill's? And where was Jill that night? I couldn't recall asking her the next day. When we'd separate during a squeeze, we usually gave each other a good accounting of our whereabouts. It also struck me as unlikely that I'd leave the beach party, but that's what I remembered happening.

Looking further back, where was Jill when I was golfing with the boys on the second day? Out shopping with the girls, she'd said. That's how I wrote it. Yet if that were true, it didn't seem possible that she went an entire day with the two other women without picking up part of a card number. She'd always delivered something.

There in the cool dampness of the library, I began to sweat. Evidently, it was easier to write about naked women and beer than what might actually have been occurring. Ignoring Jill's role on that day was possibly a deliberate oversight. The truth might be that she'd never been honest with me. If so, I'd have to start all over again, with so little time.

I heard someone—Jill, probably—telling me I was worrying over nothing. She'd always had a calming effect on me, even back at Ryerson. And for that she had my gratitude. In my assignment, I'd tried to convey what a cranky handful I'd been, not just in those last crazy days, but in general. Imagine living with a failed television actor still hungry for fame. A simple glance from her was often enough to bring me in line or reassure me. I definitely needed one now.

A fluttering motion interrupted me and something dropped onto the open notebook. I looked up to see old Steyne the mailman hustling back out the doors of the centre.

A postcard of the Forum in Rome sat on the notebook. I flipped it over and instantly recognized a handwriting I hadn't seen in a long time. Jill wrote:

> Sorry to hear about where you landed. Please understand that was never my intention. For what it's worth, I was detained too. Have I got a story to tell!
>
> Congrats on the show. xoxo.

I read it again because I couldn't believe my eyes. If before I was overheated, now I felt ill. I looked to see where Steyne had gone, as if he could explain. I was thrilled to learn Jill was still alive for perhaps a second before an anger like I'd never known erupted in me.

A year and a half of no word from her and this is all I get? A tourist postcard telling me nothing? I was better off not knowing anything. At least then there was still hope. At least then I could still delude myself that I might one day hear from her or that she'd be waiting for me when I was released.

In my dreams of her contacting me, I never considered that I might not like what I heard. Now I had even more questions. Where was she? What did she mean by *detained*? Rome isn't a prison. And why write now after so long? What did she expect from me in here?

My last question was the toughest. Yet given what I was learning about myself, I grudgingly had to ask: what did she have up her sleeve?

Day 6

Mexico City

THE BUS JUDDERING TO A HALT WOKE me. Ahead in the front windshield, a new day glowed a lustrous peach on the horizon. Closer in, below my window, the headlights of countless other vehicles shone in the dark. A pre-dawn traffic jam. We must be nearing Mexico City.

Jill remained curled into me, our limbs entwined, her chest moving in sleep against mine. I wished for her to remain under as long as possible. We faced a tricky, uncomfortable day. There was no reason to hurry into it.

I detected a foul odour and quickly traced its origin. In the mad scramble to leave Paraiso yesterday, there hadn't been time for me to shower. The strip club with the boys, the champagne party with the Vandals, the distressing chat with the cop in the hotel office—all of it had followed me across half the country. But since our cramped night on the bus was the first in many I hadn't gone to bed drunk, I felt fantastic. Ready for anything.

Except the mammoth, bewildering city we were entering.

Mexico City scared me. And not just because Jill and I were held up at knifepoint in the pretty suburb of Coyoacán. An evil resides there, a lurking madness, as if the veneer of civilization can't conceal the hate and murder that marked the modern city's founding.

By slow fits, the bus crested the last hills before descending into the mountaintop bowl containing the city. In the half-light, I discerned shantytowns straggling up the slopes. Against my better judgment, I was giving this most ancient of American cities another chance. Twenty-one million people lived there. What was two more?

When Jill woke, we shared the bottle of water we'd saved, the bus inching forward. The sun had fully risen when we pulled into a busy coach terminal. Jill explained we'd turned up in the southern end of the metropolis, at the end of a subway line.

That morning, neither of us was hungry. In the terminal departure lounge, we picked at our shrink-wrapped pastries and ordered second cups of coffee. Recalling her panicked response to the bad cards yesterday at Paraiso, I said, "Walk me through this. What's the plan?"

Our first problem was that buses to Veracruz left from a different coach terminal in another corner of the city. To reach it, we had to cross the city with our tower of luggage. The greater problem was raising the funds to get from Mexico City to Veracruz. Jill's solution involved visiting old friends from when she taught English. She was confident she could track them down. I was less so, but had no other solution to offer.

"Are these the other people we can use for card numbers?" I said.

"No, they're just other teachers I knew."

There was a small internet café near the ticketing windows. I checked my email while Jill freshened up in the washroom. Annoyingly, my father hadn't responded to my questions about the type of heart operation he was having. It wasn't yet seven thirty in the morning, and this day was already old.

Across from the terminal, a colourful maze of market stalls was open for business. Jill led us through it to a walkway rising over a depot for local buses connecting with Tasqueña subway station. Commuters blurred past us in the watery light. It would have been terribly exciting and exotic if we weren't, essentially, refugees.

The luggage made for slow progress. By the time we reached the subway station, I was sweaty and short of breath. I'd forgotten the effect of the altitude up in the mountains. "I want to get a map," I said. "To figure out where we're going."

"We won't be here long enough. Can you watch the bags while I get tickets?"

A mob ten people deep lined the subway platform. With equal parts patience and brute force, and making no friends in the process, we forced our way onto a train.

Nine stops, Jill said. No transfers. Stacked in a corner, our bags drew the ire of our fellow travellers. At six feet, I was the tallest person on the train. A few men glared up at me, a macho challenge to meet their eyes. I did not.

For the first half of its journey, the train followed an elevated track between two jammed highways. The infinite knot of streets below and the uncountable taco stands, markets, parks, monuments, and apartment buildings looped like the backdrop of an old cartoon. More roads poured into these, the epic city stretching on until it lost itself in its own satanic smog.

DF, the Mexicans call it. *Distrito Federal*. Definitely Frightening, more like. I got that sinking feeling again, washed with helplessness.

So had Jill, apparently. The strain was gouging deep furrows into her brow. "Do you remember the big park we visited near the art gallery?" she said. "The Alameda."

"The one beside that cool mural in its own museum?"

"That's it. Can you stay there with the bags while I find the people who can help us?"

"Why don't we leave the bags in a locker? Then we can both go." It wasn't the waiting I minded—that was part of the job—but the risks involved in separating when we had no means of contacting each other.

"That's a good idea," Jill said. "Only there's no lockers where we're going and things will go much faster without all these bags."

"We shouldn't separate. If this were a horror film, we'd both be killed. Badly killed."

That got the first laugh of the day, but I wasn't kidding.

With difficulty, we left the train and rose from the depths at Bellas Artes station. The streets and sidewalks downtown were snarling thoroughfares of perpetual motion. The pace never slackens in Mexico City, though occasionally it reaches a crescendo.

To speed us up, I took one of Jill's bags onto my back and led us around a grand stone building I remembered as the art gallery. We fell in pace with two men pushing carts toward the market stalls obscuring the park entrance. A few vendors called to the rich gringo tourists out so early. Little did they know.

The Alameda was a verdant island buttressed by concrete and grime. Here the city caught its breath, chatted with friends, then hurried off again. We trundled down a shady lane lined with flowering white bushes. Jill stopped in a broad circular area ringed with stone benches. In its centre was a dried-out fountain with a statue of two women pouring nothing from urns.

"You'll be fine waiting here, yeah?" Tension had stiffened her posture. For an instant, I saw her as Kattrin, Mother Courage's mute daughter, back in our school days.

"Where are you going exactly?"

She inclined her head north to where the frantic city resumed beyond many clogged lanes of traffic. Toward, if I remembered correctly, Mexico City's red-light district.

"Okay," I said. "We have to start talking about these decisions you make arbitrarily. Because, for the record, me waiting in the park feels dumb. Look what happened yesterday with the Americans' cards. Yes, I know now is not the time."

Jill looked like she was broke and homeless and had spent the night on a bus. She wasn't acting. "You're right. We have to."

I pulled her to me for a kiss. She responded with more enthusiasm than I expected, then slipped from my embrace. "Oh, Danny. This isn't some movie we're in."

"I'm going to come with you. I'm not comfortable with you being out there alone."

"Just stay here. All I'm asking is for you to do this one thing, so if you want to help, could you please just do that? Can you stay here?"

No problem, since I wasn't going anywhere with someone who spoke to me like that. She carried with her the overnight bag she hauled through Acapulco yesterday. A little voice suggested it contained all she'd need to start again somewhere else. At the moment, that might be for the better.

Eventually the pretty morning rekindled happier thoughts of our first visit together to the city. We'd stayed at the Hilton, on the southern edge of the park. Every morning, we drank coffee on park benches, and every evening we returned at dusk to let the day settle around us.

One afternoon, in a different corner of the park, we took in the colossal Diego Rivera mural of stylized Mexican historical figures promenading through the Alameda. Hernán Cortés, Frida Kahlo, Benito Juárez. Jill pointed out who they were and explained the events they represented. My understanding of life in Mexico as more raw and tragic than anything I'd ever experienced tinged my fascination with sorrow.

The full scope of Mexico's turbulent history was on display in the Rivera murals not far away in the National Palace. The flourishing aboriginal culture, the arrival of the Conquistadors, the long nightmare of colonialism, the never-ending Revolution. Rivera may have slathered his murals with blame, but he at least made sure everyone received their share.

I recalled how Jill specifically pointed out Cortés, who pulled down the vanquished Aztec city of Tenochtitlan and used the rubble to build Mexico City over it. And La Malinche, a native woman with a blue-eyed baby on her back. She was Cortés's translator and the mother of his child. Were it not for her betrayal of her own people, the conquest might never have occurred.

La Malinche's was a sad and disturbing story, not one I cared to recall. I shut down the memories and stacked the luggage around me, sandbagging myself against my imagined threats.

A tiny man in dirty jeans set up a microphone and amplifier nearby. I barely understood his account of how a trade union had violated certain articles of the Constitution. No one stopped to listen, and after half an hour, he packed up and shambled off. Church bells somewhere nearby chimed in fifteen-minute intervals. I stopped counting at two hours. I pictured Jill wading deeper into the urban morass until at last she vanished. Considering my issues with this city, the worst thing she could do was leave me alone with them to fester.

The lunch hour brought office workers into the park, then uniformed students later in the afternoon. My prospects deteriorated when a group of thuggish young men began loitering near the street. A man in mirrored shades strolled past me three times, ending his last pass-by in a brief exchange with his pals. If necessary, I would stand my ground. Although that wasn't wise in Mexico, I more feared the consequences of losing Jill's bags.

There was no lack of police officers to assist me if required. The *Policía Federal* were on patrol, as were the indistinct *Policía del Distrito Federal*. That's if they weren't in on the scam, as the cops were in Coyoacán the afternoon we were mugged. Also, a brand of cop new to me: *Policía Alameda*, men in white uniforms and Stetsons who ranged the park on horseback.

Add to my complaints an aching hunger when I was downwind from some food stalls and a dreadful thirst. A scraggly tabby sauntered past, miffed by my continued presence on his turf. You're in bad shape when you're wrangling for space with the feral cats.

I dozed off, not unexpectedly for a guy who'd recently slept so little, and woke to a horse neighing near me. An older police officer with a massive white mustache glared at me from his saddle. He wore cowboy boots, silver spurs, and had a revolver in a holster on his waist.

"Ud. tiene mucho equipaje, señor," he said.

"It's my wife's luggage," I said, in my best Texan twang. "She can't stop shopping."

The officer nodded slightly before trotting off. The next cop to pass by would suggest I move on. The evening chatter of birds couldn't drown out the familiar unease spreading within me. Didn't this just happen a year ago, after the Englishwoman? How long would I wait for Jill this time? A week on these streets wasn't possible.

Dusk brought a crisp mountain coolness, so I clawed through our bags for a sweater. Re-emerging from them, I noticed a large man in a suit ambling toward me across the circle. "Hello, Tom Walker," he said in heavily accented English.

It was the cop from the hotel manager's office at Paraiso. I was flattered: he must have seen one of my shows. Police officers often said I played a cop with such accuracy they recognized themselves on screen. I stood to meet him, arm outstretched to glad-hand.

"Tom Walker," he said again. Which was the name of the lawyer I played on Legal Ease, I realized, not the cop on Street Heat. "Is that your real name? Or are you Steve Sawyer?"

The world tilted, and I staggered back against the luggage. He wasn't here for an autograph, he was here to arrest me.

"I am so happy to see you again. Do you mind if I join you?"

Whatever identity I'd pawned off on him yesterday wouldn't work again. There was nothing I could do, save for making sure he didn't corner Jill as well.

"How do you know about Tom Walker?" I said. "Did you watch the show?"

"What show? Tom Walker is the name on your email. Tom Walker Hero at the G mail."

"You can't read my email."

"Yes, I can. The hotel manager is my friend. And I have other friends who are good with the computers."

He asked to see my identification. Here I hesitated. When yesterday we garbaged Steve Sawyer and Regina Boccia, I'd chosen another passport at random to use as identification. I crossed the fingers I drove into my pocket, praying I hadn't grabbed my own.

The winner was Warren Rudd, an American I'd played as a schoolteacher from the Midwest. St. Louis, maybe. It didn't matter. I handed it over.

"So you're Warren Rudd now? And Steve Sawyer in Acapulco. Who else are you? Are you even Tom Walker?" The cop put my passport in his pocket.

"You can't do that," I said. "You can't just take my passport."

"I think you are Tom Walker because that is the name you email to your father."

"But I didn't tell anyone I was coming here. How did you find me?"

"I had you followed. How else? In this big city? But you confused us by going to the other bus station. Why are you here? Why are you not in Mazatlán or Puerto Vallarta? That is where you like to work, yes?"

A trembling began within me. Though internal at present, I'd every confidence I'd soon be shaking uncontrollably.

"Do you have other names?" the cop said. "I am checking hotels in Acapulco to see where you stayed. Oh, and in Cozumel. And Cabo San Lucas."

A weird sort of clown in teal overalls, his whiteface smeared, had set up an amplifier of his own in the spot vacated by the revolutionary. He began a rambling monologue about the drunk bus driver who'd driven him there. I was again grateful for my limited Spanish.

"Where is the woman who stayed with you in Acapulco?" The cop kicked a suitcase. "I know she is here because these are too many bags for a man. I want to talk to her too."

My face must have sunk, for the cop visibly brightened.

"I am sorry your father is sick," the cop said. "My uncle is sick. He was like my own father to me. He raised me here in Mexico. I am here to buy him medicine. But in Canada you have the best health care. I knew you were from Canada. Yes. Ask me how I knew that."

"I don't know. I mean, how did you know?"

"Because you were so polite in Acapulco. I said to myself: he is like a Canadian. And when your driver's licence was fake, that's how I know. But you are not a polite person, and we cannot have men like you scaring tourists. You are giving my country a bad reputation."

A fair point, and not one I'd considered: our activities limited the livelihoods of honest, hardworking Mexicans. I nodded to show I was following, as if the worst I could expect was a severe lecture.

"After you ran away, your American friends were sad because now they know you are a thief. The fat one got angry, and the other one would not believe me. He said you were his friend. I told him that I would put you in jail."

We were interrupted by the clown, who shouted something after a young couple passing arm-in-arm about the boy not being able to afford the car the girl deserved. The cop didn't appreciate this distraction. "There are ways to stay out of jail, Tom Walker. You will die if you go to jail. It is very bad. There are ways even for you to stay in business in Mexico. But it comes with a cost."

Hearing this, I bent over laughing. A shakedown. The cop righted me. "Are you sick?" he asked, seemingly with concern. "Be careful."

Of course he wanted a bribe. Why else would he have come so far? If I'd been thinking straight, I'd have seen that. Still laughing, I showed him the hundred pesos in my wallet.

"You will need more than that. A lot more."

All that fine talk about freeing Mexico of criminals. "I'm small time, not what you want."

The cop shook his head. "Good trying. The price for staying out of jail is 30,000 pesos. For every month. Or I could arrest you for expired visa. Do you even have a visa?"

I turned up my palms. "Either you put me in jail, or you wait until I can pay you."

"You like Acapulco, yes? So you pay me 30,000 pesos every month to stay there. I will look after the hotel managers because they are all my friends. If not, you go to jail."

"Ten thousand pesos," I said.

Over his shoulder, from deep within the park, came the figure I most wanted to see and hoped I would not. I couldn't risk revealing my joy at seeing Jill or let him get a glimpse of her. I strode toward the fountain, knowing he'd follow. This had to end.

When the cop reached me, I took him by the arm. "Look, I'm here to see a doctor. I have heart problems, like my father." I patted my chest in illustration. "But I'll be back in Acapulco the day after tomorrow. Let's meet at the Elcano and work something out."

The cop backed me up against the fountain. "There is no

146

negotiating. Thirty thousand is the price. Bring it to the Elcano at lunch time. Do not run from me. I will find you."

"I don't doubt it."

"This is keeping you out of jail." He waved Warren Rudd's passport in my face before walking off. I sat down on the stone edge of the fountain, my head spinning with it all.

Seconds later, Jill strolled up. "Did you make a friend?"

I stared at the retreating figure of the cop and decided she already had enough on her mind. "A well-dressed beggar. Everyone in this town is on the make."

A moment blossomed, and Jill stepped into it. "Sorry about how bitchy I was earlier. It wasn't you, I promise. It's just this... you know. Everything."

"Where the hell were you? Did you get what you were after?"

"I did. My friend wasn't home, so I had to go looking for him. I should have come back and told you, but I was in a hurry to catch him."

"You scared the shit out of me."

"I know. I'm sorry. I figured you'd be okay, though."

We humped the luggage into a busy commercial district south of the park. Although I didn't see him, I assumed the cop was following us. I wouldn't have believed me.

The Hotel Fleming was on a street of hardware and plumbing stores, its lobby done in pink marble, blond wood, and mirrors. It was pricey enough to have a bellhop whose eyes lit up when he saw our bags. I steered Jill aside. "We can't afford this place."

"I figured you'd say that, so I reserved a room before I came to get you. Listen, we can't lower our standards because once you do, it's tough getting them back."

"How much did you get?"

"Enough to last for a little while."

She slipped me some hundred-peso notes for my pocket. I promptly lost one to the bellhop, who helped me get our bags up to the third floor while Jill checked us in.

Her friend was an American, she said when I asked, and had evidently been close enough to loan her a significant amount of money. I backed away at that point. If she'd wanted me to know more, she'd have told me. As I've said, there were things about our time apart I'd rather not share. And what did it matter so long as we continued moving into a new life?

147

Our tan and apricot room contained just one double bed, a pleasant surprise for which Jill offered no explanation before dropping onto it. I dove after her. We wrestled until I pinned her arms. She squirmed beneath me, screeching: "Omigod, you stink. Get off me."

In the shower, I scrubbed at forty-eight-plus hours of filth and stress, and at the nagging suspicion I should be asking more pointed questions about the money. Plush bathrobes convinced me to appreciate how her extravagance had lulled me into complacency. The grim one-star hotel I'd have insisted upon wouldn't have been half as rejuvenating.

I re-entered a room that had been converted, in half an hour, into Jill's closet. Seemingly all of her belongings were unpacked. Bras dangled from a lampshade, and socks washed in the sink dripped from the vanity. How was this necessary for an overnight stay?

I pawed through my own bag, releasing a pungent aroma of unwashed clothing. "We should send out our laundry," I said.

"We don't have time," Jill replied from inside a suitcase. "We'll sort it out in Veracruz."

Veracruz again. I'd been ignoring our destination, and the awful people meeting us there.

Jill's repacking had unearthed The Rough Guide to Mexico, which I'd withdrawn from the Toronto Public Library when she first invited me south and long thought lost. Finding it was handy since it fell to me to determine from where and when buses left for Veracruz.

I was thrilled to read that El Tajín, a major archeological site, was a few hours' drive from Veracruz. Trips to the ruins of ancient Mexican cities were—had been?—a superb way to liberate tourists' credit cards from their wallets. And a pleasure: I'd been a keen student of indigenous Mexican cultures since my visit to Chichén Itzá, near Cancun, on that long ago reading-week trip.

Since then we'd climbed so many pyramids and temples, some repeatedly, that Jill had declared us "ruined." Because we rarely left the coastal regions, I'd had more exposure to Mayan civilizations in Guatemala and the Yucatan than I'd had with Aztec and Toltec cities in central Mexico. The trip to Veracruz offered an opportunity to change that.

Jill snapped my reverie by emerging naked and sweetly scented from the shower. Her generous proportions, the dewy flesh of her tummy and inner thighs, the strand of hair before her face as she

148

bent over her luggage—there could be no returning to my reading.

Yet there I was, nose back in my book seconds later when my overture was rebuffed. Jill put on her glasses and some old sweatpants. That combination meant sleep, never sex. So much for getting back to normal.

Downstairs in the hotel restaurant, we sat by a window and ate chicken and rice with tortillas. My concern was how to sneak off to Veracruz tomorrow without the cop noticing or alerting Jill to the threat he now posed. And why had he wanted to speak to her as well?

Jill outlined her plan for the morning: an early start, then a subway to the coach terminal. I nodded, more intent on the siren song of the bustling streets that night. I was feeling better about Mexico City and wanted to return to a lively district I remembered from our earlier visit. It was to the west, I thought, not far away, where the streets were named for foreign cities, like Hamburgo and Praga, and were full of bars and bohemians. Didn't we deserve a night out?

Jill insisted we watch television in our room before turning in early. Apparently our windfall wasn't enough for us to have any fun.

Back upstairs, she swatted away my second attempt at sex like she would a house fly.

"But it'll help me sleep," I pleaded.

She rolled her shoulder in answer and was soon snoring lightly, naked save for the sheet, all her loveliness going to waste. I sighed and returned to the guidebook until a car alarm interrupted my reading. Sirens. Below our window, two men spoke of a girl one of them was late to meet. Angelica, her name was.

I tried to lie as still as possible, taking care my restlessness not disturb Jill. In my waking dream, I'd made peace with this mystifying city. We lived here in a big apartment in that neighbourhood I liked and had jobs as translators or actors or teachers. We had a good life.

A Volkswagen backfired. I heard it as gunfire and woke with a jolt expecting the mustachioed cowboy cop on horseback to clomp into our room. A light rain had commenced, a breeze moving the curtains over the bed. Now all I heard was the wet hiss of tires and Jill's steady breathing. She shifted in her sleep, her warm hands reaching for me. I slid into them.

Whoever that guy was, I hoped his girlfriend was waiting for him.

Day 7

Mexico City to Veracruz

IN THOSE LAST MONTHS IN MEXICO, I sought a formula to measure the ratio between the amount of clothing Jill unpacked in our various hotel rooms and how late we were in departing for our next destination. Variables included the length of our stay, the reason for it, and the array of options she provided herself. The greater the choice of outfits, the longer she took to decide.

She laughed at this, but I was serious. Until I had mathematical proof of her inefficiency, I was doomed to endure panicky departures and missed flights.

For a thief, Jill was oddly concerned with decorum. She intended for us to reach the Vandals' residence politely at mid-afternoon. With buses departing hourly for the six-hour ride to Veracruz, we had to leave Mexico City by ten o'clock at the latest, and that meant rising hours before that. I knew the night before that we'd never make it.

I started prodding her at eight o'clock, gave up at nine, and at nine thirty went downstairs for breakfast. It was after ten when she finally rose.

A tedious wait ensued. Irritable over missing my swim for a second consecutive morning, I gazed down at the busy street. There were so many people along it, I wasn't able to identify the cop or determine if he had anyone observing us. He'd followed us to Mexico City. Would he follow us to Veracruz? That was a chance we had to take.

At noon, hotel management hammered on the door to remind us that check-out time had passed. In doing so, they inspired a method of disguising our tracks without alerting Jill that we needed to.
Down in the lobby, I made a show of paying for another night. Then I reconnoitered a back stairwell that led to a laneway behind the hotel. When Jill was ready, we followed this route, I explained, to avoid the lobby because the manager wanted to charge us for another night.

Out on the street, she raised her arm for a taxi. "I thought you wanted to take the subway and save money?" I said before considering that a taxi was better if we were being followed.

"We don't have time for that," she said.

So suddenly, we were in a hurry.

Our destination was the *Terminal de Autobuses de Pasajeros de Oriente*—an auspicious name for a departure point. I rolled the Spanish off my tongue a few times, exploring its peaks and valleys. Its acronym was equally fun. "TAPO," I said. "TAPO. TAPO. TAPO."

The driver turned around to check on me just as Jill's hand settled on my knee. She smiled through the smoke of her first cigarette of the day. "He heard you, honey."

The station didn't disappoint. From the outside, TAPO resembled a huge flying saucer, the dozens of buses docked against it suggesting the spokes of a gigantic wheel. Underground passageways, rising like the steps of a temple, led into a massive circular interior capped by a domed ceiling. Seemingly half of Mexico was on the move within, hauling luggage, eating, chatting on phones, arguing, laughing, and chasing after kids.

I stopped to get my bearings. The ticketing windows of rival coach companies lined the curved walls. In the centre—the hub of the wheel—was seating and restaurants. It was a testament to the builders that such a large, crowded space felt so buoyant and welcoming.

"You've been here, remember?" Jill said. "We came through here that other time."

"Sure." But I hadn't. She must have been thinking of her time here before I joined her.

I led her over the polished marble floors in search of a coach line serving the Gulf of Mexico. Now that I looked, I easily spotted the many CCTV cameras monitoring the human traffic. All we could do was keep moving.

Two first-class—*premiera*—tickets on the ADO line were 1300 pesos. I wondered again how much money Jill had dredged up yesterday. As usual, she queued for tickets, and I watched the stuff. She emerged from the line flushed with frustration ten minutes later. The two o'clock bus was sold out, so we had to cool our heels until three. It was nobody's fault but her own.

Lunch—breakfast for Jill—was cardboard bus station sandwiches. By now, I greatly missed the array of nutritious foods at the resorts. When Jill ordered coffee, I asked for mine to go. "I want to check my email," I said. Of the many uncertainties we faced, my father's health crisis stood the best chance of being resolved.

"Okay. But first help me move the bags. The bus will be full, and no one ever sits in their assigned seats."

Together we hauled our luggage into the ADO departure lounge.

"This way, we'll get the seats we want." Jill sat with the bags around her like I had in the Alameda. "I'll wait here. Please don't be late."

I skipped back into the main hall, feeding off the anticipatory energy of so many travellers. Surely that upswing in our fortunes was underway. When I reached a nest of computer terminals, I took a seat between two boys playing shoot-em-up video games.

My father wrote there'd been a cancellation on the surgery list at the hospital. Bad news for someone but just dandy by him. Due to his worsening condition—about which, infuriatingly, he still didn't elaborate —the date of his surgery had been moved up.

To when? And what kind of surgery?

Taking my advice, Earl had asked a neighbour down the street for a drive to Toronto. How he'd get home he still didn't know. He was pretty nervous about the whole thing, but had been told the robot performing the surgery didn't make the same mistakes humans could.

The robot was the clue I required. By flipping through websites, I best-guessed that he was undergoing a coronary bypass by endoscopy. A robotic arm controlled by the doctor created an incision in the chest and made the bypass. How many valves were being bypassed, I didn't know. Prognosis for a full recovery was excellent. The great advantage was in not cracking the chest or having to artificially pump the heart or provide blood transfusions. Patients were usually back to work—or in Earl's case, the racetrack—in a week.

There was also an email from Kate Norwood, whom I hadn't really thought of since our time together last summer. She'd gotten my address from Earl and hoped to hear from me, despite my sudden departure last fall. I still felt shitty about that.

I logged out and paid the twenty pesos I owed, thinking: if you can't be there for him, you could at least call. I didn't have time for that. Nor had I emailed back to ask the name of the hospital he'd be in. If I never heard from him, I'd have no way of finding out what had happened.

Too late, I saw it was nearly three o'clock. I cast about for the cop again, not that there was anything to be done about him. Back in the ADO departure lounge, Jill was dragging our bags outside to the open luggage doors of the bus. The cost of my tardiness became clear when we boarded. The bus was already so full there were no double seats still available.

One of the remaining single seats was beside a young woman with a laptop. The other was between the window and a very overweight old woman. The smaller of us, Jill offered to sit there. Since I'd been late, I couldn't allow that. Maybe the old woman wasn't going all the way to Veracruz.

But she was, and she had a chronic, phlegmy smoker's cough. The worst of it came ten minutes from the station, when we were already mired in traffic. A television monitor descended from the ceiling directly over my head and a movie called *Just Go with It* commenced on it, in dubbed Spanish, at a deafening volume.

Rain began lashing the bus near the summit of the mountains. In the hour we'd been ascending, I'd felt, even in the air-conditioned chill of the bus, the air outside turning cooler and heavier.

At dusk, we pulled off the highway for a leg-stretching break at a gas station hacked out of the forest. Halfway, I figured, between Mexico City and Veracruz. A point of no return. The smokers, Jill included, were the first to clamber off the bus. The rest of us exited more leisurely into a mist that was somehow falling from a clear sky.

Expectation lit me up. I scrambled atop a pile of boulders to peer along the highway. Far beyond the western slope of the mountains, the way we'd come, a tawny twilight stretched over the central Mexican plateau. Down the opposite slope, which the sun had already forsaken, an inky blackness was steadily enshrouding the forested hills declining to the sea.

Somewhere in that darkness was Veracruz, the city Cortés and his band of cutthroats had established when they first stepped ashore five hundred years ago. Centuries of murder and betrayal followed, centuries of forced religious conversions, slavery, and a myriad other human miseries, all fuelled by a greed the invaders and the native Mexicans shared in abundance.

Hardly the place for a fresh start.

I wandered past vendor's stalls to where the clearing ended at a wall of riotous, dripping greenery. The realm of a slinky jaguar, I reckoned, who was just now cleaning a paw before making me her dinner. Since the Vandals turned up at Paraiso, I'd been dogged by uncertainty over Jill's motivation and methods. And troubled that my loyalty felt more duty-bound than practical. She wasn't making the uncertainty over our future any easier to manage.

The horn of the bus sounded. Jill waited for me by the open door, the settled mist shimmering on her rain jacket. For an instant, I contemplated hiding in the jungle, never mind the jaguar, until the bus departed.

On the remaining journey, I picked at the Shakespeare paperback I'd liberated from Paraiso. It was a slog for a television hack, one made tougher by a movie called *The Vow* blasting overhead. I recalled that *Hamlet* was about a young man who talks about making changes and then never does. From two seats behind, Jill and her new gal pal talked in Spanish too quickly for me to understand.

It was after ten o' clock when we reached the bus station in the suburbs of Veracruz. In opening the door, the driver released a wave of clammy heat that rolled up the aisle. It felt tangible, like something we'd have to fight our way through.

That fleabag hotel I thought we should get in Mexico City? We got it in Veracruz because Jill insisted it was too late to call the Vandals for a pick-up. Three hotels in the vicinity of the station turned us away before a yawning old woman checked us into a dark room with a sagging bed and a television bolted to the ceiling.

Jill stripped to her skivvies—again, not an invitation—and was soon purring softly. I lay beside her, careful not to slide into the sag, watching a dubbed episode of *Seinfeld* with the volume lower than the street sounds outside. There was much to contemplate: our escape from Paraiso, the crooked cop, our inexplicable presence in this new city. And ol' Earl Drake, alone and scared in a beige hospital room, forgotten by his son. I told myself it was more likely he'd be chatting up the nurses and not caring who came to visit him, but that didn't help.

When my head refused to shut down, I dressed again and slipped out of the room. To check for that cop, I told myself. And to be alone for a moment. I'd gone from worrying over how we'd survive in this brutal country to puzzling over the origin of Jill's money.

Down on the street, I found an internet café for the morning and place for breakfast that looked promising. And all the furtive, potentially hostile figures normally associated with the seedy environs of a bus station in the wee hours. A few cars passed, every driver possibly in the employ of that cop.

Feeling no more relaxed or sleepy, yet far preferring my more domestic demons, I went back in to thrash through the night beside Jill.

Day 8

Veracruz

JILL LOOMED OVER ME, HER SANDALED toe grinding into my ribs. "Wake up, you bastard."

Meaning I must have slept. How wonderful to start the day with good news.

She was fully processed in her tropical look: hair in a ponytail against the sopping humidity, little make-up. "Look at you," I said. "Early start, huh?"

"I couldn't sleep with you bouncing on this bed like a basketball." She offered me a take-out coffee and then a last shove with her foot. "Thrashing about. What's wrong with you?"

Over breakfast in the restaurant I'd spotted last night, she explained we'd call the Vandals at noon and pretend, like it was yesterday, we'd just arrived from Mexico City. She didn't say what we'd do after that rendezvous. I pushed my plate of eggs and beans aside. "So what's going on with the Vandals? Should I be getting card numbers?"

"It never hurts. I told you there might be another way with those."

"When will you know?"

"I'm not sure. C'mon. We just got here. Give me a little time."

After she finished eating, Jill returned to our room to pack, and I went to the internet café. There was no new email from Earl. I regretted not calling him when I could have and stalked off my frustration in the streets around the station, keeping an eye out for that cop. Veracruz hummed with the promise of French emperors, hurricanes, and pirate raids, its ragged rhythm urging me to explore. As if we were on holiday, not some dreadful secret mission known only to Jill.

The heat was a malevolent presence. It sat between us on a shaded bench across from the bus station, fanning itself with Jill's *Hello* magazine. Of the four stations we'd recently passed through, the terminal in Veracruz was the most chaotic. Semana Santa was approaching its Good Friday climax. Many people travel for it, and most, apparently, were routing through Veracruz.

Jill left to call the Vandals, stranding me with the bags. Sunlight showed their many dents and scratches. It was the luggage of drifters, not anything tourists would use. I counted them, as I'd not done so since Mexico City. Then again, because I was one short. Jill's overnight bag. Last seen with her heading north out of the Alameda.

She was gone over half an hour, quite a while for a single phone call. I watched her exit the station toward me. Even tired and perturbed, in loose travelling clothes, she drew cat calls from macho motorists. The difference when she wasn't working was that she gave them back.

"I got their machine," she said. "Then Brenda answered. Sounds like she was sleeping."

"She probably was. Hey, did we lose a bag somewhere?"

"I left one in Mexico City. I reorganized. Haven't you noticed they're easier to carry?"

Not really, since we only went from nine to eight.

The Vandals provided me with ample time to be nagged by fat blue flies, that missing bag, and how far we'd drifted off course. I was wary of discussing this with Jill, considering our predicament and her crankiness. And would a conversation even help resolve our situation? She yawned.

"This is your fault," I wagered. "You shouldn't have put those cards through so soon."

My abruptness startled her. "No, you're right. I shouldn't have."

At last, a battered black Land Rover charged the station entrance, sending travellers and pigeons scurrying before it. Brenda leaned on the horn, already impatient with us. I put my tourist face, and Steve Sawyer's identity, back on with the same enthusiasm I would a winter coat in this heat.

Brenda hugged me to her sharp frame. Somehow we'd become old friends. "That's a lot of bags for a week in Acapulco," she said, lifting one into the Rover.

Was our artifice worn so thin? I pretended that it wasn't. "I like your ride," I said. "Probably the only Land Rover in Veracruz."

"No, there's plenty. Enough so you'd think someone could fix the air conditioner."

I claimed shotgun, and Jill slipped silently into the back. Neither of us asked about Nick's whereabouts, nor did Brenda's rigid hunch over the wheel and stony expression encourage it. She sped away from the station, snarling at people in her path. I wasn't sorry to leave: whatever my future held, I hoped there were fewer bus station washrooms and diesel fumes in it.

As we drove, the Gulf of Mexico glinted an aquatic grey to our right, its desolate beach more inviting than the postcard sands of the resorts. When the laden sky opened up, saturating the landscape, Brenda calmly maneuvered around massive puddles, and I was glad of the Rover.

After ten minutes, we veered into a strip mall anchored by a large grocery store. "I need to get some things for dinner," Brenda said. "We let our girl go for the month because we're travelling so much. You're going to have to put up with my cooking."

Travelling where? And why had they invited us if they weren't going to be around?

I pushed the shopping cart as our host filled it with white bread, milk, ground beef, and strawberry jam. English food. Jill and I shared a disappointed glance.

At the checkout, Brenda slowly withdrew her wallet from her purse and peered at her cards before selecting a NatWest Visa. Beside me, Jill flinched. In the same instant, from just a glance, I had half the numbers memorized. When Brenda's hand paused over the payment terminal, I got the other half.

Still Brenda waited. Finally Jill, remembering our manners, withdrew some cash from her handbag. "Let us get these, please. Since you're so kind to be putting us up." For thanks, she received a frosty smile. Brenda did not much like her. I found myself in the strange position of missing Nick, whose charisma kept our unlikely foursome intact.

Not far from the strip mall, we turned onto a curving road of newish

158

houses with signs announcing their names. Los Pinos. El Castillo. The road ended not far along, past more houses of similar design, at the sea. A suburb of sorts, plunked down on the scrubby coast.

The Vandals' house was named Casa Soho. Why shouldn't it be? We entered a large living area filled with clunky wooden furniture. Shockingly awful canvases of abstracts in pastels shared wall space with framed gold record albums. Brenda showed us to a small room with a futon bed. The best part was the ensuite washroom. Sharing facilities with the Vandals was a horror I'd refused to contemplate.

We emerged from our room a polite hour later, cramped and restless. A hush lay over the house as we inspected photos of Nick with spiky-haired musicians from way before my time. Record albums and CDs lay about and guitars of all varieties. And lots of Union Jacks, in case anyone still didn't know.

On Brenda's smaller table of celebrity were photos of her with Joan Collins and what looked like royalty. In an adjacent office was a computer to check my email on and a stack of screenplays. A ringing phone could be heard deeper in the house, then Brenda shouting into it. She appeared in the doorway to the kitchen to say Nick would be even later. Did we want tea?

I decided to charm our host with my cheerfulness and perhaps learn something useful to our purpose. I left Jill on the sofa with *The Rough Guide to Mexico* and entered the kitchen.

Juggling kettle and cups, Brenda melted somewhat as she answered my questions. She'd starred with Joan Collins—a "dear, dear friend"—in *A Lovely Murder* in 1985. She was the most self-possessed and alert that I'd seen her, and seemingly more genuine for it.

"Our spouses get along well, don't they?" she said.

"Gina gets along with everyone," I said. "I'm the hard-ass no one likes."

Brenda lifted the tea tray. "We both know that's not true."

Poor Jill was denied the warmth Brenda showed me. We were all glad when a car roaring outside interrupted our stilted tea party. The lord of the manor, I presumed. Jill immediately attached herself to me, her breathing quick and shallow.

"Tea?" Nick bellowed. "Who wants tea when it's cocktail time?"

Martinis in hand, he led us on a tour. Jill remained glued to my side, as befitted a happy couple on holiday. Nick was likewise attuned to Jill's wariness. I gulped my drink. Equally unsettling was the increased scrutiny I was receiving from Brenda, who'd refused a drink to sip tea at the back of our graceless conga line. At last I understood the change in her: she was sober.

The roaring car was an old Porsche, the kind movie producers drive, with Arizona licence plates. "I need Mexican plates," Nick said, "'cause the cops keep stopping me for pay-offs."

Casa Soho's third mode of transportation was a Dinamo scooter parked behind the house. Remembering my role as tourist, I said: "Looks better than the scooters we rented at the hotel. Weren't they crappy, honey? They barely ran."

No one answered as we reached the sun-filled room Brenda used as a studio. She waded into it, shuffling canvases so we could follow. Only Nick did, hesitantly. Round stone Aztec faces, some painted blue tartan, others covered in psychedelic floral prints, peered out of swirling hot-pink backgrounds. The same heads appeared atop fluorescent green pyramids amidst flashes of bright yellow and orange. Jill and I gaped at each other.

"The ones on the left are sold, but they'll be in my show," Brenda said. "A student from the art college, my intern, is working with the curator on the catalogue."

She offered me a seafoam canvas smeared with crimson. "Lately I've been channelling Atlacamani, the Aztec goddess of hurricanes," she said with a familiarity that suggested they were in collaboration. "That's her in the morning, when she's demanding a human sacrifice."

I passed off the painting to Jill as I edged out of the room. A week ago, I might have enquired about purchasing one to help break the ice. Not anymore.

Next stop was a sound studio with padded walls filled with recording equipment, more guitars, keyboards, and laptops. Jill was right (as usual): there was money here. But until I heard her idea to get at it, I'd continue to wallow on stage, unrehearsed, directionless.

Figuring Steve Sawyer should be more impressed by this famous couple, I asked how long they'd lived here. Eleven years, Nick said. Six, Brenda said.

"Eleven years," Nick insisted. "Six permanently. Our first house was over the mountains in Tlaxcala. But so many foreigners moved there it was getting to be like San Miguel de Allende. Have you ever been there?"

The city he mentioned had for decades been a hub for American artists and hippies, and so not anywhere Jill and I visited. "No, it's our first …"

"If I wanted to hear English all the time, I'd have stayed in England, you know? And everyone's a sculptor or making crappy jewellery. I couldn't stand it anymore …"

He continued like this from a reclining chair in the main room, leaving Brenda to slam pots in the kitchen while he played songs from his solo records. Conspicuously absent was the slavering attention he'd previously shown Gina. Jill was brusque with him, as if they'd quarrelled, and detached from the scene when she needed to step up and run the scam she'd insisted upon undertaking. But then she'd been short with me all day as well. I filed my concerns with the rest of the stuff I was ignoring.

As I'd feared, dinner was blandly British: mashed potatoes, frozen vegetables, and fried hamburger in a thin gravy. Were it not for a jar of salsa on the table, we might have been in Leicestershire. The Vandals met my toast to new friendships with puzzled stares. The most basic social niceties escaped them. I couldn't make out why they'd invited us.

For conversation, Nick related his ordeal of riding out a hurricane in a gas station.

"Leaving me here alone with the power out," Brenda said, "and the kitchen flooded."

"Wow," Steve Sawyer said. "You don't hear that every day in Buffalo. This is what we wanted, eh Gina? The real Mexico."

"Veracruz is as real as it gets," Nick said. "But there's not much to see here."

In that, he was wrong. "There's some ruins in the jungle with these ancient ball courts that I'd love to see. El Tajín, it's called."

"I've been there." Nick offered Jill an eye roll I didn't understand. "Bit far, though."

Steve was determined. "Sounds like a great day trip. We could have a picnic."

"Brenda and I have some appointments in town tomorrow. How about the day after?"

Brenda's buzzing phone rattled the table. She poked at it, then looked to Nick. "Carlos can't drive those pieces over on Tuesday. God. I knew he'd screw it up."

"He'll have to do it sooner then," Nick said. "I'm flying to London on Monday."

The Vandals had just end-dated their hospitality. Jill and I had four days to figure this out. Unfortunately, she appeared oblivious to this development, and there was no catching her eye to pull her back in.

"Another little holiday?" I fished.

"Business," Nick said, providing a chance to ask about that audition for his movie. Steve Sawyer hadn't dragged his wife across the country just to see some ruins. But Brenda yawning, and Nick echoing her, dissuaded him. Instead, I asked if I could check my email on their computer. "My father's having heart surgery."

Hearing this, Jill shifted in her seat beside me. We generally avoided mentioning family members unless it was pertinent to our squeeze.

Nick spoke around a mouthful of potatoes. "I've a bad ticker myself. An arrhythmia. Irregular rhythm. And my dad had a heart attack. Just exploded in his chest one day ..."

His stories continued in the main room while Brenda, who refused my offer of help, cleared the table in a surly silence. Nick seemed determined to bore us into an early departure. I contemplated reminding Gina to let her mother know we'd be delayed in picking up the kids, but I couldn't recall if this version of Steve and Gina had kids or not.

Finally Nick sputtered out of breath.

"About the internet," I said. "I should get in touch with work, too, to let them know I'll be gone a few extra days."

"All right," he said, rising slowly from his reclining chair. "Hold on till I see if it's up."

For the first time in an hour, Jill looked directly at me. The glassy indifference she offered was hardly inspiring. Since this squeeze was her idea, she should at least be present for it.

Nick lumbered back into the living room. "No mate, it's not on. Our internet is out half the time. Fucking criminal how businesses operate in this country."

If Daniel Drake was frustrated by this, Steve Sawyer was more sanguine. "Thanks for checking. Maybe we can go into Veracruz tomorrow. I saw an internet café by the bus station."

"Why don't you come with us, to see the town?" Nick said. "What do you say, Ginny?"

"Whatever works for you is fine for us," Jill said.

162

"You all right, Ginny? You're all out of sorts tonight."

"Just tired. It's been a long couple of days." Jill said.

"We got to see a bit of Mexico City," Steve offered.

Nick frowned concernedly at Jill. "You need a good night's sleep, love. I hope it's all to your liking. We get up early, but that doesn't mean you have to as well."

He left the room so quickly I anticipated a sinister development in our melodrama. Enter the hired muscle, cracking their knuckles. A clock on a side table chimed nine o'clock. If I went to bed now, I'd be awake another six hours, the usual worries endlessly running through my head.

Nonetheless, I dutifully followed Jill into the bedroom.

In searching for my toothbrush, I endured a regretful pang for my last real bedroom at my last apartment in Toronto. For all of my former homes, actually, where my things were in the same place, day after day. Cupboards and drawers to put them in. Laundry machines.

"I'll ask Brenda where we can send our laundry," I said. "That's if you'll give me a few more pesos. I'm all out again."

"What are you going to say if Nick asks about your father?" Jill liked my father. Or rather an idea of him, since they'd only met twice when we were students. She'd never mentioned her own parents in the three years I'd been down south with her. Our little family was small.

"The truth. That he's having bypass surgery, and that I'm not a very good son."

"Really? No wonder you're so uptight. Will he be all right? Why didn't you tell me?"

"I was going to tell you later, when I knew he was fine. I'm more concerned about you, actually. You weren't really here tonight."

When it was very hot, Jill had a distracting habit of sleeping naked. She'd reached this state when she came up to me. "You have to tell me these things, Danny. Nothing matters more than you and me. Us. Together. But it can't work if I'm always trying to figure you out, too."

Though touched by this, I wanted to talk about her shoddy effort with the Vandals. But instead of questioning her, I placed my hands on her breasts. They were not batted away.

In bed she blurred against me, her anxiety fuelling her sudden craving. It was our first sex in weeks and inspired rather than obligatory. If I only knew the mystical combination of mood, events, and weather that led her to decide the time was right, I'd

163

be forever in clover.

That, or maybe it was the lack of a television in the room.

Afterwards, sheened with sweat, we lay listening to Nick's muffled shouting at the other end of the house. "I don't know why he bothers," I said. "She never listens to him."

"He never listens to her, either. The way you don't listen to me. Don't laugh. We might be like that one day. Old and snapping at each other."

However bleak the prediction, I was encouraged by her vision of us together when we're ancient. "And where is this place where we're snapping at each other?"

"Somewhere warm, that's for sure. Somewhere near the water."

This got me wound up. "Yeah, that much we've established. It's *how* we're going to get there that matters. Everything else is bullshit until we figure that out."

Jill put a finger to my lips. "Not now. And not here. We'll talk tomorrow."

"I don't know what you're doing."

"Let me look after that, all right?"

A thousand concerns twitched through me. "I don't like the way he looks at you."

She laughed. "It's not a problem. I looked after myself before we got together again."

I was beginning to believe that accounted for much of my concern.

Jill placed her hand on my forehead and slowly kneaded the creases there. "Stop it. You're like an old man, worrying all the time. Trust me, okay? Tomorrow we're going to have a great day. Just you and me. We haven't had a fun day in months."

She rolled to her side, then promptly rolled back. "Don't you steal my sleep tonight."

Yet I must have stolen part of it, or rather our shared stress did, for we both were awake a long time in the stifling darkness. Poor Jill was unfamiliar with the netherworld of insomnia. So we lay there not speaking, since neither of us had anything comforting to say.

Day 9

Veracruz

A HAMMERING AT THE BEDROOM DOOR yanked me from a dream. We'd been on an airplane, Jill and I, flying I don't know where but luxuriously ensconced in first class. Freedom was assured.

No, we were late. Or rather Nick and Brenda were late, Brenda having confused the time of their first appointment. If Jill and I wanted a ride into town, we'd better scoot. Nick ranged between rooms, bossing the three sluggards delaying him as Jill hustled to get ready. The Vandals possessed the magic to motivate her that I lacked.

There was no time to wonder. With just coffee in me, Nick ushered me outside to the Rover. A glassy stillness lay over the neighbouring lawns and the smooth waters of the Gulf. I got right to work. "Gonna be hot, huh? I'm sure the weather will be cooler in England."

"I won't have a chance to enjoy it. Every second is filled with meetings." He nervously drummed the steering wheel. Two women, evidently, meant twice the wait.

Jill emerged from the house first, followed by Brenda in a scooped, body-hugging black dress. Nick opened the passenger door for her. "All right, love? Big day, yeah?"

"For you, maybe. I feel like a sack of rice at the market." No one knew what to say to that. "He didn't tell you?" Brenda continued. "Today I'm signing divorce papers from my second husband in New York. So that I can marry Nick. Again."

"Twice is nice." Nick turned to me in the backseat and winked. "I've got designs on her Actors' Equity pension. There's no union benefits for knackered old musicians."

"This time I'll be keeping my eye on you," Brenda said. A wedge that large might have been useful in a normal squeeze, but this wasn't. And what kind of lawyer works on Good Friday in Mexico?

As he drove, Nick babbled about a former bandmate who'd lost his teeth through years of neglect. He wasn't going to end up like that. Few people could interrupt him. Jill Charles was one. "Can we hit an ATM?" she said. "There's one in the parking lot at the grocery store."

"We haven't got time," Brenda said. "Go to one in town."

"We've got time," Nick said. "If Gina needs money, we've got time."

Her request started my alarm bells ringing, since I thought our accounts were empty. Waiting in the Rover with Nick and Brenda, I pretended I wasn't concerned that I couldn't see which card she was using or how much she was withdrawing. Frankly, I was afraid to ask her. She'd been quiet again so far that morning, and I didn't want to set her off for the entire day.

Nick dropped us at the bus station, explaining he'd return at three o'clock. If we wanted to stay later, there were local buses plying the highway as far as the strip mall, where we could call for a ride. "Mind the pickpockets today," he said. "They'll be hard at it."

The Vandals were a cloud lifted from us. The smile Jill gave me as they drove off was the warmest from her since I returned from our separation last fall. I was overjoyed to be with her in Veracruz and not a failed actor in Toronto or an English teacher in Vietnam or a landscaper in my hometown. I would have told anyone that our predicament was just a temporary setback and that our future happiness was assured.

We were picking up where we'd left off yesterday, the city awaiting us. I briefly braved the crowded station for a map, emerging jostled and empty handed.

"We don't need one," Jill said. She took my hand. "It's just us, okay? Let's follow our feet. See where they take us."

She was right. Guidebooks, maps, tourist brochures—none of those were of any use to us by that point.

We had breakfast in a café run by a dreadlocked Dutch woman who served percolated coffee and homemade muffins, rare treats south of Texas. Then we slipped into the internet place I'd used yesterday. There was still no word from Earl. I thought about the lonely man I re-met last summer. What a time to start regretting that I'd never gotten to know my father.

"Check again tomorrow," Jill said. "If you haven't heard from him, you can ask Warren to call some hospitals for you, all right?"

A great idea and what I needed to hear. In the sultry morning heat, we sauntered toward the centre of town, linking arms until they ran with sweat, then holding hands until our fingers slipped apart. When the sweat trickled down my back, I stopped at a vendor's cart selling housewares and fingered a cloth for my neck.

"No way," Jill said. "If you put that rag on, I'll never kiss you again."

The streets became narrower and more crowded with pedestrians, the buildings older and more elegant. Balconies overhanging the street were strung with laundry, boleros blasting from windows. From a distance came the dull roar of a crowd. Despite the quickening pace of others near us, we continued to amble. Hypnotic Veracruz was a gem we preferred to uncover slowly.

Soon there were no more cars, only people, the pavement strewn with flower petals. The crowd pulled us deeper into its urgency. Some people carried Mexican flags. When I smelled incense, I knew we'd blundered into the back of the Good Friday procession. Jill knew it too and pulled me after her to follow it.

In front of an old church, some boys and girls wore white sheets and homemade angel wings. Other children dressed as shepherds were petting a cat squirming in the arms of an older girl. The passion play. The older girl set aside the cat and ushered the children off the church steps to join the parade.

Further on, men and women in white cloaks and conical hats bore tall crosses or paintings of the Last Supper. The children kept pace with us, thrilled to be part of the massive street theatre. White coffins dressed with flowers bounced overhead, as did a Virgin of Guadeloupe so large four men were required to lift her. Even larger was a statue of Christ swooning in Mary's arms, strands of scarlet fabric blood flowing from his wounds.

The procession ended at a ruddy stone building I took for the cathedral. We were in time to witness Jesus bearing his massive cross through the doors, the actor's crowned, bloody head bent with his labour. He was whipped and harried by Roman soldiers in plumed helmets, their bronze breastplates flaming in the sun. Masked priests hovered in sinister purple robes.

The faithful jostled to cram into the cathedral behind him. "Standing room only," I said.

"I've seen enough," Jill said. "We know how it ends."

The zócalo, a grand square beside the cathedral, was a fixed parade of sidewalk painters, fire-breathers, food carts, and mimes. I counted three roving mariachi bands vying for tips, and few other gringos. Most of the regal colonial buildings facing the square were hotels with cafés spreading out from beneath their porticoes. Families sat to lunch on the patios or stood waiting for tables on checkerboard paving stones littered with crushed flowers.

The crowd swallowed us, forcing us one direction, then another. Jill took my arm as a balloon vendor bumped past, pressing us together into a spontaneous kiss.

Then I saw him, in the corner of my eye. The cop, eating with another man on the patio of the Hotel Colonial. I hauled Jill behind a tree and into another kiss. (Tom Walker did that once, hiding from the bad guys in a kiss with a mini-skirted day-player.)

Moments later, breathless, I looked again. The cop was in profile to me, his head bobbing as he ate. The fear slicing through me said it was him, and that this day was always coming. Yet I had to be certain. Jill was lighting a cigarette, perceiving our pause as a break in our wanderings, not the screeching halt at the precipice that it was. "Danny, what are you doing?"

If it was him, everything changed. I'd have to tell Jill, and we'd have to leave Veracruz. What a fool I'd been to think we could evade him. To think we could avoid the sort of end we deserved. "Can you wait here a sec?" I said. "I want to use the washroom in this hotel."

I entered the patio of the neighbouring hotel so I could approach the cop from behind. I felt sick to my stomach, like I would actually need a washroom.

Even if we were still fleecing tourists, the cop's proposal would end badly for us. As in any TV movie, he'd brag to his fellow officers, who'd come looking for their piece, followed by the drug gangs. Greed being an infinite property, when the gangs weren't getting enough, they'd murder me and rape Jill.

And then the man turned to flag a waiter, and I saw it wasn't the cop who'd tracked us to Mexico City but another overweight, sad-eyed Mexican man of about fifty.

"Are you all right?" Jill said when I returned to her.

"Never better," I said, hauling her back into the party.

On the far side of the zócalo, we entered a broad boulevard filled with carnival attractions—a Tilt-A-Whirl, a bouncy castle, a rollercoaster. We lost ourselves again, Jill glued to my side.

Through the spokes of a Ferris wheel, we caught our first glimpse of the container ships and the skyscraping cranes of the port. Along a breakwall, old men cast fishing lines, and skinny boys dove after coins tossed by passersby. The boys stayed submerged for an impossibly long time before surfacing with the coins between their teeth.

I showed one boy a twenty peso coin, then followed him to the edge. For our renewed good luck, I wished, and a happy forever somewhere safe. I lobbed the coin high overhead to give the kid the best chance of catching it. He slipped into the inky green water before the coin, which disappeared into his wake.

What did Jill wish? Our hands clenched, we stared after the boy until he clambered over the breakwater with a different coin in his dripping hand. Did he mistake the coin I tossed, or did they have a stash down there ready for whenever they dove? I gave the kid another fifty pesos for his trouble.

We pressed south toward beaches flashing silver in the heat. Above the sun-drenched multitudes, an enormous Mexican flag slowly waved, the eagle holding the snake in its talons. It was a twin to the flag in Acapulco. Much had changed in our transit between them.

Vendors called out *mango, mango, mangoes*. We bought one to share in some shade, the sickly sweet fruit peeled and jammed onto a stick. Farther up the coast, a massive cruise ship slipped into port. Soon its hordes would race ashore to plunder this city by credit and debit cards. Our hours as the only gringos were numbered.

Jill shaded her eyes to watch the ship churning sideways to dock. Did it remind her of the one she worked on when she went away after university?

"We should get on one of those," she said. "All those retirees. Talk about pensions."

"Yeah, but without a contact for the numbers there's not much point."

She handed me the half-eaten mango. "I'm sorry about rushing those American cards. But I was so excited, I just had to run them through."

"So we could come here."

She sighed. "No, so we wouldn't have to come here."

I could practically hear the gears grinding in her big brain. "Did you call your contact about the cards yet?"

"No. I want to let things cool off a bit."

"Better hurry. Nick's leaving for England in a few days."

"Yeah, I heard him. We're just getting started. Cut me some slack."

"Tell me something. Do you want to leave all this? Real life means paying for things with your own money. Never travelling anywhere. No more fooling people. No more thrills."

Jill sloshed bottled water over our mango-sticky hands. "Yes. Finally. It took a while, didn't it? I don't know what I would have done if you hadn't come back for me."

Since we were being candid. "That man you were with in the lobby of the El Presidente. Last year. When I had to take off. Was he one of your contacts? From when you were down here working alone?"

"More or less. It started with modelling. Somehow I always find those sorts of people."

"Is he why you didn't meet me at the Sanborns?"

"He wanted me to do something for him. And with you gone, I couldn't say no. I didn't get back in time, then I couldn't find you."

"So why didn't you tell me that?"

"I don't like to talk about those days. And I wouldn't have run into him if you hadn't needed to prove yourself with that English chickie. Which you didn't need to do."

"Can we expect any more special guests to drop by?"

"No."

Back in the zócalo, I thought the patio of the Hotel Colonial would be appropriate for lunch. The waiter, a boy growing his first moustache, was extremely attentive to Jill and showed me the respect due the man of such a fine lady. The food was slow to arrive and not good, exactly what we expected for front row seats to the living Diego Rivera mural passing before us.

It was Jill's turn to pick at her meal. I waited for whatever was troubling her to bubble to the surface. "Thanks for understanding," she said at last. "Parts of that time, before you came here, I'm a bit embarrassed about. I can give you the details some other time."

"If you want. I'm not asking. It only matters if it affects us, which it clearly did last year. And don't ditch me again. Ever. Or make me wait a week for nothing."

"Didn't part of you secretly love that?" she teased. "All the free drama? C'mon."

While that was genuinely funny, I couldn't relax as easily. The scare over the cop reminded me we still possessed incriminating passports and identification. They were a dead weight, relics of a former life. Tomorrow, secretly, on the road to El Tajín, I'd find somewhere to jettison them and move us that much further on.

We had coffee on a quieter side street, then continued rambling in a drowsy residential district behind the beach. Here, too, I imagined homes for us and lives with defined goals and realistic expectations. Regular bed times. Just as I thought I could go on like this forever, Jill stopped at a house advertising palm and tarot readings. "Ever had your fortune told?"

Mexicans are a very spiritual people. There are shrines, seers, and wisdom witches on every corner. Jill, on the other hand, was deeply pragmatic. Her sudden interest in the mystic I couldn't figure. "We'll be late getting back to the station. They're waiting."

"Never mind them. I thought we were having fun today?"

A young woman ushered us into a front room smelling of sandalwood. Kids shrieked behind a curtain separating the rest of the house and were hushed. The woman sat us at a table covered in black lace. We watched as she lit votives decorated with portraits of the Virgin. The incense came from a shrine to *Santa Muerte* by the door.

Jill removed her wallet and glanced my way. I shook my head. The 200 pesos didn't concern me—although it should have—so much as what the astrologer might say. Granny Drake always warned against turning over stones.

"¿Ud. *desea cartas de tarot*?" the woman said.

"Yes," Jill said, laughing. "*Sí. Lo que mejor adivina mi fortuna.*"

The woman didn't think this was funny. "*La verdad es un asunto de interpretación. Si no le gusta su futuro, cámbielo.*"

Jill turned to me. "She says the truth is a matter of interpretation, and you can change it if you don't like it. Remember that."

The woman laid five cards face down on the table, then turned over three from the deck, scrutinizing each one as she went. She spoke slowly enough for us both to understand. You have come from far away, she said. Your voyage involved pleasing many people you did not like.

That struck me as obvious. Jill nodded to herself as the astrologer continued flipping cards and interpreting them. You have recently become reacquainted with some unfinished business from your past, the woman said. I am happy to tell you that will soon be over.

"Thank God," Jill said. So it went with each card for a few minutes. Jill was enraptured and unrecognizable—a con artist seduced by the same faux-emphatic gibberish she used to rob others. Why is it some people believe almost anything affirming they hear?

The astrologer began stacking her cards. The session was at an end. That was all you got for 200 pesos? Talk of journeys and enlightenment was fine, but I hadn't heard what I wanted. "¿Y nosotros?" I wagged a finger between Jill and me. "¿Cuál es nuestro futuro?"

The woman laid three cards face down on the table and turned them over individually. *La Luna*. The moon can't be bad, I thought. A five of some suit. Swords? Only the last card, on which a man fell from a castle tower, gave her pause. I didn't like the look of it either. The woman smiled through her unease. "U*ds. tendrán una vida larga y estarán contentos juntos.*"

A long and happy life together. Now that's what we'd paid to hear. Jill rose slowly from the table. "I knew it," she said. "Not long now."

Until what, I didn't ask. Her eyes glistened, and her body quavered. From never crying to tears twice in a few days. Something more profound than a few tarot cards were at work on her. Alarmed, I led her back into the leaden afternoon to search for a taxi.

Nick was in front of the bus station defending the spot he'd carved for the Rover from other drivers. I expected histrionics. Instead, he said calmly, "There you are, Ginny. It's getting late."

"Sorry about that," Steve said. "We got lost on some side streets."

Nick saw only Jill. His face was florid, his movements unnaturally fluid, and he smelled of booze. "I'll get Brenda. She signed some papers today, as you know. She's in a mood."

I waited until he'd lumbered off. "He's drunk."

"I'm sure he's fine," Jill said. "He probably does this all the time."

"All the time, sure. He can only kill us once, though."

I stamped off to wait beneath the station portico, leaving Jill to bake in the Rover. It was a crappy end to a fine afternoon. The Vandals were toxic.

It was a half hour before Nick returned, leading a doddering

Brenda. She carried a box of wine in each hand. "I'm a free woman today," she announced to anyone near the station entrance. "Free to be enslaved all over again."

Steve thought he'd lighten the mood. "So when's the happy day?"

"Ask Nick. Better tell him to hurry up or I'll get picked up by some young stud."

Nick, stowing the wine in the back, looked exhausted. If he didn't care for her, nobody would. It didn't excuse his behaviour, but it helped explain it.

I waited for him by the driver's door, my hand outstretched. "I'm driving, Nick."

A nod from Jill—one I'd be sure to ponder later—smoothed the process. He handed me the keys. Blotto Brenda crawled into the front passenger seat. "Goddamn papers don't mean anything. It's not a marriage if you don't honour your vows."

"Brenda, that's enough," Nick said from the backseat.

The Rover handled beautifully, and the hot wind roaring through the open windows compensated for the sombre silence within the vehicle. Nick nodded off, slumped against Jill. I couldn't speak against it because she seemed content to gaze out the window, the wind whipping through her hair. Beside me, Brenda hummed happily to tunes from her iPhone.

Not far from town, a hot-pink flare indicated our day was about to change. Taillights winked on ahead. I geared down and gripped the steering wheel tighter.

Roadblocks in Mexico can appear on any road, at any time. Occasionally, a cop will insist you've committed some traffic infraction or another. That may be true, but what they're interested in is your money.

I fingered the passport in my pocket, although using it might be dumb if that cop from Acapulco had red-flagged us. Which meant we couldn't use any of that identification in Mexico again. Which was another way of saying we had to leave Mexico.

Behind me, Nick roused himself. "Here we fucking go again."

A solitary officer stood in the roadway waving cars to stop. Two other cops sat on piles of bricks from a half-built house in the shade of a tree, drinking bottles of orange soda.

As I rolled forward, I extracted the last 200 pesos from my wallet, thinking: offer the bribe before your passport. That way, your name never becomes involved.

Nick coughed wetly. "Don't pay him. Just keep driving."

"I'll handle this, Nick. We can split it later."

The officer looking in at me couldn't have been more than twenty years old. "*Su licencia de conducir, por favor. Y su pasaporte.*"

"Don't pay him," Nick said. "He doesn't deserve your money."

"*Sus documentos, señor,*" the officer said again.

"He's a little cutie." Brenda craned her head around me. "How you doing, cutie?"

"Fuck him." Nick shouted out his window. "Fuck you. Corrupt fucking monkey."

The officer lost interest in me and stared intently at Nick. I noted, uncomfortably, that the two other officers in the shade were now observing us.

"*Yo necesito ver su identificación también,*" the officer said to Nick.

Nick's Spanish was horrible. "*¿Para qué? Probablemente no lo puede leer.*"

Nick had called the cop illiterate. I turned into the backseat. "I said let me handle this."

"They won't come after us because they're too lazy. So let's go."

Brenda tapped me on the shoulder, spinning me around. "Last summer, they kept us for three hours. I was so mad. But we never paid."

"It's the principle," Nick said. "They haven't earned it."

"*Yo necesito los documentos de todos,*" the officer said.

"What if they trace the Rover back to your house?" I said.

"They won't," Nick said, "because there's no money in that."

"*Todos, salgan del carro,*" the officer said. "*Ahora.*"

"*¿Qué va a hacer? ¿Disparanos?*" Nick said. "Idiots. Let's go. Just drive away."

"He's right." Jill placed her hand on the back of my neck. "They won't hurt us."

Stonewalled by Nick, the officer returned to me, his brown eyes pleading. His uniform hung off his skinny teenaged frame. This kid and I were both struggling under an illusion of control. He looked back to his fellow officers for support.

"Honey," Jill said. "Please."

Was it Nick's haranguing I most objected to or Jill's ability to steer me in any direction she chose? Some part of me had had enough of their bullshit. I slammed down on the accelerator, and the Rover tore away.

Back at Casa Soho, Brenda disappeared with one box of wine, and Nick got to work on the other in the main room. Jill and I retreated for a siesta. We were settling on the bed in our room when determined footsteps passed our door, followed by Nick's sardonic snort.

"Don't laugh," we heard Brenda say. "You're ruining my life again."

Rage-filled sound fragments reached us as our hosts scuttled between rooms, sniping and riposting: "I apologized for that years ago..." "Making me relive..." "You never forgave me ..."

It sounded like familiar territory for the grisly duo. Typical of them to lack the courtesy to take it outside or postpone it a few days. Jill curled into me, hands over her ears. We'd seen pictures of Nick and Brenda as freewheeling youngsters in the main room. What would those two make of the ogres they'd become?

A quick wet hiss and a painful shriek from Brenda abruptly ended the fight. Footsteps moved off then a foreboding silence enveloped the house.

"Did he just hit her?" I said.

"Oh God, I hope not."

I jumped out of bed, intending I'm not sure what. Before opening the door, I turned to Jill. "I've had it with these two. Can't you see how wrong they are?"

Whatever I expected to find, it wasn't Nick unfolding a Scrabble board on the coffee table. "Fancy a match?" he said.

I cast about for Brenda, all my noble intentions suspended.

"You'll be easy to beat," he said. "But Ginny is great with words."

His nonchalance made me regret my moment of compassion at the bus station. I couldn't wait to see the last of this asshole.

Hearing the softer tone of the conversation, Jill drifted in from our room. She was game.

"No Spanish words," Nick said. "English only."

I sat on the couch beside Jill, puzzled by why he'd say that. We'd given no indication we spoke more Spanish than the phrases we daily garbled as tourists. My tired brain convinced me I was being paranoid. It was a rule against Spanish words in an English game. Nothing more.

Jill started well, Nick handicapping himself with wine. My head drooped, the sun and the sea air catching up to me. Would it be rude to nap until dinner? No, not when one host was drunk and insane and the other an abusive coward. And also drunk.

Nick caught me yawning and turned his red-rimmed glare onto me. "So who's the hero of the highway today, eh Stevie? Like that role, do you? Leading man type. Action hero."

I was willing. "How'd your meeting in Acapulco go? About the movie?"

"Not bad. We're making progress. But what happened to you? I gave you that big break, and you flew away like a little bird."

I grinned through the artificiality. "I looked good, didn't I? Admit it."

Brenda appeared at the doorway to the kitchen, naked save for a paint-splattered apron. "Anyone who appreciates art should be in the studio," she announced.

The menace on Nick's face melted to reveal the full tragedy of his life.

Brenda wielded a paintbrush like it was a sceptre. "I command you all to witness."

Was there a faint red mark over her left cheekbone? Dusk was settling, and with the orangey shadows of fleeting light curving around her face, I couldn't say for certain.

Jill leaned into me and under the protective arm I offered. If we weren't dependent on this pair for our supper, it might have been funny. Nick grunted then returned to his row of letters.

Brenda pointed her paintbrush at me. "There can't be freedom until there's trust. It doesn't matter where you go." Had she compared notes with the astrologer? Then she turned and walked her droopy bum from the room.

The game continued with increased intent, Nick laying MILD down off Jill's DEMISE. After a few minutes of ominous quiet, a metallic clatter and a triumphant screech came from the studio. Nick removed his reading glasses. "Excuse me," he said.

"No," I said. "Excuse me." It was time for the shower I'd missed that morning. They'd been hard to come by of late.

The galling disappointment of every role I'd failed to land—especially in the black days after *Legal Ease*—followed me into our room. So did Jill. "I'm sorry," she said.

"Aren't they just the sweetest couple? You sure can pick them."

"It's worse today because she's upset about something."

"She thinks Nick is going to leave her for you. She's nuts. I hate it here."

Not much later, buffed and ready for more abuse, I couldn't find

176

my shaving kit. With Jill's haphazard method of packing, there was never any way to predict where my things might turn up. I opened one of her bags, remembering that I wanted to dispose of the phony passports. Since she likely wouldn't approve of that move, I needed to secure them in advance.

I soon wished I'd kept better track of my things. That way I'd never have discovered the two-inch-thick wad of pesos, secured by elastic bands, atop some underwear in one of Jill's bags. If they were hidden, she'd done a poor job.

I dropped to the bed with the bills in my hand. Fifty thousand pesos, by my quick count, in fifties and hundreds. I felt sick again. That much money meant we didn't have to be in this house. We could already be at the happy place the astrologer told us about.

And why go to an ATM when you already had thousands of pesos? The money hadn't come from there. I wondered if it had anything to do with her whereabouts that day in Mexico City or if this was Jill's emergency stash of funds. If I'd set aside money, why wouldn't she?

Or, worse. Perhaps the American cards had paid, but she'd lied about losing her contact to convince me to come to Veracruz. If that were the case, why were we here?

Sitting there, I aged considerably in a few minutes. Fresh dots had emerged in the pattern of images that resembled Jill Charles. My naiveté had finally outdone me. I placed the bills back where I'd found them, unearthed my shaving kit in the same bag, then quickly zipped it closed, wary of what else might be hidden in it.

Mostly I was sad she wouldn't tell me what was actually going on.

Back in the living room, Jill was trouncing Nick. She pulled me to her and pointed out the four-star words she'd created—EXAMPLE and QUORUM—as her hand trailed through my hair. Despite myself, I got excited for her. And by what I'd just seen in our room. Whatever she had underway, the stunning wits I thought she'd lost earlier weren't gone, just more shrewdly concealed than ever.

I could have told you Nick was a sore loser. He compensated by slurping wine at a rate that would have impressed his wife. I despaired of a long night with two drunken idiots.

Nick must have read my thoughts. "I'm afraid Brenda won't be joining us for dinner," he said. "She's taken a sedative."

"I don't blame her," I said.

"Very funny. It's nigh on dinnertime, and who's to cook for us? Why don't you send your little woman into the kitchen? Ginny? Couple of steaks, jacket potatoes."

Jill was folding up the game board. "You've got the wrong girl."

I didn't like where this was headed. I suggested the grocery store on the highway where I'd seen a hot table selling roasted chickens.

"There's a grill place in the same strip that's better." Nick dangled a set of keys at me. "Take the Rover, not the Porsche. You do not drive the Porsche. And hurry back, boy."

He wasn't far off in his description of me. I motioned for Jill to follow me to our room, where I waited, like a kid receiving his allowance, while she laid cash into my open hand. I did not mention the stash lying three feet away.

I drove recklessly fast, the speedometer bobbling around 150 kmh, as if I wanted the police to remove me from this farce. I had 500 pesos in my pocket and a car worth many thousands more. I could be on a flight north by dawn.

On the return journey, more flares and the raging crimson of emergency vehicles stopped me. An accident, which must have just occurred, for the road was clear half an hour earlier. I had a passport and driver's licence for Philip Smith, a bank manager from Cleveland. And change from dinner, nearly 300 pesos. If there was any trouble, it would just be me getting arrested, not Jill.

I inched closer to the scene. A pick-up truck was sideways in the road with a tarp over the windshield. The passenger door was open and a shoe lay on the ground before it. The kind of police that didn't wear insignia milled about. Someone had died, just not accidentally. Sadly, that worked in my favour. The cop checking passing vehicles barely glanced at the gringo in a Range Rover with take-out from a local restaurant. Nonetheless, dreamy Veracruz had suddenly been thrust into the Real Mexico I feared.

When I returned, Jill had made a salad and set the table. Nick treated us to tales of his hardscrabble origins. His father drove a bus until the drink did him in. His poor mom scrubbed the marble floors of Mayfair mansions. Plucky young Nick learned first from this singer then from that movie star. And bedded every woman (un)fortunate enough to come within fifty yards of him. No wonder Brenda had issues.

"What time are we leaving for El Tajín tomorrow?" I asked.

"Oh, that." Nick looked to Jill. "Early, I suppose. It's quite a drive."

"We appreciate it." God bless Steve Sawyer. He never wavered. "I think I'll take a swim after dinner. Could be my last dip in the ocean for a while."

"I wouldn't," Nick said. "It's not like the pretty beaches in the Caribbean you're used to."

Which was a funny thing to say to a couple from Buffalo who'd said they'd never been south of Tampa. I looked at Jill, but she was staring at her half-eaten dinner.

"I meant because there's sharks out there," Nick said quickly. "If you get in that water, you're more of a fool than I took you for."

At that point, any normal couple would politely announce they'd changed their travel plans and catch the next flight back to their lives. Jill and I didn't have that option. I set down my fork, stood from the table, and exited the house through the front door.

The evening had cooled, the moon a cantaloupe crescent on the Gulf waters. Jill caught up and walked beside me in silence until the road ended at some palm trees. Beyond them was a short gravel beach and the Gulf of Mexico.

I sat on a deadwood log in the hope of tapping into some of that big ocean calm. Small waves lapped at my feet, and the faraway lights of a container ship twinkled prettily. I wasn't even frustrated by that point. Frustration's only possible when you still have moves you can't make.

Jill settled beside me and rested her head on my shoulder. A drop of her affection melted me every time—even today, when there were so many reasons to doubt her sincerity.

"I got this crazy idea in Veracruz today," she said. "Do you want to hear it?"

"All right," I said.

"What if we attached a school to our theatre? For kids. Like a training facility. Do shows in Spanish and in English. In rep."

It was a great idea. And I'd sort of glimpsed the possibility of something similar that afternoon when I saw the kids in the passion play.

"We'd do shows for tourists and for locals, too," Jill continued. "And have a language camp like I went to last summer when you were up north. Lotsa rich parents will send their kids. We can get the schools involved. Look into education funding."

"So we've got money coming in from the theatre and the school?"

"Exactly. You'd have to get serious about learning Spanish, though."

For a minute I was lost in a dream of an acting dynasty. Lots of little Jills and Daniels gallivanting onstage like an old-time vaudeville family. Tours through Latin America. Cartagena. Buenos Aires. Big-time movie offers.

Then I remembered where I was. "It'll break our hearts every day. Same as with the theatre. We won't get rich doing it. We won't get famous, either."

"I know. I wanted to be famous once, even when I said I didn't, but I don't anymore. I still want to be rich, though. Never say never."

"So how are we going to pay for it?"

"Let me look after that, okay?"

I still wasn't convinced she could give up the drama our crimes provided and be content in a quiet "civilian" life. But I owed her the chance to try it. "Sure," I said.

"Let's really live here, Danny. Leave our old selves behind."

She kissed me, and I thought of nothing else as she did. And then I felt another idea fire to life within her.

"I still think we should try Puerto Escondido," she said. "It's getting to be about more than just surfing. Yes, I know you want out of Mexico, but that's the kind of community we should be in."

"Sounds great," I said. "As usual, all we need is the money."

Since we weren't going to find it on that beach, I kissed her again and got busy with my hands. In a single, suave move, I slid her from the log onto the wet sand. We kissed there until I began to pull at her clothing. Then she took me by the hand and led me back to the house.

Casa Soho reverberated with snoring. The deeper tone came from Nick, sprawled on the couch. The second, shriller wheeze rose from deeper in the house. There was comfort in knowing both beasts were asleep. Only if the snoring stopped did we need to worry.

In our room, she was at me before I'd closed the door, her nimble fingers opening my pants. She took me into her mouth, a fantastic sensation I hadn't known in months. I needed to slow us down, since I was in danger of finishing too soon. Jill let me take over. She always read me so well. We took our time with each other, making sure she finished, too. We'd shared everything else that day.

We lay tangled for some time, her hair draped across my chest. Soon her breathing assumed the comforting rhythm of her sleep.

Typically, I wasn't so lucky. That was fine talk on the beach. Too bad it was just talk, and so much remained unsettled. Most prominent was that wad of pesos glowing ominously in the suitcase a few feet from our bed.

Part 3 King's Reach

LATE AFTERNOON OF A TYPICALLY drab December day on the Pacific Northwest. Seamless grey sky. Rain-slick swath of highway vanishing into an icy fog. Brooding forest of evergreens.

Slicing through this desolation, our shiny orange school bus was a flash of alien colour.

Within it were the seventeen convicts presently comprising the King's Reach Players, the warden, three armed guards, and the driver (also armed). No one spoke. Seconds into our journey, the high spirits that marked our departure were shushed by an unsettling illusion of freedom.

The town of Gracechurch was a half hour drive from the prison. A few cars passed in the opposite direction, bound for Nanaimo or Victoria. Otherwise our isolation was complete. I've been at King's Reach for a year and before that was incarcerated for seven months awaiting trial. Other Players have been inside for a decade or longer. They contemplated the world beyond the barred windows of the bus with more mistrust than wonder.

After days of wrangling, Warden Carr caved to my request that the Players accompany us on a technical survey of the schoolhouse. Not that there'd be much that was technical about it. Considering how disturbing the trip had been so far, hopefully it will also help pre-empt any opening night jitters.

More cars on the road indicated we were approaching civilization. We passed a gas station from which an RCMP cruiser pulled out to follow us.

Gracechurch is tiny: a traffic light, two churches, and a strip of stores. And pretty. The waters of the Strait of Georgia glinted dully through the trees of a park, and the main drag ended at a pier replete with fishing boats. It all reminded me of faraway seaside places with Jill, the salt water smelling of what I thought had been happier days.

The red brick schoolhouse was on a side street, where a second police cruiser sat idling. The caretaker, a folksy woman in her fifties named Karen, met us on the front steps. That was brave of her, even with the police presence. The warden introduced himself before she could remind him they'd previously met at a community meeting. After his humbling, I introduced every member of the company, the warden seething, the caretaker gracious, and the Players definitely appreciative.

Behind the arched front door, abandoned scarves and hats hung from a row of hooks in a large cloakroom, conjuring a hominess that was startlingly unfamiliar. I heard the echoes of generations of kids removing raincoats and rubber boots before entering the classroom.

From the cloakroom, we entered a graceful rectangular space. Hardwood floors creaked beneath our feet, and sheer curtains over the windows diffused the pale light. For the second time, an otherwise boisterous group of men fell silent. Even motormouth Bobcat was hushed.

Waiting within was Stephen Kasey, the journalist I met last summer when I invited some local personages to the prison for a performance of *Charlie Brown*. "Thanks for coming on such short notice," I said, handing him the envelope Edith Orson had slipped me that morning.

He peered inside it. "Is this the report about expanding the prison?"

"Not sure. And not so loud, please. Why not ask him?" I gestured toward Warden Carr. "You shouldn't have trouble getting him to talk about himself."

Karen the caretaker let us collect around her. The schoolhouse was over a hundred years old, she said, and was used as a school until the mid-1980s. It was now used for special events and weddings. Various organizations called it home, including an amateur drama club. Seating for up to 130 people could be ordered from a party supplier in town.

"You hear that, boys?" said Hassan, the former arms dealer playing Stephano, the drunken butler. "The screening room only seats fifty."

"How much are they to rent, the folding chairs?" Warden Carr said.

"You'd have to call them," Karen said. "I'll give you their number."

If the warden is to be believed, sales of ten-dollar tickets are so good there might be a fourth performance added. As a gesture of good will, he'd arranged for all proceeds of the schoolhouse shows to benefit the local food bank. You can't argue with that, but turning over everything meant less money for future productions. I envisioned the Players lasting for as long as there were inmates at King's Reach. Longer than my time there, that is.

I told the Players to wander around and get a sense of the place. To look out the windows so they wouldn't when the show was underway. Some of them, like Hassan and Patrice, the arsonist playing Ariel, got together to rehearse scenes. A director couldn't ask for more. "Use your big voice," I told them. "Remember: from your centre of gravity."

The room was longer than the screening room, though not much wider. Which meant we wouldn't have to re-block our scenes. Voices carried better, like in a real theatre, taking me back to my Ryerson days. I got that rush of being onstage, which acting on screen can never provide. The Jill I knew in those long-ago days, the one I'd been struggling to remember without prejudice, would have been happy for me.

I pointed out the exposed beams in the vaulted ceiling to Carr. "We can hang lights from there. And there. Some key lights, plus a couple downstage."

The warden thumbed his phone. "How can we pay for lights if we have to rent chairs? Can you email somebody? It's a fundraiser for God's sake. The costs should be shared."

If rehabilitating men didn't work out, he could become a television producer.

At the far end of the room, behind what would be our stage, a door opened into a kitchen area. Karen was showing it to Gabriel, the meaty former bricklayer originally from Portugal I'd insisted on for Caliban.

"Mr. Drake," Karen said. "I was telling your friends that the drama club uses this as their green room."

"Then I'm sure it'll work great as one for us. Since we don't have a curtain."

"I'm making one for the screening room," Gabriel said. "There's a bunch of bed sheets in the prison laundry we can stitch together. We can make something for here, too."

At the back of the kitchen was a door and a window overlooking a sodden backyard and the dripping trees of a small park. The deadbolt securing the door easily slid open. I swung the door wide, filling the kitchen with the cool aroma of pine trees.

"Making a break for it?" Karen said.

"Are you kidding? Prison's the only place that'll let me direct."

I had questions for her about whom to contact in the drama club to borrow some lights, a selection of gels, and possibly someone to run them. I also wanted to know the watt load allowed on the house circuits, and if there were any spare extension cords in the building.

In the main room, the company was chattering like grade-schoolers on a day trip. Even the warden looked pleased. Our presence here was proof that convicted criminals were undergoing a successful transformation.

Karen offered to make some phone calls on my behalf.

"That's kind of you. I can't always get to a phone."

"How do you stay in touch with all your fans?" she said, teasingly.

Warden Carr started waving his arms in the air. "That's it," he shouted. "You've seen it. Everybody back on the bus."

So much for the rehearsal time he'd promised us. The Players dutifully filed out. "Dad's calling," I said to Karen. "Thanks for your help. Think you'll make it to one of the shows?"

"I'll be here for them all. The whole town's coming. This is bigger than Christmas."

After everyone had left, I lingered alone in the classroom, thinking here's my chance. No one would notice me gone until the nightly head count. By which point, I could be in Vancouver.

But I'd miss the great shows and our camaraderie. Most of the guys are luckless, lower-class fuck-ups who turned to crime when everything else was refused them. People like my father, I mean, and the losers he hung around with when I was a kid. Thanks to the Players, we'd each found something to like about ourselves.

There were miles to go yet. I was feeling lost and out of sorts because of all the work still to do. On our bumbling finale, on my misguided Prospero, and on the assignment I owed to Dr. K. I wasn't sleeping and had no appetite, just like down in Mexico all over again.

I took Jill's postcard from my pocket. In the few days since it arrived, my anger had subsided into a confused disappointment. Today I was obsessing over a phrase she'd written: "never my intention." I didn't need Dr. K to tell me that in a healthy relationship you shouldn't have to clarify to your partner that you hadn't planned to deceive them.

I was also stuck on a memory of her laughing as we exited the breakfast café on the morning of our day together in Veracruz. At what, I can't remember. Hopefully something I'd said. I'd have stayed in that moment forever, so it was hard to accept that even as talented an actor as Jill had faked that much sincerity.

How much of what she'd said and done was genuine? I couldn't believe she'd betrayed me, yet here I was at King's Reach, still willfully oblivious to the gullibility that put me here. And what of our theatre? I remembered her sulking for a day when I rejected her possible names for it. Was that all contrived too?

Even her postcard was a letdown. I'd gone from thinking I'd never hear from her again to wishing I hadn't. So much for my dreams of her visiting me in prison or being there to greet me when I'm released. Now all I could think about was how awful we'd been to people down south. I never figured hearing from her would leave me feeling as hopeless as when I first entered the Kent.

The sun had appeared in time to sink behind the mountains, painting the room a dusky gold. And trapping me: I hadn't seen a sunset in eighteen months.

Despite this, the solitude I so often craved, and got so little of down south and in prison, was unnerving. I got spooked when I was alone for too long, and missed the reassuring clamour of my fellow inmates. With the schoolhouse so empty and quiet, I was anxious to get, well … home, among my own kind of people.

So there was nowhere to go except back on the bus, to the life I had made for myself.

Cynthia was late to rehearsal the next day. The company was so used to her tardiness, they broke into smaller groups to run specific scenes until she deigned to appear. This she did an hour later with two attendants that I quickly chased away. They weren't permitted backstage and certainly wouldn't be at the schoolhouse. She'd better get used to doing without them.

A full dress rehearsal had been imminent until someone pointed out that Bobcat was missing. The impatience in the room became a muttered anger. "Anyone see him today?" I said.

"He was in the gym this morning," said Hassan. "Him and Dutchie."

Dutchie was another Warlord biker and a *compadre* in Bobcat's chronic drug ingestion. The other Players clustered around me, awaiting the decision I'd been postponing for a month.

"Steve Riggs, come on down," I called to one of our two understudies. A stocky, balding guy in his forties leapt from a car seat. "You're our new Gonzalo. Bobcat's out of the company. I'm sure you all know why."

"'Bout fucking time," Cynthia said. "He was dragging us down."

I held up a finger to her. "I've got one understudy left, and he can play Miranda. Everyone is replaceable. Me especially, after the bikers get done with me."

"We won't let them fuck with you," Hassan said.

Bobcat turned up at the interval. He was furious with me for starting without him, his bloodshot eyes pinpricks of spite. I walked him into the hallway, where I explained the company had decided his dedication to the production was lacking.

"Bullshit," Bobcat spat. "It's you, you actor faggot. You always had it in for me."

"If you mean I don't want you spoiling my show, you're right."

My words were wasted on his retreating form. "Better watch it," Bobcat spun and warned. "Me and the boys will be coming for you."

Back in the auto shop, Patrice and Gabriel were quarrelling over Patrice's emphasis on some of Ariel's lines. Somehow an arsonist and an alcoholic bricklayer had become experts in the pronunciation of Elizabethan English. They eyed each other warily, weighing whether their beef was worth blows. Every day, I'm reminded that I'm staging Shakespeare in what's essentially a boys' gym class. "No fighting," I said. "There's no fighting allowed in here."

A few guys stepped between them. That never happens in prison, where breaking up a fight puts you at risk of punishment. It was a testament to our fellowship. I couldn't help thinking that were it not for the Players, a few of these fellows would have been at each other's throats months ago. I could teach the warden a few things

187

about rehabilitation.

Cynthia alone exhorted them to fight and wasn't choosy who won. "Kick his fat ass, Patrice," she called. To Gabriel she said, "Don't take that from no goddamn Frenchie."

"Whose side are you on?" asked Tyler.

Cynthia giggled. "Tyler baby, I keep telling you, I'm all yours."

The tension dissipated in the ensuing laughter. I sent Gabriel and Patrice to sort it out in a corner. For me to get involved meant favouring one actor's reading over another's.

Thirty-nine delightful minutes later, I was satisfied with the running time of the second half. I finished the day's notes then dodged outside through the pouring rain to the carpentry shop. With great reluctance, the warden had paid for lumber to build a small stage. It needed to be ready for tomorrow's rehearsal in the screening room.

Gabriel and Tyler were at work within. The boards were cut, the risers half assembled. A gallon can of black paint sat on the workbench. Too bad: I'd hoped they needed help. I was dawdling, seeking distractions, and delaying the inevitable. At what cost had I removed the warden's spy from the company? The answer wouldn't be long in coming.

An afternoon hush lay over the main building. Napping inmates dreamed of the same dinner they received every second Thursday of the month. Stepping gingerly, I peered down corridors before entering them. My precautions were pointless. When it came, I wouldn't know what hit me.

In our room, Dragan lay stretched out on his bed, a small sheet of pink paper on his chest. So far that day, he hadn't pestered me to smuggle anything into the prison for him. "Your lawyer called," he said, handing an old-fashioned phone memo to me.

Robert McKeon, it read, along with a Vancouver number. So far as I could recall, it was the first time my lawyer had called me since my sentencing.

"Good news, I trust," Dragan said.

Until now, the only thing I liked about prison was the fact that I no longer continually expected, as I had down south with Jill, to be arrested at any moment. McKeon's message officially brought that worry back to me. In fact, my situation was worse because here in prison, there was nowhere to run and hide from the trouble heading my way.

There was mail, too. Four stern brown envelopes left in a neat pile by Steyne at the end of my bed. Doubtless there was a dreadful connection between them and my lawyer's call.

One letter was from a US lawyer. Two others were from Toronto lawyers, and the fourth, as I turned it over, bore a Mexican postage stamp and was addressed to me in Jill's lovely, jittery scrawl. I noted that the seal was half open and torn, as if some nine-year-old girls dying to know what was inside had clumsily steamed it open.

The envelope was made of fine Japanese paper. I smiled to think she must be doing all right if she can afford good stationery, and then tore it open. Instead of a hello or information on her whereabouts, all the envelope contained were browning pages torn from a paperback copy of *Mother Courage and Her Children*. From Scene Eleven, specifically, the second last of the play, in which mute Kattrin climbs atop a farmhouse with a drum to warn the residents of a slumbering town of an impending attack.

"Danny, hello?" Dragan said. "You're very popular. Is that about your appeal?"

If the pages were a warning, against what? I hadn't been able to promote *Charlie Brown* without mentioning myself, and interest in the Players had spiraled out over the web. And now the schoolhouse shows of *The Tempest* were sure to draw media attention. A publicist's dream, surely, yet potentially dangerous for me. Could my resurgent fame be my undoing?

I also considered that Kattrin is shot dead on the roof by angry soldiers. Was Jill letting me know about a danger she faced? That wasn't likely, considering my incarceration and inability to help. Nor was she the type to ask for help.

I still couldn't understand why she was contacting me after so long. The first answer to mind was that she hadn't been able to earlier, and there were probably good reasons why she wasn't telling me more about herself.

"No, no appeal," I said to Dragan. "Sorry. A letter from an old girlfriend."

I tossed the telephone memo into a wastebasket and went digging in my locker for my notebook.

Down in the resource centre the elephant that follows me everywhere settled into the desk beside mine. This elephant is an attractive woman of average size and shape in her early thirties with a delicious mess of dyed blond hair mounded atop her head. Despite the damp wintry chill in the room, she was as warm and sunny as she'd been on that sweetly distracting day in Veracruz.

No, wait. Not the blond hair. The honey auburn colour from our student days.

Listen to your gut, Dr. K had said. Which I couldn't feel with my pounding heart telling me I'd been too hard on Jill in what I'd written about our last days together. That I'd gone from protecting myself from the truth about her to portraying her as overly manipulative and bitchy. Or was that the truth?

Dr. K's deadline had motivated me to work ever harder but progress was still laboured. It wasn't simply that the writing was dangerous, that I'd revealed enough to put myself away for a long time. That postcard had left me even more confused over how to interpret what had happened in Mexico. Every event and conversation had to be carefully weighed.

I should have noticed, at least by Mexico City, that she wasn't telling me everything and had probably led us to Veracruz deliberately. There were so many questions I could have asked instead of dumbly watching her and Nick play Scrabble or running out for dinner. I'd been lulled by that restorative day together when I should have been sharper.

Contradictions abounded. What about the bag of coffee she bought in the zócalo because she liked it so much? As if we had room for souvenirs in our overstuffed bags. As if we had a home where we could serve it to our friends at brunch. A year and a half later, that bag of coffee caused me much distress while writing. Eventually, it became proof that she fully intended for us to be together after Veracruz. Why else would she buy coffee for us?

Which of course flies against everything I've believed since landing in jail.

I leaned Jill's card and the paperback pages against the computer monitor before me. To my mind, they emitted a summery odour of coconut sunblock and rum that flowed into every corner of King's Reach, muting the gamey man-reek. Soon powdery beach sand was pouring over my desk and across the floor of the resource centre. Beyond the windows, pine trees transformed into royal palms, and the muddy ground sprouted flowerbeds. The sun came out, and the sea moved closer and became warmer. Kids played in the surf, and adults relaxed beneath striped umbrellas.

From there, it was an easy step to any of the hundreds of hotel rooms Jill and I had shared, and to Jill in the bath smelling of guava shampoo and lavender. Or a dripping Jill, wrapped in a towel, showing me possibilities for an outfit for the evening. This dress or these pants and this top? And me peering around her at the television, chaffing because I didn't want to have dinner with some boring oil executives from Alberta.

And so goes another installment in my foolish dream of a reunion with Jill Charles. Happy endings that will never happen. What else have I got to look forward to in here?

And let's not forget all those letters under my bed. Feeling especially doomed, I closed the notebook to better enjoy my fantasy and gave up any hope of meeting Dr. K's deadline.

Other work remained. Having finalized the cast list with Bobcat's expulsion, I turned to the playbill for *The Tempest*. Deleting Bobcat's name was easy. Less easy, for a guy who could barely two-finger type, was incorporating logos from our community sponsors and getting the text to line up beside them. I'd have to ask Edith Orson for help.

Next I turned to the book of spells—called a *grimoire*—that Prospero uses to control the elements. His cloak I had from Margot, and his magic staff Gabriel was making. Yet despite hours of research, I couldn't fathom the alchemy, numerology, Hebrew, and occult philosophy required for Elizabethan magic. It must have been simpler in olden times.

The resource centre was deserted by this point, the space filled with the sick light and drone of the overhead fluorescents. Night again. Somehow it's always dark out here on the gloomy West Coast. There's rarely any twilight, just shades of grey.

The grimoire was a craft project, involving cardboard, construction paper, sparkly star stickers, scissors, and white glue. I'd just entered a groove with it when Gabriel eased his powerful bulk up to my table. "Party's starting, boss," he said. "Figured you'd want to go."

"I do. Thanks. I'll be along in a minute."

"Sure. You can't work all the time, eh?"

He was right. It made sense to enjoy myself while I could. I grabbed my notebook and my copy of the script.

By the time I reached the dining room, half the prison population had assembled to say farewell to the mailman, Steyne. The kitchen staff had made a cake and fruit punch. Steyne never spoke about himself, but according to Edith Orson, he'd been in prison for much of his adult life. That might explain his obvious trepidation at leaving this comfortably limiting world behind. After yesterday's unsettling solitude at the schoolhouse, I could appreciate his fear.

Dragan had a bottle of brown liquor and was spiking glasses of punch for two dollars apiece. I bought one for Steyne, who regarded the crowd skeptically. With no Warlords in attendance—there is no profit in sad old men—I let myself relax and was speaking to Edith about finding a camera to record the shows when a guard told me the warden wanted to speak to me in the kitchen.

The great man was making himself a sandwich on one of the large stainless-steel tables. "Who said you could kick someone out of the show?" he said. "And why can't you remember you're an inmate like all the others?"

I'd been expecting a barrage like this. "You'd rather he flub his lines on stage? Or nod off? Or maybe start a fight with someone?"

"Hold on, Danny. I care less about Bobcat than you think. It's your attitude I don't like. This is the thanks I get for being so lenient with you?"

"The new guy is way better. You may not like how I operate, but you're going to love what you see on stage."

The warden disappeared into a walk-in refrigerator, emerging after a moment with a big jar of mustard. "I'm sure I will. But you're not listening. You've got bigger problems. Why don't you open that file there."

A beige file folder sat atop a table beside the warden's sandwich fixings. I flipped it open to reveal photocopied pages of the notebook I held in my other hand. My assignment. For an instant, before fear and shame rushed in, I was genuinely confused. Everybody knows personal writing is hands-off.

"Pretty stupid of you to write it all down, don't you think? Now I know everything."

"I made it up," I stammered. "For the shrink. So I wouldn't have to talk about myself. That's what everyone said I should do."

The warden contemplated his sandwich while he chewed. "It's like you're confessing to all the gossip I've heard about you. People are going to want their money back. Not that they'd get it, because if I give this to the police, you'll be going down for a very long time."

For a moment, my regret was greater than my fear. It was the warden's idea that I visit Dr. K in the first place. Now the doc's process, to which I honestly submitted myself, had confounded my situation. I should have changed all the names and locations. I stood pursing my lips, sweat forming in my palms. "There's nothing to prove."

"You sure? Sounds pretty convincing to me. And the girlfriend. Wow. Little hottie I bet, huh? Betcha miss her."

A welling sympathy for Jill—wherever she was—threatened to undo all of the work I'd done in her absence. I hated that she could still do this to me. "You'll never find her."

"No? You'd be surprised by the traces people leave nowadays. Nobody disappears anymore. And is that her real name you're using in there?"

"So what do you want?"

"Nothing, for now. That's what you don't understand. You're nothing in here."

I picked up the photocopied pages and read from the opening. As I've said, I was happy with the work I'd done with the first few days at Paraiso. It was only after the Vandals turned up that everything became confusing.

"I'll take that for safekeeping, thank you," Carr said. "If you feel like crossing me again, remember what I can do to you. Oh, and I still want that walk-on. For the opening night."

Day 10

Veracruz

PEARLY PINK SMEAR TO THE EAST. LOW clouds glowing a pretty Easter mauve. In those last crowded days down south, I definitely preferred a sunrise to a sunset because it offered the best chance of some solitude. The gulf waters were a sheet of black glass and unreasonably cold. My last swim in the ocean was brief. Within minutes, I'd wrapped myself up in a towel to watch for the sharks Nick had mentioned. To my mind, there was a greater risk of encountering them on shore.

Casa Soho slumbered on while I made coffee and noisily cleared the dinner plates from the night before. That roused a haggard Jill, who complained she'd slept poorly again. I poured a coffee into her, then nudged her into the shower with a reminder of how long I'd wanted to see the ruins of El Tajín.

Nick emerged with awful news: Brenda was joining our excursion. Her search for an appropriately devout ensemble lasted two agonizing hours. I doubted the spirits of the ancient people of El Tajín, gone from this world eight centuries, would appreciate the fuchsia mini-skirt and torn Green Day t-shirt she eventually chose to wear.

During this interval, I endured Nick in his pajamas strumming the same few chords on a guitar until I could scream. It was eleven o'clock, the coolest portion of the day ending, when we trooped outside to find he'd raised the hood of the Rover. The unidentified problem cost us another half hour of him poking at the engine and muttering to himself.

So no surprise when, twenty minutes down the road, a sharply whispered argument began in the front seats. "It's three hours there," Nick said. "That's too far without air conditioning."

"But you said you would," Brenda said.

I knew what was happening. "Tell me I'm not hearing this," I said.

Nick looked into the backseat. "It's the holiday traffic, mate. Too many locals getting drunk and driving. Tell you what. There's some other ruins just as good that are closer."

"You knew it would be busy when you agreed to drive us." This prompted Jill to tap my thigh, warning me to back off. Nick was offering up the ruins of a less ancient town. It was stupid of me to believe he'd keep his word. "Do you mean Zempoala?" I said.

"That's it. Be there in half an hour. It's too fucking hot, Stevie, and we don't want to tire ourselves out for the casino tonight."

"What casino?" Jill said.

"The one on the cruise ship that docked yesterday. You probably saw it. They've all got them now, the big liners. Did you bring your ball gown, Ginny?"

"The last time we went, you lost 10,000 pesos," Brenda wailed.

Steve Sawyer took one for the team again. A pillar of patience and obedience, he opened the guidebook in his lap and cleared his throat. It was time for a history lesson.

The ruins at Zempoala were less grand but more historically significant than those at El Tajín, and perhaps more thematically resonant for our foursome. It was at Zempoala that the newly arrived Cortés forged an alliance with a band of natives—arranged with the help of his lover and translator, the beautiful La Malinche—that led to one of the greatest sellouts in history.

Five hundred years ago, the Totonacs of Zempoala were made subjects of the Aztec empire centred on what is now Mexico City. Enter Cortés & Co., stage left, looking for allies in the region to challenge the Aztec supremacy. For their part, the Totonacs saw in the Spaniards a chance to rebel against their native overlords and regain their independence.

It was from Zempoala that Cortés launched his epic campaign against the Aztecs. Without the Totonacs' assistance, it's unlikely the Spaniards would have defeated the Aztecs. The entire history of the Americas might be different were it not for the Totonacs' famous betrayal of their Aztec cousins, thanks in part to La Malinche's treachery.

Only Jill acknowledged my reading. I pretended it annoyed Nick, but I doubt he heard it over the roaring open windows and the Ramones blasting from his iPod.

The road was a straight swathe hacked from jungle and grassy scrub. Nick had lied about the traffic, too. It wasn't busy at all. A hot wind wagged the palms at the edge of the forest. We were deep in the Real Mexico now, and that had me on edge.

We left the highway, heading inland. Minutes later, a poor town began straggling along the road: sun-blanched billboards, the cinderblock skeletons of unfinished buildings, and skinny dogs barking from the shade. A sign welcoming us to Zempoala and the *Zona Arqueológica* turned us down a leafy street. The ruins were on the edge of town and surrounded by a fence. There was only one other car in the parking lot. "Maybe it's closed," Nick said optimistically.

Admission was a hundred pesos each, paid for by Jill. A young man in a khaki uniform offered brochures in English. Only I took one.

What little interest in the ruins I'd generated evaporated upon encountering a low, circular wall of grey igneous stones poking up from the grass. There were other piles of the same rock scattered across a sun-scorched field. Even I was disappointed, and I'd suspected it would be lame. A green wall of forest stood on three sides, ready to reclaim the land.

Peacocks wandered at will, as they might have centuries ago, the drooping plumage of the males leaving broom-like trails in the dust. Brenda chased after one then left off to flop in some shade with a sketchbook. It was so hot my lungs ached when I breathed. Nothing about the site conveyed the energy and drama of the events that occurred here. I couldn't picture Cortés & Co. destroying the pagan idols or marching out to war with their cannons and armour. There was just grass, rocks, and dust.

In staggering between the ruins, I sensed again the mysterious gravity between Jill and Nick. It wasn't a sexual heat, but a silent language they shared, like they were siblings. I hated it and knew I was missing something. A subtext or a big plot point. We were all in the same movie, but each of us had different drafts of the script.

Nick and I stood squinting at Jill as she scrambled atop the stubby pyramid. At least there was no mistaking how little he liked me. "So when's that audition you mentioned?" I said.

Nick's sneer said I should know better. "Why not get your agent to send in your reel?"

As he turned away, the glaring sunlight on his sweaty face showed a raised red welt over his left cheekbone. Was it Brenda who'd smacked him? If so, good for her.

Jill caught the end of this exchange and frowned. I told her what I'd asked Nick.

"Oh honey," she said. "There is no movie. But Nick thinks you think there is one."

"What? Help me with this."

She was serenely composed beneath her wide-brimmed straw hat, a happy lizard in the heat again. "It'll take too long to explain. Just don't push him too much, 'cause he's cranky. But keep doing what you're doing. I hope you're not too let down."

I couldn't deny that I was. So long from a television camera, the chance of fame rang in my ears louder than the alarms blaring over Jill's handling of the Vandals.

The Totonacs, were there any still around, would tell you that greed and pride were also their undoing. Scant years after welcoming the barbarian Spaniards and selling out the Aztecs in the process, war, starvation, and European diseases like smallpox had decimated their population. Zempoala was abandoned and swallowed by the jungle. The only winners were the Spaniards, who in confronting the many warring peoples in Mexico, had effectively employed Jill's favoured divide-and-conquer tactic.

Despite my misgivings, there in that burning field, I was struck by Jill's brazenness and the extent of her control. She had a dozen flaming balls in the air, like some kind of ultimate improv. It was thrilling, all the moreso because I knew it was being done with our future in mind.

Back to work. In the gift shop, Steve Sawyer mused aloud about buying a poster of a Totonac warrior in full regalia for the kids back home. Peacock feathers, powerful totems for native Mexicans, were on sale for twenty pesos each. One lay trampled on the floor. Nick picked it up, brushed some dirt from it, and presented it to Jill.

"Thanks," she said. "But shouldn't we pay for it first?"

"Why? They don't think enough of it to keep it off the ground."

"*Señor, son veinte pesos,*" the woman behind the counter said. Like most of the people we'd seen in modern Zempoala, she had strong native features.

Nick treated the woman to a sarcastic wave then led Jill from the shop. I paid for the feather, stunned by the ignorance I was enduring for the sake of these clowns.

Outside, Nick and Jill had reached the Rover, Brenda trailing. "What was that all about?" I called across the parking lot to him. "You just take what you want from these people?"

"Piss off out of it," Nick said. "There's a good man."

Nick started the Rover and reconnected the iPod. I paused to recall that he was merely a means to an end before climbing into the backseat beside Jill. Her hand on my thigh conveyed her thanks for having turned the other cheek. Essentially, she'd asked me to let her run the Vandals on her own, and I'd assented. My only job was to be patient.

We stopped for lunch at a taco stand, the four of us crammed at a picnic table in the brutal sun. Brenda paid with the same NatWest Visa she'd used at the grocery store. I burned the last few numbers I required and her pin number into my brain.

Pork fried with onion and dressed with cilantro and green salsa in fresh tortillas. A cold beer to wash it down. I was feeling much better and was soon eyeing the tacos Nick hadn't touched. He looked parboiled in the unrelenting heat. He was nearly an old man and didn't take care of himself. The women fussed over him, insisting he eat. I loaned Brenda my floppy hat so she could fan him. I did not say: maybe you shouldn't smack him around so much.

"How about I drive back, eh Nick?" I didn't need him suffering heat stroke or a heart attack behind the wheel. "You can have a rest."

He set the keys to the Rover on the table beside my plate.

All three of my passengers nodded off before we reached the main road. Fine by me. I leaned forward in my seat to let the hot rushing wind dry my shirt.

The temperature in Casa Soho wasn't unbearable thanks to the ceiling fans Brenda had left whirling. Jill and I retreated to our room for a badly needed siesta. I snuggled up to her, my hand tracing her splendidly naked body before resting between her breasts. Her cleverness had me quite worked up. If I'd wanted her before, in the ordinary way of a busy couple who aren't making enough time for

198

themselves, now I was mad for her.

"Don't." She slunk away from me. "It's too hot, and you kept me up again last night."

Our host woke us an hour or so later with some awful eighties synth-pop. He had a jug of margaritas prepared and was already much revived for it. I joined him in one, unexpectedly excited about the evening ahead and willing, with so much at stake, to forget our earlier spat.

Jill showered first, then started her make-up. When I emerged from my shower, Nick stood partway in our room speaking to her. With Jill still in a towel, wet hair stuck to her neck.

Seeing me, Nick excused himself. I closed the door behind him. "What did he want?"

"Just talking about the casino. Brenda's not much fun to go out with." She clicked her tongue at a wrinkled dress she'd unpacked from the bag I'd discovered the wad of pesos in. "Now, what have you got left to wear?"

The chinos I'd earlier hung up would do, though my good lavender shirt was again crumpled. While Jill flattened the creases with a spritz bottle, I dug out a dark wrap dress that I liked her in and showed it to her. "This one, please," I said.

A happy Jill accepted the dress in exchange for the shirt and then waved me away.

Nick inspected me in the living room. "Not bad, but you're going to need a jacket. I forgot to mention that. Wait here a sec." He returned with a sharply cut vintage tuxedo jacket, the frayed lapels a rich plum velvet. "From when I was a younger man. I'm too fat for it now."

It fit pretty well and no doubt had wild stories of marathon concerts, partying in LA, and adoring groupies. I was honoured to wear it for a night.

After another drink, Nick disappeared into his office, emerging with a bag of cocaine. About twenty ounces, I'd say, recalling my television days. I wasn't surprised by it at all.

"I trust you're okay with recreational drug use." Grinning wickedly, he carved lines with a Banamex Visa card I'd waited a week to see. "We keep a bit around for entertaining."

He was lying again. No one has that much cocaine lying around just for guests. I wasn't okay with it, but I was more interested in Nick's card, filing away the number on it as well. Extraneous, isolated bits of information were sliding into place. I didn't like the pattern that was emerging.

Jill arrived to refresh her drink. How was it possible, when I'd last seen her tired and distressed by her dirty clothing, that she now appeared so stunningly put together? She flinched at the sight of the cocaine. Her cat was coming out of the bag, too.

"Ah, Regina, don't you look beautiful." Nick handed her a tightly rolled 500-peso bill. "I was going to send your young man after you."

Jill and I had a moment there. The no drugs rule was likely the last we hadn't broken. We'd wandered far off the map. I don't know if she wanted permission, or understanding, but I gave it to her. She held her hair with one hand, and with the other hoovered up a line. Then she offered the rolled bill to Nick, who indicated it should be passed to me. I hesitated.

"C'mon," Nick said. "If you want to be a movie star, act like one."

Jill brought me to it. Her eyes said we needed to do this. But her eyes did not say all would be well for following her direction. They never did, actually.

And so I snorted cocaine for the first time in many years.

Everyone immediately became shiny and witty. I forgot how worn out and scared I was. Cocaine is a fantastic drug. As soon as you've done some, you regret not having done it sooner. Cocaine says: I'm a fantastic drug, have some more. So I did, and quickly I thought I was the most fantastic guy in Mexico.

Of course, I knew it was a veneer. My anxiety would return, exponentially so, in the creepy insomniac hours before dawn, when I'd regret every molecule I crammed up my nose. Until then, I couldn't think of any reason not to have a great time. The party guy role, the one that distracted limes while Jill worked the room, was as comfortable as ever.

Nick and I became the best of friends. I loved his jokes, and I loved his music. We heard remixes of the same poppy punk tracks and stories of him partying with other rock stars, probably in the jacket I was wearing. We drank more margaritas. Brenda wandered in, this time fully clothed beneath her painter's apron. She poured herself a drink, frowned at the cocaine, then left again.

"She'll come around," Nick said. "You'll see."

Brenda returned with a platter of guacamole and chips, English cream crackers, and unwrapped slices of American processed cheese.

Nobody touched it.

Nick suggested a restaurant for dinner, vividly describing their lobster platters and fish in a special "Veracruzano" sauce of chilies and chocolate. "That's what I'm having," I said. "Whenever we travel, I always try the local delicacies."

Jill nodded. "Yes he does," she said. "All the time."

I saw the living room as if for the first time and strummed the very guitars that had made Nick's music. Finally, I appreciated the depth of vision in Brenda's abstractions of Aztec warrior gods. How fantastic, I thought, to have met such fantastically talented people.

Jill beckoned me toward our bedroom. I'd have followed her anywhere.

In the washroom, she pawed through her make-up bag while I floated upon her aromas, now magically enhanced: lime and tequila, Camel cigarettes, cherry lip balm. I wanted to snort coke and smell her all day.

"You're doing a great job with Nick," she said. "I know it's not easy."

Never mind him. I was also less concerned about the money I'd seen in that bag. Drugs could be useful that way. "I've got two of their card numbers. When are you going to call your new contact?"

"Soon, Danny," she said distractedly. She stared at her image in the mirror. As I watched her, an unsettling desperation twisted her face, and she clenched her eyeliner pencil like a dagger. "It's going to be so good. He's going to pay so much."

"What?" I said. "You all right? I mean, considering."

She allowed herself a last once-over in the mirror before turning and marching out of the room. "Never better," she said.

We didn't make it to dinner. I don't recall why. Probably no one was hungry.

The cruise ship was visible from many streets away, its sleek, white rows of decks rising taller than nearby freight cranes and refinery towers. I scanned for its name: *Arcadian Epic*. Well, exactly.

Nick drove past a canopied gangway leading into the ship to park behind some ocean-going containers in a vast open space. He shook a small mound of coke from a vial onto the back of his hand and made it disappear. I leaned forward, practically salivating.

"Greedy, greedy," he said. "Ladies first."

Jill got the next bump, then it was Brenda's turn. Part of my enthusiasm for the night fizzled out at the prospect of contending with a coked-out Brenda. Finally Nick shook out a fourth bump and passed it back to me. My pessimism vanished instantly.

The *Arcadian Epic* resembled a floating resort. The guests were older, on average, but they likewise bumbled between pools, restaurants, and spas, dispersing their surplus cash. We passed a dance underway in a ballroom, retirees from Lethbridge and Poughkeepsie grooving to the Bee Gees. Jill was right about the credit cards we could have accessed.

Although I had only been in one other casino—to drag my father from it—I thought the one on the *Arcadian Epic* was small. A row of slot machines, another of gaming tables, and a few seniors shuffling beneath the ceiling fans. An empty bar. Bingo might have been more popular.

Jill's entrance attracted some admiring glances, and an Asian man in a burgundy jacket. "Champagne, little man, and four glasses," Nick said to him. "And not flutes, proper champagne cups. One bottle now, a second on ice."

Adrift for months on the good ship geriatric, the waiter welcomed his fervour.

Jill bought chips with money I wasn't officially aware we possessed and offered me 500 pesos' worth. I wasn't budging. The cocaine was bad enough.

"I get it," she said. "But if you change your mind, let me know."

Nick nudged me along the line of tables. He was the prince of punk again, circa 1981. "Be Sean Connery," he said, "in *Dr. No*. Walk like him. Feel everyone looking at you."

I tried to shake him off, but he squeezed my arm tighter, the reek of cocaine acrid on his breath. "Be a good man and play nice," he hissed. "She deserves it."

The "champagne" was a sweet sparkling Peruvian wine. I ordered a beer and leaned on the bar, enchanted by a radiant Jill enjoying herself and the seductive ping-ping-ping of the one-armed bandits. It was the perfect accompaniment to the chemical happiness bubbling within me. Nick and Jill settled at a blackjack table, from which Jill kept turning to confirm my presence. Nick was a bad joke that would end. In the icy certainty of a cocaine euphoria, I knew all would be well for us.

Brenda joined me in watching them. She seemed sober, or was at the point of inebriation where she could pass as such. "What a nice couple. Like the good old days, huh?"

I'd had enough. "Look, lady. Gina's not cheating on me. Not with your husband, not with anyone. So if that's your problem, you can stop being a bitch to my wife."

"You just don't get it, do you? Or maybe you don't want to."

No, I didn't. Nor did I care to talk to her. I stalked off. This would be over soon.

Although guests like ourselves were restricted to the casino and adjacent lounges, no one stopped me from wandering around on deck. The *Arcadian Epic* afforded a sweeping view of brilliant Veracruz stretching into the black nighttime. Closer in, I marked the zócalo by the Ferris wheel and the colourful shimmer of the carnival beneath it. The coke said that's where we needed to be, in the wild heat and press of the real party. I went to get the others.

The number of gamblers had doubled in my absence. I searched for Jill, growing concerned, until Nick grabbed my shoulder. "There you are. She's been asking after you."

Jill dominated a different table, shiny with happiness like the girl whose performances used to blow us away at Ryerson. As then, I could scarcely believe she'd chosen me. She beckoned me forward for a quick kiss. Before her on the table was a large pile of chips, some 3,000 pesos by my quick count. "Our luck is back," she said. "I got it back."

In her voice was the confident laughter I'd missed for a year. The zócalo could wait. "I'm glad one of us did," I said

A crowd of spectators ringed the table. They were retired janitors from Idaho pushing walkers, not monocled Russian counts in exile. Nonetheless, they'd come to admire Jill's winning ways. Elbowing aside an old woman in a teal track suit, I made more room for her to play. With every card the dealer turned over, she glanced slyly my way. A fox in a henhouse, she made it look easy. I could be forgiven for thinking we'd turned a corner.

Then the lights went out, plunging us into a complete blackness. In the shrill rush of excited voices, a frightened male voice near me yelled out, "Jill."

A male voice that did not belong to me, the only person in the world who knew the woman claiming to be Regina Boccia was actually named Jill Charles.

A male voice that sounded remarkably like the one belonging to Nick Vandal.

By *blackness*, I mean its official definition: an absence of light. I could not see my hand in front of my face.

Panic flashed through the crowd. A few people enabled the lights on their phones, illuminating only the flushed faces of seniors.

I called out for her—for Gina—my voice lost in the clamour of others crying out names in many languages. There was a rush to the exit, and I shrunk back to what I thought would be a wall. I never found it and instead kept walking backwards. I only stopped when I no longer sensed the motion of others. The borrowed jacket I wore exuded an oniony odour of stale perspiration—not mine—and fear. Nick's cry confirmed what I'd dreaded most, a truth so awful I'd refused to consider it. My heart knew otherwise, though.

When the lights came back on, I was alone by the bar. A waiter explained, in English, that the problem with the power had been corrected. Games underway when the lights went out would be started again rather than continued.

Jill was nearby, her chips collected in the skirt of her dress. That's my girl, I thought, before realizing I had no idea who that girl was at all. Nick was with her, standing guard. She turned a slow circle. Looking for me, presumably. Nick's eyes met mine in an instant of understanding. How curious that he wanted to protect her as much as I did.

With what I'd heard written on my face, I headed to the exit. I couldn't stand for her to learn that everything she'd ever said or done was now suspect.

I reached the deck I wished I'd never left. The sprawling city I contemplated had turned into a squalid, hostile place. Nick's slip of the tongue had brought the focus I required to make sense of the whole rotten affair. In as much as there was sense to make. I stormed around to the far side of the boat to stare at the moonlit waters of the gulf. Life preservers lined the railing. From this point on, I figured, it was everyone for themselves.

I heard Nick behind me before he spoke. "Don't jump, Stevie. Oh God, how would we ever get along without you?"

"My name's not Steve," I said.

He tucked a champagne bottle under his arm while he fussed with the vial containing the coke. "She's looking for you again. I told her you'd be crying somewhere."

"Why did you call out her name? How do you know it?"

Nick got the bump onto his hand and sucked it up his nose. Then he shook his head, his face contorting in pleasure and pain. "Say again?"

"You heard me. You know what I mean."

For an answer, I got a washed-up English rocker licking cocaine residue off the back of his hand. His indifference led me to doubt what I'd heard in the casino. In the hysteria, the word *Jill* might have sounded like anything else.

"Give me the keys to the Rover," I said. "You're too drunk to drive again."

"I've already given you more than you deserve." He dangled the car keys before me. When I took a menacing step closer, he punched out with the hand holding the bottle, landing a weak blow to my shoulder and sloshing champagne onto my neck.

In my years of television semi-stardom, I was saddled with a reputation for softness because I insisted on using stunt doubles for my fight scenes. To my mind, if someone wanted to save me the trouble of tumbling down a flight of stairs, and be paid well for it, they were welcome to it. I'd been fighting since I was six years old and didn't have anything left to prove.

Except I didn't always have that luxury. On low-budget shows like *Street Heat*, it had been up to me to toss rapists headfirst into holding-cell walls and trade punches with rampaging meth-heads. To avoid injury, I listened closely to the stunt people and learned their tricks.

Nick dangled the keys again. "You want to go home, little boy? This too hot for you?"

I responded with a classic thrown punch, the stuntman's bread and butter. My right hand sailed just under his nose then stopped. He was so astonished by his nose not erupting with pain and blood that he dropped the keys. I scooped them from the deck and left him there.

Downstairs, the power outage had sucked the gaming spirit from the room. A line had formed at the cashier. Jill looked relieved to see me again. I joined her as she cashed in her chips for nearly three hundred American dollars.

"Is this the new us?" I said. "Are we card sharks now?"

"No. What makes you think that? And where did you go? Nick saw you walking off."

"Nick, yeah." I showed Jill the keys. "He'll be here in a minute."

Her concern made me question what I'd heard again. "Are you all right?" she said. "You're acting kind of weird."

"Just fine."

"No more coke, okay? Yes, I know it was my idea, but see how everything worked out?"

Nick returned subdued, even vaguely contrite. And reeling drunk, the champagne having caught up to him. We unearthed Brenda delighting a table of old women in the ballroom with tales of life on the London stage. As if they recognized her.

The clock in the Rover said it was two in the morning. I'd forgotten how drugs made time disappear. The Vandals lolled about the backseat. Jill sat up front with me and took my free hand in hers when I wasn't shifting gears. She must have known I'd heard. I'd been right beside her. Not that you'd guess by her casual demeanour. I was furious. Yet since she'd asked me to suspend my judgment while she worked, I had to sit on this. Which was also smart of her.

True to form, Brenda had to be wrangled into the house. The thunderous dueling snores recommenced shortly after our return. Who sleeps with a headful of coke? Not me, that's certain.

Jill changed into a t-shirt and got into bed. I stood anxiously in the bedroom doorway, thinking I couldn't confront her because I wasn't certain about what I'd heard. I parked myself on the living room couch hoping my absence from bed might let Jill get some rest. An old spaghetti western on the Vandals' television did a poor job of quieting the anxious din in my head.

Be patient, I told myself. Have faith. That's what she'd asked of me, right?

Wanting to see if there was any word from Earl, I nosed into Nick's office. His laptop fired up all right, but required a password. The desk was strewn with screenplays and letters from lawyers and production companies. It all felt legitimate, and my snooping left me even more confused. How did he know Jill as Jill?

I flung open drawers and sifted through stationery supplies. I found the cocaine, a small brick-shaped bundle wrapped in plastic. There was enough that if Tom Walker were prosecuting, he'd conclude the Vandals had a sideline in distribution. While that might have alarmed me yesterday evening, on this new day, it barely got a second glance.

There wasn't any cash. The props people on my shows always supplied drug dealers with scads of ready cash. Had there been any on hand, I'd have stolen it, woken Jill, and ran.

In the bottom drawer were business chequebooks from banks in Mexico, London, and Zurich. (Switzerland, huh? Tom Walker would have called Interpol.) Beneath those were envelopes of photographs. Holiday snaps, mostly, and from years ago, judging by the negatives. I flipped through the first envelope at hand and was about to return it to the drawer when a photo of two young women caught my eye.

One of them was Jill.

My whole world went black. The photos, save for the one of Jill and her companion, spilled from my hand to the floor.

I knew that girl. I met her at Ryerson and fell hard for her on a university trip to Cancun. The Jill with the messy pile of auburn hair, the men's shirts, and the secretive smile.

She wore a lemony dress and stood by a table covered with beer bottles. The flash had caught her staring, red-eyed. It was dusk and there were palm trees behind her.

On the back, a male hand had written: *Gina & Paula. Isla Mujeres.* 2001.

I recalled the older men Jill hung around with in Cancun. Did she meet him then, or when she disappeared from school? Or was that another group of Nicks entirely? What mattered was that there was a photo of a younger Jill in the possession of a man who, so far as I'd been led to believe, she hadn't met until a week ago.

The poor thing, I thought. Trapped so young and still trapped today.

I flipped through the fallen photographs. There were no others of Jill, but there was one of the man I'd seen Jill with last year in the lobby of the El Presidente. Or was it him? I couldn't be certain, and by this point I was desperate for any kind of explanation.

I took a mental photograph of my own. There was a grainy quality to it, a grit-your-teeth edginess like the end of a coke bender. My photo saw everything at once: how things were and how they were going to be.

My compassion in no way lessened my anger. I started for the bedroom, to get answers, then reconsidered. That would have been the wrong approach, at the wrong time. Confronting Jill also might have woken the Vandals, who would in no way have contributed positively to the situation. I dropped the photos into the drawer, except for the one of Jill and the other girl. That I stuck in my jacket pocket.

What did she do with him? Or for him. Scam tourists? Prostitute herself? The dots had been there all along, but I'd chosen, even in our school days, not to fully connect them.

The blue glow of dawn was a presence I felt before it coloured the windows. The first birdsong commenced. Daniel Drake, champion insomniac, had crossed through another night.

There remained hours to kill—until what I didn't know. I went outside to the front porch and sat in a plastic garden chair. Thin clouds hung over the gulf, glowing faintly pink again. It was the same sunrise as yesterday, except everything was different now.

Day 11

Veracruz

THE GULF WATERS WERE CHOPPY THAT fourth morning in Veracruz. If I swam, I'd have to be mindful of the undertow. But getting my trunks would have woken Jill, and I couldn't see her.

I wound up on the scooter, the Dinamo, the key for which I found in Nick's suit jacket. Some distance might clear my head. I headed toward central Veracruz. It was Easter Sunday, and traffic was almost nonexistent.

At that hour, the deserted, garbage-strewn zócalo was half in shadow and reeking of spilled beer and trampled mango skins. A muggy thunderburst, not far off, would help with that.

Chairs stood atop tables on the restaurant terraces, waiters sweeping beneath them like they had every morning for centuries. Nick had left coins in the cache under the seat of the Dinamo. I thanked him for a coffee at the Hotel Colonial. Veracruz coffee is among the best in the world, and for a few delicious moments, I forgot about the photo in my pocket.

There were likely dozens of internet cafés in Veracruz. Equal parts familiarity and customer loyalty brought me back to the one by the bus station. I parked the Dinamo on the sidewalk out front, the better to keep an eye on it.

There was no new email from my father. I counted back four days since I last had word from him at the bus station in Mexico City. Soon no news would no longer be good news.

Warren wrote that his many auditions had finally paid off: he'd secured the lead in a big-budget American cable series shooting in Toronto, a political thriller with a sci-fi edge. I swallowed hard and read again. Of course I was overjoyed for him. I didn't know an actor or person who deserved it more. I just would have preferred hearing his news on a different day.

The series would shoot around the tour of his play, *Bumpercars*. I congratulated him, though I stopped short of writing that I was coming home. I really wanted to see that play and couldn't understand why I remained so stupidly loyal to Jill.

The answer of course involved the deeper drama underway within her. She may have wanted to squeeze the Vandals, but she also wanted revenge. As furious as I was, her courage made her all the more attractive to me. I just wished she'd chosen another time and a different means of confronting her old demons.

There was also another email from Kate Norwood. She and Judah both missed me, she wrote, and there were things that needed to be said. I scanned the rest. Phrases like "the way we were headed" and "our responsibilities" convinced me to log off. She definitely had a point. I could have handled that better. However, I presently had my hands full with another woman thrashing through a personal crisis.

Outside, the cloudburst I'd predicted was moving off, the street gleaming in the sunshine. Then my world went dark as a blow to the gut doubled me in half and a hood of some sort went over my head. I was thrust forward, my knees slamming against something hard.

A vehicle. Someone got behind me and forced me face first onto a carpeted floor. His boots followed, kicking me in the head when I raised it. The cop from Paraiso, maybe. Or a colleague of his. Consumed by Jill's schemes, I'd forgotten him.

Two feet pressed onto my back as first one arm and then the other was stretched behind me. Probably I was on the floor of the backseat. The plastic zip-tie, which I expected—bad guys on television always use them—was duly cinched around my wrists. A vehicle door opened and closed ahead of me. Two men, I deduced. One to manage the cargo, the other to drive.

A semi-familiar voice boomed above me: "*Llévanos al puerto.*"

The port area. That's not good, I thought. The glib lies I'd handed him in Mexico City would not work again. There was nothing to do except make sure he didn't find Jill, presuming he hadn't snatched her already. (Tom Walker might ask how far I'd go to protect a woman who didn't consider me worthy of the truth.)

The vehicle—an SUV, surely—rolled forward. Breathing was difficult with the cop's feet crushing my spine and me panicking. I took deep breaths, slowly adjusting my rhythm and turning my head to gasp through the bottom of the canvas bag. At least the vehicle had air-conditioning, the first I'd enjoyed since the bus that brought us to Veracruz.

We reached highway speed, staying there long enough for me to consider all the mistakes that had brought me to this point. And to endure the stench of stale breath, sweat, and fear in the canvas bag over my head. How many other poor souls had worn it in their last moments? It wasn't death I feared—not yet—but a kidnapping for ransom. All the drug cartels were into them now as side excursions into terror. So far as the cop knew, Jill and I were rich criminals whose families luxuriated in wealth in the distant north.

I pictured my father in his La-Z-Boy watching a Blue Jays game while the phone rings and rings in the kitchen. He finally answers at the seventh-inning stretch, hears the demands, then says he doesn't have the money. Nothing doing, the cop says. Give us the money or your boy is dead. Earl says call back after the game then never answers the phone again.

I wouldn't blame him. Regardless of his parenting skills, this was my own mess.

After about ten minutes, the vehicle decelerated and made some turns. At last it stopped. My breathing had settled, less so my coca-fried brain. The door at my feet opened, and I was hauled by my jacket collar into a putrid fog of salt, rotten fish, and diesel fumes.

The cop whipped the hood off. We stood beside a silver SUV midway down a wharf where men unloaded the morning's catch off commercial fishing boats. I blinked in the sudden brightness, my shaky hands pulling sunglasses off my forehead. A rational voice whispered: there are many people here. You're not going to die.

That might be true, I countered, if I were anywhere other than Mexico.

The second man cut the tie on my wrists with a large knife. "Come walk with me, Tom Walker," the cop said. "Do you like the fishing?"

He tugged me past the boats toward the end of the wharf, his henchman orbiting, pine tar gummy under our feet. In the rainbow-slick water below, a predatory creature tore at the fish heads and other scraps tossed from the boats, seagulls reeling and screaming overhead. I gagged at the fear in me, and the smell. I'd rather be shot than get dumped in that water.

Near the end of the wharf, the cop lifted my passport from my jacket pocket and tossed it into the water. So much for Philip Smith.

"Hey," I said, half-heartedly. We both knew there were more of those.

"Where is your wife? Regina Boccia. Or maybe she is Patty Harper?"

"I don't know. We split up."

That got me a blow to the right cheekbone from his henchman. Then two more to the gut that left me sucking wind. The few fishermen on the wharf began to leave their boats.

"Patty is Regina, your wife. Or whatever her name is today. I thought she might be your wife, but I wasn't sure until I saw the hotel videos. I used to know Patty from the old times."

That figured. Oh Jill. I couldn't see the point in stringing this along. "Look, I'm not going to tell you where she is."

The cop shrugged. It was all bullshit. "I know Patty. She's the boss. I must talk to her."

I threw up my hands. "Can't you just leave us alone? We're leaving Mexico. My dad is sick. You know that, right? We're going home because he's dying."

That earned me another blow to the head, this time from the cop. He held my face by the chin. "Tom Walker, I will hurt your face so you cannot work. You must know this."

That they didn't have Jill was great news. Unfortunately, she was now my only currency. In any movie I'd seen, that's a tough spot. I was also aware that neither of us would last long after they had her in their clutches.

"Does Patty ever talk about Raul from Condesa Beach? I will talk to her because we used to have an arrangement like I told you about. She knows how to do the business."

We'd reached a short wooden plank linking the last boat to the wharf. The cop started across it, leaving me on the wharf with his colleague. "If you don't want to take us to Patty for business, we will go out on this boat and talk about it there. Do you understand me?"

I did. Traditionally, Mexican drug lords and rogue cops employed a chainsaw to extract information from people. I wondered what the nautical version of that tool might be. Some kind of nasty pole with sharp hooks? I'd stepped out of myself by this point. I was already a ghost, watching events unfold as I hovered overhead.

"I will find her without you, okay? She will work for me again. Maybe you will, too. You must choose that." The cop stepped onto the boat. "Tom Walker, do not go on this boat. It will be no fun for us, but worst for you. Please let's go see Patty, okay?"

In answer, I started down the plank toward him. The cop was genuinely disappointed by this. His colleague followed, his sudden weight wobbling the plank beneath me. My arms went out to steady myself as I shuffled forward out of the other cop's reach. One last wobble, and off I dove, down into the filthy water, my legs already kicking.

So, technically, the previous morning's swim hadn't been my last dip in the ocean.

I swam under the boat and surfaced on its far side. But the cop had anticipated this and was waiting there, lunging at me. So I dove again to emerge beneath the pillars of the wharf, and then swam between them toward shore. The water wasn't as cold as I feared, but it tasted worse than it smelled, and it was filled with unspeakable detritus that I pushed out of my way.

Realizing the cop would be waiting by the shore, I turned back to sea. Near the end of the wharf, I treaded water beneath another boat. To the north was the menacing metal web of the Pemex oil refinery, and Veracruz. Where Jill slumbered, presumably oblivious to this latest development.

For the next ten minutes or so—the longest of my life—I bobbed between sea-slimy pillars and fishing boats, vigilant for any footsteps overhead.

From such a poor vantage point, there was only one way to determine whether my would-be killers still stalked me. I pushed off into open waters, heading south, away from Veracruz. I told myself that if I didn't look back, and so didn't see them, they weren't following me.

When I was growing up, Easter was only rarely observed in the various apartments my father rented. Earl never hid eggs for me to find, though occasionally, if he was flush with cash, there'd be scads of chocolate on Sunday morning. We'd eat it until he regretted his indulgence and banished me, rain or snow, to a soggy spring playground to burn off my sugar high.

During high school, while I was living with my grandmother, he would sometimes turn up unannounced for the Christmas or Easter dinner he knew she'd be cooking. He'd bring a case of root beer, a frozen banana cream pie, and gifts like country music records he thought I'd like. One year, I received two suits he'd received in lieu of a debt payment. Neither fit me.

We'd hear of his adventures with his musician pals and big wins at racetracks in the States, stories which accounted for maybe a week of his months-long absence. I was old enough to judge that all was not right with him. However much I lacked for his absence—there were times when having a dad may have been useful—there was nothing I could do about it. After dinner, he'd roar off in his ailing Duster, and me and Granny would have no word of him for a long time.

Those old days dogged me down the quiet streets of suburban Veracruz, where they took Easter very seriously. Scarcely a person or a car had passed, nor had I seen a bus moving in any direction. The sun beat down. I wished I'd brought my hat because you never know when you'll have to escape from a crooked cop in a Mexican city.

I'd waded ashore about half a mile south of the fishing wharf, all alone on a muddy beach. I still carried Nick's jacket, probably because it had that photograph in it.

Easter was also observed, I suspected, in Omaha, where my American friends would be enjoying a last day off before returning to their weekday routines. No doubt there'd be an egg hunt for the three Umberger boys, then church if Lori could coax Cal from the garage. Over at the Biddles', Shauna would be marshalling a cranky Evan to consider transforming the spare bedroom, presently filled with unused exercise equipment, into a nursery. Perhaps they'd stop at the paint and wallpaper superstore by the highway exit to the Umbergers', where they'd been invited to dinner. If there was time, maybe a preliminary trip to Baby Gap.

I'm sure they'd say I deserved the jam I found myself in. I thought I did. If it was any consolation, I believed that much worse was headed my way.

The cop had left me no choice but to confront Jill over that devastating photo. He was resourceful and would find me again. In the hours it took to plod back into central Veracruz, I determined

214

that I was leaving—leaving Veracruz, leaving Mexico. By week's end, I wanted to be waiting tables at a restaurant in Toronto or cutting lawns in my hometown again.

With Jill or without Jill, I meant. Much depended on what she had to say for herself. I'd let her know the danger she faced. Hopefully she'd see reason and come north with me. Despite everything the photo potentially represented, I overwhelmingly wanted her to choose to leave with me. Or she could stay and take her chances. I didn't owe her more than that.

In the short term, my priority was to avoid leading her friend Raul to Casa Soho. I figured all he knew was that I visited the internet café by the station, or else he would have snatched me sooner. His mistake was in not following me to Jill.

I also needed to destroy the remaining pieces of identification and passports. Daniel Drake, failed actor, would have to carry me from here. And there was the coke in Nick's desk to consider. For what he'd done to a young Jill—and how many other troubled girls, the fucking creep?—I would have loved to see him shackled in a Mexican jail. But the chance Jill might also get arrested was too great.

The Dinamo was still in front of the internet café. I watched it for as long as my post-coke paranoia dictated I should before sauntering into the bus station. If the cop was watching, let him think I was catching a bus.

I sat in the waiting area until I distinguished the kids who hung out in the station, thieving and begging, from the kids who were passing through. I asked a boy if he knew the internet café around the corner, and if he could wheel the scooter to the front of the station for me.

"*Veinte pesos*," he said.

"*Cinco.*"

"*Diez, y una vuelta.*"

Taking the kid for a ride wasn't a bad idea if it made me look less like the Tom Walker the cop might be following. "*Cinco, y una vuelta. ¿Qué me dices? Sí o no.*"

Once on the bike, I turned confusing circles of local streets, the kid on the back yelling with joy, until I was satisfied I wasn't being followed. I kicked the kid off near the zócalo and gave him the twenty pesos he wanted. Fellow thief—farewell.

It was late morning when I returned to Casa Soho. The Rover was gone from the driveway, the house silent within. Maybe the cop actually had beaten me there and hauled them all away.

Jill's note sat atop the luggage in our bedroom:

> **Gone for breakfast. Where are you? Stay here and don't go anywhere else. I'm worried.**
>
> Love, J

J she'd signed it. Not Jill, not Gina, but J, like she did when we were being ourselves. What did that mean?

I found the phony passports in a bag beneath some dirty tops and extracted the one belonging to Jill Charles. I'd never looked at her passport before—why would I?—and was suddenly terrified it would reveal even more lies. But she was born in Montreal on the day and in the year we celebrated as her birthday.

Exhaustion hammered into me. I was woozy, too, like I had sunstroke. Our bed was unmade and littered with her clothing. I plunged into it, totally overwhelmed—in the seconds I remained awake—by her comforting aromas.

Voices woke me. Jill's voice, particularly, in the friendly tone she used to control someone. That would be Nick, presumably, since she wasn't speaking to me. Was it possible she had actually been in control, or a willing accomplice, when I believed she was a victim? I didn't want to consider that.

The voices were in motion, in preparation for something. Then Jill was beside me on the bed, her cool hand in my sweaty hair. "Hey sleepyhead. I thought I'd miss you."

I curled onto her lap and handed up the photo of her and the other girl. "I remember that dress," I said. "You loved it so much you wore it in *Rocky Horror*."

Jill released a heavy sigh.

"This is where you need to come clean," I said. "And where I decide whether you're being honest or not. Everything's hanging on what you say next."

"Danny, I don't have time to explain. Nick and I are leaving now."

"To where?"

"Nick's not going to London. I am. Tonight. On an overnight."

I sat up and rubbed my eyes, as if that might bring everything into focus. "Because you're couriering drugs, right? Is that what you used to do for him? When you came down here?"

The distress in her eyes let me know I wouldn't like what I heard next. "Not back then. He used me to find things out about other men, like who their girlfriends were and where their money was. Then he'd take it. He'd get the dirt on them and make them pay."

My boiling blood abruptly turned cold. How she acquired that information, I didn't care to learn. "What about teaching English? Was that all a lie?"

She gazed at the photo, an internal battle clearly raging, before handing it back to me. "No. After I got away from him I taught for a while in Mexico City. But I couldn't make enough to live on. Not like I'd gotten used to. And I missed you, so when I heard you were struggling in Toronto, I thought we could do what I learned with Nick. Then we could be together."

"Without you being a call girl, you mean?" I didn't want to believe her, but who'd make that up? I was shouting now. "Or maybe you still are?"

"Honey, now's not the time for this." She got close enough to kiss me then gently put her hand over my mouth and whispered, "Listen carefully. I'm not meeting the person Nick expects me to. I'm going to take Nick's coke and sell it to someone else. This is how we're getting out, all right? This is our ticket to a new life."

I realized why we'd hung around the Pacific coast so long, and why Jill abruptly dropped the Americans when the Vandals turned up. "You set all this up, didn't you? Were you ever going to tell me any this?"

"No. Never. Not if I didn't have to. I hate myself for it. For all of this."

"So we're in the deepest shit of our lives because you were young and stupid?"

"If you want to look at it that way. But we're also going to make a lot of money."

"Why? Do you even want our theatre? Or any of the things we talked about?"

"Of course. Why do you think I'm doing this?"

She began filling one of her bags with clothing and toiletries. I liked things better when I didn't know what was going on. "You're crazy to make it personal," I said.

"I'm not coming back here. You have to leave, too. When Nick gets back tomorrow morning, he is going to be very pissed off with me. With us." She handed me a wad of bills considerably smaller than the one she'd offered a year ago in Acapulco after I screwed up with the Englishwoman. Her casino winnings. "Sorry. It's all we've got."

"What about that big stack of money you didn't hide very well?"

"That was a test run. In Mexico City. So Nick could trust me. And to buy me a stake."

"So that's why you left me in the park that afternoon?"

From outside came the long peal of a car horn. That would be Nick, in the Rover.

"Danny, I have to go," she said. "I made Nick stop here so I could see you. Or leave you a note. I'd have told you sooner, but I didn't want you to worry."

"No, you wouldn't. And you didn't want me to stop you. Hey, do you remember Raul from Condesa Beach? He says you were friends, but he wasn't very friendly to me."

It was Jill's turn to look horrified. "Does he know we're here? In this house?"

"In Veracruz, yes. In this house, I'm not sure."

"Stay away from him." She brightened a little. "So when were you going to tell me?"

"Never. If I didn't have to." I handed her the passport belonging to Jill Charles. "You'll be needing this. But is it really you?"

"Yes." She slipped it into her handbag.

"Where am I going to go?" I said.

"Go to your father's again. I'll find you there."

"Haven't we been here before? How do I know you're not lying?"

"You don't. But I found you last time, didn't I?"

Yes, she had. In fact, she wasn't asking any more of me than she had all along.

The horn sounded again.

"I have to go." She was pleading with me to let her. "Or we'll be late for the meet, and then none of this will happen."

"Let's just walk away," I said. "Or let me go instead. They cut people's heads off."

"It has to be me. The flight's in my name. There's no other way."

Her determination was greater than my own. Regardless of the many risks involved, there'd be no future of any sort for us if she didn't make an end to what had happened to her down here before I joined her. "Okay," I said. "How can I help?"

"Come say goodbye to Nick and me like I'll be coming back in a few days. And then pretend we'll be flying back to Buffalo, all right? Steve and Gina. Can you do that?"

"Yes. One last time. Then never again."

"No. Never again. I promise." She offered an unabashedly goofy smile. "It might be a week or maybe two before you hear from me. I'm sorry it's happening this way."

At the door, she wrapped her arms around me. I'd never felt such need from her. "One thing," she said. "There's a little photo album in one of my bags. I don't have time to find it. Can you get it and bring it with you?"

"Of course."

I followed her into the living room, where I was struck by a disquieting tranquility. Then I guessed why. "Wait. Where's Brenda? Is she going with you?"

"No. We dropped her off at some college."

Outside, Nick stood by the open driver's door of the Rover, texting into his phone. He never expected me to hop into the seat behind his. "Where's he think he's going?" he said to Jill.

I'd decided to put what Jill told me to the test. "Take me with you," I said. "I wanna go on a drug run too."

What I never expected was for Nick to grab me by the throat and throw me to the ground. Jill got between us instantly. That was smart. This time I would have hit him for real.

She held me at arm's length while she addressed Nick: "Touch him again, and you will fucking regret it."

Nick was winded from the exertion. "I don't want to see him again," he said.

"We'll leave tomorrow when I get back," Jill said. "Just like you agreed. If you're going to renege on our deal, maybe I'll change my mind about doing you this favour."

"No. You can't. Not now. Everything's arranged."

"Then you'd better remember your manners. Now get in the car."

Nick did as he was told. She had him, I saw. A victim no longer.

I walked her around to the passenger door and handed her up into the seat. She placed her bag on her lap, her hands trembling slightly. "Are you all right?" she said.

"Never mind me," I said. It was all happening too fast. "How are you?"

"I'll be fine." She kissed me quickly, and it wasn't hardly enough. Her steely gaze betrayed how much she loved the rush she was chasing. She pulled her door closed. "See you tomorrow, okay?"

"Tomorrow," I repeated. It didn't feel right in my mouth.

She waved from her window as the Rover rolled down the driveway. A cheerful resignation on her weary face, like she was glad her truth had finally been revealed.

Goodbye, my love.

I staggered back indoors, dizzy with disbelief. Yet hadn't I suspected for a week something of this magnitude was afoot?

Jill had left me roughly 2000 pesos, which wouldn't get me farther than Mexico City. I stormed into the living room. An iPod on the coffee table might be pawnable, but Nick's stereo equipment and his guitars were too bulky to transport.

I paused in the kitchen to drink some cold coffee. Roiling within me were all the questions I never got a chance to ask, and my fury at having been kept in the dark for so long.

Add to that my overwhelming shame over how ready I'd been to abandon her.

In the room we'd shared, I upended her bags onto the bed. Deep in an inner pocket of one was a photo album the size of a paperback novel, secured with elastic bands. Fearing more cataclysmic surprises, I opened it slowly. Soon I was breathing easier over baby pictures, a family shot with who must have been the younger brother she never mentioned, a kid's birthday party, and—I swooned—a school portrait of Jill age eleven or twelve in thick glasses and a ponytail. I'd seen a couple of the photos in our university days but hadn't known about this little album.

Probably there were other personal items she would want. But which dress did she love most? And which facial toner could she least live without? I decided everything that remained was replaceable. The lighter we were, the farther we'd travel.

I crammed the photo album, my shaving kit, and my hat into my knapsack. Anticipating a lot of waiting in my future, I grabbed the three-in-one volume of Shakespeare. Unlike Hamlet, I was getting on with the job. At the last second, I grabbed that bag of coffee so we could drink it in celebration next week and to make sure the Vandals didn't get it.

Despite the clammy night heat, I pulled on Nick's jacket. There might still be snow on the ground where I was headed. I re-found the extra passports in the tangle of clothing on the bed and filled my pockets with them.

Cocaine is currency, I told myself as I rushed into Nick's office and hauled open the drawers of his desk. But the small brick I'd seen earlier was gone, prompting an unexpected concern. If that was what Jill was couriering, it wouldn't bring us enough money to open a theatre and start a new life. A sudden fear that she was out of her depth, that Nick intended her harm, quickened my panic. And my helplessness. I needed to leave now with what I had. The Dinamo alone was enough to get me home. Or to some place where Warren could wire me funds.

I was contemplating the destruction I'd wreaked on Nick's desk when Brenda's voice spun me around. "What are you doing?" she said. Despite her predictable level of intoxication, her approach was regal. "Are you going somewhere? Take me with you."

"I'm just trying to get on the computer," I said. The wall protecting the frightened girl was collapsing. I didn't care to see what was on the far side of it.

"No, you're leaving. And I know why. You found out they knew each other before, didn't you? I thought they did, too. That's why Nick wanted to go to Acapulco."

"I don't know what you're talking about," I said.

"Yes, you do." She got uncomfortably close. "You're just like him. You and Gina. Or whatever your names are. Con artists."

"We're actors," I said. "You heard us talking about Nick's movie."

"I wouldn't count on that movie if I were you. The American investors are suing him over it. That's why Nick went to Miami."

"Miami?" It was like the cop hit me again. "No. Really?"

Someone was lying. Whether it was Nick to Brenda, or Brenda to me. Or maybe Jill had lied to me, possibly to protect me. Or herself. At least, I hoped that was why.

Brenda sobbed into her hands. "Nick can't go back to England because of it. Take me with you. I can't live like this anymore, but I don't know how to leave."

I thought of a question I would have asked Jill if it had come to me in time. "The people at the party in Acapulco. The Mexicans. Were they drug dealers?"

"Not all of them. Look, you've got to help me get away from here."

My wellspring of pity bubbled up for this second victim of Nick Vandal. I couldn't leave her with him. Then I surprised myself by showing Brenda the old photo of Jill.

Without her reading glasses, Brenda held it at a distance. "See. I tried to tell you at the party in Acapulco. You didn't want to listen."

No, likely I didn't. Who would? Then I made the last and easily the largest in an unfortunate series of mistakes by saying, "Let's go. If you're coming, we're leaving now."

"Let me get a few things." She hurried from the room. "I'll be right back."

I used her absence to visit the washroom. A deranged man stared back from the mirror. I splashed water on his face and freshened up with some deodorant. That would have to do.

Brenda waited by the front door, holding my knapsack and a large shoulder bag of her own. I was impressed, having anticipated dragging her from her studio.

"Is there a second set of keys for the Porsche?" I said.

"Not that I know of. He doesn't let anyone else drive it."

As we stepped outside, distant headlights turned from the highway onto the road to the Vandals' house. The waning moon was bright enough for me to see the vehicle was silver and boxy like an SUV. What a season finale this was turning out to be.

I mounted the Dinamo and called to Brenda. "Now or never. I'm not waiting."

She clambered on behind me, wrapping her arms tightly around me and pressing far too closely to my back. Already I regretted rescuing her.

Halfway down the driveway, I saw it was the heavy-set cop behind the wheel of the SUV. I gunned the Dinamo, driving straight for the enemy. Raul may have honed his brand of thuggery growing up in the barrios of Mexico City, but I doubt he'd passed many evenings as a bored teenager playing chicken in pick-up trucks on dusty Ontario side roads.

The SUV rounded a curve before the road straightened in front of Casa Soho. Raul must have anticipated the danger, for he slowed and swung as far right as the narrow road allowed.

I countered, tracking left, forcing him to suddenly swerve back into the centre of the road. I met him there, face on, until at last, the Dinamo racing toward the truck, he chickened out. The SUV swerved sharply enough that it left the road. I chanced a backward glance in time to see it bounce through a drainage ditch and crash through a wire fence into a heavily rutted field.

The Dinamo screamed in the night, its tiny headlight showing the way.

Part 4
King's Reach

IN THE DAYS AFTER OLD STEYNE'S farewell party, a multitude of concerns robbed me of sleep. I wished I could be like other inmates, snoring my sentence away.

There was my anticipated thumping from the Warlords, which everyone was waiting for. There was my portrayal of Prospero, whom I'd neglected to focus on while directing the show. Thankfully, my colleagues were so focused on their own performances that only I knew how clumsy and uninspired my interpretation was. There was the warden's trump card, revealed if not yet played. What a fool I was to leave my notebook lying around, and what a failure the project was because there was no chance I'd complete my assignment before Dr. K's deadline.

But mostly there was the mail from Jill and my concern for her well-being when overwhelming evidence suggested I should be grateful she was no longer part of my life.

One night, as Dragan snored contentedly, I plotted a spin-off entitled *Tempest Too!* In it, a now-ordinary Prospero, reinstalled in Milan, grapples with the loss of his magical powers, the vagaries of aging, and the political fallout from Miranda's hasty marriage. There'd be a forthright and calculating duchess to keep him in line, a young woman to also serve as a rival to Miranda. And walk-on comic relief from Ariel.

A sitcom in codpieces. That was my solution to these

approaching crises.

Sleep eventually comes to even the most seasoned of insomniacs. The last time I looked at Dragan's alarm it was nearly six in the morning. The next thing I knew, he was shaking my bed. "Get up," he said. "It's nine o'clock. I'm tired of tiptoeing around here."

"I hardly slept," I said, lurching upright.

"Sleep at night like everyone else."

"I'd like to." My roommate had been moody and snarky of late. His smuggling of a woman into the conjugal cabin—by now a legendary feat—was under review and might get him transferred back to the Kent or delay his parole. He was also pissed at my refusal to get involved with his smuggling business, despite all the help he and Margot had provided me.

There was enough time to shower before seeing Dr. K, who'd be pleased I put my foot down over Bobcat. Too bad he was going to be disappointed about my assignment. What I'd do without his counsel, I didn't like to imagine.

Just outside my room, I met the man who'd replaced old Steyne as the prison mailman. "Hold on, Danny," he said. "There's another handful for you today."

Among the beige business envelopes he handed me—there'd been a lot of those lately—was a pink envelope without a return address, postmarked Cancun. My old stomping ground. I brought it to my nose. Coconut sunblock. Dusty-sweet make-up. Bourbon. All my troubles evaporated as a secret joy curled my lip.

I tossed the serious letters under my bed and carried on. Ahead of me in the main corridor, Dragan stepped from the room used by the chess players. He beckoned me forward. "Come see this board. You will not believe it."

"I'm late," I said, even as I followed him into the room. Whereupon he abruptly turned and exited, the door slamming behind him. Facing me was Bobcat and a bulky sidekick.

There wasn't even time to whimper or taste the sting of my roommate's betrayal.

The sidekick held a metal stacking chair aloft. I raised my hand, still clutching the pretty envelope, to protect myself, but he came under it, the chair crunching against my ribs. Bobcat attacked simultaneously, his fists landing blows to my other side.

One at a time, I thought. I'd handled two bullies at once before, though those boys were considerably younger and weren't speeding on meth.

The sidekick swung the chair again, smashing it into the same side of my body. In the instant it took to recover my footing, Bobcat hit my eye hard enough to raise a shiner. Now I was angry. I swung out. They never count on that. Everyone foolishly assumes the actor is a wimp. I hit Bobcat twice and the sidekick once, before a third blow from the chair dropped me to my knees. I struggled to rise, and for my trouble got Bobcat's boot to my right ear.

That's enough, I figured. Schoolyard wisdom said it was time to let them think they'd won. I balled up to protect my head and waited for them to get bored of hoofing me.

The chair came down, again and again, until the door flung open and words were exchanged. One more boot crunched into my ribs as the chair clattered to the floor.

Footsteps approached. A guard righted the discarded chair and lifted me onto it. Someone must have alerted him.

The guard peered down at me. "Danny, do you need a doctor?"

"No," I said, sputtering blood running from my nose.

"Do you want to file a report?"

"No way," I said, struggling to stand. "This never happened."

Snitching would trigger another beating as well as an investigation that could jeopardize the show. Bobcat just wanted the last word and to send a message to the other inmates.

The guard steadied me as a few of the chess players filed into the room, stepping over the blood spilled on the floor. Others waited in the hallway with their game boards. Dragan, the coward, wasn't among them.

I ducked into a washroom to staunch the bleeding from my face. It was too early to fully assess the damage, though I hadn't lost any more teeth. My knuckles were cut, an ear was torn, and light flashed on the periphery of my vision when I moved my head. At least the beating had eliminated one of the day's worries before my first coffee.

I ran into Dr. K in the hallway leading to the room where we met. Evidently, my ten minutes of grace were up. "Sorry I'm late," I said around a paper towel pressed against my battered bottom lip. "How's this for an excuse?"

"What the hell happened to you?" He held the door open for me to enter.

"Remember the biker you told me to kick out?" I said, carefully lowering myself into a chair. If my ribs hurt this much now they'd be agony tomorrow. "I told you this would happen."

"You did. But I didn't tell you to kick him out. I told you to deal with it on your own. Which you obviously did. So congratulations."

From my limited experience with shrinks, I've learned they'll gladly take the credit if their idea works out but will never accept responsibility if it fails.

"Tell me what happened," he said.

That much, I decided, must have been obvious, so I told him about Dragan's role. I was raging now. The small-town scrapper was back. "Before you ask about my feelings," I said, "let me tell you I'm pissed with myself that I didn't see this coming. Dragan's tight with the bikers."

"You need to stop identifying with the real criminals around here. Try to remember you're an artist."

"Am I, really? Let's face it. I'm not a very good actor. I just got lucky."

"That's the pessimism talking. The last time you gave up on yourself, you ended up in Mexico. Actors get dry spells. That's part of the business."

"Sure, but when a dry spell lasts this long, you're done."

"Not necessarily. You're choosing that definition. Who's the letter from?"

My left hand gripped a crumpled and bloodstained envelope. Only now did I remember smelling creamy piña coladas in the hallway before I was jumped. I brought it to my nose again.

"I think it's from Jill," I said, with an unexpected satisfaction.

"It's from Jill, and you haven't opened it? Why not?"

"I was busy. And I haven't much liked what she's had to say, so I guess I'm in no hurry."

"You mean there've been others? Why haven't you brought them here?"

"Because I haven't seen you yet." I set the letter on the table between us and waited for Jill to work her magic. "It's from Cancun. That's where we met. Did I ever tell you that story?"

"No, you didn't. Will it be in your assignment? Which is due at your next session."

I tapped the letter. "How can I finish telling the story when it's obviously not over? I'll have to wait and see if I get more letters."

The doc laughed. "That's good. Kind of romantic, too. Nice try."

I dabbed the paper towel at my bleeding lip. I didn't like that Jill was in Mexico. The drug violence had escalated since I'd been gone, reaching south into areas previously unscathed like Veracruz. And I didn't like that I was worrying over her safety while I was in prison, or that I was comforted that she was still part of my life when she wasn't at all.

At least she wasn't in Acapulco. That city had become a tragedy.

Dr. K carefully lifted the letter by an unstained edge and peered at the handwritten address and quaint postage stamp. "There's no return address. Why doesn't she want you to write her back?"

Because she doesn't want to be found, I wanted to say. Whether that's due to some scheme she's got on or some trouble she's in, I can't say and not knowing is driving me nuts.

"Because she still cares about me?" That was the simple conclusion I'd drawn from the "warning" pages from *Mother Courage* that arrived a few days ago.

Dr. K handed the letter back to me. "If you say so. This isn't helping you. We need to talk about these letters. There've been others, you said?"

"Can you fit me in tomorrow?" I said. "Since I was late this morning? And since you're going on holiday. I know it's last minute."

Dr. K consulted his phone. "I can. Early again. That means your story assignment will be due. We need it in here. Is it going to be ready?"

"Yes," I lied.

"Can you bring those other letters too, please? We need to understand the hold she's still got on you."

"Okay." I brought the letter to my nose again. It smelled like paper and blood. "Did you smell the ocean? You smelled the ocean on this letter, didn't you?"

Dr. K made a note in his book. "Sure I did," he said.

From my appointment, I went to the screening room to help Gabriel and Tyler install the stage. My lip stung, my pulped eye throbbed, and my ribs ached. The aspirin Dr. K offered me from his briefcase had had no effect. Something stronger was required—an OxyContin or a Percocet or two. The irony being that Bobcat and the bikers controlled the drug trade hereabouts.

Gabriel had finished hand-sewing a stage curtain from the

cornflower blue bedsheets he'd found in the laundry room. He and Tyler were suspending it from the ceiling with wire when I arrived. My battered face brought their work to a halt.

"Guess you knew that was coming," Tyler said.

My side hurt too much to do any lifting, so I directed them in arranging the risers. When one proved too wide, we returned it to the carpentry shop for trimming. The delay proved inspirational. "What's the plan for opening and closing those curtains?" I asked.

"Fishing line," Tyler said, "tied to the top and bottom and pulled from both ends."

"Yeah, but that could snag. We should get a proper curtain rod."

Within minutes, we'd scrounged enough lumber to build a frame across the screening room to serve as a proscenium arch. I was pleased with my idea and wished I'd received more than Gabriel and Tyler's grunted approval of it. No, what I wanted was for Jill to be impressed. Like an idiot.

Back in the screening room, we took measurements, bearing in mind the frame had to be disassembled and brought with us to the schoolhouse. Now of course Gabriel's curtains were too short. And we still lacked a curtain rod and grommets. Maybe Margot could bring us some. There were still three days until we opened here at King's Reach.

"We need to make new curtains and dye them black," I said. "The blue ones Gabriel made we can cut up and use for waves in the shipwreck scene."

"I'm not sure if I can sew that quickly," Gabriel said. "But I know who can."

Handsome young Tyler was sent to entice Cynthia Sweet from her boudoir with an offer to practice the scene in which they kiss. Cynthia didn't appreciate the deception, and it took a half hour of flattery for her to agree to make us new curtains with her sewing machine.

When the boys returned to the carpentry shop to start on the frame, I sat to rest a moment, my head pounding. For a second, I couldn't recall why. That's the thrill of live theatre: in the sprint to the opening, you forget everything else. If this were television, I'd be lounging in my trailer complaining about delays while other people worked.

At rehearsal that afternoon, I asked Brooks, our sole remaining understudy, to play Prospero again. My lip was still bleeding, and

I wanted to steal from him. In his fifties, he was better suited for the role of a jaded man arranging a last-chance escape. A man old enough to understand that it was his own mistakes that got him exiled and that forgiving his enemies was crucial to his salvation. None of that meant squat to me. It was clear I'd miscast myself.

I also wanted to see how Brooks handled Cynthia's Miranda. The director in me let her exaggerated mannerisms interfere with my performance. I had to remember that Miranda is the best thing to come off the island. Whatever Prospero does, he does for her.

By the finale, when Brooks snaps Prospero's broom handle/ magician's staff, I wondered whether he should have the role while I understudied him. Not only was he excellent, the desire to perform had curiously left me. It wasn't an uncomfortable sensation, just one totally unfamiliar to me

There were many other wrinkles in the show, all of which, my immense pride in the boys welling, I was prepared to overlook.

That evening in the dining room, my bashed face drew stares from my fellow convicts and fresh taunts from the bikers. It was so high school, I expected to be called to the warden's office to explain. Earlier that week, an enterprising inmate had taken bets on how long it would take the bikers to hurt me. During the meal, Hassan sheepishly revealed he'd successfully predicted five days and nine hours. The pot was close to $300. "Hope you don't mind," he said.

I held out an open palm. "I won't if you donate some money to the show. The costumes and make-up aren't free, you know."

After dinner, I went for a gentle swim to help loosen my stiffening muscles. Before dressing again, I examined myself in the ghastly florescent light of the washroom. The skin around my eye was purpling nicely, and my entire left side was a magenta darkening to black. Since mid-afternoon, it had hurt to breathe.

I passed the rest of the evening in the resource centre with Prospero's magic book, copying and puzzling over spells and incantations from the internet. I was finding Elizabethan magic quite absorbing.

At lights out, I returned to my room. I'd postponed this confrontation long enough. Dragan sat on his bed, his laptop perched on his knees. With his reading glasses on, he more resembled a kindly uncle than a mob wannabe who'd lured his roommate into a savaging.

"How you feeling?" he said. "Sorry, eh? Nothing personal. For me, I mean."

"No? You sure it's not because I won't help you at the schoolhouse?"

"No. I found someone else for that. I didn't want to set you up, but they threatened Margot. Those crazies. I only work for them because we need the money. That's what I mean nothing personal. You don't look so bad."

"I've had worse."

"Haven't we all. You turning in?"

The beating had dampened something within me. Tonight I would sleep. "Yeah."

But sleep was coming whenever it damn well pleased. Like every night, for weeks now. The only difference was that Dragan, one of those blessed few who go under immediately, also remained sleepless. I placed a hand over my left side, gingerly poking for which ribs felt most damaged. I might need to have them examined after all.

"She's cheating on me, did you know that?" Dragan said. "Margot. She told me last week. Some guy from daycare. I don't want to lose her, Danny. Or my girls."

"Did she tell you this before or after she found out that you were banned from the cabin?"

"Yes, after. And she's not leaving me, is she? She's just fucking some guy. I don't blame her. Look what I did to her. But I tell myself this, and I can't take my own advice."

"That's your macho European bullshit. You're worse than a Mexican. Tell her you're sorry for what you've done. Then you guys can fix it when you get out."

"Yeah. Thanks, buddy. Listen, if there's anything you need, just let me know."

"Since you asked, can Margot visit again? We need a few last-minute things."

Bizarrely, I only remembered Jill's letter long into the shadowed hours of wakefulness following Dragan's confession. Bobcat and his buddy must have given me a concussion. Or—and this was Dr. K putting ideas in my head—I didn't want to read whatever the letter contained. A frantic search in the dark unearthed it in the back pocket of my jeans. I pulled them on, rummaged for a shirt, and hurried down the hall to the resource centre.

In the pooled light of a desk lamp, I carefully sliced open the envelope. A photo spilled out first, honey into my hands. A radiant Jill posed in a white sundress before a scarlet wall of blooming hibiscus, her skin an even brown, her hair the lovely dark blond mess I liked best. My entire world, searing with longing, narrowed to the four-by-six rectangle of paper before me. Her beauty was liberating. I felt like the judge from my trial had suddenly laid a hand on my shoulder and said: "Daniel, there's been a mistake, you're free to go."

After the photo came a sheet of dove-grey paper graced with a few lines. Jill wrote:

> I've arrived and settled into a place. At last.
> Everything is going according to plan. All we need
> is you. From what I hear, you better get moving.
> Love, J xoxo

What a wonderful message, and what a shame I didn't understand it.

The plan I remembered was that she'd look me up at my father's house a week or so after her switcheroo on Nick. Which she may well have. Sadly, I wasn't there then. Considering all we'd shared together, she might have tried a little harder to get in contact with me.

Perhaps she'd changed her mind and sent the details in a letter that was lost in the mail. She often forgot to tell me things then got annoyed when I didn't remember what she hadn't said.

Or maybe the letter wasn't lost. Maybe those nine-year-old girls had held it back instead of steaming it open. I examined the envelope, but it was too late to determine if anyone had tampered with it.

I looked again at the photo for clues. Beyond the wall of hibiscus was a deserted beach, huge waves rolling ashore. Jill on a beach. Nothing new in that. She looked peaceful and happy, and that made me happy too. I was softening again and falling under her spell while my body ached from the consequences of not putting my own needs first.

I returned to my room to continue not sleeping. There was plenty of time to be confused about Jill tomorrow. The old-timers say not to get wound-up by situations on the outside, there's enough to worry about in prison. But they'd never met Jill.

The following morning, I examined the business letters piling up under my bed. The ones I received the day before were from law firms in Maine and Iowa. Soon I'd have letters from every state in the union. I recalled from an episode of *Legal Ease* that in the United States a person can be tried in a civil court for a crime for which he has not been criminally convicted. It was cold comfort that these new legal troubles effectively nullified the warden's threat to expose the truth of what Jill and I had done. The lawyers wouldn't be after me if they didn't already have definitive proof. I stuffed the letters back under the bed.

Two hours later, en route to that additional meeting with Dr. K—our last, apparently—I met Warden Carr on the stairs to the administrative wing.

He peered at my face. "Why didn't you listen to me? Now look what you've done."

"I've done? You could have prevented this and didn't."

"Careful. Don't forget our chat in the kitchen." He clicked his tongue disapprovingly. "I hear you've been receiving a lot of interesting mail. Care to tell me what it's about, or will I have to find out another way?"

I continued past him up the stairs. It appeared Dragan was another of the warden's spies. And it wasn't like Carr had been threatening Margot. My opinion of the big Serb had nosedived in the past twenty-four hours.

Edith was at her desk outside of the warden's office. "You just missed him," she said.

"I know. That's why I'm here. Did you get it?"

"I did. This morning." She inclined her head toward two chatting colleagues then handed me the beige file folder the warden had wagged at me in the kitchen. "Are you nuts?" she whispered. "Writing all that down."

"I guess so," I said, flipping through the photocopied pages of my notebook. For all the good retrieving it did me now. "Was it the only copy?"

"It was the only copy in his office. If he's got one at home in his sock drawer, I can't help you. He's going to suspect it was me. You know that, right?"

"Yes, I know." I grinned so widely my split lip cracked open again. "Thank you, Edith. You totally saved my ass. Again."

Tomorrow, Dr. K was leaving for a two-week vacation. He'd miss every performance of *The Tempest* and wouldn't return to King's Reach for a month. We'd already discussed how I was disappointed by his absence yet understood the arrangements were made long ago.

He eyed the pages slipping out of the folder. "Is that for me?" he said.

"Not yet. Sorry. It's not finished."

"Really? I told you it had to be today. That we're through talking in circles here."

He was genuinely upset, and I regretted making him feel that way. Not only had I never told him the entire truth, I'd expected him to help me regardless. How could he fix me if he didn't have the proper tools? "There wasn't enough time, doc. And then the beating yesterday and the letter."

"Right. The letter. So let me ask you outright, since we're done, why did you go to her? Since you knew what it involved, what you were getting in to."

I guess I must have gaped at him.

"Don't play dumb with me. We both know you're not a criminal at heart. You like people so much you actually trust them. So why go and do that? And why stay?"

Despite my remorse, I still couldn't tell him the truth. "Because I needed her. And she needed me. Everything is better when we're together."

"Can't you see how you served her purpose?"

"You can look at it that way. But even if that were true, why would she be writing me now? I think she's just reassuring me. Letting me know she's still out there."

"Or she's luring you back to her."

"But why? I'll be in here for another three years, and that's only if I get early parole. I'm no use to her at all right now. So I've got to believe she still cares."

That seemed to satisfy him. And while that may have been another dangerous fantasy I'd created, it helped settle the matter within me. It was also a relief to finally share how I still felt about her with someone.

We chatted amicably for the rest of our time together. He opened up about his kids and the pressures of his job. I felt a bit like the grifter of old, looking for that wedge, and was very glad I wasn't. I appreciated his candour, even if I was only receiving it because we were through.

At the end of our session, I told him how much I appreciated his help, especially with the shows. I think we might have become friends if the circumstances were different.

"My pleasure," he said. "And there'll be other shows. I'll see those."

"Not with me performing. I'm done with that."

"You mentioned that yesterday. Do you mean never acting again?"

"Maybe not. Ever since I played Snoopy again, it's like I've come full circle. That's why I can't find Prospero. My heart's not in it. It's a weird feeling, like I'm floating. I've been acting since I was a kid. It's the only way I know how to be."

I didn't say I wanted to do more directing. Yes, every actor wants to direct, only I feel I have the skills, like a gift for manipulation, that are suited to it. Time to put them to a better purpose.

"Well, you've got three years to figure something else out," he said.

"Hey, if I finish my assignment and get it to you, can we hang out again?"

"Only if you lay it out honestly. If I get to meet the real Daniel Drake."

That wouldn't be difficult. Henceforth, I wasn't going to be anyone other than myself.

We shook hands at the door. "Take care of yourself, Daniel."

"I will. Have a great trip, doc. Thanks for everything."

If I ever see Jill again, I'll tell her it turned out I was one of those actors who was only in it for the money and the fame.

Halfway through lunch, a guard approached me in the dining room and told me I had a visitor waiting. My soup spoon clattered to the table as I leapt out of my seat. It couldn't be Margot, since it was only that morning that Dragan emailed her with my final requests for building supplies. And since I didn't know anyone else on the West Coast …

Obviously, the letter was a herald. That's what she meant about a plan. I skipped behind the guard down the dirty corridors I call home. Blood pumping with such fervour I might pass out. My day had come. Our day, I should say. Our reunion. The wait was over.

A last corner and I entered the gloomy dinginess of the visitors' lounge. The room was empty save for a couple talking with their son and an old man with his grizzled head slumped against the back of a chair. She must be outside smoking, I thought, as my father lifted his head and said, "Danny, my boy."

I staggered to a halt, disappointment creasing my face. If Earl saw it before I wiped it away, I couldn't tell. I sank into the seat adjacent to his. "Hey, Dad. What took you so long?"

He'd grown jowly and heavier since I'd seen him last. He was unshaven, and what hair he had left spiked from his scalp. He'd heard of my arrest and trial. The whole town had. No doubt he'd enjoyed the temporary notoriety it provided him. Now, of course, word had reached him of the shows we were doing. It was further proof my aspirations will be my undoing. It little mattered I was getting out of acting. I was still playing a dangerous game with fame.

The last we'd communicated, he was undergoing heart surgery. My own heart was hammering. The real world was intruding, and I burned with shame over the mess I'd made of things. If seeing Earl had rattled me so thoroughly, part of me was glad it hadn't been Jill waiting for me.

"How's the ticker?" I asked.

"I'm like a man of thirty," he said, plugging coins into a coffee vending machine. We stood in its wan orange light waiting for our cups. Earl opened his shirt to show me his scar. "That's where they cut me. Then they insert a wire and pump up your veins like you're a big balloon."

The couple with their son tactfully ignored the spectacle. I didn't care. No one cared about decorum in this place, so why should I? We walked our coffees back to the worn couch.

"Looks like you had a disagreement," Earl said. "I hope you got a few shots in yourself."

"There was more than one of them. I did what I could."

"That's all you can do sometimes. Sorry to see you locked up in here. But you know what? I'm kinda proud you're a chip off the ol' block."

"I'm glad you finally approve." With that attitude from my single parental unit, it's a wonder I didn't end up in prison sooner.

Earl's periods of incarceration were a badly kept secret. While I was living with Granny Drake, we once went two years without hearing from him. Granny thought he'd found a woman. I maintained he was in jail.

I finally asked about his absence. Turns out I'd been right all along.

"Burglary. Out east. And resisting arrest. But that was bullshit. All of it. I got set up."

There was that naiveté I'd inherited. "For how long?"

"Two years less a day. In Dorchester. Boy, that's a tough joint. Toughest I've been in. Take it from me, stay out of that one."

"I'll try."

He drifted a few more years after his release, primarily in New England. He was more of a loser than a criminal, but losers often end up as criminals.

I barely saw him in my teens and twenties. He came back for good when I was twenty-seven, near the end of my television glory, arriving after Granny died, on the night of her wake. He called her house collect from a gas station ten miles south of town. He had no money for a taxi, and with night falling, his thumb couldn't take him any further. One of Granny's cousins volunteered to pick him up. I barely recognized the skinny, bearded vagrant claiming to be my father.

The man who owned Granny's house wanted to renovate it and carve it into separate apartments. That would leave Earl, now in his early fifties and less employable with each passing day, homeless and penniless. Three days after the funeral, I paid cash for a draughty bungalow across the street from the county fairgrounds and handed the keys to him.

His sudden presence didn't entirely sit right with me. "I can't believe you came all this way. How did you afford it?"

"I won money on a bingo scratch card. And my girlfriend helped. Valerie. You don't know about her. I met her online, with the computer you left me. She lives in Vancouver. Two trips for the price of one. Why not?"

So seeing me wasn't the real purpose of his trip. While that smarted, I wasn't angry. Neither bright nor handsome, Earl got lucky once with a girl who, by all accounts, was a real gift—my mother— then lost her. I was happy to hear he was finally moving beyond that.

Yet some part of me must have felt let down, and that hung between us. "Guess I'll get going," Earl said. "I've got a ways to go."

Beyond the windows, the weak afternoon light was fading. We'd chatted nearly an hour. "Where are you staying?"

"In Vancouver. With Valerie. I have to catch the ferry."

I would have asked him to stay longer if that were possible. "Hey, did a woman call for me since I've been in jail?"

"No, no woman. But I've been down in Tucson. Valerie's got a timeshare down there."

"Nice," I said. That meant, possibly, that Jill had been detained as she'd written. It might also have meant she never intended to contact me. I chose—again, and always—to have faith in her.

"Yeah, it is. But you reminded me. There's been reporters knocking on my door saying awful things about you, Danny. And lawyers keep asking who owns the house. They're calling from all over the place. Texas. California. Even England."

"Don't let them bother you. Some people think I owe them money, that's why they're asking about the house. It's a good thing I put it in your name, isn't it?"

I walked with him to the security desk, which marked the extent of my range. "Thanks for coming," I said. "The best show for you to see is opening night. I'll make sure there's tickets for two at the door."

"See you next week, then. You'll like Valerie. She's looking forward to meeting you."

We had a kind of hug by the doors. I couldn't recall when we'd last done that. "I'd walk you to your car, but ..."

"Next time. Don't sweat it, eh? Keep your head down. Do your time."

Spoken with the eloquence of a seasoned con. "Hey," I said. "When I get out of here, can I come stay with you? Just for a little while. Until I get things sorted."

Earl's doughy face softened even further. That may have been the question he was hoping I'd ask. "Of course you can. It's your house. You bought it."

"Nah, it's your house. Your home."

His progress across the parking lot, a hunched figure in the drizzle, put me in mind of other parking lots, long ago. And of his Duster, crammed with our belongings, and of highways. I watched him squeeze into a tiny Ford and wanted to be going with him. Things hadn't worked out here, so we were bound for another town. That's how it works for guys like me and Earl.

Day 12

Veracruz

TOM WALKER NEVER GOT A SERIES finale. He was last seen in a bar agonizing over prosecuting an eighty-seven-year-old woman who'd euthanized a husband ravaged by Alzheimer's. Also troubling him that night was his foolish affair with a colleague—played by Hannah Dyer—while his wife struggled through postpartum depression. Deep in crisis, Tom vowed to the bartender he'd regain control of his life and fulfill a youthful dream of becoming an attorney for human rights.

Unfortunately, Tom's fans never learned if he made good on that promise. The abrupt cancellation of *Legal Ease* left characters stranded in their storylines and loyal viewers fuming.

In the steamy Veracruz night, my own ending felt haphazard and incomplete. How to account for speeding on a stolen scooter with a drunken wacko as a passenger—a wacko on whom I was counting to have enough money to fly us both out of the country. (Technically, the Dinamo wasn't stolen so long as Brenda remained on it.)

We were racing south to the city, intending I'm not sure what, when the scooter began sputtering and losing power. Everything might now be different if we hadn't been approaching the eagle logo and Mexican green and red of a Pemex gas station.

Brenda paced her gangly legs by the pumps. In the minute it took to get the nozzle into the gas tank, I felt her anxiety boring into me. "Why didn't you fill it up before?" she said.

239

I averted my eyes to gaze along the road ahead. There was still a long, long way to go. When I looked back, Brenda was still there. "Go pay for this gas," I said.

"I don't have any money. You didn't give me time to get any."

"You've got credit cards. Please go inside and pay for the gas."

In her absence, a battered pick-up truck, its back filled with kids, pulled in beside me. The kids leaned over the side to admire the shiny scooter, so I restarted it and revved the engine for them. They liked that almost as much as I did. Thank God all it needed was gas.

More cars rolled up: teenagers out for a night, two older women in a Toyota. To make room at the pumps, I drove around to the sales booth. Brenda was within, arguing with the young female clerk, her frizzy mane mimicking her angry gestures. She waved for me to join her. As if I could solve whatever problem she'd created.

Given the facts on hand, it's difficult to fault myself for the decision I made next. I tossed Brenda's bag at the booth, spun the Dinamo around the pumps, and tore off back the way we came. North. Away from Veracruz. It was dangerous to pass the Vandals' house again and risk the wrath of Raul the cop, but I didn't want to go anywhere I'd already been.

A glance back showed Brenda sprinting after me, mouthing words lost to the drone of the bike. It was running more smoothly for her absence and wouldn't miss her either. I looked back again, and she'd been reduced to a tiny dot of fury.

Beyond the afterglow of Veracruz, the lonesome darkness was absolute. The Dinamo's dim headlight showed only the road and a few slumbering villages straggling along it. Hunched over the handlebars, I was a trash can of conflicting emotions, negotiating relief, confusion, joy, disappointment, and sorrow. Anger, too. Lots of hope. It's a wonder I kept the bike on the road.

After a few hours, the bike began emitting a nagging whine, reminding me it wasn't made for long hauls on the highway. The arrival of another honey-orange dawn, this one no less beautiful or uncertain than any other in the past week, was welcome. By my count, ten days had passed since I first laid eyes on the Vandals at Paraiso.

To my right, the shoreline I'd been hearing and smelling for hours materialized in the gathering light. Mile upon mile of unspoiled beach, between forest and sea, begging to be developed. Imagine resorts like grains of sand along every coastline in the world. Imagine the limes to be squeezed.

Few other cars shared the road, and none, mercifully, were the police. What they'd make of a helmetless gringo on a stolen bike with a pocketful of phony passports, I didn't care to learn. Nor did I like my chances of remaining unnoticed in daylight.

I pulled into a beach-side rest area. In the violet shadows beneath some palm trees, I piled driftwood and dried fronds and got a small fire going with matches I found beneath the seat of the Dinamo. Then I turned out the pockets of Nick's jacket onto the sand, separating "my" passports and pieces of identification from those Jill had used.

I burned me first. David Masters. Colin Spencer. Hardly the most imaginative of names. They were like characters in a play waiting for me to interpret the role. The passports burned easily, flames licking pages stamped with phony visas, though twice I burned my fingers on plastic from melting social security cards and driver's licences. I never liked these versions of myself and was glad to see them go.

A boy of about ten cautiously crossed the sand toward me. Behind him, discernible in the half light, was a house hidden from the road by a grove of palms, a fishing skiff drawn up beside it. A woman stood in the doorway, watching me.

The kid advanced to within a few yards, attracted more by the Dinamo than my little pyre of passports. My welcoming nod got no response. I couldn't blame him: I must have cut a disturbing figure on his beach at dawn.

I returned to the business at hand, torching Sandra Webb, Regina Boccia, and Patty Harper. A different woman stared back at me from each photograph. Where was Jill this new day? Brenda's comment about Miami made me question whether Jill had told me the entire truth. There was no making sense of this. All I could do was get out of Mexico and wait at my father's house. I closed my eyes to it all as a wave of tiredness rolled over me.

When I looked up again, the kid and another boy were kicking a football along the shore. Once everything was burned, I carefully extinguished the fire with sand. The boys had reminded me I was a guest on their beach and should treat it respectfully.

The highway turned inland not much farther along the road. Fifteen minutes later, I reached a town called Gutiérrez Zamora in the foothills of the mountains. In the pretty downtown, the day's business was commencing on streets leading to a placid lake. The buildings around a central plaza were painted the heart-warming colours of happy endings: canary yellow, dusty tangerine, and creamy lime. Flowers in planters. Trees and shrubs in lovely springtime bloom. I liked it there.

Facing the plaza was the ADO terminal, where I learned from an old woman that the next bus to Mexico City, an express, left at noon. A one-way ticket was 530 pesos. Needing much more than that, I drove the scooter over narrow streets until I spotted an auto shop bulwarked by piles of tires. Three men in coveralls smoked cigarettes in the sunshine before an open garage door. I gunned the bike past them into an empty bay.

One of the men was beside me instantly. "¡Oye! Ud. no puede conducir así aquí."

I'd done some calculating on the road. "Quince mil pesos por el escúter," I said. "Cash."

The man glanced at his colleagues, who ambled toward us. My desperation poured as freely as my sweat. I had to stop showing my hand so early.

The man examined the bike then looked to his friends. "Tres mil."

"¿Estás bromeando? Es nuevo, y vale veinte mil por lo menos."

Another man closed the bay door, bringing a gloom like night. Whether he did this to better facilitate our haggling for the bike or to strangle me for it, I would shortly find out.

"Diecisiete mil," I said weakly.

So it went until we settled on 10,000 pesos. It was enough for the bus ticket and a flight north. What else did I need?

The man purchasing the bike had to visit a bank. In his absence, the other men fiddled with their phones. I expected the police to arrive and waited with my legs astride the Dinamo, protecting my only asset, ready to race off at any sign of trouble. But there wasn't any, and I was paid in full.

Bus ticket in hand, I was stabbed by vicious hunger, and couldn't remember when I'd last eaten. The tacos I ate from a cart in the plaza were memorable only in that they were my last. I waited on a bench in the shade, enjoying the limpid morning. My head ached where the cop had hit me, and I'd acquired a sunburn on yesterday's march through Veracruz. I amused myself by fantasizing about my reunion with Jill and wondering what she and Earl would find to talk about other than duping people. And what a worldly trilingual Montrealer would make of my near-trash small-town Ontario roots. She must love me, I figured. I felt pretty good sitting there in that plaza.

The woman who sold me the ticket lied about the bus being an express. Or perhaps I misheard. The bus I boarded terminated an hour later in a small mountain city named Papantla that was quite near, as it goes, the ruins at El Tajín I'd so wanted to see. There I waited for and boarded a different bus and did so again another hour down the road. By dispiriting stages, I eventually reached Mexico City and the flying saucer-shaped bus station, TAPO, from which Jill and I launched our escapade in Veracruz.

At Benito Juárez International, I staggered into a marvellously chilled departures terminal like the lone survivor of a doomed jungle safari. Certainly, I looked like one. I passed the British Airways counter where Jill would have checked in for her red-eye to Heathrow. Two security guards followed me to the Air Canada counter, which seemed to satisfy their curiosity in me.

Air Canada's flights to Toronto were sold out for the week. There were a few seats left on a flight to Vancouver that evening and a flight to Montreal later that week. Waiting wasn't an option. I considered Delta or American Airlines to Buffalo or Detroit and a bus over the border, before recalling the hornet's nest I'd poked with Cal and Evan. Staying out of the United States seemed advisable.

Vancouver, then. No worrying about sunburn there. There was a fluster over my paying cash, but Daniel Drake's legitimate passport smoothed over any difficulties.

In the departure lounge, over tepid cups of coffee, I pictured Jill asleep in a posh London hotel, with a big stack of cash for a bedmate. While Nick got a phone call that sent him into an apoplexy of rage. For an alternate potential outcome, I could have consulted the crime tabloids lying around. They were filled with lurid photos of murdered drug cartel victims. One rag described how two assassins dressed as police officers had gunned down two real cops in the very departure hall in which I waited. Oh, Mexico.

For the first half of the flight, I sat quietly reassembling the pieces of Daniel Drake. I was an actor who in recent years had not received many roles. Well, none. They made television in Vancouver, most notably the private investigator series spun-off from *Legal Ease* starring Hannah Dyer. Potentially, this move might herald the relaunch my career required.

Wired on caffeine, I asked a flight attendant for a calming glass of wine. She was my age and heard my request with a distant sympathy. The wine cost eleven dollars, payable by debit or credit card. My damp clump of pesos counted for nothing. The attendant looked back toward the galley. "I'll buy you this one, okay? You look like you could use it."

After she left, I felt pretty low. I believe I was having one of those moments Jill used to describe as overdramatic. By now, I'd convinced myself she'd waited until the last minute to tell me of her plans to avoid messy scenes like, for example, me tearing up on a plane.

If she'd wanted to ditch me she'd have done it cleanly and far earlier. And she wouldn't have entrusted me with her photo album. Aching badly for her, I chanced another peek within it. There were ticket stubs for concerts in Montreal—Beck and Portishead at the Forum—and one for *Angels in America* in New York in 1995. Jill and her brother looked alike, but neither kid looked like their parents. I got stuck again on bespectacled, pre-teen Jill, searching that girl's face for the promise of the woman I knew.

The flight was filled with migrant agricultural workers bound for orchards and farms on British Columbia's lower mainland. Small men with thickly calloused hands. I made friends with some of them, and for the last two hours of the flight, filled in as many of their customs declaration cards as I could. Some of them were illiterate and grateful for my assistance.

In the line for customs in Vancouver, I got tangled with a group of Indians freshly arrived from Mumbai. My old heart was clattering and gasping in my chest. I have a gift for choosing the slowest lines in banks, grocery stores, and customs halls. This one was no exception, though to change halfway to another might attract unnecessary attention. I could smell myself, despair and fresh sweat over the stink of dead fish and old sweat from Nick's jacket.

Then I remembered there was nothing to fear.

Nationality? Length of trip? Purpose of your trip? Anything to declare?

The customs officer was a middle-aged man, who stamped my passport with a brisk, northern efficiency. That he barely glanced at the photo in it disappointed me. People needed to know Daniel Drake was back.

Then I was power-walking through the baggage claim area, elation and relief shaking through me. Oh brave new world, I was thinking. We were free and clear of the life we both despised. The future I'd always wanted for us lay beyond the door to the arrivals area.

I racked my brain to recall if I knew anyone in Vancouver who could loan me enough money to get to Toronto. How about Hannah Dyer or the former producers of *Legal Ease*? I wasn't kidding: if they hadn't bungled my show, I would not have been in this predicament.

I couldn't afford a hotel room. A soggy cardboard box in a park would be a paradise compared to being murdered on a fishing boat. I'd visit a bank to get a new credit card in the morning. They gave those out to anyone.

Outside it was raining. I gulped mouthfuls of the cool, wet night air. I'd only been to Vancouver once before, on a day-long press junket around the time Jill and I broke up after university. Presumably it was smaller than Mexico City, so of a manageable, non-terrifying size. I predicted a long walk ahead and debated converting the last of my pesos into an umbrella. Otherwise, I was in for a soaking.

I heard their footsteps first, rapidly approaching me from behind. Then a rush of motion spun me around. Two men in their forties stood before me.

"Can we see some identification?" one of them said. The other was removing some handcuffs from his coat pocket. For an instant, I thought this was a joke, that this couldn't be happening, even as I offered my passport with a fatalistic dread. Had I really thought I'd get away with all that I'd done?

The first officer glanced back and forth between my passport and my face, inches from recognizing me. From *Street Heat*, probably. A lot of cops admired the accuracy of that series. "Hey hey, you're that guy," he said. "From that show."

I nodded soberly, desperate to conceal a stupid grin. What an auspicious welcome home it was turning out to be.

"Can we look inside your bag?" the officer with the handcuffs said. "Where is it you're arriving from?"

I handed my knapsack to him. "Mexico."

The first officer removed my shaving kit, the bag of coffee, and my hat and placed them on a newspaper box. Then from a side pocket I never use, he pulled the small plastic brick last seen in Nick's office. He ripped a corner of it, revealing a hard, yellow-white substance.

"Uh oh." The officer poked me in the shoulder with the brick of cocaine. "Not good."

"That's not mine. Honestly. I have no idea how it got there."

"Sir," said the officer with the handcuffs, "we're placing you under arrest."

So much for the new me. No wonder Brenda had been so anxious to catch up with the scooter.

I tried to run, but the officers each hauled me back by an arm. I heard the shriek of a cornered animal and assumed it had come from me.

"Where you going, Danny?" the first officer said.

"Daniel, please," I said as the cuffs tightened over my wrists. "I use Daniel now."

The police kindly provided a ride into the city, where I spent the night as their guest. They gave me food and my first shower in days. Also a cot, where I lay awake reflecting that my strained behaviour must have red-flagged me the instant I entered the airport in Mexico City. The lazy security guards there did me a favour in letting me get on that flight. My prospects would have been infinitely more bleak if Brenda's stash had been discovered in Mexico.

In the morning, two other men and I were driven to a courthouse where I met with a lawyer who told me a different lawyer would be handling my case. He advised me to plead not guilty and not say anything else. I was arraigned on charges of importation with the intent to traffic a controlled substance. A date for a pre-trial hearing was set for two weeks hence.

Bail wasn't even considered. I had very few belongings and just a handful of pesos to my name. I also lacked proof of a fixed address as I'd refused to divulge where I'd been staying in Mexico, with whom, and for how long. The lawyer told me that even if I'd had money, the Crown would have recommended detention because the amount of time I'd spent abroad made me a flight risk.

Never having been arrested before, I was more overwhelmed than scared. Mostly I was dumbfounded by my stupidity in letting Brenda play me when I was so close to freedom. She must have placed the cocaine in my bag at Casa Soho or somewhere on the road to Veracruz. So who was the drug mule?

My main concern was what would happen when Jill reached my father's house and learned I'd never showed up? I tried to call Earl all that first day but never even got an answering machine. After my last attempt, I hung up the payphone and rested my frantic head against the cool concrete of the wall beside it. There was no other way to find her. She'd vanished just as completely, and perhaps as deliberately, as she had years ago from our Toronto apartment.

That evening, I was astonished by the media attention my arrest was garnering. It was a top story on the evening news, which ran clips from Street Heat and Legal Ease. I'd been out of the television business so long, I hadn't even considered I'd still be tabloid fodder. I watched on a television in a common room with some fellow detainees, many of whom now considered me in a new light. From that moment, I was a marked man in the penal system.

The following morning, my face was on the front page of all the local newspapers. Someone had leaked the photo taken at the police station when I wasn't looking my best. I was also the subject of conversations, and the predictable sort of jokes, on the radio call-in show the guards kept on at their work station.

Curiously, my arrest coincided with a debate underway in the media over the difficulties former teen and child performers encounter after their careers end. Fame is a sort of prison, apparently. Safety nets for former actors, including counselling and job-retraining programs, were suggested. All of which ignored the fact you can never replace the eternal rush of gratification the spotlight brings. Once in it, people chase after it the rest of their lives.

Nor will it let you go. On the third day of my incarceration, I was contacted by a savvy LA agent interested in my plans after my trial. Getting arrested might have been the best thing for my career in years.

A week after my arraignment, a pricey defense attorney named McKeon offered to defend me for free. His sole interest was his own glory, which was acceptable if he brought my case to a swift conclusion. I didn't care since I was still expecting Jill to rescue me at any moment.

McKeon decided to seek leniency from the court. He would approach the Crown to see if they'd accept a guilty plea to the lesser charge of just possession. My spotless record, combined with an intent to undergo drug counselling, could result in a suspended sentence. I'd be placed on probation and have to perform community service or serve a few weekends in a detention centre. The great news was that I could be free in a matter of days. I was ever more anxious about meeting Jill since McKeon couldn't reach my father either.

Although, by this point, I was concerned about her, the unavoidable truth was that someone who consumed as much trash media as Jill couldn't have failed to hear that I was in jail. Either her scheme had failed—perhaps badly—or she had never intended to connect with me. I didn't know which was worse, and the silence was maddening.

Then came the first indication of greater trouble heading my way. A woman from Calgary reported on an infotainment show that she knew me not from television but from a resort in Cuba where her Visa card was mysteriously charged $3000. The next day, a man in Tacoma reported much the same, as did a woman in Seattle.

Every evening for a week, I watched the television in mute horror as a dozen people came forward to accuse me. I recognized them and couldn't begrudge them their right to report a criminal. Each victim expressed how inconvenient the losses had been, how ashamed they felt for having been robbed, and how they were now having trouble trusting people and sleeping. I wasn't sleeping, either. It was no longer possible to delude myself that the only victims of our crimes were the card companies and their vast oceans of cash.

The possibility of extradition to the United States or, worse, Mexico became a waking nightmare. The police visited me. I denied everything and refused to name my companion, variously described as my girlfriend, fiancé, or wife, the mother of our two, three, or five children, a dental receptionist, a teacher, a nutritionist, named Regina or Debbie or Sandy. When none of my accusers could prove I'd stolen from them, the police withdrew without filing charges.

Eventually another has-been actor landed in a juicy drugs-for-sex scandal, knocking me from the spotlight. Still, it was only a matter of time before the banks and card companies dug up the necessary proof of our crimes. My dream of reviving my acting career was hopeless. What I'd done with Jill would darken the rest of my days.

When it finally began, my trial was nothing like those on *Legal Ease*. In the real world, trials are tedious and subject to many delays, and there is no trailer with satellite TV to retreat to when you're bored. Whole weeks passed in which nothing was achieved, providing ample time for me to regret my crimes and not simply because I'd been caught.

In a surprise move, the prosecution called Hannah Dyer as a character witness. The applause she received cut right through me. Hannah testified that in the years we worked together, she often suspected I was using drugs, to the detriment of my performances.

Not true. She was the cokehead, and the source of anything I ever put up my nose. After I broke it off with her, I didn't touch anything stronger than aspirin until the casino night in Veracruz.

I observed my trial as if through a distant window. A man who resembled me sat in a borrowed suit beside his lawyer, apparently engaged in the proceedings underway. This wasn't happening because I was supposed to be building a new theatre company, and a new life, in a tropical paradise with Jill.

And where was she? Months had passed without word from her. What's worse is that I worried more for her than I did myself. I hated that. And I missed her, so very badly. The various pieces of the woman I thought I understood had fallen apart again. Had she meant anything she'd said to me?

The solution was to ignore the facts and believe we'd be reunited. As if she'd soon turn up in the visitor's gallery of the courtroom, in a smart suit, beaming her support down to me. I'd returned to Mexico to rescue her, so why wouldn't she step in to save me?

McKeon proved to be worth what I paid for him. He was late on trial dates and totally unprepared for some key prosecution moves. The Crown would only reduce the charges if I provided information on my drugland associates. No chance, I told McKeon. I didn't want to create a connection between my present situation, what actually went on down south, and the woman I wouldn't name. My refusal to name my co-conspirator sparked rumours of links to Mexican drug cartels. Anyone halfway informed on the subject would know that if I were even remotely linked to the cartels, I'd have been disembowelled and hung from a bridge.

Around this time, I got into my first fight since grade school. It began over some seating arrangements in the dining hall of the detention centre and might have been avoided if I'd simply moved to a different table. How could I have guessed it would be the first of many prison fights? In that moment, all I knew is that I felt more alive than I had in months, and my refurbished pride insisted I could handle anything that came at me.

McKeon's revised plan to get the case dismissed by questioning the right of the police to search me in front of the airport failed because they have much broader powers in sensitive locations like airports. Thereafter, he basically folded, having garnered the publicity he'd sought for himself. He was a terrible lawyer, really, the last of a long string of bad luck.

The trial judge was the sort of old biddy Tom Walker used to torment and eventually charm. She shared none of the opinions of the celebrity-pandering media. Quite the opposite: her summary cited my high-profile career and the luxurious lifestyle it afforded. By her estimation, wealthy entertainers such as myself should accept our leadership roles in the community. She also cited the quantity of drugs seized and how it was brazenly kept on my person. Despite my unblemished record, she sentenced me to the maximum time allowable: twelve years, with no chance of parole until I'd served a third of my sentence.

At first, I didn't understand her, as if she wasn't speaking English. Then McKeon repeated my sentence to me, and everything crashed into me. The pain and damage I'd inflicted on others. Jill's betrayal. My abandonment. My isolation. I dropped back into the chair beside McKeon. And all in a hopeless pursuit of some easy money and a woman who wasn't worth the trouble.

McKeon decried my punishment as excessive. With the court officers leading me away, he promised to file an appeal of my conviction. And then never did.

The judge's sentence returned me to reality. I didn't want to go to prison, but I'd made such a mess of things there was nowhere else to go. Some enforced contemplation might help define new goals. I was getting away with far greater crimes, so I'd quietly do my time in a distant corner of the penal system.

Some illusions were difficult to relinquish. The next day, I was scheduled to be transferred to the Kent Institution, a maximum-security prison where I'd wait until a place was found for me in a less secure institution. I had no capacity to comprehend the sort of hell I was entering and distracted myself with various conceptions of prison from all the mediocre television I'd helped make. I still half-believed Jill would appear and take me away from everything.

En route to the Kent, the driver of the transport van told me the inmates were preparing a special reception for me. Despite hard lessons learned in the time I'd already spent locked up, I was still sufficiently deluded by fame to believe they were fans of my shows.

And then the driver told me of the sort of welcome I should really expect.

Part 5 King's Reach

OUR SECOND EXCURSION TO Gracechurch, for our opening night there, was far less comfortable than our first. Warden Carr refused to provide additional transport for our stage, costumes, and props, forcing us to cram everything and everyone onto the prison bus. (Less the warden, of course, who drove his Buick into town.)

Players and guards piled over each other, legs spilling into the aisle, arms poking from windows. A few older, overweight inmates grumbled about their creaking backs but most were still too high from our triumphant seven show run in the screening room at King's Reach to care about comfort. I sat squashed under the mainmast of the ship, my knapsack and Prospero's props on my lap. We could have been on a donkey cart and I'd have been happy.

The cramped ride reminded me of when we took our university production of *Mother Courage* on the road to other colleges. With Jill behind the wheel of a panel van, no one dared complain of being squeezed between set pieces in the back. She had more passion for performing than anyone I've known. I like to think she'd be proud of my recent conversion to theatrical purist.

A winter dusk was descending when we reached the town, this time accompanied by two RCMP cruisers, one leading, the other following. More cops awaited us at the schoolhouse. With my ribs still sore from my beating, I supervised the off-loading of the bus.

How directorial of me, I thought.

Soon we discovered that despite my friendly emails, the local theatre troupe had only provided us with three lights. I showed Patrice and Hassan how to suspend them from the ceiling beams and got the others assembling the wrecked ship and hanging Cynthia's patchwork curtain. A Christmas tree and other decorations had gone up since our technical survey. With the blessing of Karen the caretaker, we transferred some golden rope lights from the windows to our stage and proscenium. I wanted them on for the joyous daylight of the scene that introduces Miranda. And every time she appeared on stage, for that matter.

When the work was done, a brittle tension mounted. Everyone was anxious to get started. A few guys ate the sandwiches the prison cook had packed for our supper. Half the Players hailed from British Columbia and would have family and friends in attendance. The prison shows had been previews: this was the night that mattered.

The first patrons began trickling into the schoolhouse, their excited chatter further animating everyone backstage. I told the boys to start dressing and doing their make-up. The kitchen/green room was so tiny, and so much of it was lost to Cynthia and her many costumes, that they had to process themselves in shifts. Soon, it felt like a hockey dressing room, all sweat, bravado, and fear.

I slipped onto the front steps for some air, nodding to the police officer on the door to let him know I wasn't going far. That's where Karen found me, handing me a letter addressed to me, care of the schoolhouse, in a familiar handwriting.

"I guess one of your fans doesn't know where you're living these days," she said.

I looked at the letter. There wasn't a stamp on it, nor had it been postmarked.

Karen laid a hand on my arm. "It came not long after your visit that afternoon. For what it's worth, no one else knows it's here."

I tore it open and removed a single sheet of yellow notepaper. Jill wrote:

> The Tempest, huh? Ambitious. But why not
> Shakespeare's new play? It's called The Third
> Night. It's got a nautical theme too, with boats and
> harbours. Get it?
> Karen seems cool, so I think it's safe to write you

here. I miss you like crazy and can't wait to see you.

I did it, honey. We did it. I got the stuff to my other old friend, the man you saw me with in Acapulco when you were with that English chick. (I'm still pissed off about that!) I was ready to meet you until Nick sent some people after me. I called the English tax police on him, so I had to disappear for a while. Now I'm back.

You always sucked as a thief. That's one of the reasons I chose you. I knew you'd lead me out of this mess. Now I'm going to return the favour.

See you soon. Don't forget. One night only! The Third Night. Please try it! I promise you won't be disappointed.

Love, J

I stood re-reading the letter until the words meant nothing and the page was half-soaked with raindrops. "See you soon?" Never mind her troubles with Nick or that it sounded like she'd succeeded. Did this mean I was going to see her? Tonight? I was ready for anything, just maybe not that. I looked for answers among the patrons hurrying into the schoolhouse out of the rain.

Back inside, I elbowed myself a spot at the make-up table and with trembling hands started applying the foundation I needed for my damaged face. Although the swelling around my eye had gone down, the bruising remained a captivating whorl of raspberry and lemon.

Beside me, the Montreal mobsters playing Alonso and Antonio knotted thrift-shop ties. As corporate executives, everyone wore business suits save for the island's residents: Prospero, Miranda, Ariel, and Caliban. For Ariel, Patrice had dyed a prison jumpsuit sylvan green, while Gabriel's Caliban wore a sky-blue fun-fur costume that Margot, who delivered it last week, said was used by a character on a children's television show. My too-young Prospero was in jeans, a lavender shirt, and the old tuxedo jacket that had travelled with me since Veracruz. And Cynthia wore whatever she chose—vintage ball gowns, cherry-red hot pants, schoolgirl uniforms—depending on her mood and how long she had to change between scenes. She was the oddest Miranda I've seen, yet absolutely captivating in the wonder and innocence she conveyed. And isn't that the point of her character?

A welcome waft of fresh air reached me. Brooks the understudy had opened the back door so he could smoke. He watched as I unpacked Prospero's sparkly dragon cloak, the staff, and the book of magic spells. "Your tale, sir, would cure deafness," I said to him, quoting Miranda from Act I.

Brooks replied as Prospero: "To have no screen between this part he played and him he played it for."

"Sounds like you're ready," I said. "How about the second show? Tomorrow. Give me a break for the night." Not only did Brooks deserve to display his talents, I fancied sitting among the paying public for a show, like a real person.

"Throw me in. Anytime."

It might be tonight as well, I thought, because presently Jill had me so wound up I could barely remember my lines. The more make-up I slathered on, my hands actually trembling, the more my gut knotted itself. It's easy to gallivant before convicts. Tonight we performed for a real audience, the first I'd faced in over a decade. Years of lame work on television then "acting" at the resorts had softened me.

No. I could handle the audience—any audience. It was Jill I wasn't ready for.

What was she trying to tell me? Whatever the message, it must be sincere. I read the letter again quickly before stuffing it into my knapsack. So she'd been here, to the schoolhouse, and hadn't visited me at King's Reach? Karen could confirm that, but I was wary of further involving her in my affairs.

A prison guard, the same one who kindly failed to report my beating by the bikers, strode into the room. "Danny. The warden wants to see you at the front."

"Can you tell him he needs to be back here getting ready?"

"No, I can't. He wants you up front, so let's go."

I was shirtless, my face half-painted. Near to hand was a jury-rigged clothing rack for Cynthia's costumes. I lifted down a plain blue terry-cloth robe.

"May I?" With Cynthia, it was wise to ask first.

"Take any of them except the green one. My little Manny gave that to me."

The lover she bludgeoned to death. Let's keep that in perspective.

The schoolhouse was nearly full of patrons, people from a distant, half-remembered world. How strange they appeared, some finely dressed for their evening, and all equally oblivious to the fragility of their freedom. I glanced about for Jill, never expecting her to be among them because I'd have sensed her presence before I saw her. And because nothing so greatly desired ever comes easy.

In the cloakroom, other people milled about drinking wine, the lights of a television camera glaring. A pre-show reception, to which I hadn't been invited. Nor had I anticipated it, marking a further decline in my thinking into that of an ignorant, myopic convict.

I stopped the guard from entering the cloakroom. "I can't go in there dressed like this. It's bad form."

The guard considered this. "All right. Stay here. I'll be back in a second."

Curious, I stuck my head into the cloakroom again. I saw Edith Orson chatting with Stephen Kasey. I saw reverends in clerical collars and people who must have been mayors, councillors, and other Gracechurch worthies. I also saw many cops whose overtime fees, combined with the free-flowing wine, must have gobbled up the money for the lights the warden had promised us.

I did not see Jill Charles and was both disappointed and relieved. Puzzled faces swivelled my way. I badly wanted a glass of that wine.

Finally, I spotted my father, and with a bittersweet near-weepiness, beckoned him to me. I hadn't realized how much I'd been hoping he'd be here tonight. With him was Valerie, a petite redhead in her fifties with a wide smile.

We'd barely said hello when the guard returned. "Let's go, Danny," he said. "Warden says you're supposed to follow me."

I said goodbye to my father then apprehensively followed the guard down the steps into the crowd, thinking: I used to be good at this.

The hot light of a camera spun onto me, and a microphone was shoved in my face. I knew the woman wielding it. In my heyday, she'd interviewed me for *Legal Ease*. More recently, she'd gleefully reported on my conviction. "Congratulations on your comeback," she said. "How do you respond to people who say you've still got a lot to answer for?"

Years ago I'd had a publicist to shield me from questions that barbed. Now I had a prison guard to lead me away, the local big-shots clearing a path for us.

Warden Carr was speaking into a phone held by a young woman.

He prattled on until the girl became more interested in my presence than in the credit he was taking for my work. Carr dismissed her then said to me with a scowl, "Next time, you come when you're called."

He prodded me before two jowly, balding men in dark suits. His superiors at Correctional Services, I assumed. Neither of them shook my proffered hand, nor introduced themselves, reminding me that convicted criminals don't merit the usual personal courtesies.

"Carr tells me you're a stubborn sonofabitch," said one man. "You'd have to be, to get anything out of him."

"There's lots of people aren't sure about this," said the other man. "Don't fuck it up."

"We won't," I said. "The men have worked really hard at this."

"That's what I was saying the about their rehabilitation," Carr said.

The first man cut him off. "Why aren't you doing the Shakespeare play I like?" he said to me. "With the wood nymphs and the king of the forest. I took my wife to see it back when we were dating. That sweetened her, let me tell you."

"A *Midsummer Night's Dream*?"

"That's the one. Women love it."

"I like *Hamlet*," said the second man. "'The rest is silence.' I remember that line from high school. That's a good fucking play."

Have you heard of *The Third Night*? I wanted to ask them. Because I hadn't, and it seemed there was a lot hinging on it.

"*The Dream* would be a great show for next summer," I said. "We could build a stage on the front lawn, rent some bleachers. That way it pays for itself."

"Could make for a fine night," the first man said. "Carr, you should follow up on this."

The veteran reporter's camera caught up to me, its light illuminating the steam escaping the warden's ears. "That's enough," he said. "Danny and I need to get ready."

I got the handshakes I'd earlier been denied. "Nice meeting you," the first man said.

"How much time do you have?" said the second man.

I glanced into the classroom. "Not much," I said.

The warden laughed. "He's got two years until he can apply for parole."

"Plenty of time," the first man said.

"I'm hearing you might be with us a lot longer than that," the second man said. Then they both chortled.

256

No one knew that better than I did. An email from my lawyer earlier that week had informed me that the police in a number of jurisdictions were re-opening their investigations into whether I'd stolen credit-card data from people while they were on holiday in the Caribbean. He told me to expect to hear from him again soon.

Out of their earshot, the warden said, "When should I come and get ready?"

"Now," I said. I'd caved to his request for a walk-on because there wasn't anything to be gained in being selfish. An additional character in the opening shipwreck scene was a small thing compared to the other changes I'd made to the play.

Most of the seats in the classroom were now full. Above the general chatter, I detected certain words: "Danny Drake," "*Legal Ease*," and "looks so young." I swallowed a grin. It had been a long time since I'd heard that.

Maybe Jill simply meant she was coming on the third night. It didn't matter. She was back. She'd waited. No, she was waiting. She was waiting for me to get out of jail, and probably knew I'd be here for an awfully long time.

By the stage, a woman of maybe forty stepped between me and the curtain. She held a phone. "Sorry to bother you," she said. "Could I get a photograph of us?"

The warden paused on his walk to the green room, then thought better of interfering.

The boys' nerves were considerably steadier by the interval. They kibitzed in the green room, sipping the bottles of water Karen had provided and smoking out the back door.

They'd turned in an inspired performance, our best so far. As I predicted, the audience loved Gabriel's woeful Caliban. And while Cynthia's Miranda was only politely received—I guess you have to know her—I stood by my casting. Who else was there for the role?

By this point, I thought I understood what Jill meant in her letter. It was the boat that twigged me, the one Prospero wrecks in the storm and then repairs to get everyone off the island. What a final act Jill had planned. What a decision I faced.

Since receiving her first letter, I'd realized that she couldn't have known or predicted what Brenda would do. And that the rumours of our crimes in the media understandably forced her to keep out of sight. That was my tough luck as well. Now I was gambling that the plan Jill referred to in her earlier letter wasn't to meet at my father's after she'd completed her double-cross of Nick. She was referring to our plan to start a small theatre company together. Her earlier letter assured me that she still cared. This most recent letter was asking me to act on that belief.

At least, that was the latest story I was telling myself.

"How we doing, boss?" Tyler asked. "You think they like it?"

Feeling lavishly Shakespearean, I clambered atop a table. These guys had crossed oceans and deserts. Some rarely laughed before we started this voyage. Now all of them had at least one thing about themselves to admire.

I started by thanking them for their hard work. "I've been acting since I was thirteen, in I don't know how many shows, and with I don't know how many people. In all that time, I've never said: this is the best thing I've ever done, and the best group I've ever worked with."

Their cheering silenced me. Grateful arms hoisted me from the table onto the shoulders of Cynthia, who paraded me around the room. We carried on like this until a guard appeared in the doorway. "What the hell are you doing in here?" he said. "You're freaking people out."

I'd forgotten how we must have appeared to the good folk of Gracechurch, who'd each paid ten dollars to be entertained. Alarming them was disrespectful. Actors are nothing without their audience.

In the end, the decision was easy. What choice did I have? And who wouldn't take that risk to be happy? So it was simply a matter of choosing the right moment and the right magic. All those red-eyed nights of research paid off handsomely.

I waited until the climax of the third and final night at the schoolhouse, when the boys had nearly ten great shows behind them. Years of reading lame television scripts had taught me the value of creating a diversion to distract from your real purpose. The trick was in waiting until the final scene, when everyone is on stage and the boat off the island has been magically restored and is ready to sail.

With every character in place—Ferdinand and Miranda in each other's arms, Caliban returned to his master by Ariel, and Prospero standing proudly at centre stage—I employed some Elizabethan hocus pocus to momentarily suspend audience and Players alike.

A poof of smoke and a dazzling burst of light was all that was required to get everything back to the way it was. My fellow Players began moving very slowly. The audience, already transfixed by our playing, was now entirely motionless and seemingly all the more enraptured.

I threw down the magic staff—unbroken—and ran from the stage.

A second later—these spells don't last long—I was in the green room, grabbing my tuxedo jacket and throwing my knapsack over my shoulder. I slipped out the back door, closed it behind me, and raced toward the tightly packed trees behind the schoolhouse.

Their darkness enveloped me. After such a long confinement, my heart sang to be on the move again. I was raised on the road, and that's where I belong.

I never once looked back.

Epilogue

Dr. Kyle Moran
c/o King's Reach Correctional Institution
Gracechurch, Vancouver Island
British Columbia, Canada

Hey Doc—

Surprised to be hearing from me? I wanted to reach out to you sooner, but as you can probably appreciate, I've been laying low.

Enclosed please find a completed copy of the assignment you gave me. It's quite late, occasionally enhanced, and totally absorbing. Jill took it with her to the beach this morning and devoured it in one sitting. A page-turner, she said.

I'm sure you've been grilled by the authorities on whether you had prior knowledge of my intentions. All I can say is the *why* of my escape must be obvious. It was only a matter of days before I was charged for robbing many people. The *how* I never fully understood myself. That's magic, I guess.

I'd like to thank you for all your help. I was in rough shape when I rolled into King's Reach, battered, exhausted, depressed. Our conversations and your efforts at motivation showed me how to rebuild myself. I hope my escape didn't make things difficult for you. The work you do should be free from interference. If it's of any use, please feel free to show this letter to your bosses.

I'd also like to apologize for not being totally honest with you or as introspective as you asked me to be. I'm sure you can appreciate the reasons I couldn't discuss what Jill and I did down south. I'm sure that internal conflict was why I had so much difficulty writing. I never intended any disrespect to your methods or your profession.

With more free time at hand, I've been contemplating the issues you said I was reluctant to confront. There still isn't anything to be done about my poor dead mother. Nor my relationship with Jill. Yes, it's too bad she had to resort to the drug trade to rescue us. And it's too bad she went so long without contacting me, but she had her reasons. Yet that doesn't mean our reunion wasn't always foremost on her mind.

Even you'd agree the results were spectacular: a jubilant, career-capping performance, the audience thundering their approval as she makes a final exit from the stage.

As for stages, in a perfect world, I like to imagine that Brooks the understudy filled in for Prospero in the last few minutes of the show I abandoned. Not much chance of that, is there?

The rest of that night must have been awful. The police locking down the building, my broken-hearted colleagues shackled and led onto the bus. I ruined a lot of evenings, I know.

I suspect the guys' reactions to my escape were mixed. As an actor, what I did was inexcusable. As a convict, it's understandable, even admirable. Not every inmate can do their time. There's no shame in setting yourself free. Prospero certainly understands that, and the need to seek rejuvenation. Whatever else he's doing, he's getting himself and Miranda off that island. All the same, I regret any pain I caused.

You'll notice there's no return address on the envelope and that it was mailed in Florida. Just for fun, pretend you can write me back. I'd like to hear you found a job that got you home to spend time with your wife and sons. Please also tell me that the King's Reach Players are still in operation. Gabriel would make a fine director. So would Hassan, if he allowed himself broader interpretations of the text.

Thanks to the media, actors are the most conspicuously troubled of artists. I could tell you a story about a naïve and unhappy girl who was lured south on the promise of an acting career. Apparently, I wasn't the only student at Ryerson who placed fame and wealth ahead of art, the difference being I wasn't half as ashamed about it. In the spirit of

261

rejuvenation, all that matters now is that Jill had a plan, and it worked.

In the green room of our new rehearsal and studio space, we've also established a lending library for books in English. Since there's nothing else like it in town, people are always stopping by for books and magazines, and that's getting the word out on our project.

This morning after my swim, I met some American surfer kids dropping off boxes of books they'd found somewhere. Among them was a stash of old mystery novels for teenagers that allow readers to guide the story themselves by choosing directions for the young detective to follow at various points in the book. In this way, readers can reach different endings to the book, some satisfactory, others not, and all based on decisions made earlier.

These choose-your-own-adventure books were all the rage in my fourth grade class. Flipping through one, I recalled how I always cheated when I read them. I'd start by choosing the ending I liked best before backtracking through the various story crossroads to determine how that ending was achieved. Then I'd start the book at the beginning, confident I'd plotted the surest route to happiness and fulfillment.

Inspired by my find, I'd like to offer you, by way of conclusion, and thanks, three different endings. You choose whichever you prefer. Or think we deserve.

The first and least desirable unfortunately remains a possibility. Picture me in a Mexican jail, where I'm serving an eternity of consecutive ten-year sentences for credit-card fraud. No Jill, never again. Beatings and buggerings daily. Enforced drug abuse. Starvation and unidentifiable infections. The best I can hope for is a terminal illness or to be slaughtered in a riot.

The second ending opens on a foggy night along a wet stretch of Pacific coast highway. Enter Jill and me in a stolen car, racing hell-bent ahead of some police cruisers, their red lights strobing off the wall of pine trees lining the road. We take a curve sharply, the skidding car barely under Jill's control. Ahead of us, more cops maintain a roadblock. A last look between the doomed lovers. Jill swerves, and the front left wheel rises on a guardrail, forcing the car into an airborne corkscrew spin. The cops fire after us, shattering the back window. We remain aloft, the car spiraling as we sail over the roadblock.

Freeze frame. Will we escape? Tune in next week.

The third ending is by far the most satisfactory. If I were reading the book, I'd choose it then work backwards to achieve it.

Start with me running through the dripping woods behind the schoolhouse toward the lights of central Gracechurch and the black waters of the strait beyond it. Trailing pixie dust from Prospero's cloak as I go. Is this what Jill meant when she mentioned the harbour on the third night? It's a risk that could result in years added to my prison sentence. But then so too will all those fraud charges amassing against me.

It's raining of course, perhaps hard enough to qualify as a storm. I cross the deserted main drag and sprint onto a pier that contains just two darkened, shuttered boats. Not good, I think, staggering to a halt. I'm so out of breath it's a few moments before I discern the greasy hammering of an approaching engine. A spotlight turns on and scans the pier until it finds me alone on this narrow stage for anyone pursuing me to see.

Then the light goes off as a boat clunks against the pier. I leap aboard it, and Jill is beside me, at long last, a smugly self-satisfied grin on her face.

The *Serena*, from Bellingham, Washington is captained by an old woman who imports BC skunkweed into the States. Because she wasn't informed she'd be abetting a prison break, and because the prisoner is wearing stage make-up and a cape, a few anxious minutes pass that are finally broken by the sound of approaching police sirens. It's not these but the joyous reunion of two rain-drenched lovebirds underway in the stern of her boat that convinces the captain to cast off.

And so, the trail of sparkles ends on the pier as the boat speeds on through the night.

Flash forward to me and Jill in our own secluded tropical cove. Add some baby Daniels and Jills gurgling healthily in the shade, and Earl watching them while placing his bets online. Be sure to include fifty close friends, a barbecue, and cocktails. If it's easier, picture it as a beer commercial. Living in one of those isn't a bad goal to have in life.

As the director of the commercial, I'm entitled to a helicopter shot. I'd hold it until everyone is waving goodbye, then pull slowly out until the cove is a tan crescent of shoreline in a sea of emerald and azure, and all the people on it grains of sand in a story already told.

Thanks again for everything, doc. See you on the beach,

Daniel

Thanks to

Steven Stack, Sarah Kekewich, Conan Tobias, Randy Morgan, Maria Meindl, Mignette Garvida, Stephanie Fysh, and David Robbeson.

Jim Nason, Heather Wood, Deanna Janovski, and everyone at Tightrope Books.

All my friends and colleagues in the Toronto film community who gave me work when I needed it and also understood that writing comes first.

The taxpayers of Ontario, who made funds available to me through the Ontario Arts Council.

About the Author

Andrew Daley was raised in Orangeville, Ontario and moved to Toronto to attend university. Aside from a year in England, he's lived there ever since. He's done a variety of jobs and seems to have settled in the film business. His first novel, *Tell Your Sister*, was published by Tightrope Books in 2007.